Copyright © 2023 by Mary E. Chambers

This book is a work of fiction. Names, characters, and incidents are either products of the author's imagination or are used fictitiously. Any resemblance to actual events or persons, living or dead, is entirely coincidental.

All rights reserved. No part of this publication may be reproduced, distributed, or transmitted in any form or by any means, including photocopying, recording, or other electronic or mechanical methods, without the prior written permission of the publisher, except in the case of brief quotations embodied in critical reviews and certain other noncommercial uses permitted by copyright law. If you would like permission to use material from the book (other than for review purposes), please contact the author or publisher. Thank you for your support of the author's rights.

Books may be purchased in bulk quantity and/or special sales by contacting the publisher.

Published by Mend Matters Publishing

978-1-957097-30-0 (pbk)
978-1-957097-31-7 (ebk)
978-1-957097-32-4 (hc)

FIRST EDITION

Copyright © 2023 by Mary E. Chambers.

This book is a work of fiction. Names, characters, and incidents are either products of the author's imagination or are used fictitiously. Any resemblance to actual events or persons, living or dead, is entirely coincidental.

All rights reserved. No part of this publication may be reproduced, distributed, or transmitted in any form or by any means, including photocopying, recording, or other electronic or mechanical methods, without the prior written permission of the publisher, except in the case of brief quotations embodied in critical reviews and certain other noncommercial uses permitted by copyright law. If you would like permission to use material from the book (other than for review purposes), please contact the author or publisher. Thank you for your support of the author's rights.

Books may be purchased in bulk quantity and/or special sales by contacting the publisher.

Published by Mynd Matters Publishing
715 Peachtree Street NE
Suites 100 & 200
Atlanta, GA 30308
www.myndmatterspublishing.com

978-1-957092-30-0 (pbk)
978-1-957092-31-7 (hdcv)
978-1-957092-32-4 (ebk)

FIRST EDITION

solo
love lost and found

MARY E. CHAMBERS
Critically-acclaimed author of *Tulip (a love story)*

Lola

love lost and found

MARY E. CHAMBERS

*To my husband, children, and grandchildren,
our flowers continue to bloom.*

ONE

Mama and Papa Gone

They say, "Life doesn't come with a manual; it comes with a mother."

Solo ran as fast as her little legs would carry her. Arms flailing wildly, her flowing blonde hair, loose from the lengthy braids, slapped against her face. Dirt flew up from the land in a cloud of smoke as she ran faster and faster. The chickens, confused by the unexpected commotion, noisily scattered as she passed by. Max, with his tail wagging and mouth open wide, ran beside Solo as if they were playing a game. Solo ran. Tears flew from her eyes like rain. She ran. Out of pure stubbornness, she refused to turn around. She never looked back to see if her Mama was coming after her or if she had walked away. Regardless, Solo didn't care, she was too caught up in her own emotions.

Through her pain and heartbreak, Solo could hear Misses Chiles and Faith calling out to her, but she continued to run back to her empty cabin. She knew no one would be there, but it was her home, and she wouldn't leave, no matter what, and no one could make her.

Solo cried out, "LET THEM ALL LEAVE!" She was glad they were all gone. "MAMA CAN JUST GO!" Solo yelled. "Let her go, I don't care." *Let Mama run away just like that mean Papa.* Hate filled Solo's little heart like flames in a fire. Her hatred for her Mama and Papa was like bee stings. Each worse than the one before. She wished they would both just die. She was too young to realize there was no coming back with death.

How Solo wished she had never been born. Papa left her and now Mama was leaving her too. Papa hated her. Now Mama hated her. No one loved her. Misses Chiles always told her God loved her. But Solo cried to herself wondering, *If God loves me so much, then why does everyone keep leaving me and why do they treat me so mean?* That very moment, Solo decided she even hated God just as much as she hated her Mama and Papa. God couldn't have loved her either. So, God could just get out her life like Mama and Papa. She didn't love God anymore. She would never again pray to that mean God who made her. What good did he do her? Misses Chiles said she was a different, beautiful flower made by God.

"Why?" I didn't ask God to make me different," Solo voiced aloud. "SO GO, GOD! GO AWAY!" Solo cried.

With all the strength she had left, Solo pushed the door open. It still smelled of her family's last supper together. The cabin was cold and vacant. The wood stove no longer housed a fire. Solo looked around through tear-filled eyes. Snot dripped from her nose, and she felt flushed from running. Her heart was beating fast, and her two hands were balled into tight fists. The beds were bare of sheets and blankets. Exhausted, she threw herself onto the bed she once shared with Little Henry. She could still smell his scent and recalled how they would whisper in the still of the night about different things. But Papa loved Little Henry and Little Henry loved him.

"I hate you Little Henry and you are not my brother anymore!" Solo proclaimed aloud.

She felt conflicted about hating Little Henry, but she knew in her heart she hated Baby Cecila who was now going to live with *her* Faith. Why couldn't she live with Faith? Why did Mama give Baby Cecila to Faith too? Mama loved Baby Cecila. She was always going on about how much Baby Cecila reminded her of her dead Mama. On and on she would carry on to anyone who would listen. Mama was always telling Baby Cecila, "You look just like your Granny...yeah you do! Your Granny, God rest her soul, sure would have loved you."

What was so special about that Baby Cecila with her black skin and nappy hair anyway? Plus, she was ugly. *"I'm the pretty one,"* Solo mused. She was determined, somehow and some way, Baby Cecila would pay one day. Solo cried until her chest hurt.

There was a slight creak as the cabin door opened. Hesitantly, Faith entered the soulless abode. She looked around and recalled how the dark and empty room was once the home of her friends, Tulip and Malcolm, and their children. Faith allowed her mind to wander as she thought back to the day she helped her Mama and Papa fix up the cabin for Malcolm and Tulip. It was a wedding present and she had to keep it a secret. Oh, how she wanted to tell Tulip about the cabin. It was so hard for Faith to keep a secret from Tulip because they shared everything and never kept anything from one another, just like real sisters. In fact, in many ways, Faith felt like Tulip was more of a sister than Hope and Charity, even though she loved them dearly. But Faith promised her Mama and Papa she would not tell Tulip or Malcolm about the cabin. It was a secret she had to keep.

For Faith, Malcolm and Tulip's wedding day was even more special because she got to help her Mama decorate the cabin with scented candles and Tulip's favorite flowers—lilies. She knew the flowers would make Tulip happy, and she wanted happiness for her. The cabin also presented an opportunity for Faith as well. Of course, it was a gift to the happy couple, but Faith also secretly hoped it would grant her some privacy with Ben. Her wishes were granted as he was now her husband. They stole kisses, embraced closely, and got lost in each other's eyes. While they had gotten caught up in passion, they knew it was a sin and did not get too carried away. Restraint was extremely difficult because they were in love. The very next week, Ben came courting and the rest is history.

Faith smiled, remembering their courtship. Now, they just wanted a family. God had not yet blessed them with children of their own, so having Baby Cecila brought joy to their home. Faith knew she and Ben would treat Baby Cecila just like their own child. But Solo, that was another story. While Faith loved Solo, she knew Solo was a handful. On many occasions, Tulip had shared the problems Solo caused between her and Malcolm. Faith did not want to bring any problems into her own household. She believed her own Mama and Papa were best to take care of Solo. She needed a firm hand.

Solo was lying face down on the bed crying her poor heart out. Faith digested the scene. How small and vulnerable she looked with her curly hair cascading down to the floor. Solo didn't seem to move, but Faith saw her petite body quiver with each whimper. Faith knew Solo's heart was broken after being abandoned by her parents. She was just a child. Now, a motherless child. At that moment, Faith was overwhelmed with motherly compassion for Solo.

Solo knew someone had entered the cabin. She didn't dare look to see who it was in fear her Mama had returned. She wanted whoever it was to see her brokenness and feel sorry for her. As Solo heard footsteps approaching the bed, her heart palpitated harder. Faith knelt beside her, gently stroking her hair. Solo knew it wasn't her Mama, because Mama yanked and brushed her hair hard. Sometimes it made Solo cry. It had to be either Faith or Misses Chiles. Solo relaxed ever so slightly and continued whimpering while enjoying the little bit of consoling being offered.

"Solo," Faith said sweetly, "I know it hurts that your Mama must go away and leave you and your brother and sister. I know you're probably scared. But you're young so it's hard for you to understand why your Mama and Papa had to go away."

While talking, Faith continued to stroke Solo's hair. "You are kin, and we will take care of you, Little Henry, and Baby Cecila just like your Mama and Papa did. So don't be scared. And before you know it, your Mama and Papa will be back and everything will be just like it was before. But, while we wait for the Lord to grant that day, just know I am here for you and will take care of you."

With that, Solo turned to face Faith. With the sweetest, most innocent smile she could muster, she wrapped her little arms around Faith's neck and whispered hopefully in her ear," So I can live with you and Ben now!"

> *I wouldn't have it any other way,*
> *so please don't go*
> *and stay.*
> *Don't leave me to wonder alone in this vast emptiness.*
> *To justify my mere existence.*
> *For without you, there is no me.*
> *Come be with me, let's move in unison to the music we play*
> *and live life day by day.*
> *Our song will be our dance.*
> *The lyrics flowing free with every movement.*
> *Only we will understand.*
> *For it's me and you,*
> *and you for me,*
> *until this world sets us free.*

TWO
Solo's Birthday

"Stay still and quit your wiggling," Faith playfully scolded Solo. "One would think you never had a birthday before." "But I ain't never been thirteen," giggled Solo.

It had been seven years since Tulip left the children in the care of her family. Little Henry was now almost eleven and Baby Cecila (who was just called "Baby") was nine. Little Henry stayed with Misses and Mister Chiles, while Solo and Baby lived with Faith and Ben. Faith and Ben had still not been blessed with their own children but had come to think of Solo and Baby as their own. While Faith still loved Tulip, deep down in her heart she dreaded the day Tulip would return for Baby and Solo, who now called her Mama Faith, and her husband Papa Ben.

Misses Chiles warned Faith not to get too close to the children, because one day, rest assured their Mama or Papa would come back for them. Although there had been no word from Malcolm, Misses Chiles knew Tulip planned to return for her family, and rightfully so. When she received the first letter from Tulip, she was pleased.

September 21, 1935

My Dearest Misses Chiles,

Please accept my apology in the delay in writing this letter. You know I don't have much reading and writing teaching, so I had someone to write this letter for me. First, I want to thank you from the bottom of my heart for taking care of my children. I long for the arms of my babies and please let them know their Mama love them and will be back soon to get them.

It was long and hard, but I made way to New York City. I have not found Malcolm and probably never will in this place with them strange ugly tall buildings, so many kinds of folks, talking and dressing funny. Too noisy and busy, can't think straight. Not clean at all either. Work is hard to come, so I don't have any money right now to send you. But I will send some when I can.

Don't know how long I will be here. As soon as I get some money, I will make my way to Maryland to find some kin. Give Mister Chiles, Faith, Hope, and Charity my love. That's all I have say for now.

Love, Tulip

P.S. Nice lady help me write this letter. No address right now for you to write back. Please know that I will write you again soon. Please read this letter to my babies.

Misses Chiles didn't know if Tulip was still in New York City. Her kids had stopped asking when their Mama was coming to get them, especially Solo, who seem to resent even speaking her name. Misses Chiles was sure Baby didn't even remember her Mama or Papa, and Henry, sweet Henry, never asked any questions.

But in her recent letter, Tulip mentioned she'd met a man named Carson and had feelings for him. She wrote:

June 9, 1936

He has been very good to me and knows that I am a married woman, so to speak. I know only a couple of years have passed since Malcolm and I have lived as man and wife, while my feelings for Malcolm have not changed. I wondered if he is even alive or maybe remarried. Does he still love me and the children? Why has he not come back? I am so conflicted especially since my feelings are growing for Carson and he has strong feelings for me. We have agreed to take it slow and not rush things. I know that it is a sin to be with another man being a married woman and all, but in my heart, Malcolm and I are no longer man and wife."

Misses Chiles was happy Tulip had found someone who was good to her and maybe could help her return home for her children. But, for the sake of her own daughter, Misses Chiles dreaded the day Tulip would return. If, or when Tulip returned, Misses Chiles knew Faith would be devastated and heartbroken to lose Baby and possibly even Solo. Solo was a difficult child and despite all their efforts, all was not well between Solo and Faith.

To further complicate matters, Misses Chiles was concerned for her husband, who over the years had grown so fond of Little Henry. For Mister Chiles, Henry was the son he never had. They all loved the children so dearly, even that mean-spirited Solo. Misses Chiles made the sign of the cross even thinking that child's name.

"Nevertheless, right is right," Misses Chiles said out loud. She knew how much Tulip missed and loved her children and while she hated to admit it, it would be best if Tulip came back for her family, sooner than later. With a heavy heart, Misses Chiles prayed.

Faith finally finished the last touches of Solo's birthday dress. She stepped back to take a good look at the dress, and she caught her breath. The dress had completely transformed Solo from a little girl to a stunning, fully developed young woman. The dress clung to her curved body and accented the right parts. Faith didn't know the dress would be so breathtaking, and maybe just a little too inviting for the wrong attention. But she admitted to herself that Solo looked lovely. Faith watched as Solo danced and spun around. Solo loved the dress and she felt pretty. The dress was her favorite color, pink, and was adorned with white and pink ribbons and ruffles. Solo took note of the dress's low cut in the front and thought to herself she should stuff the void with some paper so her breasts could sit up high. Solo turned and hugged and thanked Faith. Faith and Ben had ordered Solo's dress from the Sears and Roebuck catalog as a birthday gift. Faith tweaked it by adding a few extra ribbons and bows. They wanted to give her something special for her birthday, even though Faith felt she didn't quite deserve it.

Solo continued to spin around and around until she was dizzy. Her long blonde hair flowed across her face with each movement. At thirteen years old, she stood five feet, seven inches, with nice-sized breasts, a small waist, big thighs and calves, and wide hips. Her blue-gray eyes were now completely gray, and her complexion was more of an olive color, a nod to her mixed race. Town folks complimented her on her looks, and some would give her treats for no reason at all. Solo would give them each her special smile. She knew she was special. The older boys at her schoolhouse tried to touch and kiss her, always wanting to stroke her hair. Sometimes Solo would lift her dress and let them have a little feel. She was a real flirt. The girls thought she was fresh, but they were just jealous because Solo was pretty, and the boys frolicked around her like newborn puppies. But Solo didn't care about the girls, she only cared about one thing, and that was herself.

In honor of Solo's birthday, there was to be a party at the Chiles' farm. There hadn't been a big party since Tulip and Malcolm's wedding (*Ben and Faith were married at the local church house*). Solo knew some of the children from her schoolhouse would be coming because their families knew the Chiles' and everyone liked to get together to eat, drink, dance, and be social with neighbors and kinfolk. There would be plenty of food, music, and lots of dancing. Solo couldn't wait. She loved to dance and thought pretty good on her feet. Mama Faith was always getting on her for dancing about. But, since they lived close to town, Solo sneaked and peeped under the door of the local beer garden and watched the men and women dance. Sometimes it got so good it consumed her, and Solo would dance right out into the middle of the road without a care of who saw her. Some of the men watched and clapped and egged Solo on, all the while licking their lips and eyeing her with their own sexual desire. Solo thrived on the attention, and it made her move her body even more. Now the women, seeing such display, shook their heads in disgust. One bold woman walked up to Solo, grabbed her, and gave her a hard swap on her backside. Solo just laughed and ran off in glee.

So today is my birthday. I will dance, dance, and dance. Solo mused. As Solo eyed herself in the mirror, she thought she might even let one of those boys go a little further than a touch between her nice shapely breasts, and maybe let one or two of them kiss her on the lips. Solo grew flush with those thoughts. At thirteen, her young body and curiosity screamed for more. For what exactly, she didn't quite know. On occasions, Solo would sneak and watch Mama Faith and Papa Ben kiss and hump naked. Mama Faith would moan and turn her head from side to side. Papa Ben did all the humping between Mama Faith's legs. Solo didn't know if Papa Ben was hurting her or not. Mama Faith didn't cry. But, seeing them embracing, humping, and kissing made Solo get moist between her legs and touch herself. It felt good. Solo wanted Papa Ben to do the same to her. Once, when Solo brushed up real close to Papa Ben and let her backside rub up against his privates, what the schoolboys called theirs. Papa Ben realized what was happening, pushed her away, and scolded her. Since that day, Solo knew Papa Ben would not hump on her, so she turned her attention to the silly, ugly boys at her schoolhouse.

Solo was also aware that some of the older townsmen, both white and colored, watched her with lust in their eyes. She would sway her little hips from side to side when she walked by and give them a coy smile. Being a quick study, it didn't take her long to learn she could get things from them. So, when she wanted candy from the store, Solo would let some of the men touch her between her legs or hump her backside, while she ate her candy. Sometimes they wanted her to touch their private thing. She would if they did not take it out their pants. Solo wondered why it was always hard. She never let the townsmen kiss her lips, many of them were stinky and smelled of drink. If they got too rough, Solo would haughtily remind them if they hurt her, she would not let them do it anymore.

Solo smiled to herself. *For my birthday present to me, I will let one of those silly boys or men have their way with me."* Knowing the silly boys didn't have any money, she reconsidered. *But the men got to give me a present.* Solo laughed to herself.

As they were getting closer to the Chiles' farm, Solo could hear the faint sound of music. She stood up in the wagon to get a better look. "Sat down Solo!" said Faith. "Else you fall in the water and mess up your pretty dress."

Solo rolled her eyes, ignored Faith, and defiantly continued to stand up in the wagon. She looked towards the Chiles' farm and suddenly recalled her former home. A home she did not miss.

Years ago, the old rickety bridge Tulip and Malcolm had perilously crossed to get to the farm had been widened and reinforced, making it safer for people to cross. Since the river was a low tide, Ben moved the wagon and horses slowly through the river. Solo continued to stand. She was not afraid of the water since she knew how to swim. Sometimes when Solo was visiting the Chiles' farm, she would go to the river, take off all her clothes, not caring if anyone was watching, and swim naked. The water felt so good on her body. In the water, she could touch her body and please herself. But for some reason, it thrilled her to think somebody was watching.

"Solo!" yelled Faith. "I am not going to ask you again. Sat down, please!" Finally obeying Faith, Solo thought she better sit because she didn't want to mess up her pretty new birthday dress or her hair for that matter, which had taken her all morning to fix. Plus, she was wearing her new ribbons bought with her earnings from the townsmen.

Solo felt Baby looking at her, so she stuck out her tongue at her and rolled her eyes. This made Baby sad. Solo still hated Baby and resented the fact that she lived with Mama Faith and Papa Ben. Every chance Solo got she would let Baby know she did not like her, and she was no sister of hers. This would really upset Baby because she so wanted her big sister to like her and be her friend. Baby knew they didn't look like sisters. Solo's skin was white, like Mama Faith and Baby's skin was brown just like their Mama Tulip, a mama Baby no longer remembered. She had these big old sad looking brown eyes that gave the impression she was always on the verge of tears. Thick lips and a wide nose rounded out her features. But when Baby smiled, her whole face would crinkle, and you knew then she had a heart full of love. Always kind to everything and everyone. However, Baby was rather short in stature and very small boned, so some folks nicknamed her "Tincey." She had very small facial features along with short, curly, and thick brown hair which was always neatly braided. Baby was very smart as well as an avid reader. She could do numbers much better than some adults. But she was also reserved and could always be found either helping Mama Faith or sitting in a corner reading a book.

On the other hand, Solo didn't care about books, numbers, helping Faith, or being a goody two shoes like her sister. Solo knew Baby could read way better than her and everybody thought she was so sweet. So, Solo took pleasure in tormenting Baby whenever she could. Solo knew Baby would just run and cry and tell Mama Faith or Papa Ben. Of course, Solo would deny it. She knew Mama Faith and Papa Ben loved Baby more than her, but why? Solo didn't have an answer. *Today is my day*, Solo thought to herself as she looked towards the Chiles' farm.

Over the years the Chiles' farm had managed to prosper a little. There was a new barn with a couple more horses and other livestock. Mister Chiles had a new wagon. He wasn't quite ready for an automobile yet. There was even a new dog named Betsy since Max had passed on. The little cabin Tulip and Malcolm once occupied still stood down the path. It had decayed some from age, but Little Henry still called it his home and found comfort in going there. He would sit for long periods of time. He had grown tall for his age. In fact, he was a couple of inches taller than Solo but lanky. Little Henry had a long sharp nose and thin lips. His skin was smooth and silky brown. Many folks commented on how Little Henry was the spitting image of his Papa Malcolm, whom he still remembered fondly. He hoped one day he would see his beloved Papa walking up the path to their little cabin. So many years had gone by, yet Little Henry would still sit in that cold, lonely cabin waiting. Not that he was unhappy, because Little Henry loved Papa Chiles, who had been very good to him and showed him a lot of things, like shooting a gun, hunting, fixing a roof, plowing, and doing other odd jobs in town. Recently, Papa Chiles talked of a Depression, so work was hard to come by and many town folks were leaving for the fabled New York City. Little Henry was told that was where his Mama and Papa were. He thought one day very soon he would leave and go there to find his Mama and Papa. But for now, he had to help with his sister Solo's birthday party. Something he was not looking forward to as he hated being around her.

The evil we spin cannot be seen by the naked eye,
but rather lies deep within;
We try hard to hide the contempt we feel,
but sooner or later it is revealed
as easy as a white potato peel;
Say what you want and believe all is good,
for it's the fool who is doomed,
and plead it on being misunderstood,
while continuing on a path of life with a cloud of darkness
that's in full bloom.

THREE
The Party

Solo carefully jumped down from the wagon and was about to run off towards some of the girls and boys from her schoolhouse. Faith called out, "Solo, I know it's your birthday, but don't go running off without helping us take some of this food to Mama." Faith looked at Solo with her hands on her hips.

"But..." Solo protested.

"No buts," Faith chimed in as Ben and Baby looked on.

"I don't wanna mess up my dress," said Solo.

"Help or stay in the wagon Solo," said Faith.

Solo looked at Ben who had walked off with Baby while carrying packages. She glared at Faith with such hate and made a silent promise to get her back. Solo reached in the wagon and grabbed a tightly wrapped bundle and stomped off towards the party, leaving Faith staring at her back.

There were so many folks there and tables piled with all sorts of food and drinks. As Solo walked up carrying the bundle, she smiled sweetly because she knew all eyes were on her. "How pretty you are," some of the ladies called out to her in envy. "Such a pretty child," they said as Solo walked by them in her beautiful party dress. Solo caught a glimpse of her brother Little Henry staring at her. She rolled her eyes. Misses Chiles was instructing Baby and Ben where to put the food Faith had prepared. There hadn't been a party at Chiles' farm since Tulip and Malcolm's wedding day so, it was good to see her neighbors and friends. But secretly, Misses Chiles hoped this party would change

Solo's behavior and show her how much she was loved. Faith had shared with Misses Chiles about the constant back-talking and disrespect from Solo. Additionally, Misses Chiles had heard talk about Solo and men in town. But she had refused to believe such gossip. Solo may be a handful, but she was no slut.

"Well, how pretty you look, my dear," Misses Chiles said as Solo approached her carrying a bundle.

"Thank you, Mama Chiles," said Faith as she twirled around.

"That is about the prettiest dress I've seen in a long time," said Misses Chiles. For a moment, Misses Chiles recalled the dress Tulip had worn to the dance with Malcolm, how pretty and happy she was. The thought made her smile.

"Why are you smiling Mama Chiles?" asked Solo.

"Just remembering happy times," Misses Chiles said sweetly while pulling Solo into her arms for a hug. Being hugged by Misses Chiles made her feel uncomfortable, so Solo pulled away quickly and walked away.

As she walked away, Solo was furious Misses Chiles would touch her. "Misses Chiles is always so touchy," Solo thought, "I hope she didn't mess up my hair." Solo quickly made her way to the house and found the mirror on the wall. She looked at her hair and was satisfied it was still perfect. Solo looked to see if anyone was coming and reached under her dress to retrieve the rags she had hidden in her undies. She took the cloths and stuck a piece of the material under each breast. This made Solo breasts raise up high and puff out of the dress like mounds of melon. Solo clapped her hands with delight. With one more look over in the mirror, Solo proclaimed, "Now I'm ready," and walked out the door.

Solo stopped and looked up to the sky and exhaled. She wanted to take in the day. "This is the most perfect day for my birthday party," She thought. The sky was a clear blue with a sprinkle of white puffy clouds throughout. The sun was beaming bright with narrow rays of sunlight shining through the trees. There was an easy wind, which provided a slow, steady warm breeze. Leaves gratefully rustled gently in return. Birds perched on tree limbs appeared to look down at the festivities.

Solo saw several girls running towards her with their breasts bouncing, wearing their ugly, plain homemade dresses. *The best they have*, she figured. Each girl had a big bow pinned lopsided on her nappy head, like *that* would make her look better. Their shoes were old and dirty. Solo felt superior and looked at them with disgust as they approached her. These were the girls from her schoolhouse. Some were older, a couple were younger, but none were prettier. Solo put a big old fake smile on her face and waved at the girls. Once the girls reached Solo, they stopped in their tracks. With their mouths gaped open, showing yellow teeth, eyes wide they each looked Solo up and down. The oldest girl, Telly, who was fat with buck teeth and skin as black as coal, spoke first.

"Wow, you sure look pretty Solo," she said admirably, looking admiralty Solo up and down. Telly thought it was the most beautiful dress she had ever seen, and she hoped one day she could have a dress just like it. Solo, not one for small talk, especially with stupid girls, simply said "Thank you" and walked off towards the music. The girls stared at her as she walked, each wishing they were her.

Solo was ready to sneak a forbidden drink and dance. She did not have time for talking with some silly, ugly little girls. She felt the excitement brewing in her very soul. She was an animal in heat about to explore.

There were so many people, with more people yet arriving, yelling, greeting, hugging, and kissing. As the food was eaten; more food was laid out. Games were played and men folks headed deep into the woods for a drink. A fiddler was playing the music, someone else was singing, and there was even a horn. Children were running about; some were even chasing poor Betsy, but the dog seemed to be enjoying it. Solo surveyed the crowd of people. She caught the eyes of some of the schoolboys looking at her, but no one had asked to dance. She noticed the townsmen, who she knew on a personal level, would slightly peek at her. Solo rolled her eyes. Some of the men and women were dancing, little kids were jumping to the music. But no one asked her to dance.

Noticing her brother Little Henry talking to one of the older schoolhouse girls, Solo ran over to Little Henry. She grabbed his hand forcibly and said, "DANCE WITH ME BROTHER! IT'S MY BIRTHDAY!" The girl Little Henry was talking with, stepped back, she knew of Solo's temper. Little Henry pulled back and replied, "Stop it, I don't dance, now leave me alone." Little Henry glared at Solo, and she knew better than to force the issue.

Solo heard her name being called. She looked up and saw Misses Chiles walking up with a very handsome man. First, Solo was annoyed because her brother had rejected her (*she made a mental note to get him back*). Now Misses Chiles wanted to talk, and all she wanted was to dance.

"Solo," called Misses Chiles, in her usual sweet voice. *So, entreating* Solo thought. "Solo, dear, I want you to meet a friend of your Papa and Mama," she continued as she approached Solo clearly looking annoyed. But suddenly there was a transformation in Solo's demeanor as she looked at this hulk of a man approaching her. She thought, *I may be only thirteen, but I certainly know a good-looking man when I see one.* She felt a wetness in her Secret Garden watching this man approach. Solo threw her head high and poked out her rag-filled bosom. Solo felt hot and she hoped she wouldn't pass out.

"Solo, this here is Mister Jessie Freeman," said Misses Chiles excitedly. "He was a very good friend of your Mama and Papa." Jessie looked Solo up and down and just knew he was going to go straight to hell with his thoughts. Now her Mama Tulip was a looker, Jessie thought, *but this girl right here, Lord give me strength*. Solo stood tall and poked out her breasts to full attention as she looked at Jessie.

"Do you dance?" Solo asked. Misses Chiles looked befuddled. Jessie was taken aback but recalled how he and Tulip were known to tear up a dance floor. With that thought, he grabbed Solo's hand, stopped, and respectfully turned and asked Misses Chiles "Is it ok?"

Misses Chiles too was taken aback by the sudden change of events, "Sure, by all means, Jessie. Solo loves to dance, just like her Mama, but mind your manners; she is only thirteen. So off they went to shake a leg.

Solo moved quickly with Jessie, but not before turning to give Misses Chiles the evil eye. She just had to tell him her age (*another mental note, she will pay for that*).

Jessie turned Solo about, and boy could she move. Solo twisted and turned and kick up her feet. Her hips swayed from side to side to the rhythm of the music. People stopped dancing to watch Jessie and Solo. Jessie picked up Solo and flipped her around like the new dance craze and she kept up with his every move. Hair flying, dress held high up to show off those pretty legs. The men, boys, girls, and women all watched Jessie and Solo. Faith and Ben watched and thought maybe Solo was being just a little too fresh, but they knew if they tried to stop her, it would cause a big ruckus. Mister Chiles and Misses Chiles watched also and had their concerns as they looked at the expressions on some of their guests' faces. Baby watched her sister and was glad to see her having fun, maybe this would make her nicer. However, Little Henry didn't like it, so he walked down the path to his old home, the dark cabin.

Solo was in heaven. Her heart moved as fast as her feet. Sweat beaded up on her forehead and her hair began to curl up from the heat. She didn't care. She had never met anybody who could dance like Jessie. They managed about three dances until finally Jessie said,

"Come on girl, you got to give this old man a break."

Solo laughed and said, "You don't dance like no old man."

Jessie laughed and replied, "Well I am a lot older than you and I need a drink."

"Do you want me to get you a punch?" Solo offered.

Now that is funny Jessie thought as he walked away. "Thank you, little lady, but I have something in my automobile that will take care of my thirst."

"You got one of those automobiles?" Solo asked hurriedly while she caught up with Jessie.

"Sure do, 1932 Ford. Won it from a fellow in a card game," Jessie replied smiling.

"Can I see it?" Solo asked with her best innocent smile. "It could be a birthday gift," Solo went on.

Jessie paused for a moment and looked at Solo. Better judgment told him to walk away, but he thought to himself, *what harm would it do to show his friend's daughter an automobile for her birthday?* Plus, we around friends and kinfolks. Jessie smiled at Solo.

"Sure, why not?"

The party was in full swing, and everyone was enjoying the food, fellowship, and music. Even Mister Chiles and Misses Chiles were dancing and smiling at each other. Faith and Ben were socializing with friends and Baby was jumping rope with some other girls. Little Henry was nowhere in sight. So, hardly anyone no one noticed when Solo slipped off with Jessie, happily skipping along. Hardly anyone.

To Jessie, this was all innocent. She might have been about the most beautiful girl he had ever met, besides her Mama, but she was a girl even though she was in a woman's body. He thought Malcolm was a fool, leaving such a nice, sweet girl and kids. Last he heard; Malcolm had run off to New York City. Jessie had come around a few times to visit Tulip after Malcolm left her and the children. She was friendly but clearly heartbroken over Malcolm, so he thought best to leave it alone. Plus, his fast lifestyle was not for a good woman and children. However, he did let Tulip know she could call on him anytime and on occasion even gave Mister Chiles a little money (*he said was from Malcolm knowing that Mister Chiles would not take his money*) to help out Tulip. So, letting his friend's daughter see his pride and joy automobile was no harm. Jessie figured he was headed that way for a drink after all that dancing. Little did Jessie know the web Solo was weaving in her young mind.

Dusk was slowly falling, and the sun was settling down. By the time Solo and Jessie reached his car, the sun had set and there was a slight chill in the air.

"This is a pretty automobile," squealed Solo as she allowed her hand to slowly side down the body of this black beauty.

"Yea," said Jessie proudly, "It's my baby" as he reached in the back to retrieve a flask.

Jessie leaned against his baby, opened the top of the flask and took a long swig, and exhaled.

Solo watched and asked, "Can I have some, please?" Her voice was syrupy sweet. "It's my birthday," Solo went on. "Just a little, please?" she begged.

Jessie, Jessie, he thought, but against his better judgment, he handed Solo the flask and she drank the liquor without flinching. After the liquor stopped burning down her throat, Solo felt warm and giddy. She loved the feeling. Jessie took the flask and took another long swig. They both laughed.

*To be young, to be free, to be loved,
to be untouched by any pain or misery.
No worries, every wakening moment is pure enjoyment and
full of richness only the heavenly beings spun;
In our hearts and dreams, fantasies are our truths,
unrealistic, and never fulfilled, but in our reality it's real,
and always fulfilled;
Destined to be disappointed in the journey of life; so, the
question remains, is this all for real or just for not;
I love you and you say you love me but only time shows what
it is truly meant to be;
So, we pray, we hope, we hang on when we know the end is
drawing near;
We give it all, but it does not stop the unfathomable life of
reality;
Because nothing is ever truly what it could have been
because we eventually come to know in living, there are no
guarantees.*

FOUR
Too Young Too Fast

For weeks to come after the party, Solo dreamed and dreamed of Jessie. After drinking that nasty, foul liquor in Jessie's automobile, bumping into each other along the way, they returned to the party feeling giddy and laughing aloud. Jessie knew she was too young to be drinking, but what the hell, a lot of girls her age drank, plus it was her birthday. The music was in full swing, and everyone appeared to be having a good time. A crowd had formed near the music, some were dancing, and others were just listening and nodding their heads. Even though Solo didn't like the taste of that nasty liquor, she liked the way it made her feel, plus she had drunk liquor before. Feeling the effects of the liquor, Solo wanted to dance and shake her butt. She noticed some of the men folks and schoolboys eyeing her, so she figured it was a good time to show off her dance moves. Solo literally yanked Jessie, *who didn't protest* but was taken by surprise as he had his eyes on some of the women moving to the music and pulled him to dance with her. Solo and Jessie danced and danced. Other men and boys tried to cut in to dance with Solo. While Jessie didn't mind (*because he wanted to entertain some of the women*), Solo pulled Jessie closer and wouldn't let him go. She only wanted to dance with Jessie. Some of the women and girls noticed Solo and Jessie and began to whisper amongst themselves, but Solo didn't care. It was her birthday, and she could dance with whomever she wanted. Besides, Solo loved how Jessie was a good dancer and knew how to hold her just right, never too close, but close enough for Solo to wiggle her backside close to him and lean her fake big breasts into his strong, muscular chest. Solo kept reliving and reliving her time with Jessie.

While at school, Solo constantly daydreamed of Jessie and she would forget where she was because school was the furthest thing from her mind. This caused some problems, particularly with Misses Beckon. A colored teacher in her mid-thirties, so short in stature that many of the students towered over her, Misses Beckon didn't appreciate Solo's lack of attention. As she walked by Solo, Misses Beckon tapped her long yellow ruler on Solo's wooden desk, making a loud rattling sound in the process. Seeing Solo jump in fright from Misses Beckon's ruler hitting the desk made the school children burst out in a fit of loud laughter. Having these stupid children laugh at her really infuriated Solo, who didn't see the humor and certainly didn't like being laughed at. Rightfully so, Misses Beckon was added to Solo's growing list of people she would get back at one day.

Solo walked around in a daze thinking about Jessie. She thought of how she could sneak away to find him. All Solo knew was he stayed somewhere in town. If only she could get away from home to find him. Since the party Solo had not been able to go anywhere except school with those silly kids, even though some were older than her. For some reason, Faith was keeping tight reins on Solo and wouldn't let her out her sight. Unbeknownst to Solo, Faith and Ben had watched how Solo flirted with Jessie at the party. They knew Jessie was a grown man and Solo was too young. Faith and Ben agreed to make sure to keep a close eye on Solo and her coming and goings.

Solo felt as if she would go crazy. So, she was happy when she saw Misses Chiles' buggy coming up the road. Solo knew Faith would be distracted by her Mama, giving her time to sneak away. Solo graciously yelled to Faith her Mama was here and ran down to greet Misses Chiles.

Solo ran so fast, she was out of breath. Hair was flying about and her face, flushed. Misses Chiles looked in bewilderment at Solo.

"Slow up there," Misses Chiles yelled out to Solo.

Misses Chiles was afraid she would fall and hurt herself. Besides, Solo was never that eager to see her. Even Faith, who was watching from the front porch, was a little puzzled at the sight of Solo running to greet her Mama, knowing she usually just sunk off somewhere when Mama came for a visit. Faith knew Solo always thought when Mama came to visit, she was coming to take her back to her home. Somewhere Solo did not want to live. Solo was never happy to see Mama. Faith welcomed this response as a pleasant change.

As Solo approached Misses Chiles' buggy, she announced "I wanted to see if you needed any help, as she grabbed the horse reins.

Well, this is the first, thought Misses Chiles, *maybe things are taking a turn for the better.* "That's very nice of you Solo," Misses Chiles said sweetly, "but please slow down running in this heat, don't want you to have a heat stroke."

Solo looked and smiled at Misses Chiles, but when her back was to her, Solo frowned, and a sly grin smeared across her face.

"Hey there Mama," yelled Faith, who stood on the porch covering her eyes from the sun. "What brings you out here today?"

Misses Chiles got down slowly from the buggy and stood a moment to catch her breath as Solo led the horse and buggy to the barn.

"Do I need a reason to visit my family?" Misses Chiles asked, laughing.

Faith smiled at her Mama. "Well let's get out of this heat and get you a cool drink."

As they were walking into the house, Misses Chiles called out towards the barn, "Solo dear, got another letter from your Mama!"

Over the years, Tulip continued to write to Misses Chiles. She was now with a man named Carson. Though they had not married, they had two children (a boy and a girl) together. Occasionally, the letter would include a couple of dollars. Tulip and Carson were still in New

York City but planned to go to Maryland and find her family. In her letters, Tulip always said she would return for her children as soon as she and Carson could get the money together, but so far that day had not come. Misses Chiles told only Mister Chiles and Faith that Tulip had birthed more children. Mister Chiles just shook his head and walked off. Faith was secretly happy that Tulip had other children and had not returned because she and Ben never wanted to give up Baby. Only Little Henry asked Misses Chiles to read his Mama's letters to him (*He never asked about his Papa*). Solo didn't care and was never around when a letter was being read. Baby really did not remember her Mama or Papa.

Misses Chiles wanted Solo to read this letter from her Mama. She thought it was past time Tulip knew her Mama had another family. She knew well it was going to be hard for Solo to accept, but things needed to be set right and Solo was old enough to understand. Misses Chiles motioned for Solo to come in the house so her Mama's letter could be read.

The mention of a letter from her Mama made Solo's hands tighten into fists. She stomped her foot and kicked the dirt.

Solo heard the call from down by the barn and talked to herself out loud, "I don't care about no letter from her. She is not my Mama and I wish everyone would stop calling her that. What Mama would go off and leave her children? I hate her and I will always hate her." Solo knew Misses Chiles would wait for her to come into the house so she could read that stupid letter. She couldn't leave right now. "Shit, Shit!" Solo yelled as she stormed out of the barn.

May 15, 1939

My Dearest Misses Chiles:

Enclosed you will find $5.00. I know that it's not much, but with the children and Carson working odd jobs it's *the best we can do. This depression has made work hard for everyone. I hope to send more soon. Good news, I found my family in Maryland. We left New York City and moved to a little town in the State of Maryland, called Saint Mary's County, where Carson's family is from and believe or not, I found my Mama's cousin George Allen living down here. We are staying on at one of Carson's brothers and Carson goes oyster and crab fishing to earn our keep. Saint Mary's County is much like my memory of my home in Connecticut, very rural. From what I've gathered so far, Indians were here first, and the Roman Catholic religion is throughout the land. Believe it or not, we are not that far from Washington, DC where the President lives. Maybe one day we can all meet him. So, with that said, Carson and I think that as soon as we get a little money saved, we will come for the children. I can't wait for all my children to be together under one roof. Lord, can you believe seven children, yes seven, I recently had a set of twins, a boy and girl.*

Well, enough about me. How the children? I know that Solo is a hand full. What about Little Henry? I know that he is a good boy and helping you and Mister Chiles around the farm. Baby Cecila is seven now. Where have the years gone. I know she is still sweet. So much time has gone by that it hurts my heart. I hope that my children haven't forgotten me. How is their schooling? Please give Faith, Hope and Charity my love. Can you have my children write me and send their letter to the address in this letter? Don't know how long I will be living here, but for now I am here.

**32456 Leonard Town Road
St Mary's County, Maryland**

I will write again soon and let you know when we plan to arrive. Give kisses and hugs to my babies.

Love, Tulip

Solo listened to Misses Chiles read her Mama's letter with disinterest. But she heard her Mama had gone and got herself a new man and more babies. Well, that suited her just fine. Solo thought to herself, *If Mama thought she was going take off to some place called Maryland with her a brunch of nappy-head kids, well she got another thought coming.* Solo knew she needed to move her plans up quickly before she was forced to go live with her Mama. She wished Misses Chiles would hurry and finish reading that silly letter.

Finally, Misses Chiles finished reading the letter and turned to look at Solo. Misses Chiles reached out and took Solo's hands in hers. "Solo, I know this is shocking to hear your Mama has a new husband, (*she didn't exactly want to say Tulip was living with a man in sin*), and you have new sisters and brothers. Just know your Mama still loves you, Little Henry and Baby, and soon she will be here to make you all a family. I know this is a lot to take in, but Faith and I are here if you need to talk."

Solo got up and went over to hug Misses Chiles.

"Can I have the letter, so I can write Mama?"

Misses Chiles handed Solo the letter and thought, *Finally Solo is coming around.* Solo took the letter and smiled. She then turned and asked Faith for some writing papers and a pencil. Faith told Solo where to look for the items in her dresser drawer. Solo went into Faith and Ben's bedroom and found writing papers and pencils neatly stacked in the top dresser drawer. She walked into her bedroom and hid the items under her mattress.

"Mama Faith," said Solo, "I looked and looked but I can find the writing papers or pencil in your drawer."

Faith excused herself from her Mama to look for the items. Solo held her head down and smiled as Faith walked past her. Faith looked and looked through her dresser drawer but could not find the items.

"Did you find them?" asked Solo knowingly.

"No," Faith replied with her hands on her hips looking puzzled.

Knowing Faith wanted to get back to her own Mama, Solo, so demurely asked

"Do you mind if I go into town to purchase some writing paper? I will be quick about it."

Faith, still looking puzzled mumbled, "That's fine Solo. Just tell Misses Tate to put the items on our bill."

Solo wanted to jump for joy, but she didn't want to seem too excited.

"Ok, Mama Faith, I will just grab a hat and be on my way, I will be quick."

Faith and Ben's modest five-room house was no more than a mile outside of town in a small community with about ten other similar homes. Ben worked in town at the sole bank as a clerk and made pretty good money. Faith stayed at home, but she taught some of the local townspeople writing, reading, and numbers, but lately, many could not afford her services. So, she and Baby would make baked goods and sell them to the local store. Of course, Solo would not demean herself with baking and selling goods.

Over the years, since Malcolm and Tulip had arrived, the town had flourished with new businesses and many more people; colored, white, even Asian. There were more rooming houses, a local beer garden (*drinking, dancing, gambling*), a dentist, small diner, church, train depot, bank, local jail, and courthouse. Several homes and a small schoolhouse sat on the outskirts of the town. Even with the Depression, the town managed to survive.

From Faith and Ben's small community, the town was no more than a mile. Walking on a good day would take about 30 minutes, but today, Solo made it to town in 15 minutes. She had rushed so sweat was running down her face, and the pits of her arms were saturated. Her white ruffle blouse was clinging to her skin and clearly accented the outline of her breast. Solo had stopped along the road and changed into some shorts she hid under her skirt. The shorts were yellow with black polka dots, and they were way too short and tight. The shorts made Solo's behind look like two ripe, large round melons. Even some of her butt cheeks popped freely and were visual. Solo didn't want to look a mess, so she took some time to fix herself up as best she could. She wiped the sweat from under her arms and fanned feverishly to dry her blouse. She tried her blouse in a knot, so it showed off her small waist and flat stomach. Solo spat in her hands and wiped the dust from her legs and feet. One more look over, Solo was ready.

As Solo walked into the town, some of the men folks both colored and white whistled, and some tilted their hats. Solo gave them all a flirty smile. If she had time, Solo would have chatted with them, but she was on a mission and had to find Jessie. *But, where?* She thought. Solo stood and looked around. She noticed a few young colored men kneeling in a circle on the side of one of the rooming houses. Solo crossed the road. Some of the white women who passed her shook their heads in contempt. Solo looked at them and rolled her eyes. If they knew she was colored, they probably would have been insulted, but they just thought Solo was a fast little white girl who needed a good spanking. Solo sashayed, over to the group of colored men. They were so engrossed in their game, they didn't notice her walking up.

"Excuse me," Solo announced her presence.

A couple of the young men looked up from the dice game but held tightly to their crumbled dollars, and gave Solo a once over from head to toe. One even let a low lustful groan.

Staring at Solo hard, one of the men asked, "Ain't you Malcolm's and Tulip's youngin?"

With hands on her hips and looking the man right in his eyes "Yes, I am" Solo replied rather flirtatious. "What of it?" she smirked still looking at the man.

Another man chimed in, "A few weeks back we were at the Chiles' farm for that gathering, and she was dancing with that fellow Jessie."

Solo was excited they knew Jessie, maybe they could help her. "Well do you know where I can find Jessie?" she asked rather hurriedly.

The man was taken back by this mere child's request (even though she could give any grown woman a run for her money), so he looked at her, shaking his head, and said, "Now why do you want to trouble your pretty little self with an old man like Jessie? Ain't you a little too young?"

Solo didn't want to get Jessie in any trouble, and she didn't want it to get back to the Chiles she was asking around about Jessie, given his age and so. So, she lied, "Mister Chiles ask me to find him. They need him for some work."

The man responded, "Well last I heard he was at Miss Kit's rooming house, which ain't but about 30 feet or so on from here on the left." The man rolled dice and howled, "My baby needs new pair of shoes!"

All the men yelled "NO!" as the man reached down and grabbed the money laying on the ground.

Solo thanked them. They were not listening, even though a few of them looked up to check out her butt cheeks hanging from her shorts, which were clearly too tight and short.

It was a steamy hot day, so the door to Misses Kit's rooming house was open to let in whatever breeze was possible as well as flies, bees, birds, and even stray dogs looking for a handout. Solo walked in and looked around at the large open space with a long wooden table surrounded by ten mismatched chairs. The wood floors were covered with beautiful rugs and white, laced, ruffled curtains blew freely with the breeze coming from the many large open windows. A brilliant chandelier with lighted candles hung from the ceiling. There was a large staircase, so Solo preceded to walk up the long row of stairs. Above the stairs was a spacious landing with a couple of chairs and tables. There was also a long hallway with eight or more closed doors with numbers on them. Solo didn't know which door to knock on. As she was about the knock on the first door, it suddenly opened, and a nicely dressed colored woman walked out. She was startled so by Solo standing in front of her door, it made the woman jump.

"Little girl," the woman said with her right gloved hand on her heart, "You gave me such a fright."

"Sorry Mam, I didn't mean to frighten you, but there was no one downstairs to help me." Solo went on. "I am looking for my brother Jessie. I was told he lived here."

The woman thought for a second and finally said, "Oh Jessie, well yes, his room is two doors down on the left, but he may be out right now. Sister, huh? The woman laughed, closed her door, and walked down the stairs without looking back at Solo.

Solo counted the doors and when she reached Jessie's door, she stood there just staring with her hand held high ready to knock, but she didn't. Doubt had entered Solo's head. *What if he thinks I'm just a silly girl? What if he doesn't like me and tells me to go home?* Solo stood for a few more moments and then knocked hard. She knocked again and put her ear up against the door. No answer. Solo knocked again. *Maybe the woman was right, he's probably not here.*

Solo turned to walk away and suddenly, she heard a voice yelling, "Hold your britches, I'm coming! Man can't even take a shit in peace." Solo froze and Jessie opened the door.

"What in God's name are you doing here," Jessie asked, looking around to make sure no one had seen her.

Thinking Jessie was displeased, tears formed in Solo's eyes. She hung her head down, and sheepishly said, "I wanted to see you again."

Jessie, dumbfounded, scratched his head and looked at Solo and boy did she look good. "Get in here, with your fine ass!" Jessie said grinning like he just won a big poker hand.

Solo nervously walked into Jessie's little room which housed a small bed, a nightstand with a lamp, and a chair and table near the window. On the table were a bottle of liquor, a tin cup, cigarettes, matches, a deck of playing cards, a few dollar bills, and some loose change. Jessie told Solo to take a seat. Solo looked around and decided to sit in the chair near the window. Sitting made her little polka dot shorts rise up further. Jessie walked over to the table, grabbed the bottle and poured some liquor into the tin cup, and pushed it towards Solo. Jessie took a big swallow of the liquor from the bottle and continued to look at Solo like he was trying to decide something.

Jessie finally spoke. "Your family know you here?"

Solo considered her options. "Well not here exactly."

Jessie took another, longer swig from the bottle and looked at Solo. "So why did you want to see me?"

Solo reached for the cup and took a sip of the liquor. It felt warm going down her throat. She felt nice and relaxed. She took another sip but decided to drink it all, which made her gag and cough.

"Hold on now," cautioned Jessie, "Don't make yourself sick." Solo smiled.

"You are so pretty," Jessie said. "But you're so young, and you're my friend's daughter."

Solo, gaining courage from the liquor, stood up and walked to Jessie. She began to unbutton her blouse while looking Jessie straight in his eyes. Jessie started to protest, but Solo put her index finger to his mouth. Her gray eyes looked into his very soul. Her nearness made his nature rise. Solo carefully laid her blouse on the bed. She was now standing in front of Jessie topless with her breasts on full display. While she had let boys and men touch her breasts through her clothes, she had never shown her bare breasts to anyone. Jessie looked at her naked chest, full, high, and round. Her nipples were pink and hard. He reached up and stroked her breasts and Solo gasped. How many times had Jessie thought about doing this very thing to Tulip? Never in his wildest dreams did he ever think he would do it with Tulip's daughter. It was like having Tulip.

Jessie walked over and pulled down the window shade. The room was semi-dark, just a little sunshine managed to seep through the opening of the shade. Jessie walked Solo over to the bed and pulled back the blanket. Solo stood in front of Jessie and began to slowly take off her shorts and panties. Jessie watched Solo with full anticipation, aching to see her naked body. After Solo had removed her clothing, she slowly lay down on the bed, fully exposing every inch of her body. Solo didn't attempt to pull the blanket to cover herself. She took pleasure in Jessie looking at her body with lust in his eyes.

While it wasn't the first teenage girl Jessie, being a man in his 30s, had been with, he thought to himself this girl could not be just thirteen with a body like this. She was built and shaped better than some grown women he had spent time with. Jessie looked at the bushy blonde hair covering Solo's private area. It seemed to glisten and sparkle. Solo's beautiful, long blonde hair was spread out around her face. Jessie thought she looked like a white goddess with her shapely, long, pretty, and smooth thick legs which were now open wide, inviting him in.

Jessie disrobed hastily, almost ripping his clothes off. He stripped down to bare bones and his manhood swung above Solo's head. Jessie gently mounted Solo. She seemed so delicate, and he didn't want to hurt her. Once he lay on top of her, Jessie kissed Solo's nose, her cheeks, and then those nice perfect lips. Solo's mouth parted to welcome Jessie's kisses. She gently kissed his back. Jessie stuck his tongue into Solo's mouth. This made Solo jump a little, but her tongue hungrily met his. Jessie moved from Solo's lips to her nice, firm breasts. Solo breasts were not big, but her nipples were hard and fat. Jessie passionately kissed each one. With each kiss, Solo moaned and turned her head from side to side. Jessie slowly sucked each nipple. This made Solo moan more. She felt as if she was going to explore.

Jessie moved from Solo's nipples and kissed her stomach, letting his tongue savor her like melting ice cream on an August day. Solo's body quivered from Jessie's kisses. She was terrified and began to tense up because this was something she had never expected, let alone, experienced. But, being so caught up in the rapture, her body responded to Jessie's kisses. Jessie sensed Solo was overwhelmed. He reassured Solo he would not hurt her, and only wanted to make her feel good. He asked her to trust him. Jessie proceeded to move down Solo's stomach. He kissed the mop of the curly hair draping Solo's Secret Garden. Then Jessie kissed in between Solo's thighs. Solo sat straight up in terror.

"You can't put your mouth there," She gasped.

Jessie didn't respond, but gently laid Solo back down and kissed her on the lips. He went back down between her thighs and began to lick and suck. Solo screamed out. Jessie, frightened someone would hear, covered Solo's mouth with one of his hands. Solo was biting his fingers and tossed her head about. No longer could he hold back, so with his big, hard manhood, he pushed himself into Solo's tight, wet private. Solo screamed out.

I didn't know what to expect, but I didn't want it to stop;
The invasion of mind reacting to the sensation of body, was more than you could bear, but the emotions running through you, screamed out and loss of control was the option.
Give into and feel it flowing freely, no costs, but only rewards, if it's not forced upon you
It builds, lingers, and then explodes, leaving you in wonder, satisfaction, but for some ungodly reason, there is still a linger and wanting for more.

FIVE
Solo and Jessie

Over the next year, Solo and Jessie kept up their secret rendezvous. For Jessie it was just sex, however, for Solo it was love. No one ever had ever made her feel like Jessie. His kisses would make her so dizzy, sometimes she thought she would faint. While Jessie wasn't the first man or boy who had touched her, it was only Jessie she let go all the way. Solo felt it was natural to let him have it his way. Besides, she liked doing it as much as Jessie. Plus, she and Jessie were courting and one day, sooner than later, Solo dreamed Jessie would ask her to be his wife and they would live in a nice house and have plenty of little Jessies. Just the thought, made Solo all hot and bothered. Most nights, while Solo lay in her bed, she would open her legs wide, put her fingers between her thighs, and gently touch herself, imagining Jessie touching and kissing her breasts, which would bring Solo to full ecstasy. Solo would cover her mouth to muffle her screams. During the day, Jessie was her every thought...*where was he, what was he doing, when would she see him?* On and on, nothing but Jessie was on her mind.

Sometimes Solo snuck away and met Jessie by the river. Hand in hand they walked and talked. Mainly Jessie talked, and Solo listened. Solo would bring a little food so they could have picnics. Jessie had big plans. He talked of making his way to the Big City (New York City) to make a lot of money and become a rich colored man. Solo sometimes felt a little jealous because Jessie never mentioned her in his plans. She didn't mind too much because she would follow him anywhere. When

Solo had not managed to sneak off somewhere with Jessie, daydreaming of him consumed every waking moment of her young life. Solo walked around with her head in a cloud, singing, smiling, to herself so much sometimes she would not even hear Mama Faith calling her name. Mama Faith shook her head and wondered what in the darn world was wrong with that child. She was relieved she was not causing trouble or fighting with Baby. Mama Faith would just sigh and tell Solo to get her head out the clouds.

Baby, however, knew her sister Solo well, and sometimes she would follow her and watch as she and Jessie made out. She was very careful Solo didn't catch her because surely, Solo would hurt her. So, Baby kept the secret to herself, but on occasion and just to get her sister back for being mean to her, Baby teased Solo for dreaming about her boyfriend. Of course, Solo denied it, but Baby kept repeating it and saying she was going to tell (*of course she knew better*). Even though Solo knew Baby could no way know about Jessie, the thought of Mama Faith and Papa Ben founding out about her taking up with Jessie made her mad and caused her to turn red with anger. If they found out, it would be the end. Also, if Baby ever discovered the truth about her and Jessie, being the tattletale she was, Baby would definitely tell Mama Faith and Papa Ben.

It was hard for Solo to get away from home. For her not to draw attention to long periods away from home, Solo arranged to meet Jessie in the woods closer to the house. That way, neither Mama Faith nor Papa Ben would not get suspicious. Occasionally, Solo skipped school. Solo felt she didn't need any more schooling because one day she would be Jessie's wife and he would take care of her. When Solo wanted to skip school, she made Little Henry and Baby promise her they would not tell she was not in school. Solo knew Baby was such a little tattletale, but Little Henry didn't care one way or another. Solo lied and told her brother and sister she had to miss school so she could work and make money to help Mama Faith and Papa Ben. Baby didn't promise Solo. She did not believe in lying to Mama Faith and Papa Ben and the Preacher said lying was a sin and when you lie the gates of Hell would open for you. Baby feared going to Hell. Furthermore, she didn't believe what Solo said about wanting to help at home because Solo was selfish, and she only helped herself. So, when Solo asked Baby to promise she wouldn't tell on her for not going to school, Baby crossed her fingers behind her back and nodded. As far as Baby was concerned, she did not make a promise she could not break. Baby was determined to find out what Solo was up to.

Solo was laying in Jessie's arms, sweating profusely from hours of intense, heavy lovemaking. Since Solo started her affair with Jessie, she only had eyes for him. She didn't care that Jessie was old enough to be her father. Many girls married men much older than they were. Besides, Solo didn't care what people thought, but Jessie did and didn't want to cause any trouble with Mister Chiles. Their affair had to remain a secret, for now.

Solo sat up in the bed and wiped the dripping sweat from her forehead. The room felt hot and smelled of sex. Solo threw her legs over the bed and peeked out the drawn window shade. The sun would be setting soon. She realized it was getting late and needed to get home before Mama Faith returned from visiting her own Mama. Solo was supposed to be at home helping Baby prepare supper for the family. Mama Faith had left very strict instructions because she didn't want Solo wandering off like she had been in the habit of doing. Of course, as soon as Mama Faith left, Solo told Baby to get started on supper and she would be back soon. Baby protested but Solo ignored her. Now, Solo had gotten caught up in her lovemaking with Jessie and let too much time pass. Solo looked down over at Jessie who was fast asleep and snoring loudly. She reached down to wake him, but her head started to spin, and she felt dizzy. Solo realized the liquor she drank with Jessie made her feel sick to her stomach. Since taking up with Jessie, her liquor consumption had really taken off. Solo reached over and shook Jessie's shoulder.

"Jessie, Jessie," Solo shook him awake, "Get up, I don't feel too good, and I got to get home. Jessie, wake up," Solo whispered.

Jessie didn't respond to Solo. She continued to shake him but got no response. Solo had to get going. She pulled the cover closer to Jessie's face and bent down to kiss his lips. Solo almost vomited because Jessie's breath reeked of foul-smelling booze. But he was still cute.

Solo quickly got dressed and opened the door to Jessie's room. She looked up and down the hallway just to make sure it was clear. Jessie had warned Solo about being careful and not to let anyone see her at his place. After she felt it was safe for her to leave, Solo ran as fast as she could down the stairs and out the front door. Solo was walking as fast as she could to get home. She was just about out of breath and had to slow down a little. Solo hoped Baby had already finished supper. Hopefully, Mama Faith and Papa Ben had not made it home, but she had to hurry because it was later than she expected.

As Solo got closer to the home, she became aware of a faint smell of smoke. Way above the trees, she could see smoke rising to the sky. Solo thought someone was just burning timber, but the smell of smoke only got stronger and stronger the closer Solo got to her house. Solo could see the smoke rising above the large oak trees, making circles of clouds in the open sky. She heard the cracking of burning wood. The smoke was getting thicker the closer she got to her home. Solo's heart began to beat fast. Beads of sweat began to form on her forehead, her eyes stung from the smoke, and her throat was burning as she inhaled. Solo covered her mouth and tried to suppress her cough.

Through the smoke Solo could see wagons and horses on the road near the house. Many people were running about. She heard shouting, and then more shouting. Then she saw it, her specious home all ablaze with an orange and yellow fire billowing from every direction. The fire was angry and evil...the devil himself. It was burning hard and fast. Solo stood frozen and a single tear slid slowly from her eye down her cheek to her mouth leaving a salty taste on her lips. A line of people had formed a human chain and passed buckets of water from the well to throw on the raging fire, but the fire was just too furious and growing larger.

Solo gathered her thoughts and began to move toward her home. As she got closer to the burning home, she recognized some of the locals from town as well as some strangers she did not know. Some people began to stare at Solo and whisper. Others made the sign of the cross. Thinking the sisters had been lost in the fire, someone shouted, "She here!"

Solo felt herself running towards the fire. As she got closer to her burning home, several of the men grabbed her and held her tight. "Now slow down now girl. There is nothing you can do here."

Solo was hysterical, kicking, sobbing, screaming "WHERE IS BABY? WHERE IS MY SISTER, BABY, BABY?" She and Baby had their differences, but she didn't want her dead, not like this. "LET ME GO!" Solo yelled at the men. "MY BABY SISTER IS IN THERE! LET ME GO!" Solo was kicking and continued to scream at the men. But the men held tight.

Faith was several yards away from her burning house being comforted by some of the women. Her face was streaked with black soot from the fire which had not only destroyed her home but had also possibly taken her babies. No one had seen Baby or Solo. Everyone felt certain they could not have escaped that monster of a fire. Faith watched as Ben and the townspeople, both young and old, worked hard to put out the fire. When she and Ben had arrived home the house was already in full blaze. Ben tried to enter the house, but the fire fought him back. Faith had looked around for the girls. She screamed and called out their names. Echoes of her screams ringed loudly throughout the woods, birds flew away rapidly beating their wings, dogs barked indicating danger. Maybe they went to town for help, Faith thought. She called out to her husband, "I don't see the children!" The fire and smoke were pushing Ben back from the house. Ben also yelled out for the children. No answer. He quickly ran back to Faith telling her to bring water from the well. "HURRY!" he had yelled. As Ben ran towards his house, he saw people coming up the road by foot and by buggy alike. He knew he would need all the help he could get, so he silently thanked God and prayed the children were safe. Hopefully, it was not too late.

It was too unbearable for Faith to watch her home burn down as well as the dreaded possibility Solo and Baby were consumed by the roaming fire flames or smoke. Thank God Little Henry was away working at another farm, he was safe. She had been a good mother and loved the girls as if she had borne each one herself. It was incomprehensible that God would make her suffer by taking the girls in such a cruel manner. How could she tell Tulip? With this thought, Faith dropped to her knees on the hard dirty rocks and muddy ground (from the well water) and prayed. She prayed to God the children He and Tulip had entrusted in her care had not perished in the fire. Faith prayed out loud, not caring who heard her.

"GOD PLEASE!" she begged. "LET MY BABIES BE SAFE! YOU ARE A MERCIFUL GOD! PLEASE DON'T TAKE MY BABIES. PLEASE, I BEG YOU!"

Her head ached, her eyes were blood red, her knees hurt from the hard ground, and her throat burned from breathing in the thick black smoke, but Faith felt no pain…she prayed. Like a sweet blessing from above, she heard one of her girl's voices calling out. Could it be possible? Was she hearing things? Faith stood to her feet and brushed away the dirt, mud, and rocks stinging her knees. With tears streaming down her dirty face, she looked around and yelled out, "BABY, SOLO!"

Ben stopped what he was doing and turned in the direction of his wife's voice. Solo, hearing Mama Faith calling out her name, broke away from the men who were holding her and ran towards Mama Faith, who in turn, was running to her.

Mama Faith, with snot flying and tears running, hugged Solo tight and proclaimed, "Dear God, Solo, you girls are safe, I thought I had lost you both."

Faith kissed Solo's forehead, cheeks, and hair then drew her so close they almost became one. As Faith gathered Solo into her arms, Papa Ben watched as his wife kissed and hugged Solo. Tears fell from his eyes because one of the girls had survived, but he also knew one had not. Faith and Solo, mother and daughter, embraced for what must have seemed like an eternity. Faith stroked Solo's hair and rocked her from side to side, praying and thanking God for this blessing. Suddenly, as though hit by a thunderbolt, Faith withdrew her arms from around Solo, pulled back, stood for a moment looking at Solo who was sobbing uncontrollably. In a daze, Faith turned around slowly to look at her burning house then looked back at Solo. Faith's brain was having a hard time registering what was happening; her mouth could not form words. It was hard for her to breathe with her heart racing. It seemed like hours had passed, but only seconds had. Faith struggled to find her words. She took a deep breath, looked at Solo, and asked nervously "Where is Baby?"

Solo could not look at Mama Faith, but the question she asked cut like a sharp knife slicing deep into her flesh. Solo heard what she thought was the cry of a wounded animal. The cry was so primal, it made Solo's skin crawl. But it wasn't a hurt animal's cry, it was Mama Faith's pain. With her head hung low, Solo listened to Mama Faith sobbing and screaming with both arms extended toward her burning house. Mama Faith repeatedly called out Baby's name, as she crumbled to the ground on her knees. The woods grew quiet, there was not a sound. There was no motion. The only sound was the cry of agony, suffering, and pain. The women folk gathered around Faith to comfort her. They folded their hands and prayed for God to comfort her in this time of great tragedy. They knew all too well there is no greater loss than one of losing a child.

Ben heard his wife's screams; he saw as she fell to the ground. He dropped the water pan, spilling its content down to the ground. As fast as his legs would take him, Ben ran to the woman he loved more than anything on earth.

As people gathered around Faith and Ben, Solo slowly moved back. No one comforted her. It was like she was invisible. The smoke burned Solo's eyes and throat. Mama Faith's screams were more than Solo could bear. Solo looked with pity and sorrow at the woman who she loved more than her own Mama. Solo knew Mama Faith loved Baby like her own and losing Baby would surely break her heart. Now Baby was gone, and it was her fault. Mama Faith and Papa Ben would never forgive her if they found out she had left Baby alone to start the stove for supper. Many times, Mama Faith warned Baby to be careful the fire didn't catch her clothing. Solo thought of Baby screaming as the fire burned her pretty, brown soft skin, and the thought made her shiver. Though she didn't have much love for her little sister, the thought of Baby suffering did make Solo sad. Solo looked at her home, which was now just a pile of burnt rumble. She looked and Mama Faith and Papa Ben clinging to each other and sobbing. Solo turned and ran.

Solo ran as fast as she could. Tears streaking her face, hair flying wildly in the wind, arms flinging. She was running away from everyone and everything. "They never loved me anyway!" Solo screamed out loud. Not Mama, Papa, Misses Chiles, Mister Chiles, Mama Faith, Papa Ben, not even her own sister and brother. How could her own mother and father leave her like she was a piece of trash, discarded and given to the first taker? Mama or Papa never came back to get her. They didn't care about her. Why was she ever born? Truly, they did not want her. Solo continued to run faster and faster. The wind hit her face like rocks. Tears blinded her eyes. But still, she ran away from the pain. In the distance, Solo heard Mama Faith and Papa Ben calling her name and pleading for her to come back. But Solo continued to run. How could she tell them she'd left Baby in the house to cook supper while she was away doing the unspeakable with a man twice her age?

As Solo continue to run, her thoughts flowed through her mind like an overflowing river. It was Baby's own fault the house burned down. *Stupid girl! She should have been more careful, always so fast to do things. Baby, always the goody two shoes, wanting to please Mama Faith and Papa Ben. She probably couldn't wait to tell Mama Faith I ran off and left her alone to cook supper. Served her right she burned up. Good riddance, I am glad she's gone. It wasn't my fault. I didn't mean to stay so long with Jessie. Baby should have waited for me to return.* Solo's head was pounding with pain and her chest was beating too fast from running. She needed to stop thinking and rest. She looked and realized she had reached town.

The sun had settled down and it was now growing dark. Solo was alone in the dark. Thank goodness no one was walking around town. Many of the townsfolk went to help with the fire and others had most likely settled in for the night. *I don't have any money, what will I do, where will I go? If I go back, Mama Faith and Papa Ben they will be mad because they lost their precious Baby. they will blame me and send me away to that awful place for children who were not wanted.* At school Solo had heard some of the children talk about this old, dirty mean place where children were sent when they didn't have anyone to take care of them. They talked about how the children were raggedy, beaten, and had no food. It was an awful place to be sent. *I will not go to that place, but where will I go?*

Solo stopped, looked, smiled, and said "Jessie."

Let your heart run free,
we are truly as young as we want to be. Travel in your space
and do what is placed in your spirit to do;
The time is right now, and it is yours to spend as you see.
Looking back is wasteful, because the only thoughts of the
old cliché "what will be, will be;"
Rather, dear one, look ahead and grab hold and make your
world the best it can be; Yesterday is no do-over, tomorrow is
maybe my friend, this moment is the time you have;
So, keep it moving forward, put forth the effort, and make
your life the best it can be; Taste it, live it, feel it, this thing
called living. For, as it is said, as it is true, life waits for no
one, only those who live as dreamers and fools;
Surely, I hope that is not you!

SIX

Liar, Liar Pants on Fire

Solo hurried up the stairs to Jessie's room, taking two steps or more at a time. She knew for sure Jessie would help her because he loved her. Jessie talked about leaving this old nothing of a town. Now Solo could go with him. Nothing was here for her. Jessie was now her life. By the time she reached Jessie's door, Solo had to stop to catch her breath. She knew she looked a mess, so she wet the hem of her blouse with spit and wiped her tear shrieked face. She gathered her hair into one long braid. She smoothed out her clothes. She tried the door, but it was locked. Solo gently knocked on Jessie's door and called out to him.

"Jessie, Jessie it's me, Solo, open the door," she begged. She put her ear up against the door to see if she heard movement from inside, but it was quiet. Solo knocked a little harder and called out a little louder. Still no answer. Panic began to set in. Solo's mind was racing. *What if Jessie heard about the fire and ran away fearing they might blame him?* Solo just knew Jessie wouldn't leave her though. So, she knocked harder and called out to him louder.

Finally, Solo heard a muffling noise and Jessie's door cracked open. "WHO IN THE HELL IS IT?" Jessie angrily demanded. He hated being woken out of his sleep. *What could be so important?*

"Jessie, it's me, Solo. I need to talk with you," Solo pleaded.

"Solo, that's you girl?" Jessie asked while rubbing his eyes. "What in the tarnation you are doing here at this hour?" He cautiously opened his door. The room was dark, and the smell of musky sex, smoke, and liquor lingered in the air, giving the room a foul smell. Jessie had still been sleeping, exhausted from drink and liquor. Solo entered the room and quickly closed the door behind her. She was glad the room was dark because she didn't want Jessie to see her in such sight.

Jessie walked over to the table and reached for the lamp. He needed some light to focus on Solo. As Jessie reached for the lamp, Solo yelled "No!" in protest, pulling his hand away from the lamp.

"What is wrong with you girl?" Jessie was puzzled by Solo's actions. Then, as if a light bulb went off in Jessie's head, he turned in Solo's direction and asked, "What are you doing here at this hour anyway? Did something happen?" Suddenly, dread entered the pit of Jessie's stomach, like a snake creeping slowly up his back. He grabbed Solo forcibly by the shoulder and pulled her close to him. His breath was hot and reeked of too much stale alcohol. Jessie's voice quivered as he asked, "Did Mister Ben find out about us?"

Solo hesitated before she answered. Her mind was swirling. Apparently, Jessie hadn't heard about the fire. How could she tell him about fire and Baby? She needed to think quickly.

"SOLO!" Jessie yelled, causing her to jump. "DID YOU HEAR ME? DOES MISTER BEN KNOW ABOUT US? SPEAK UP, GIRL!" Jessie demanded with fright and a sense of urgency. He reached and turned on the lamp so he could see Solo's face. She looked a mess, and this frightened him even more.

"Yes!" Solo quietly answered meekly.

"Yes, what?"

"Yes, Papa Ben knows about us, and that's why I'm here, to warn you," Solo lied. "Papa Ben and some of the men from town are coming after you and they are going to send me to one of the awful homes." Solo continued, "Jessie, we got to go before they get here. Please Jessie we need to go."

As Solo was pleading with him, Jessie was pacing back and forth trying to wrap his head around what Solo was saying. He had planned to leave for New York City soon, but he was trying to save up a few more dollars, and he surely had not planned to take anyone with him, certainly not this young girl. Jessie thought about what he had gotten himself into. He should have used better judgement and not messed with this girl. What had he gotten himself into?

Solo watched as Jessie paced back and forth, offering no response. Suddenly, Jessie knelt, reached under his bed, and pulled out a battered old brown suitcase. Without a single word to Solo, he set the suitcase on his bed and commenced to throwing what little clothing and toiletries he had into the case. Solo was overjoyed with happiness because Jessie was packing, and they would be able to leave this nothing of town for the big city.

Solo realized she only had the clothes she was wearing. "Jessie, I rushed here to tell you so fast, I didn't have time to pack. Can we get me some new clothes in the big city?"

"Hold up Baby Girl," said Jessie.

"He stopped packing and looked at Solo. "Now, I barely have enough money for me to make it to New York City, I can't have you trailing along. It's best you just mosey on back home and make amends with your family, I am sure everything will work out."

Solo was speechless and she felt herself growing hot. She thought to herself, "*He can't just leave me here.*" Solo watched as Jessie took one last look around the room then picked up the suitcase from the bed and moved towards the door. Solo began to panic and moved as quickly as she could to block the door. Jessie cast a hard look at Solo and knew what she was up to. He was frustrated and he didn't have time for any of her silly games.

"Solo," Jessie said as calmly as possible, "Now you know I am fond of you, and one day you will find a nice young man your age and settle down. But you can't go with me and that's that. Now move away from the door because I need to make haste."

Tears slowly streamed down Solo's face. She couldn't lose the one person she loved. Solo reached out, took Jessie's hands into hers and choked back tears. "Jessie, I am with child, your child. That's why I can't go back home. Papa Ben and Mama Faith called me awful names and told me to leave their house. I have nowhere to go. See, you must take me with you. I won't be no bother and plus, you know my Mama lives in New York City, and she will take me and the baby in. So, please Jessie you have to take me with you." Solo threw her arms around Jessie's neck and held on tight. Such a good liar, she thought to herself as she held tight to Jessie.

Jessie dropped his suitcase to the floor and let his arms fall to his side, while Solo held tightly onto his neck. Jessie was stunned. "*A baby? I am not ready to be nobody's Daddy. Surely Mister Ben will shoot me or force me to marry Solo. How did this happen? What was I thinking by fooling around with this girl? This is a mess.*" Jessie reached up and had to pry Solo's arms from around his neck. His neck was wet from all her sobbing. Jessie placed his hands on Solo's shoulders.

"Listen., I will take you to New York City to find your Mama. But hear me clear, afterwards, we are done and you must promise me you will tell Tulip, I mean your Mama, the baby is someone else's. You got to promise me that. You know Tulip and your Papa are my friends, and they will not take kindly knowing I was messing with their daughter. Solo, do you promise?" Jessie demanded.

Solo's head was hanging low, so Jessie did not see the slight smile across her face. She was elated. This on-the-spot plan was working. "Yes, I promise Jessie."

"Solo, I am not playing, and you better keep your promise," Jessie stated with authority.

Solo threw her arms around Jessie's waist proclaiming, "Oh, Jessie, I love you so much, thank you, thank you. You won't be sorry, and I will keep my promise, please don't worry."

Jessie pushed her away a little too hard and looked at her. What choice did he have? He was stuck.

"Come on," Jessie replied, "We need to get moving. Just know it won't be an easy trip and we may have to pick up some odd jobs along the way to earn money for gas and food. And little girl, just know you will work for you keep, this here ain't no free ride. So, no complaining."

Solo smiled and nodded. She dared not say another word, in fear Jessie would change his mind. Solo felt for the very first time in her short life true happiness, and it was because of Jessie. *Just wait and see*, Solo thought to herself. She had no intention of looking for that awful Mama of hers. Jessie will surely marry her, wait and see. For a fleeting moment, Solo allowed her thoughts to go to her siblings. Baby, how she must have suffered when the fire burned her skin, the mere thought made Solo shiver, and Little Henry, he will be missed a little. The Chiles' were good to her. So were Mama Faith and Papa Ben, but it's over now. Jessie is her life now. So, she smiled and closed the automobile door. Just like that, Solo left that life behind her.

Lies, Lies, more lies, is it even worth it, the lies we tell are like being caught up you're your own fictitious spider web;
A continuous entrapment, like a never-ending story, that all started with a big fat fib;
Needed from the beginning, even creative and beautiful in some way, but lies always fray,
but seems to linger forever in a day;
Not meant to be mean, maybe even kind, but many found a little lie is needed time to time;
So tread lightly with your white lies, because the truth will be known when the lie is untold.

SEVEN
Big City...New York City

In the early 1900s in New York City, a Negro man was accused of killing a White patrolman. Needless to say, in the minds of the Whites, this was an unfathomable and unforgivable act by a Negro. The reason the Negro killed the White patrolman was never substantiated. For the Whites, there could never be any justification for the killing of one of their own, a man serving the law at that. Therefore, the reason was of no consequence and the killing had to be avenged. The white community was enraged and demanded justice. Bent on vergence and self-righteous, a mob of thousands of angry whites took the law into their own hands. It was like a red cloud descended over New York City, and Whites were out for the blood of Negroes. As a result, this act caused a history-making murderous, racist riot between Negroes and Whites. There was no place for the Negroes to hide from the onslaught of thousands of Whites. While the Negroes tried to protect their community and family, they were outgunned and outnumbered. Resulting in hundreds of innocent Negroes (men, women, and children (old and young) unjustly descended on by Whites who were seeking to rend their form of justice. The Whites' cruel violence resulted in mass casualties and outright murder. Not only did the Whites kill defenseless Negroes, but they also confiscated their merger processions, and burned their homes and businesses. How naive were the Negroes who thought they had left such treatment and brutality in the Jim Crow South? So stupid to think their lives would be better in the Big City. So, in 1943 when Jessie and Solo arrived in

New York City, the effects of the 1900 race riot were still evident and they found Negroes were fairing no better than when they were in the South.

Jessie and Solo saw the look of defeat on many of the faces, but even more so, the City itself was of a different kind of beast. New York City was a cultural shock for Jessie and Solo. Long gone were the gentle winds, the sweet smell of the Magnolia trees. They were accustomed to tall trees providing needed shade on a hot sunny day. The clean fresh air, open fields with roaming animals, beautiful flowers, and peaceful birds chirping away were now gone. Instead, they were welcomed with New York City's tall, ugly stone structures looming before them, which gave off a ghostly, dark, uninviting gloomy appearance. No trees, no crisp breeze, no beautiful flowers. Instead, New York City was loud and noisy. The dirt-paved streets were crowded with a combination of people, automobiles, wagons, horses (including their droppings) cats, and dogs. There were so many people moving about and some shouted out their wares for sale… "Got fresh meats! Get your vegetables! Juicy, ripe fruit for sale!" Some people were just simply shouting at each other in their attempt to communicate over the deafening City sounds. Children ran about playing tag, oblivious to the chaos of their surroundings. But what Jessie and Solo found most shocking were the foul smells attacking their nostrils with such force, they fought back the urge to spill their guts. The smells were an intoxicating mix of aromas of different foods, animals, human and nonhuman waste, decay, and just plain bad odors.

While there was some racial mixing in New York City, it was ethnically divided, even for the wealthy. Most Blacks and West Indians lived in lower Manhattan in an area called San Juan Hill, which was "a bit of Africa." In Tenderloin, Blacks Southerners lived in proximity to Irish immigrants with whom they competed for low-wages and low-skilled jobs. It was well-known "the animosity between the two groups was high." However, the Red-Light District was "the heart of the black middle class and a haven for artists and writers whose presence earned the neighborhood the name of "Black Bohemia." The Red-Light District was where the races mixed because of the offering of an array of nightlife, hard liquor, drugs, dancing, gambling, and fast women. Many Black musicians and dance girls (with lighter complexions) were hired to entertain the wealthy as well as criminals.

But most Negro men found employment at the shipyards where goods were both exported and imported, as well as distributed and delivered to the many businesses. For Negro women, there was high availability of domestic work in the homes of wealthy whites. Some Negro women were fortunate enough to become independent laundresses and/or seamstresses or even beauticians (limited to other Negro women and sometimes Negro men who wanted their hair permed and curled). But laundry businesses were mostly ruled by Asians who provided work opportunities for Negro women to wash, iron and sew. Cleaning for the wealthy and caring for their children was still the job for colored women as well as the newly arrived immigrants. Negro men found chauffeur jobs. However, there were plenty of employment opportunities for other races who wanted to work.

In New York City most of the neighborhoods were ethnically segregated based on race (i.e., Whites, Negroes, Asians, Jews, Irish, Italians). Initially, in the late 1800s, tenements were built to provide housing for the thousands of newly arriving immigrants (Jews, Irish). The tenements were small, crowded, and not well-maintained, but the tenements offered the arriving immigrants a roof over their heads, and they were affordable. With so many people cramped together; the tenements eventually became "slums." However, the immigrants worked hard and pooled their resources and in time they moved on to better living conditions. The run-down tenements were left to the new immigrants…Negroes.

The tenements' landlords took advantage of the Negroes. The tenements were slums, so it was not uncommon to see poor living conditions. Most of these places were small, crowded, rodent-infested, and dangerous fire hazards. Rent was high, and landlords did not pay attention or keep up the conditions of the property they rented to Negroes or these new immigrants. Regardless of the conditions, for those with limited resources, it was better than living on the streets; especially during the hard New York City winters to which Southern Negroes were not accustomed.

So, in the early spring of 1943, Jessie walked into the front door of their tenement apartment. The smells of the different ethnic foods being cooked, combined with stale acholic, and fresh urine, assaulted their senses.

Many tenants left their doors open to keep an eye on their children or just to chat with each other or visitors. In the summers, the hallway provided a cool breeze for the hot, cramped apartments. Some of the women hung about in their doorways fanning from the heat, scantily dressed and flirted with the passing men. Most of the time the flirting was innocent, but in some cases, the women flirted to earn some much-needed money, food, clothes, or even a drink. Children played freely in the long poorly lit hallways with peeling paint, screaming, laughing, and running about. Some men and young boys gathered in the corners rolling dice and drinking, which sometimes resulted in loud arguments and fights.

While the tenement was the slums, it was relativity safe and clean. However, rodents ran about freely in search of food and cats stayed in the hunt for rodents.

Jessie felt lucky to find this place for him and Solo. The travel to New York City was not easy, rather it was long and hard and used up most of Jessie's hard-earned cash. He was almost down to his last penny. Of course, Solo didn't have a dime to her name. Along the way, they did pick up work here and there, which provided a few pennies for gas and food. Solo complained most of the time about her hair or being tired or hungry. She was lazy and didn't want to work. Most of the time, she wanted to drink and complain.

When Jessie and Solo arrived in New York, they had very little money left for a nice place to live, but Jessie was able to find work at the shipyard unloading goods from the various ships when they arrived at the port. The work was hard, long, and backbreaking. Jessie was glad he was young and strong because many Colored men would stand in line all day and would not get picked for work. First, the whites, then the Chinese, sometimes the Irish, and then the Colored. The pay was not fair for the hard work and long hours, and he was certain the Coloreds got less than the others. Fortunately, he could count and made sure he wasn't being cheated like many of the others. Given their current financial situation, the tenement was the best they could do for the time. He hoped Solo would find her kin and move on. But in the meantime, they needed money.

Jessie had to walk up three long flights of steps to get to his and Solo's apartment, which was located at the end of the long hallway. As he hurriedly walked by, some neighbors yelled greetings. A few ladies winked at him. But Jessie knew to just keep moving, head down, no eye contact. He turned the knob to his apartment, which was always unlocked, and walked in. There she was, sprawled out on their makeshift bed. The room was musky and hot. Curtains were drawn, so the room was semi-dark, with a little daylight allowed. Clothes were thrown about, dishes unwashed and the smell of stale cigarettes lingered in the air. Jessie looked down at Solo. Damn, he thought, I wish she wasn't so pretty. Some folks in the tenement thought she was either Mulatto or Creole. Others thought Solo was poor white trash who fell in love with a Colored man and was now unwanted by her own kind. They would just shake their head at Jessie like they felt sorry for him because they knew he was a dead man walking. Some of the men were outright disrespectful and whistled at Solo or made crude comments about her body or what they would like to do with her, which Jessie just ignored, but Solo relished. However, for the Colored women, it was a different story. They showed blatant contempt for Solo and would roll their eyes when she passed by them and they in turn mumbled under their breath. Solo seemed to take pleasure in their attitude, and as she walked past them, she tossed her beautiful blonde hair and smirked, which didn't help matters.

Jessie placed the large bundle he was carrying on the floor and stood looking down at Solo, either she was fast to sleep or drunk again. Her drinking had greatly increased since arriving in New York City. He watched as her nice plump young breasts rose up and down. Her beautiful blonde hair cascaded down to the floor. Her long, beautiful legs were hanging slightly off the unmade bed. Jessie felt conflicted about his feelings for Solo. In the six months since arriving in New York City, Jessie had come to realize he had been tricked into bringing Solo with him. It had all been lies. Neither Ben nor Mister Chiles were coming for him. Even her being in the family way was a lied. Jessie was relieved because he was not ready to be anyone's father. No baby was coming, nor was Solo trying to find her Maw. A few months back, Jessie ran into some fellows from back home and learned about the fire and the death of Baby. There was even talk about Solo having something to do with it all considering she had run off. Jessie thought to himself what a fool he was to be hoodwinked by a sassy little girl. He was so blinded by her beauty and sex. But, no more. THAT he knew for sure. Little did she realize, there would be no more free rides and Jessie would no longer be the fool. Things were about to change.

"Solo, wake up girl. Have you been drinking and sleeping again all day? Dammit, git your black ass up! I'm sick of this shit. We been here for six months, and I been busting my ass for the both of us. For what?"

Jessie walked towards the apartment window. He pulled back the raggedy curtain to let in a little light. Jessie looked down and briefly stared at the people moving about. He turned and looked back at Solo, he noticed she had not moved. He walked over to the bed, reached down, and shook Solo's shoulder as hard as he could. "WAKE UP!"

"OK! OK!" Solo yelled back as she slowly raised from the crumpled bed. "Hold your horses, will you! My head is killing me, and your yelling is making it worse." Solo lowered her head into her hands.

"I don't have time for your whining, I need you to get up, NOW!!"

Solo looked up at Jessie through red, strained eyes. She hadn't slept well because of the reoccurring nightmare. Always the same—smoke, fire, burning, screaming, someone calling her name, a hand reaching out to her. She would always wake up soaking wet and sweating before the hand touched her. Jessie told her sometimes she would scream in her sleep.

"What's the rush, Jessie?" Solo stretched out her arms and yawned. Jessie decided it was best to change his tune a little. He knelt in front of Solo and took both of her hands in his. He reached up and brushed the hair out of her face and smiled. "Same dream again?"

Solo looked sad and nodded her head yes.

"Well maybe this will make it all better," said Jessie smiling like a little boy. He reached down and picked up the package he had brought home. "I got you a gift," he said with a wide grin.

Solo greedily reached for the package. "For me?" she squealed and put her hands to her face.

"Yes," Jessie said, "for you, but it's for a purpose. You being such the good dancer you are, I mean you're the best I've ever seen, except for Tulip, I mean your Maw." He allowed memories to briefly occupy his mind. "So tonight, my sweet, your dear Jessie is taking you out on the town and we are going out to dance."

Solo leaped to her feet, grabbed the package, yelled, and jumped up and down like a happy child getting a birthday gift. Solo was making such a ruckus, the neighbors knocked on the wall and yelled at them to keep the noise down. They were tired of Jessie and Solo constantly yelling and fighting. They didn't know this was happy noise.

Solo held the package close to her chest. It had been a long time since someone had given her a gift.

"Go ahead," Jessie prompted. "Open the package."

That was all the encouragement she needed. Tulip ripped open the package, not worrying she could damage the goods inside. Out spilled a pair of shiny red patent leather high-heeled shoes, black silky stockings with a black garter, a black silk slip, and a red straight silk dress with a long front line and a split in the back. Solo was floored. It was the prettiest dress she had ever seen. There were even matching undies. She was overjoyed. Seeing how happy she was, Jessie felt guilty he lied to her about going dancing. Sheepishly and softy he admitted, "I got you a gig, I mean a job."

Solo stopped twirling around and looked at Jessie with a puzzled look.

"A job? What kind of job?" she asked.

Jessie smiled and proudly announced, "A dancing job of course, so you need to get all dolled up with these pretty new clothes, so you can make a good impression. I hope the size is right for everything. I tried my best to describe your size to the store lady. So, get moving, I need to have you there by seven." Jessie was all business by this point.

Solo stood with her mouth gaped open and stared at Jessie. Suddenly, she was consumed with fear. She absolutely loved dancing. She danced every day around their small apartment. Even when she and Jessie went out to dance, people would clap for them. Solo thought herself to be a very good dancer with all the right moves, but it was for fun, not for work, at least not for her. She never thought she could make money dancing. But, come to think of it, she always noticed men watching her dance. That she really liked, and it gave her a thrill.

Solo finally said to Jessie, "A job...you got me a job. A dancing job? But, Jessie, I've never danced for anyone before, only for you. I don't know if I'm good enough or if I could even dance for other people. What if they don't like me or laugh at me?" Solo asked with a sense of dismay.

"Now, now, stop all that foolishness." Jessie pulled her into his arms, and affectionately stroked her hair. "No one is going to laugh at you. You are a good dancer. Besides, I will be right there with you. Look at this job as fun, while you make a little money, and you know we need the money. So, stop worrying and go get dressed, we need to get there soon." Jessie patted Solo lovingly on her bottom and pushed her into the small bathroom.

> *Yes, I say bring it on, I welcome this thing with open arms;*
> *I am ready to be free, to enjoy and let in this thing that may*
> *be the very key to my life's needs;*
> *No fear, no doubt, no fleeing,*
> *I will be breezing through this thing like a sunny day,*
> *doused by a sudden onset of summer rain;*
> *Do not fret, or fear for me, rather pray for me, because my*
> *life is a choice for where and what I want to be;*
> *Like mother nature, I control my destiny;*
> *and only the "almighty" can make this thing meet my most*
> *ultimate needs or be the demise of me; which is to be loved*
> *by only you for eternity.*

EIGHT
Feeling Yourself

"Slow down Jessie, you are going too fast, and you know how hard it is to walk in these high heels," Solo complained.

Jessie had to make up for the time Solo took getting ready. But he had to admit, it was worth the wait because Solo looked stunning. When she walked out of the bathroom, Jessie couldn't believe his eyes. The dress fitted her to a "T" as well as accented her womanly curves. Who would believe she was just fifteen years old with a body that would bring any man to his knees? On top of that, she looked like a white girl, which was an extra bonus.

Jessie looked back at Solo, while still walking fast in front of her.

"Stop complaining, Solo. I told Mr. Big I would have you there by seven and it's already seven and we still have a way to go. Speed it up so we can get there already."

If only I could take off these high heels and walk in my bare feet like I did back home, then I could walk faster and keep up with Jessie, Solo thought to herself. But the City streets were dirty, littered with trash and broken glass. No way was she going to risk walking with bare feet on these streets. Solo tried her best to keep up as well and ignore cat calls and whistles from men as they passed. She liked the attention. However, the women she passed gave her evil looks of envy. This made Solo smile and hold her head up higher. Still, she wondered, *who in hell is Mr. Big?*

"Jessie," Solo protested, "please slow down, I'm all sweaty and my makeup will be messy."

Jessie slowed his pace a little. It was important to him Solo make a good impression. This gig was important because he wasn't making that much money on the shipping docks, so he needed Solo to get this gig.

"Jessie," Solo called out.

"What now?" Jessie answered.

"Who is Mr. Big?" she asked.

"Well, Mr. Big is a very important Colored man who owns businesses here in the city, like Spots where people can go and dance and have fun after a hard day of work. It's been said all sorts of people go to these Spots. Some are very important people and even white people. Now you have to be invited to these Spots so it's very important you don't go running your mouth about where you're working. Do you understand me, little girl?" Jessie was forceful with his reply.

"But, Jessie, I don't understand why I can't tell anybody, especially if they want to come and see me dance," Solo recanted.

"Because you can't and that's all you need to know," Jessie replied angrily. "Now stop with all the questioning and get a move on. We are almost there. Remember when we get there, I do all the talking. But, if anyone asks your age, you're eighteen years old. Remember, you are eighteen years old. Don't want no problem with you being underage, given you are only fifteen there about, but it's is our little secret." He gave Solo a wink. "You look pretty, so smile and show those pretty whites."

Solo wanted to ask more questions, but she knew Jessie was getting all bothered, so it was best to keep quiet for now. However, she was curious about Mr. Big, and the job. She wondered why this was such a secret.

Finally, Jessie stopped at the entrance of a long alley full of discarded trash and debris. The alley looked dark and mean. Solo noticed cats were on top of trash cans looking for food and scurrying about. Also, several men were lying on the ground. They were dirty and their clothes were ragged. A few didn't even have on any shoes. Solo turned to and looked at Jessie who was adjusting his own clothes.

"Jessie, I am scared, this place doesn't look right." Jessie hadn't even noticed the men on the ground, let alone the unsightly appearance of the alley.

"What you scared for girl?' he inquired while smiling. "Them just bums, who down on their luck. They don't mean you know harm, plus you know I'm carrying, so no need to worry. Just stay close to me."

Solo gripped Jessie's harm and held on tight. She had never seen bums before.

"Come on now, the place is right down here a way. Watch your step and don't mind them bums."

Solo tried not to look at the bums as she walked by, but they looked at her with blood-streaked sad eyes and matted hair. A couple even smiled, showing yellow stained teeth. The alley stunk of urine and discarded rotten food. Solo put her head down and walked holding on to Jessie.

"Ok, we're here. This is the place."

Solo was confused because she didn't see anything except doors with no windows, and stairs leading down.

"Solo," Jessie said grabbing both of her shoulders, "Let me get one more good look at you." Jessie looked her up and down and grinned with approval. "Boy, you are a beauty. Now remember, you let me do the talking and remember, by chance anybody asks you, you is eighteen, just like we told the landlord, and don't forget."

"But, Jessie, I don't feel good about this. Look at this place, how is this a place to dance?"

"Now, what you worry about the outside for girl, you are dancing inside, just you wait and see," Jessie replied excitingly. Jessie told Solo to be careful going down the steps. After walking down, a flight of steps they came to a heavy metal door with a small, closed window box. Jessie knocked on the door twice. To Solo's surprise, the little window opened showing off two rather large eyes. The eyes first looked at Jessie, then lingered on Solo. She felt naked under the gaze.

"I'm a guest of Mr. Big," said Jessie. The eyes disappeared, and the window closed with a bang. Suddenly, the big metal door cranked open. Jessie stepped in, pulling Solo with him and the door slammed shut behind them. Solo jumped. Her heart was beating so fast, but Jessie seemed relaxed and calm. The eyes were suddenly in front of them. The owner seemed to be a big, black, wooly-headed giant. Everything about him was large, his head, nose, lips, eyes, ears, hands, biceps, and more. He even had a big old rear end. Solo slowly moved behind Jessie.

"Follow me," the eyes said. Down a long dark hallway they walked, but Solo got the sense they were not alone. The thought made her skin crawl. She was so nervous and needed answers, but before she could open her mouth, a door opened to what seemed to be another world.

Wow! Solo mouthed to herself as her eyes grew wide in amazement. She had never seen such a place, let alone been in one. While it was dark and smoky, the place had an air of elegance. Solo noticed a large, magnificent bird, a kind she had never seen before, sitting in a cage. The bird had beautiful colors of blue and green, with large wings. Solo tugged at Jessie's jacket and whispered in his ear, "Is that a bird?"

Jessie was rather preoccupied with meeting Mr. Big and offered an agitated response.

"It's a peacock and don't be so stupid!"

She thought, *Hmm...a peacock? Funny name for a bird, but pretty.* Solo was surprised by Jessie's tone but didn't let it stop her from taking in her surroundings. She thought it was an odd place for dancing. There were different colored lights all around. Music was roaring from the band on a small stage. The room was filled with people dressed to the nines, both men and women. Some of the women were sitting on men's laps, their dresses pulled up to expose as much thigh as possible. *Modesty be damned.* The men's hands seemed to disappear up the women's dresses. Solo turned away quickly because she didn't want to stare. Drinking, smoking, laughing, talking, dancing, you name it, were all in full swing. The place was exciting, and Solo could barely contain herself. She felt her heart racing, the heat from the room made her sweat, and her already fitted dress was now certainly clinging to her body. But it was so very exciting. She had never, ever, been anywhere so exciting. Both men and women looked in her direction. Some nodded and smiled with cigarettes hanging from their lips and drinks in their hands. She wished she could have a smoke and a drink.

Solo was so caught up, Jessie shook her shoulders to get her attention.

"Solo," he nudged, "stop lagging and keep up!"

They followed the man with the eyes down the dark hallway. However, Solo wasn't keeping up, so Jessie decided it was best to pull her along. Finally, they reached a closed door and the man with the eyes said in a deep voice, "Wait here." He knocked twice on the door and walked in. It seemed like an eternity had passed since Jessie and Solo stood waiting outside the closed door. They could hear the music and talking coming from the other side of the door.

Jessie smiled at Solo and said "Now remember what I told you, let me do all the talking. Don't start mouthing off. Just let me talk." Solo wanted to ask why. She wasn't no child and didn't like Jessie treating her like one. Instead, she just nodded. Finally, the closed door swung open. Jessie walked in with Solo so close behind, he felt her hot breath on his neck. Solo looked around the room, which was brightly lit with beautiful furnishings. There were no windows, which gave the room a very closed feeling. The hardwood floors had a nice shine. Along the wall was a beautiful red velvet sofa with two matching chairs, adorned with two matching tables and lamps. The man with the eyes quietly closed the door and stood in front of the door with his arms folded in front of him. Solo then noticed the large desk positioned in the middle of the room, with a rather short, stocky man, with a thick mustache, and small beady eyes sitting behind it. There were two other rather big men with expressionless faces standing directly behind him. Their muscled arms were also folded in front of them, but their eyes looked straight ahead and showed no emotion. These men made Solo fearful, she crept even closer behind Jessie, as if she was trying to disappear.

The small man behind the desk looked up at Jessie and Solo, smiling invitingly.

"Now who do we have here?"

His greedy eyes ignored Jessie and were firmly fixed on Solo, but she was so close behind Jessie, the man couldn't even get a good look.

Jessie finally answered, "Mr. Big, my name is Jessie and this here is my lady, Solo." Introductions made, Jessie reached behind him and pulled Solo to his side.

Jessie continued, "I want to thank you for this opportunity. You won't be sorry. Solo is not only a good girl—I mean woman—she's an excellent dancer as well as good to look at."

Solo smiled because Jessie had never referred to her as his lady, and now he even called her a woman. As Jessie continued to ramble, Mr. Big tuned Jessie out and focused solely on the lovely young creature blessing his presence. He had seen and been with some beautiful women in his time, colored and white and everything in between. But standing before him was by far the most beautiful creature ever created by God. He let his eyes slowly roam over Solo's perfectly shaped body, his eyes resting on her perky breasts. Her long golden hair caressed her arms, giving her a look of a goddess. Her beautiful green-gray eyes were hypnotizing. Her complexion was golden, and her skin was flawless. Mr. Big's eyes traveled down to Solo's wide hips.

Finally, he said, "Turn around." Solo's feet were planted so firmly to the floor, she couldn't move. She looked at Jessie who was urging her to comply. Slowly she turned as if she was a toy in a music box.

"Stop," commanded Mr. Big. His small, nubby fingers were raised high. Solo had her back to him, and she was now facing the man with the eyes, who was looking directly ahead, but not making eye contact with her. Not many things frightened Solo, but this whole scene was making her quite uncomfortable. She wanted to leave but she could barely move and dared not speak.

"Dear, turn around and face me," Mr. Big's voice bellowed. Solo slowly turned around with her arms straight down and hands each tightened into a ball. Her head hung low.

"Look at me, dear. I am not going to bite you. What is your name?"

Solo nervously raised her head and looked at Jessie.

"No dear, don't look at him, look at me and tell me your name."

Solo was conflicted and didn't know what to do so Jessie spoke up.

"Again Mr. Big, her name is Solo. She's just a little nervous."

"Did I ask you to speak?" Mr. Big asked Jessie, clearly not requiring an answer. Jessie, sensing Mr. Big's warning, nudged Solo into compliance.

"I'm called Solo," she meekly responded.

"How lovely, and the name suits you. How old are you? If you don't mind me inquiring."

Solo hesitated but recalling Jessie's warning she managed a meek, "I'm eighteen, Sir."

"Now, please dear, don't *sir* me. You'll make me feel old. My friends call me Mr. Big or MB and if you're going to dance here, you have to be my friend. Don't you want to be my friend?" asked Mr. Big seductively.

Solo knew men, and she knew what that statement meant. Her mind was racing. *Why not* she thought, maybe it's time for a change and little fun. She raised her head in full confidence, flipped her hair over her shoulders, smiled and looked directly into Mr. Big's eyes, and responded.

"Yes, I want to be your friend."

"Great! Those formalities are out of the way." Mr. Big leaned back in his chair and put his feet up. "You are hired. Now, understand, you will not only dance with the customers, but you will drink with them so they can buy more drinks. That's how we make money. The more they drink, the more money we make. They will tip you with cash, and that's yours to keep. Now, the liquor and a pretty girl may make some men get a little touchy. That's for us to handle. So, no need for you to get upset, we will be watching over you. You are expected here every night, except on Sunday. Seven o'clock pm, at the latest. Don't know what time you will be leaving. It'll will depend on the crowd, but we will make sure you get home safely. Now, Betsy, where is Betsy?"

Mr. Big looked at the man with the eyes. "Vick," *(he had a name)* "get Betsy in here."

As Vick left, Mr. Big continued talking directly to Solo. He said, "You can drink, but drink quick, it will be watered down. Don't want to chance you getting drunk. I expect you to dress sexy, just like you are now. Keep your hair down. Stay clean, meaning bathe, and always smell good. I will give you a cash advance to buy some clothes, but you will have to pay it back with interest. Do you understand?"

Both Solo and Jessie shook their heads in agreement. The door opened behind them, and in walked Vick followed by a very tall, heavy-set colored woman, with extremely large breasts.

"Betsy," Mr. Big apologized, "Sorry to bother you. I know you busy with the customers.

"Yes, I am MB…and tired," Betsy stated rather salty.

"I know Betsy", replied Mr. Big, "but I got someone here I want you to take under your wing. Betsy hadn't noticed the two standing there. She turned quickly to look at this stunning creature, the man wasn't bad either.

"Little young ain't she MB? Don't want no trouble with the law." Betsy was observant as she looked Solo over.

"Don't worry, she's legal and I will handle the law, you just handle the workers." Mr. Big smiled knowing Betsy well. She would teach Solo the ropes.

"What's your name child?" Betsy continued to look Solo up and down. She knew a cash cow when she saw one.

Solo looked at Jessie and then Betsy and responded, "My name is Solo."

"What the hell kind of name is *Solo?*" Betsy asked, laughing out loud. "What kind of name is that? How do you say it, *Solo?*" Betsy continued to laugh.

Solo was furious. No one ever laughed at her name, and she decided then and there she didn't like this woman and she would make her pay.

Between her fits of laughter, Betsy realized she had offended the poor girl. "Ok, sweetie, I don't mean to make fun of your name, but that is truly going to be a conversation piece for our customers."

Mr. Big, sensing the tension in the room, decided to keep the meet and greet brief.

"Ok that's enough, we're done here," he announced.

He extended an envelope to Jessie. While still holding on to the envelope, he looked at Jessie sternly in his eyes, leaned in closer to his face, and stated, "You have that pretty little thing here tomorrow, and don't be late, and you make damn sure she gets some of this money."

Jessie, feeling the meaning, just nodded. Mr. Big released the envelope and said, "Ok everyone, out, we got a club to run."

Everyone then exited the room.

Jessie tucked the envelope in his pocket, grabbed Solo by the elbow, and pushed her through the door.

New life in the day, no time to play,
just time to find your way;
If it's fame you seek, open the doors wide and let it in and
see if you weep;
For you will be judged, the world will not be your friend,
can you handle letting them in;
Stripped down naked, vulnerable as can be, smiling like you
like it, is this what you want the world to see;
Not free in this life to be what you want to be, being out
there ripped you down, made you doubtful, feel like now
your life is no bigger than bee…yep that's me!

NINE
Make that Money

Jessie could not believe his good fortune. He needed a drink. It was time to celebrate. He turned to Solo who was trailing close behind him, looking around with her eyes wide open.

"Come, baby. Let's have a little fun before we leave." Jessie was in good spirits and asked Solo, "Do you want a drink?"

Solo was so relieved Jessie asked, she was dying for a drink. Everything was happening so fast, and she was so nervous she could have passed out right then and there. Jessie spotted an empty table and motioned for Solo to follow him as she continued to take in everything. The joint was even more crowded than when they first arrived, and it was jumping. Both white and colored folks were smoking, drinking, laughing, talking, dancing, flirting, and just having a good old time. Solo noticed the men looking at her very approvingly. However, the women looked at her with envy.

"What you having?" asked a young colored girl, wearing red lipstick and a very tight blue dress which barely contained her busty bosom. The girl leaned in close to Jessie and smiled. In the process, she managed to roll her eyes at Solo. Jessie was grinning so hard right back at this girl. Solo looked at Jessie. He seemed to be hypnotized by this girl who was spilling out her too-small dress. Solo elbowed Jessie in his ribs as hard as could. Jessie jumped and looked at Solo, who was obviously pissed at him.

"We will have whatever you are serving, bring a bottle and two glasses." The girl seductively responded, "That will be two dollars, sweetie."

Jessie turned his back to the girl as he rifled through the envelope Mr. Big had given him. There were a lot of bills, so he carefully pulled out a five-dollar bill. He didn't want to be flashy with the money because he knew there were some good-for-nothing, low-lifes in there who would be waiting for him in the alley to rob him blind; Jessie had been around the block a few times, he was no fool. So, he folded the bill as he handed it to this sexy girl and said, "make the drink a double and you keep the change."

The girl looked at the bill and smiled, "Yes sir," she said as she sashayed away in her too-tight dress with her jiggly big ass being tossed from side to side. Jessie let his eyes follow that big ass as he lit his cigarette and took a long, slow drag. *Yes*, he thought to himself smiling, *My kind of town.*

Solo's foot tapped to the music and her butt bounced up and down. She wanted to get out there on the dance floor and shake her stuff. Maybe Jessie would dance with her when he stopped gawking at the ugly girl with her out-of-shape, big ass. Solo noted his disrespect. She was the best-looking girl in this joint. As she looked around the room, a few men winked and smiled at her. But suddenly, Solo's eyes stopped directly on Misses Betsy who was staring directly at her. Solo quickly turned away from her penetrating gaze. She felt a little hot and unnerved. Something wasn't right about that woman.

"Solo, Solo," Jessie said, shaking Solo's shoulders.

An annoyed Solo looked at Jessie "What? I'm sitting right here, why are you yelling my name," Solo asked sharply. "If you hadn't been so busy staring at that ugly girl's behind, you wouldn't have to try and get my attention."

At that very moment, the girl walked up and placed the bottle of liquor on the table and sat down two glasses, giving Jessie a wink as she walked off with her hips moving to the music. Jessie didn't dare let his eyes linger on the nice, gorgeous ass. Instead, he poured both him and Solo a drink from the bottle. Solo had her back to Jessie, so he gently turned her to face him and lifted her chin to make eye-to-eye contact. He handed her the other glass and said, "Here's to the most beautiful lady in this joint." After the toast, he drank the shot of liquor straight down. The liquor was strong, and his throat felt the fire, he coughed a little. Solo laughed seeing the liquor make Jessie flinch. She raised her glass of liquor and swallowed the burning substance quickly and smiled.

Jessie looked at her and slapped his knee. "Now that's a real woman for you. Come on baby girl, let's show these folks how to cut a rug." He grabbed Solo's hand and pulled her up out of her seat to the dance floor, which was small and crowded with other patrons. Jessie turned Solo about, and she threw her beautiful blonde hair about her head, kicked up her legs, shook her butt, and snapped her fingers. Jessie thought to himself, *Boy, she can really go.* People on the dance floor began to stop and made room for Jessie and Solo. They clapped and chanted "Go, Go, Go." This made Solo move even faster, with hips twisting, fingers snapping, dress raised up to show her beautiful legs and thighs, and butt shaking. She was giving it her all. Jessie picked her up and spun her around. He was recalling another woman who moved like Solo.

With her back against the wall, Betsy smoked her cigarette and watched Solo on the dance floor. She slowly let her tongue move across her lips. Now she had seen a lot of girls come through the place who could dance and was good to look at. But this thing right here was something totally different. Betsy looked around the room and watched how the men and women were enjoying Solo's dancing, as well as her good looks. MB had struck gold with this young thing. *And it's going to be my pleasure to take her under my wing*, Betsy smiled to herself and took a drag of her cigarette.

Jessie and Solo were exhausted from dancing so much. They

finished their drinks and began the long walk home. It was a little chilly outside, but they didn't feel the cold. They held each close and smiled. Solo hadn't been this happy since her thirteenth birthday party where she met Jessie. She leaned her head on his shoulder. Jessie was talking so fast about everything, but the only thing she could focus on was her hurting feet. There were killing her. How she wished she could take off her shoes like she did back home. The thought of home made her briefly pause. Regardless of the pain, Solo didn't dare walk on the dirty city streets barefoot. Jessie was so focused on the money Solo would make, he didn't realize she was behind him moving at a snail's pace.

"What is it? Are you hurt?" he asked, with actual concern in his voice.

"No, I'm fine Jessie, but my feet are killing me in these shoes."

Jessie took one look at her and immediately swept her up in his arms.

"Jessie, have you lost your mind? Put me down," Solo demanded as she laughed.

"Nope, my love, tonight I'm your prince in shining armor, the king of the jungle and you are my queen," Jessie said with a wide grin.

"At the shipyard, I carry loads way heavier than you anyway," he added.

"Still yet, we have a long way to go, and you can't carry me all the way," Solo said as she wrapped both her arms around Jessie's neck and laid her head on his wet shirt.

"Watch me!" Jessie challenged.

When they finally reach their apartment building, Jessie slowly eased Solo down. He was exhausted, but he was still smiling. Solo sat down and took off her shoes and looked up at her hero. Together, hand in hand they made their way up the stairs and walked down the long hallway to their small apartment. The building was quiet and dark. A few crickets scurried about. Jessie was glad it was late because he didn't want any trouble. He had the envelope with the money safely tucked in his shoe, but still, he kept watch.

When they reached their apartment, Solo threw her arms around Jessie.

"I just want you to know I appreciate everything you do for us. I feel so safe with you, and I know you will take care of me. I love you so very much. You are my family, and I will always do what it takes to keep us happy. I know you could have any other woman, but you chose me. You were my first (*for going all the way*) and I will always be your lady."

Jessie felt his heart was going to explode. He didn't plan to fall in love with this girl. He just wanted to get her to her family. But now he had caught some feelings for her. Maybe she wasn't that bad to have as his lady. At least there were no babies. He wasn't ready for no family or wife. He thought to himself, *Right now I'm just ready to have this sweet thing.* Jessie took the key and unlocked the apartment door while he and Solo kissed passionately. Her body clung to his. He took his foot and kick open the door, while Solo continued planting kisses on his face and neck. He took his foot and kicked the door closed and reach back with one hand and clicked the lock.

Solo pushed Jessie back on the bed and threw her head back while laughing. Using her sexiest voice, she offered herself to him.

She mumbled hotly in his ear, "You want some of this, baby?"

Jessie could only nod as he rushed to disrobe.

"Slow down baby," urged Solo, "and let me help you."

Jessie laid back on the crumpled, unmade bed and let Solo finish undressing him. She slowly took off his shirt, folded it, and laid it aside. Next came his shoes, socks, and his pants, which she also folded. She did not remove his underwear. Done with the task of undressing him, she straddled him and slowly lowered the top of her dress so her bra was fully exposed. So was ready to get this thing happening. Jessie reached up to help her remove her bra. Solo took his hands, kissed them, and placed them down on his chest. She reached behind her and carefully removed her bra. Her perky breasts spilled out, fully exposed and raised to attention. Jessie reached up to touch her breast, but Solo lovingly swatted at his hand. *What a tease*, Jessie thought.

Still straddling him and with her chest fully exposed and her dress around her waist, Solo began to move in methodical, steady movement. She needed music, but she didn't want to stop. Her panties were now wet, so she stood up slowly.

"Where are we going?" Jessie asked confused.

Solo looked at him seductively and let her dress fall to the floor. She walked over to the record player and placed the needle on her favorite album by Billy Holiday. With only her panties on, she swayed to the music and let her long golden hair fall about her face and breasts. Jessie could only stare. Slowly she walked over to Jessie, who by now was fully nude and fully erect. Solo looked down at him and thought to herself, *Let the fun begin.*

***

Solo woke up and reached out for Jessie. She felt around, but the bed was empty. Yet, there lay a flower, a tulip, with a note, which read:

"Take this money and go to the following places listed, they will be expecting you. I got some business, so I may not be home around 7:00 to take you to the joint. Make sure you do exactly what's listed in this note. By chance I don't make it home, get dressed and go without me. The address is in the note just in case you forgot. Don't be nervous, you will be fine, and Betsy will show you the

ropes. If I don't make home to pick you up, I will be there to take you home. Don't go off with NOBODY and be careful and watch yourself. By the way baby girl, last night you were great!"

Solo's heart was racing. *WHAT THE HELL!* She threw the money and note to the floor. She thought to herself, *How can he expect me to do all this? He said he would be here to help me. I can't do this by myself. I just won't go, that'll show him.* Solo paced back and forth, shaking her head from side to side. She had to decide what to do. Talking out loud, she surmised, "I want to dance and need to make this money. However, I can't travel the streets by myself, I don't even know where to start. What to do? What to do?" It dawned on her, maybe one of the ladies in the building could help. She had to get her hair fixed and buy some new clothes. But who would she ask? Solo mentally ran down the list of women, the ones she knew anyway, and one stood out. "Yes, Maybelline," she announced to herself.

Solo considered the idea. Maybelline appeared to be around her age, but much more mature and sophisticated. Jessie seemed to like her, and she was also pleasant. No need to waste time. Solo picked up the note and money and hurried into the bathroom to wash and get dressed. Maybelline's apartment was on the same floor as Jessie and Solo's. The door was usually open, but this morning it was closed. Solo gently knocked on the door.

"Who is it?" a voice yelled from the closed door.

Solo hesitated," It's me, Solo.

"Who? Speak up?" Came the reply from the other side of the door.

Solo cleared her throat. "Ahem, it's me Solo from down the hall."

"Oh." Maybelline recognized Solo's voice. "Hang there for a minute."

Solo replied with a barely audible, "Okay." She was so nervous.

After what seemed like forever, Maybelline's apartment door opened revealing an exotic domain. Burning incense filled the space, giving off a strong, sensual, hypnotizing aroma. Different color pillows cascaded about on the floor and a round bed covered in purple and gold linens. No lamps were on, but candles were lit everywhere. The place was inviting and different from anything Solo had experienced.

"Now to what do I owe this occasion?" asked Maybelline as she bowed before Solo. Maybelline thought Solo was one of the most beautiful colored girls she had ever met. She didn't understand the relationship between her Jessie, whom she had bedded herself on several occasions. The girl was very young, clearly naive; and Jessie was a fully grown man, with great skills for pleasing any woman Yet here he was robbing the cradle. Maybelline shook her head in disgust and thought to herself, *N—rs ain't shit*. Anyhow, she liked Solo, and it wasn't her fault she was with this cheat of a man.

Solo looked at Maybelline and took a deep breath and handed her the note Jessie left. Maybelline, who was not much of a reader, tried to make sense of the note. She knew of the places in the note and figured Jessie was pimping Solo out. Maybelline smiled and looked at Solo who was looking like a scared rabbit.

"Yeah, I know the places," Maybelline announced. "Give me a minute and we will be on our way." Solo was relieved.

When they entered Mz Ethel's hair shop, a little girl greeted Maybelline and she handed her Jessie's note. The little girl walked over to an older big, black, busty woman, with a big kind smile. Her name was Mz Ethel, and she was known for doing all kinds of hair, both Colored and White women *(of course she had to go to the White women's houses because they would not dare have their hair washed in the same bowl as a Colored)*.

Mz Ethel walked up to Solo. "So, this is the pretty thing who crazy Jessie was going on about. Come here, chile. You is as cute as a button.

What are you White, Colored, Indian, Mulatto? We gets them all in here. Don't be scared, I don't bite. Mz Ethel is going to take real good care of you."

Solo was frozen in her spot. Since Mama left, she had to take care of her hair as well as Baby's hair. Maybelline, sensing Solo's reservations, egged her on.

About three hours later, Solo looked in the mirror and she could not believe the transformation. Mz Ethel had worked magic on her hair. Solo smiled.

"I look beautiful. Thank you, Mz Ethel. Thank You, Mama. What do I owe you?" Solo asked.

"For you, my dear child, five dollars," replied Mz Ethel.

Solo turned her back, pulled the money from her bra, and handed Mz Ethel a wrinkled five dollar bill. Solo had no way of knowing Jessie had paid Mz Ethel in advance. Maybelline and Solo thanked Mz Ethel and went on to their next stop, which was Misses Kay's dress shop.

Misses Kay was a petite Asian woman who stood no more than four feet tall. She owned a seamstress shop on 171 West 31st Street. She kept a supply of ready-made dresses or could make a dress to your specifications. She specialized in serving the working women of the evening. Her dresses made head turns. And she was no fool. When Maybelline and Solo entered her shop, the overhead bell rang. Misses Kay stood up and bowed and smiled, displaying brown stained teeth to the two ladies. She was familiar with Maybelline and watched her carefully, but she didn't know this other pretty who stood before her. How she would love to dress her and accent her shapely body.

Maybelline spoke up, "Good Afternoon, Misses Kay, it's good to see you. This here is my friend Solo. She needs some of your magic for an evening event."

Misses Kay thought to herself, *Evening event, tsk, serving men, always serving men.* Bowing, she said, "I will make her beautiful, because just maybe her beauty will keep her safe."

Misses Kay looked at Maybelline and smiled before saying, "Yes, I have a dress for her. Come follow me."

After leaving Misses Kay's the time was drawing near for Solo to get to the spot. She was excited and rushed to her apartment, hoping to find Jessie. There was no Jessie. Maybelline told Solo not to worry and assured her she would help her and get her to work. Unbeknownst to Solo, Maybelline once worked for Mr. Big. She wanted to offer some words of advice but thought the better of it. She didn't want any problems herself. She had gotten out.

Maybelline helped Solo with her makeup and got her dressed. Solo's transformation made Maybelline gasp. Solo was stunning. Maybelline almost wanted to cry, because she too, was once just as stunning, and she knew what would come Solo's way.

Maybelline smiled at Solo. "I got you a ride. Are you ready?" Solo was still a little apprehensive without Jessie, but she didn't want to be late on her first day and disappoint Mr. Big. *Where could Jessie possible be?* He knew how important tonight was. *Well, who needs him? I can do this.*

Solo turned to Maybelline. "Yeah, I'm ready."

Maybelline had gotten Solo a ride with someone she referred to as one of her "Johns." This particular "John" was dark-skinned and heavyset with a big belly hanging over his belt. Solo didn't know if Maybelline had more than one man friend named John or what. Maybelline quickly hopped in the front seat of the car and moved over very close to the man. She motioned for Solo to get the back seat of the car. Solo hesitated and thought maybe this wasn't such a good idea. She considered waiting for Jessie. While Maybelline had been nice to her, this man was another story. He seemed a bit gruff.

"Get in, come on Solo, you don't want to be late, do you? Get in and shut the door, it's getting a little chilly," said Maybelline urged, as her hand inched slowly towards the fat man's crotch. Solo was conflicted, *What the hell,* she thought, plus it was getting a little chilly, and she didn't have a proper coat to match her fancy dress. This city weather was so unpredictable.

Solo hopped in the back seat of the car. As she sat, her dress crept up, exposing her shocking thighs. This made her uncomfortable because the fat man named Johnny Boy kept looking at her through the rear-view mirror. Maybelline was so busy chatting away, she didn't even notice. Solo was familiar with the look she was getting from this disgusting fat man. It was the same look she used to get from the men back home. Sometimes, it was rather annoying especially when she wasn't interested and best believe, she was not interested in this fat man. Solo looked at him and rolled her eyes. Hopefully, he got the message.

Maybelline told the man to stop at the entrance of the alley and turned around to face Solo.

"OK, honey, this as far as we can go. You know where to go from here. Stop by my place tomorrow and let me know how things went. Go 'head, hop out and go in there and shake that ass, make that money."

Solo was scared to move. She looked down the dark alley. "Can't you take me a little closer? I have on these high heels, and with no coat. I might catch a chill, plus the alley is really dark and creepy." Solo pleaded.

"Don't be a silly rabbit," Maybelline said as she threw her head back and let out a fake laugh, "It's not that far, plus Mr. Big don't care for cars driving up to his place, draws the wrong attention, if you catch my drift."

The fat man finally spoke, "Come on, get to moving. I got to get going."

Solo gave him a mean look and stepped out of the car and slammed the door. The fat man yelled, "Damn it she could have broken my window! If anything is broken Maybelline, I am taking it out of your hide."

Maybelline let out a hearty laugh. "Come on sugar, she's just a child, didn't mean no harm." The car sped away leaving Solo shivering from the night's cool air.

How she wished Jessie was here. She thought to herself, *Boy, you wait until I see that no good n—r.* Solo peeked down the dirty dark alley. Of course, a few critters scurry about, but she didn't see any humans lurking. It was getting late, and she needed to get moving. She wished she could take off her shoes and make a run for it in her bare feet, but the alley was just too dirty. Solo took a deep breath and willed her two feet to move. With her head up high, she moved as fast as she could down the alley. Except for the noises from cars on the main street and dogs barking in the distance, the alley was relatively quiet. No one would expect a night spot to be located there. It was a well-kept secret.

Solo's high heels made a clicking sound as she briskly made her way down the alley. Apart from the city noises, the alley was no different than the long down roads back home. Solo's eye caught a raggedy, big, black cat astride on a discarded box. It carefully watched Solo as she walked by. She hoped it wasn't a sign of bad luck.

"Best to keep my eyes focused forward," she said out loud. She didn't look back or sideways, just forward. After what seemed like an eternity, she finally saw the door she and Jessie had entered through the first time. Her feet were now hurting really something awful, and she felt a chill. Nevertheless, she was ready and excited for this adventure. She wished she had one of those little mirrors so she could check herself out. Instead, she carefully patted her hair and pulled it down and straightened her dress with her hands. She reached down the front of her dress and pushed up her breasts so they could sit up nice and high. She rubbed down her stockings to smooth out any wrinkles and checked for any runs or snags. *That will have to do. If that good-for-nothing Jessie was here, he could check me out and make sure I'm in good shape. He ain't but I will show him. Just wait til I get some money in my pocket.* The most wicked smile spread across her lips. Solo raised her chin high, tossed her hair, and gingerly knocked on the door, as if not to disturb anyone. Just as before, through the small slit, the same beady eyes peered out at her, seemingly annoyed. The eyes slowly traveled down Solo's body, taking in every detail. With a quick slam, the window slit closed, and the door jerked open. With no questions asked, the big man motioned for her to enter. Solo stepped inside, relieved to be out of the unnerving alley, and so ready to show her stuff and make some money. *Where in the hell was Jessie?*

> *To be young, to be free, but so naïve;*
> *Your youth is your armor,*
> *use it to shield against the wannabes;*
> *Time is on yourself,*
> *plan wisely to accomplish all things as foreseen;*
> *Like an unpredictable sunny day,*
> *there will be obstacles that will come into play;*
> *Why? Devils' playground some say, but listen to God's voice*
> *so you will not be lead astray;*
> *Because as surely as I say, one day, you will wonder, what*
> *happened that day making me go that way;*

TEN

Awakening

Like before, Solo followed the muscular man, Vick, who she learned was Mr. Big's bodyguard, down the long dark hallway. Her high heels clicked and her tired legs stretched as she tried to keep up with Vick. She was so excited with anticipation, it was hard to control the nerves and keep her legs from trembling. Hot sweat dripped down her neck to the center of her back. Her skin glistened from the moisture. Solo thought to herself, *Thank God I have good hair, so I don't have to worry about my hair kinking up.*

Suddenly a wave of fear engulfed her very soul, and she began to panic. With her heart racing and pounding, she worried, *What if they don't like me or even worse, what if they laugh at me? Where is Jessie? He should be here to watch out for me. Just wait until I see that good-for-nothing Black ass of his. That m—f— is going to get a damn good piece of my mind.* Solo smiled and her eyes turned green, as she thought, *Better yet I will show him.*

The music and laughter were getting closer. Solo could feel the heat radiating toward her. She blinked to adjust to the lights as they entered the night spot. The smoke was so thick, a cloud of smoke hung from the ceiling. Vick had disappeared, leaving Solo to fend for herself. The music was defyingly loud, and everyone seemed to be talking at the same time. Solo's feet would not move, it was like she was glued to the floor. Looking around for either Betsy or even Mr. Big, Solo realized some of the men were looking directly at her. While she was no stranger to looks from men, this was different.

Betsy saw Solo as she entered the room looking like a scared little mouse. *Wow,* Betsy thought to herself as she licked her lips. *Her dress is hugging that nice young tight body. But I got to move slow because she is very green and don't know her own worth. Give it time and she will be mine.* Betsy sauntered up to Solo, who had the look of a deer caught in headlights.

"Hello, my dear, follow me." As Betsy and Solo made their way through the crowds, catcalls and whistles rang out. Solo blushed from the attention. But Betsy kept moving with her hips swaying. Solo copied her movements and followed Betsy with her hips swaying. Solo smiled and loved it.

Solo followed Betsy into a room where she was surprised to see young girls and a few older-looking women. They all stopped what they were doing and stared at Betsy and Solo.

Betsy made her announcement. "I want you all to meet the newest member of our family. Her name is Solo and before y'all start, no she is not White, and yes, she is young and her name is strange. With that all said and out of the way, please teach her the ropes and watch out for her. She's a lil' green and this is her first time out the stable. As MB always says, 'We all family, so play nice and make that money.'"

Betsy exited the room leaving Solo standing alone with all eyes on her.

The room was quiet. Finally, a small, short, colored girl, with a big pretty smile and large eyes and a very large wiggling rear end, walked over to Solo and said in a very childlike voice, "Welcome to our family. My name is Jewel, and I am pleased to meet you." She held out her hand to Solo and smiled.

Solo looked Jewel up and down, rolled her eyes, and walked away. Bewildered, Jewel stared as Solo walked away but the others knew right then that Solo was not there to be family.

One of the older women, with a pretty face and large bouncy

breasts, clapped her hands and said very firmly, "Okay my beautiful goddesses, it's almost showtime."

Solo looked on and listened carefully as the older woman spoke. She didn't know what was expected of her, so she thought it was best just to listen and follow the others. The older woman continued.

"Tonight you will make some poor soul's dream come true and make a few dollars while you're doing it. Remember Mr. BM's rules: no asking the customers for money, but you can accept tips. No leaving the spot with customers, unless approved by MB. No touching the customer's private area while dancing. No oral stimulation of the customers. No exposing body parts. Keep drinking within limits. Report all problems with customers to me directly. Always be a lady, polite, and respectful. Follow these rules and you will be safe as well as keep your job. Break the rules and you are OUT!"

Everyone nodded except Solo. She just stared and thought to herself, *We will see!*

Betsy walked into the room and shouted, "Okay ladies, get your asses ready to shake. It is show time! We got a full house tonight, so there is plenty money to be made. Remember, I will collect your tips and anyone holding out will suffer the consequences. Push those tits up, stick out those asses, and get ready."

The women all laughed. Solo watched as they filed out of the room. She stood back because she still wasn't sure what was expected. Jewel, noticing Solo's hesitance, walked over to her.

"Hey Solo, just follow my lead. Don't be afraid. MB and Betsy won't let any harm come to you. Just greet the customers, be nice, dance, talk, and remember to smile. Don't get upset if they want a little kiss or squeeze your tits or even pinch your ass. They are here to have a good time and then go home. Don't drink too much and remember to give your tips to Betsy to hold. However, remember to try and keep track of your money, that's very important. At the end of the night,

Betsy will give you your share. Do you have any questions?"

Solo looked at Jewel and took a deep breath. She had to decide quickly, to either leave right now or go out there and make some money. Solo nodded and thought, *where in the hell is my man?*

For living life is like a road, sometimes it's straight,
narrow and bold;
You will find your days may drag on,
offering both warm and cold;
Laughter and sadness will come into play because it is part
of the human soul and meant to be that way;
But, as you navigate, and try to find your path,
there will be bumps coming into play;
Others will have more, some will have less, but it's the road
that's the test and we will take;
Your spirit will be shaken, but not forsaken, because it is
real, not fake;
Our journey is destined, our paths are predetermined, and
living may be like a piece of cake;
Some things will come easy; hurt feelings will be forgiven,
dreams will become realities and your road becomes a dead
end like a bottomless lake...

ELEVEN
A Star is born

Solo was sweating and nervous. It was too much to remember. What if she forgot something? What if the customers didn't like her? Would Betsy tell her to leave and put her out? Jewel saw Solo was still hesitant, so she poured a little liquor into a cup and slowly walked over to Solo.

"Here, drink this down quickly," said Jewel, handing Solo the drink. Solo was no stranger to drinking, but as she sniffed the liquor in the cup it attacked her nostrils and made her eyes water. Jewel let out a hearty laugh. "Go ahead," Jewel encouraged Solo, "you can thank me later."

Looking at Jewel, Solo threw the drink in her mouth and closed her eyes. The liquid burned her throat and lungs, and her stomach was on fire. Solo felt dizzy and then warm all over.

"Now that's some powerful stuff," remarked Solo.

"Yes, it is, replied Jewel, now let me see what you are working with."

The liquor taking effect made Solo laugh aloud.

"Now follow me." Solo let Jewel lead.

Following Jewel, Solo entered the spot, and it was in full swing. The air was thick with smoke, liquor, sweat, and the smell of lust. The three-piece band was playing loudly, backing up a large, heavyset, older colored woman with thick everything. She belted out the songs loudly. Several of the ladies were already dancing with customers, a few were even sitting on customers' laps, both men and women. Solo, however, was focused on the dancing. The music was so inviting, she felt her hips begin to shake in rhythm with the music. Maybe it was liquor she drank, but she was ready to bust loose and couldn't contain herself. Solo noticed Jewel waving at her to come out to the dance floor, but Solo didn't feel right dancing alone. She looked around and noticed several men and women eyeing her up and down. How badly she wanted to dance. Just as sudden as the thought, she felt her hand being pulled towards the dance floor and she followed without hesitation.

The young negro man turned and turned her. He was a good dancer. He picked Solo up in the air and brought her down between his legs. Solo was throwing her head back so her long golden hair could swing back and forth. She was so caught up in the dancing, she didn't notice the other folks backing off the dance floor. It was just her and this young man now, cutting a rug. Solo kicked up her feet, shook her rear end, twirled her hips, snapped her fingers, smiled, and threw her hair to the music. The crowd was going crazy, people clapped, shouted and money was being thrown to the floor. Finally, the music stopped, and people clapped even louder. Solo looked around and realized the young man was gone and she was dancing alone on the dance floor. Sweat ran down her face and she noticed Jewel and Betsy motioning for her to pick the money up from the floor. Solo started scooping up the dollars and pushing them down into her bra. Before, she could catch her breath several men were asking her to dance or buy her a drink. Solo was so flattered but wondered how to choose. So, Betsy seeming her dilemma told the men to give Solo a minute to catch her breath and she would be available to spend a little time with each. Solo was so relieved Betsy intervened because she had no idea what to do with so many requests.

Betsy walked Solo off the dance floor and put her hand out and smiled. Solo reached down in her bra and handed over the money. She didn't have time to count it, so she didn't know how much it was. Betsy took the money and smiled.

"Good job for your first day. Boy, you can really go on the dance floor. I'm going to ask MB to give you a solo dance each night. Good job. Now, here's what I want you to do. See that nice-looking fellow in the yellow suit? Go over and join him for a drink. Be pleasant, smile and make conversation. He is not a dancer, so don't worry, but he is a good tipper. I will let you know when to leave him. Now go and have some fun."

After Solo walked away, Betsy motioned to the young Negro man who took Solo to the dance floor and handed him a few dollars. "Well done," she said with a smirk. The young man put the money in his pocket and walked back to the kitchen.

As Solo walked over to this strange older man, she felt hands reaching out for her, touching her hands and arms while discreetly sliding across her bottom. Men and women nodded at her, which made her blush all over. Men were just fine, but women were a different story. She recalled how the men at home loved to see her walk swaying her hips. So Solo slowly walked through the crowd very slowly, teasing, moving her hips from side to side. She had a sexy smile on her face, and she held her head up high. When Solo, walked by, one man fell backward. Laughter rang out. Nevertheless, Solo just kept walking tossing her hair every now and then. Finally, she reached the man Betsy had pointed out. He was an older gentleman, fair-skinned, *(could pass for white)* well-dressed, hair slicked back, mustache, nice eyes, big hands with long fingers with rings on each. Solo had never seen a man with rings on every finger.

The older gentleman rose from his seat as Solo approached him. He knew she was just a mere girl in a woman's body, but oh man what a beauty.

He tipped his hat., "Theodore Southern at your service and pleased to have you join me." He took Solo's small delicate hand, bowed, and kissed it.

"What a pleasure to have your company. Please sit. You must be exhausted from your dance, which I must add was delightful," he continued. "I must say, you are as lovely as your dancing."

As if on cue, the waitress walked up and asked if they would like a drink. She never made eye contact with Solo; she spoke directly to the man. Mr. Southern ordered two drinks, without even asking Solo if she wanted a drink (*it was the rule, two drinks must be brought when one of the ladies joined a man's table*).

Solo was impressed by this nice, older gentleman, and he had referred to her as a lady. Even though he was older than what she preferred, he seemed nice, and he was a gentleman. So, she thought to herself, *this job may not be so bad after all.*

Solo was unaware Betsy was pleased with Theodore Southern requesting her. This meant big bucks. She would wait to inform MB about Mr. Southern spending time with Solo. The longer she waited, the bigger her share of the pot. Betsy smiled at the thought of this becoming her big payday. If Solo played along, this could mean plenty of money for them both.

Mr. Southern looked at the beauty before him and felt a rising. She was a jewel. "My dear, please forgive me, but if you don't mind me asking, what do they call you?"

Solo was so impressed by his formal talk and mannerisms, she blushed and meekly replied, "They call me Solo."

Not quite sure of what he heard, Mr. Southern asked again. "I'm sorry dear, but with it being so loud in here, could you repeat that?"

Solo leaned over close to him and her bust dipped out of her dress.

"Solo is my name!" She looked into Mr. Southern's eyes real long and smiled.

"How pretty, but very unusual," Mr. Southern said.

The waitress placed the two drinks on the table and Mr. Southern handed her a bill and told her to keep the change.

"Thank you, sir, thank you," the waitress said as she quickly stuck the money in her bra.

Solo picked up her drink and took a quick sip. She also gagged. It was much stronger than the drink Jewel gave her earlier. Once again, she felt the slow burn down her throat to her stomach and then the warm feeling all over. She felt good and was ready to dance. "Do you dance sir?" Solo asked flirtingly.

"On occasion, but I much rather watch a good dancer like yourself, and dear please, call me Theodore," he stressed.

"Oh!" Solo blushed. "I love to dance; it makes me feel free and happy." Solo took another sip of her strong drink. This sip was not as bad at first. As she felt the warm liquid entering her body, she was feeling the effects, which were rather nice, she thought.

Mr. Southern leaned in closer to Solo, and looking directly into her eyes, he whispered "I like to make you happy."

Solo was so taken aback by his comment, she blushed. His comment was so unexpected, she didn't know how to respond. So, she just smiled and looked around. She then spotted Jessie glaring directly at her. He didn't look pleased which made her happy.

Solo thought to herself, *that ass hole finally showed up. Well, I'll give him something to think about for the next time he decides to abandon me.* She quickly stole a glance at Jessie and then she looked back at Mr. Southern.

Solo said demurely, "Mr. Southern, I mean Theodore, I am flattered you want to make me happy, but we just met, and you don't even know me. I am at a loss for words. So let me show you how much I appreciate you."

Solo rose from her chair and walked around the small table to face Mr. Southern. Seeing this beauty standing directly in front of him, made him squirm in his seat and made his nature rise, which was a very welcoming feeling, and a slow smile embraced his lips. Solo gracefully raised her hands about her head and began to move her hips slowly and seductively to the music. She swayed back and forth, letting her hair fall over her face while looking directly into Mr. Southern's eyes, and she bent over in front of him so her long beautiful hair would fall in his lap. Jessie's mouth dropped open. *What the hell is she doing?!* It was as if she was going down on him. Solo continued with her slow grind. The crowd began to whistle and urged her on. This made her body move and shake. Everyone on the dance floor stopped to look at Solo's performance.

Betsy ran as quickly as she could to Mr. Big's office. Being overweight and excited, she was out of breath by the time she reached the door. She forcibly opened the door without knocking. Mr. Big jumped, and he reached for his gun. "MB, MB!" Betsy mouthed as she tried to catch her breath.

"What the hell is the matter with you, Betsy?" Mr. Big yelled directly at her, "And what is all the commotion?"

"Come with me quickly MB, this you got to see," Betsy summoned.

"Now what?" Mr. Big mumbled to himself as he placed his gun in his belt. "Betsy, this better be good for you to burst into my office. If not, your fat ass is mine."

"Oh, don't worry MB, just you wait and see. Now hurry and follow me."

"Now, you know better than to rush me, he said looking sternly at Betsy. But, sensing her excitement, he figured he better get a move on.

As they approached the entry, Mr. Big could hear the chanting and catcalls from the crowd. Everyone was on their feet, so with Betsy leading the way, Mr. Big had to push people aside to see what causing so much raucous in his place. He certainly didn't want no trouble, even though he was well equipped to handle it. Betsy pushed the crowd and yelled at them to move, so the boss, Mr. Big, could have a clear vision.

The crowd quickly parted, mainly in fear. There she was in the center of the room, long blonde hair flying in every direction, dress raised to show off her nice, thick, shapely thighs, rear end shaking, tits jumping up and down. The unlit cigar Mr. Big was chewing on slowly slipped from his wet lips to the floor. His mouth remained gaped open as he stared at Solo.

Mr. Big couldn't believe his eyes. Was this the same shy thing he met briefly only just yesterday? She seemed to have transformed overnight. She was stunning as she moved and twisted about the dance floor, which was completely covered with money being thrown in her direction. But Solo was so caught up in the music and dancing, she was oblivious to the money. She loved dancing, but mostly the attention from the crowd encircling her, and she didn't want to stop. Mr. Big motioned to the band to slow down the music and pointed to Betsy to scoop up the money before some good-for-nothing jerk took the liberty. Mr. Big moved close to the dance floor and caught Solo in his arms as she spun around. Solo was a bit startled Mr. Big had his arm around her waist, holding her close and in a tight grip. Fear engulfed her, so she stopped dancing and stood perfectly still as sweat casually dripped down her face and made a slow steady stream to her breasts, which were heaving up and down. Solo was so nervous, she thought she would pass out right there on the dirty dance floor, but most of all, she hoped she hadn't offended Mr. Big. She did not want to lose her job.

The crowd was momentarily quiet as they watched Mr. Big taking hold of Solo, but they commenced to yell for her to continue her entertaining performance. Mr. Big waved his short, nubby hands in the air and yelled "Let the little lady catch her breath, she will be back. My people this is her first night and we don't want to wear her out." Some folks mumbled in agreement, and soon laughter permeated throughout the spot. Mr. Big continued, "Now I ask you, wasn't that great?" The crown began to clap and nod in agreement. "I know you all must be thirsty, so drink up, tip the help and enjoy the music and this pretty little thing will be back to entertain you shortly."

Mr. Big took Solo's hand in his and quickly made his way to the office. Through the commotion, Mr. Big didn't notice both Jessie and Mr. Southern were watching him as he took hold of Solo. Both men felt a flicker of jealousy. Jessie knew Solo was his lady, and she was faithful, so he wasn't worried, only concerned for her safety with Mr. Big. She was still a kid and still wet behind the ears. Mr. Southern thought to himself, *in time, she will be mine.* He held his hand up high for service. He needed a drink, a good stiff one and he needed to get a word to Mr. Big quickly.

Jessie carefully watched as Mr. Big took Solo from the dance floor while being mindful not to take his eyes off them. He had a strange feeling, so he quickly moved to follow, only to be stopped by two burly-colored men with bad hair and breath. They stopped Jessie by the entrance leading to Mr. Big's office, folded their arms in front of their massive chests, and stared at him as if they were daring him to make a move. Jessie knew what that meant, so he would just have to wait for Solo to return. He hoped Mr. Big wouldn't try to touch her. He hoped she was safe. *What about her tips?* He saw how Betsy had quickly scooped the money from the floor. He knew the game. He only wanted Solo's fair share. But what was *fair* among crooks? Betsy was surely in that number.

Betsy walked around and gathered the money from the dirty floor. The money thrown to Solo. She was impressed; it was the most money she had seen for one girl in a long time. A chill ran over her when thought of a time long ago. She picked up the dollars and placed most of the money in her dress pockets. She always ensured she had pockets to store the money the girls earned for tips, which she secured with rubber bands, but she made sure she stuck a few bills securely down her front for herself, even though she would take another cut. It was only fair. MB made his money from the girl's watered-down drinks and all the other extras the customers paid for. But only if the girls were willing to make a few extra dollars, and most of the time they were. Betsy knew MB personally made sure to take care of those girls who refused a customer request for a little one-on-one time.

A sly smile came over Betsy's face as she thought about how this young pretty little thing was going to make her rich. She just needed to teach her a few tricks of the trade and together, they would make plenty of money. But there was one potential problem. Jessie. Betsy noticed Jessie had been watching Solo's every move, but more importantly, he watched the money. Betsy knew for women, there was always a Jessie. Some of the girls had husbands, boyfriends, pimps, girlfriends...you name it. She knew the type all too well. And they were all the same—greedy, controlling, abusive, but most of all, trouble. Best to nip this in the bud right now. She would ask MB to give this Jessie some odd job to keep him busy and away from the spot, particularly when Solo was working. The customers didn't like when the girls' men were lurking about, especially, a girl like Solo. Yes, Betsy smiled. Exactly what needs to happen. Make Jessie disappear. She could have Solo to herself without any inferences from her so-called man. This is a cruel, cutthroat business and a young pretty thing like Solo could get eaten up very quickly by these blood-thirsty wolves. Betsy had seen it happen many times, including to herself. But, not this time, thought Betsy as she shook her head from side to side, she wasn't going to let it happen again. Especially not to Solo, not this time.

Solo felt as though Mr. Big was dragging her along, as they moved quickly down the dark hallway. She couldn't wrap her mind around what was happening. She wondered if she had done something wrong. She was only dancing. *Was he mad at her? What if he forced himself on her? Should she fight or just let him have his way with her? Was he going to fire her?* She needed to do what she had to do to keep this job.

Finally, they reached Mr. Big's office, and he gently released Solo from his grip. While his hands were rather small, with stubby fingers, her wrist was aching from his tight hold. Solo stood very still with her head hung low and eyes cast downward as Mr. Big walked over to his looming desk. It was comically large for such a small man. Mr. Big didn't sit, but rather pulled two glasses from his desk drawer as well as a bottle of brown liquor. He expertly poured liquor into each glass, careful as not to spill a drop of this special substance. He handed one glass to Solo but she was too nervous to take the glass. Mr. Big walked up real close to Solo, his eyes scanning her body. His hot breath brushed across her face. Because of his closeness, she smelled his heavy cologne and almost gagged. She swallowed hard.

Mr. Big reached down and took Solo's hand, wrapping her fingers around the glass. Solo was trembling so hard; she was a nervous wreck.

"Drink!" he commanded.

As much as Solo liked liquor, right now she would much rather be out there dancing, drinking, and flirting with the menfolk. Also, Jessie was out there, and she didn't want to make him mad. Why did this man frighten her so? Mr. Big looked at Solo as though he could read her mind. He steadily held the glass to her lips as they parted in submission. She let the warm liquor fill her mouth. The liquor tasted different from others she had at the spot. This liquor tasted like pure gasoline. A few drops slipped from the corner of her mouth. With his index finger, Mr. Big wiped the liquor from her chin and put the wet digit in his mouth as he looked Solo in the eyes. Solo was hot and felt faint. She thought she might pee on herself and felt moisture between her legs. She didn't know if she had wet herself or if she was aroused.

Suddenly, there was a thunderous pounding on Mr. Big's office door.

"WHAT, WHAT?" an annoyed Mr. Big shouted.

Vick slowly opened the door. He partially entered the office and spoke low and slow, dragging his words. "It's that lady's fellow, he wants a word."

"SHIT!" yelled Mr. Big. Just when... *Well another time,* he thought to himself. Mr. Big, without saying a word, waved his hand to Vick to let Jessie in as he walked behind his desk and sat. Solo stood still too afraid to look around but let out a slight breath because Jessie was there, even though she was still mad with him.

Jessie walked nervously through the door, not knowing what to expect. He looked Solo up and down, but she didn't turn around. "Mr. Big," said Jessie, "didn't mean to disturb you, but I wanted to see if Solo was done for the evening?" Jessie's question made Mr. Big angry, the balls of this boy.

Mr. Big slowly rose from his chair and placed both hands on his desk, leaned towards Jessie, and shouted "DONE, WHAT THE HELL DO YOU MEAN DONE? SHE IS DONE WHEN I SAY SHE'S DONE! LET THIS BE THE FIRST AND LAST TIME YOU COME HERE INQUIRING ABOUT HER WORK SCHEDULE. SHE WORKS FOR ME AND DON'T FORGET. SHE IS DONE WHEN I SAY SHE IS DONE! NOW GET THE F—K OUT OF MY OFFICE!

Jessie stood for a minute. Vick opened the door wide and looked at Jessie. Solo turned to look at Jessie as he walked through the door. Betsy entered Mr. Big's office and walked past Jessie who was upset. *Good,* she thought to herself.

"MB," Betsy called out, out of breath from walking so fast, "I need a minute with you, alone," she said nodding at Solo.

"OK," Mr. Big instructed, "You can get back to work, but you are not off the clock until Betsy tells you, not that no good man of yours. You understand? If you want a piece of advice, you need to dump him."

Solo was speechless, so she just nodded.

"Good work tonight and you have earned a place here." Mr. Big waved his hand for her to leave.

Solo finally could breathe. She turned quickly and as she almost skipped past Vick, she gave him a wink and a slight smile. So much had happened in just one short night, at that moment Solo realized things for her were about to change. *Good or bad?* The question to be answered. But she would enjoy the ride. She smiled.

> *As life will have it,*
> *time changes things and people will come and go;*
> *When the goings are good, the ups have you on a speculator*
> *high, but now here are the lows;*
> *How you deal with the ever-changing tides is what helps you*
> *firsthand deal with the blows;*
> *So tread carefully, be thankful, don't always be receiving, be*
> *giving, because as God commands,*
> *you will reap what you sow.*

TWELVE
The Letter

Since leaving her children with the Chiles, Tulip stayed in touch with the Chiles through letters. Like two ships passing in the dark, sometimes long periods of time would pass between their communication, Regardless, Tulip always found a way to send Misses Chiles a letter, and likewise Misses Chiles would write to Tulip. However, the last letter Misses Chiles wrote to Tulip took more than a year to reach her because Tulip had moved. Tulip learned of the fire and of Baby Cecila's horrible death. Tulip read the letter over and over to make sure what she was reading was real. The news shook Tulip to the core. The Chiles' letter drifted from Tulip's hand as if it was dancing in the wind and made its way to the floor. Tulip screamed out in pain and went to a place she had not been in years, "The field of flowers." Tulip felt the old forgotten fears creeping into her soul. She wanted to retreat to the fields of flowers, she wanted to scream out for her Mama, but she had to stay strong. So instead, she prayed to God. Since marrying Carson, Tulip had fully embraced her faith and remained a devoted Catholic. God had saved her, and it was in God, not man, she put all her trust. Tulip fell to her knees and began to pray to God that Baby wasn't dead, not gone from this earth. "Baby, Baby" Tulip screamed out, "I have forsaken you. My beautiful Baby."

While Tulip had other children, Baby held a very special place in her heart because she was the last child created out of love between her and Malcolm. Losing Baby was like losing Malcolm all over again. The realization she would never see Baby again was hard to digest. She would never again kiss her sweet, cute brown face. *What was she like? Was she a good girl? Did she still love her Mama and Papa?* So many questions would never be answered. Now, Baby was gone to heaven. Tulip prayed to God and asked Malcolm to watch their baby girl. The grief of never seeing her little girl again was unbearable. Tulip was heartbroken, but she didn't blame the Chiles. Rather she blamed herself for leaving her children. It was her fault Baby died. Not the Chiles'. Her children were her responsibility, not the Chiles'. The Chiles were good to her and the children. She knew they thought of the children as their own. They, too, must be sad and heartbroken. How selfish of Tulip to only think about her loss and pain. She didn't want to admit it, but the Chiles were truly Baby's Mama and Papa. This thought was like a knife plowed into her heart. She must do the right thing and go get her children. The Chiles had done enough and losing Baby was like losing their own flesh and blood. In their reality, Baby was their child. So, Tulip prayed for them.

Not only did Misses Chiles' letter let Tulip know about the loss of Baby, but Misses Chiles went on to write about a lot of changes. Little Henry was gone away to join the Army at the age of 14 after lying about his age. She also learned Solo had run off, not so much as leaving a note. Everyone had assumed she had run off overcome with grief about Baby and was confident she would return home soon. But, after a few days, Mister Chiles went looking for Solo. Over time they learned Solo and Jessie had taken off together. He had heard rumors Jessie was messing around with Solo, but he refused to believe it because Jessie had been such a good friend to both Malcolm and Tulip. So Baby was put to rest without the respects of her big sister Solo, Mama, or Papa seeing her to heaven.

Tulip just couldn't wrap her mind around why Solo would just run off after the death of her little sister, leaving her brother alone to grieve. Could it be Solo was still the same mean-spirited, selfish child? Or maybe something even worse. The thought sent chills through Tulip's body. Besides, it still didn't answer the question as to why Solo, a young girl, would run off with her Papa's friend Jessie, a man twice her age. Tulip was so confused. What had happened to her children over the years? No one ever mentioned there were problems. Tulip threw up her hands, shaking her head, as the warm tears slid down her face like raindrops from the sky. There were no babies for Tulip to retrieve from the Chiles. No little arms to wrap around her. No children to run to her and call out, "Mama!" Tulip let out a quiet cry. Was God punishing her for leaving her children? *No,* Tulip thought, God loved her. God knew her heart. Like Malcolm, she must look for Solo. This time will be different. She was determined to find her daughter. Even though all she knew was Solo was somewhere with Jessie in New York City. Tulip could not just pick up and go to New York City, there was no money for another trip. But she needed to let Solo know she was there to get her and wanted her to come home.

Tulip got out her pencil and paper. She began to write, "The Letter."

December 1944

Dearest Daughter:

This letter is from your Mama. I pray God finds you in good health. I am so sorry I did not return, as promised, for you, little Henry and Baby, who is now an angel in Heaven. It broke my heart to leave my babies, but I was no good without your Paw. I had to make sure he was ok. I am so sorry to say, but I never found your Paw, I tried. God knows I tried. But I couldn't find him, I couldn't bring him back home to us. With my spirit broken, limbs weak, just plain down and too ashamed to return home with no money, no dignity, but most of all without my man. I didn't want to live.

I know it may be hard to understand all of this and maybe one day you will. Just know I tried to find your Paw and when I didn't, I had no money to come home, and I no longer wanted to live off others' charity. I had to work to make money to eat. I did some things as a God-fearing woman, that pains me. I was so lost. However, the fact remains, I knew you and your brother and sister were in a loving home. I knew Mister and Misses Chiles would take of you all until I returned for you. I vowed to return one day to get my babies and I did. But as fate would have it, I am too late, and my babies are gone. My poor baby girl lost in a fire. God have mercy on her soul. Why did you run away? I know you were sad to lose Baby, but your brother needed you. Were you afraid? You should not have left your brother all alone.

I don't mean to scorn you, because I know grief and what it means to be afraid. So, I do understand, because I ran away when I was afraid. I was so afraid to live without my Mama, so I ran. Then your Paw. I ran again. Maybe you felt like you were not loved. I thought your Paw didn't love us anymore and I know you also felt the same. Believe me, Solo, I looked for your Paw, but he was nowhere to be found because little did, I know, God had called your Paw home. See that is why he couldn't come home. I know after your Paw hurt your arm it was not good between you. I know you blamed yourself for Paw leaving. I also blamed myself. But it was not my fault or yours he left or never came back.

I know this is very hard news for you to hear. I was hoping to tell you and your brother and sister in person. The fact is time changes things. After I learned of your Paw's death, I didn't want to live. You see your Paw was the first man I loved. He was my life. I lived for him. He filled my very existence. There was no me without him. After learning of his death, I wanted to run back home to my babies. But, instead ended up with bad nerves and had to be hospitalized. I was so tired and confused. I could not take care of myself, let alone you and your brother and sister. I was ashamed of myself for leaving you all behind. So, I just pretty much gave up on life. I care about nothing and nobody. When I left the hospital, I commenced to drinking hard liquor, being with no-count men, just plain sinning. Basically, I just lived a sinful, lowlife until I met Carson Michael Barnes. He gave me faith. I stopped the drinking and gave my life over to God and married this good man. My husband, he is a good hardworking man. Not as handsome as your Paw, God rest his soul, but he is pleasing to the eyes. While he hasn't turned his life over to God, he is a good provider and good father to our children. He knows about my old life with your Paw. He loves me and wants to be a father to you and little Henry.

While my life is not perfect, it is good and steady. I've had some schooling, as you can see from this letter. Some think I am a pretty good writer. I don't know about all of that, I just write what I feel. Your new Paw and I have a home, here in Maryland near his kinfolks. It's not much to speak of, but it's clean and decent. Your new Paw is trying to get a job with the railroad, and we will be moving up to the City. Oh, I'm going on. Almost forgot, you now have two more brothers and two sisters. These youngins are more than a handful. Just as busy as you and your brother and sister were. Your brother Paul is the oldest, just turned 8. Not as sweet as my dear Henry. Next is Veronica. She is 7 and reminds me of Baby. She was followed by the twins, Magdalene and Joseph, who are 5 years old, and more than hand full. Two babies at once almost tore me apart. All named after Catholic saints. Your Mama has been baptized as a Catholic as well your brothers and sisters. We attend St. Mary's Church, but not your new Paw. He is not much on church. When you come to live with us, I will get you baptized Catholic.

We are not rich, by no means. Really not much better off than most colored folks around here, but we manage and get by. With four kids, times are hard, but we are making it work together. My husband is a good, hardworking man and provides for his family.

Oh, in all my talk I forgot to mention little Henry. Well, I guess he no longer little Henry since he went up and joined the Army. You know he was always older than his years, so I am sure they believed he was older. Anyway, he is gone, like you. No babies here for me at the Chiles'. However, I did visit Baby's gravesite. The Chiles' made a beautiful burial site for my precious Baby, and Lord knows that I am greatly appreciative. I know they also grieved for the passing of Baby.

Our old home has new folks now, so I didn't visit. There

it was still standing, such a beautiful and heartwarming sight. Old memories can flood back and there you were our beautiful, blonde bouncing girl with the most beautiful green eyes. What a beautiful child you were. As a little girl, you were outspoken, never minded your folks, but we loved you just the same, even though you and your Paw had some rough spots, but no need to cry over spilled milk. Time has a way of healing things. So much time has passed and here you are grown young lady now, on your own. I am sure you're driving the boys crazy.

To speak of, there's silly talk back home you had run off with your Paw's old friend Jessie to New York City. Folks said you were sweet on Jessie and spent time sneaking around with him. I hope that's not true and if it is true, I know Jessie to be a good and honorable man and looked at you like a daughter. I have so much to say to you, but I can't put a lifetime into this one letter. I am going to write my address down so you can know where to find me and come to live with your family. I don't have much money, but I know me and your new Paw (he and the little ones can't wait to meet you) could scrape up to send for you. I can't wait for you to meet your new family, so sorry it's been so long, and I hope this letter finds you in good health. I hope not too much more time goes by until we see each.

You can write me at Mrs. Tulip Barnes, Box 45611, Dorchester, Maryland.

May God be with you.

Your loving Mama

THIRTEEN
Truth Be Told

In 1944 Solo had been working at the Peacock for more than a year and things were going well. Actually, things were better than ever. She was the most sought-after girl, rather, woman at the spot. Her dancing had improved greatly and weekly she performed for the crowd. This made her the happiest, besides the money. Mr. Southern was her special friend, and he even slipped her a little extra for a quick feel here and there. Solo didn't mind, because it was no different from the men back home feeling her up, except now she was getting paid with real money instead of treats. Even after Betsy and Mr. Big's cut, she was making good money for her work at the spot. Jessie seemed happier since more money was coming in. There was enough money to help Jessie pay the rent, which was way too much for the dump they lived in, but it had to do for now. A few dollars spent on food, and even some to buy herself a few nice things.

Things were beginning to work out. Even the dreadful nightmares were subsiding. Always the same, smoke, fire, burning, screaming, someone calling her name, a hand reaching out to her. Solo would always wake up soaking wet and sweating before the hand touched her. To his annoyance, sometimes Jessie had to wake her up from the bad dreams. Solo knew the source of her nightmares, which she could never share with Jessie. If Jessie ever learned the truth about why they had to leave home, he would hate her for sure. For now, she just needed more sleep. Lately Solo was always tired and sleepy. She understood the late hours, smoking, and heavy drinking may be culprits, but something in her body felt a little off. Maybe she would talk with Betsy, and she could recommend something to give her more energy. But, for now, she just needed to lay down and get some rest before Jessie got home.

Jessie slowly opened the door to the cramped apartment. He was surprised the room was dark, and he expected to see Solo running around busy getting herself ready for her so-called job. He didn't like Solo working at the Peacock, not one bit, especially the special attention paid to the customers. Jessie had to admit the money she earned was needed, but he still didn't like it. He particularly hated Betsy, who was always watching him, and Mr. Big, that low life. Why couldn't she take on one of those domestic jobs, like the other young Negro girls? No, she'd rather be shaking her tits and ass. Well, things were about to change. Jessie shook his head trying to shake the thoughts away when he realized he still had the envelope in his hand Jimmy Mack from back home had given him. He quickly stuffed the envelope in his jacket pocket, carefully so as not to tear it.

Jessie's eyes adjusted to the darkness of the room, it smelled stale and sweaty. He quietly made his way to the nearest lamp and flicked on the light. To his surprise, his dearest Solo was sprawled a crossed the makeshift bed. Usually, she made sounds when she slept and thrust about, but for some reason, this time she was quiet and still. Jessie stared at her. He took in every feature. His breaths quickened. How fast she had changed from the skinny cute, long-legged, sassy girl. Still sassy, but in the almost two years since arriving in New York City, she had blossomed into a shapely woman. *She is stunning*, Jessie observed. Her beautiful blonde hair cascaded down to the floor. Her long muscular legs dangled off the bed. Her long eyelashes cast a shadow on her high cheekbones. Her skin was creamy and clear. She could pass for a white woman, but that body was no white woman. Jessie's heart pulsated and his feelings grew. He wanted to bend down and kiss her soft, thin lips, which were unusually small for a colored woman.

Instead, he sat down on the bed and whispered passionately in her ear. *"Sweet, sweet, Solo!"*

Hearing her name, Solo sat straight up, hitting Jessie full in the face with her forehead. Jessie jumped up and yelled in pain. Solo grabbed her head with both hands.

"Jessie, I'm sorry," Solo silently protested as she shook her head back and forth. "I am so sorry, but what were you doing leaning over me? You damn near scared the crap out of me. Wait, what time is it?"

Solo spoke loudly with a sense of urgency as she leapt from the bed to her feet. The motion made her head spin and she felt dizzy. Solo gathered it was from the head collision with Jessie. She sat down to collect herself, not saying a single word to Jessie. Once she felt her senses coming back, she began stripping off her clothes. But she still felt sick to her stomach, she wanted to throw up.

"Why in the hell didn't you wake me?" Solo yelled. "What time is it?! My god! Mr. Big told me I only had one more time to be late. What time is it, Jessie?!

Jessie slowly looked down at his prize procession, the watch he had won some years back at home off this old Jew in a crap game. How he loved that watch. To his disappointment, he learned it was not real gold like the old Jew had said, but it shined like real gold and kept accurate time and it was his.

"It's seven o'clock," Jessie grunted, as he continued to rub his forehead. He needed to talk with Solo, but it had to wait. Now was not a good time, plus she wouldn't listen right now anyway. Jessie knew the contents of his pocket had to wait.

Solo felt nausea rise to her throat and her head started spinning, so she slowly made her way to the bathroom. This sick feeling and throwing up were getting more frequent and on top of that, she was getting thick, and some of her clothes were tight. Plus, she was always tried. Solo figured it was probably from all the liquor, greasy food, and sweets. How she loved sweets, especially those little cream-filled cones. Her mouth watered from the thought. "But enough is enough," Solo said aloud talking to herself. She would start putting water in drinks and cut back on the greasy food and sweets. Even though men didn't mind a woman with a little weight on her, there was no extra money for new clothes, so she had to watch her weight.

Solo stripped out of clothes and filled the basin with water and washed her face and the essential body parts, no time for a full bath. She would just spray a little more perfume. Jessie was amazed at how quickly she could transform herself. She was a good-looking woman and he had feelings for her. But there were some troubling things he had recently learned.

"Solo, kick off a little early tonight. I need to talk with you about a few things," Jessie said slowly.

Solo continued to move around the room, looking for various items. She didn't respond to Jessie because she was too preoccupied with getting herself dressed and off to work. To make matters worse, she'd missed her ride with nasty Maybelline's man, Johnny Boy. Maybelline had asked for him to give her a ride. He usually just waits a few minutes for her to come out before he would pull off. Always saying, "Time is money," while trying to feel her up. But she needed the ride. She shrugged it off. Jessie would have to take her, even though he couldn't come in the club. He could drop her off nearby, and she could walk the rest of the way. Not too far away, because she couldn't walk too far in those high heels in the dirty alley and there was always someone lurking.

"Solo, did you hear me?" Jessie yelled, irritated at her lack of response.

"Yeah, why are yelling? I am not deaf, I heard you. ok, but I'm trying to get dressed and I'm not feeling well and your howling is not helping." Solo sarcastically responded.

"I just need you to come home tonight before the sun comes up," yelled Jessie, "Is that too much to ask?"

Solo stopped what she was doing and put her hands on her hips and looked directly at Jessie.

"As a matter of fact, it is too much to ask. How in the hell am I supposed to leave early when I am going in late? Now you answer that Mr. Smart Man!"

Jessie and Solo stared at one another without moving.

"I am getting tired of your back talking and you not doing what I ask you to do," Jessie said as he moved closer to Solo. "I am not asking you. I am telling you to be home early tonight. If not, I will walk into that club and drag your ass right out."

Before she could respond, the smell of his liquored, hot breath made her gag and she had to move quickly to the toilet to throw up. Fortunately, she didn't soil her dress, but the taste in her mouth was foul and she felt sick. Jessie didn't expect that response and was concerned. He had noticed changes in Solo's body like the thickness around her middle, the fullness of her breasts, and the roundness of her behind, but he just thought she was moving from being a girl to becoming a woman. Even though she had mood swings, it was not abnormal for her. But he had noticed the changes. With a little concern he asked, "Are you coming down with something or are you in the family way?"

The thought genuinely shocked Solo. She hadn't thought about the possibility she might be…she could not even form the word in her heart. Her hands went down to her stomach. *Is it possible?* she wondered. Her Jessie had been so careful, but Jessie wasn't the only person she had been with. Mr. Big always used a rubber on his thing, Mr. Southern only wanted her to kiss his private and a couple of others were too quick to even care. No, this could not be happening. It had been a few months since she last bled, but with no women to talk to about such things, Solo just figured it was supposed to be like that sometimes.

"No, no!" Solo yelled out so loudly, it frightened Jessie, who was deep in his own thoughts.

A tide rushes in and brings destruction along its path, not caring what it takes along the way;
Not able to foresee what was coming and unable to avoid being an unwilling victim seeing it simply as faith;
Didn't want to leave,
hurt would only prolong my unwanted stay;
It takes all and leaves little, there is no vision, no clarity and you have no say;
Lost sight of what could have been, unavoidable series of unplanned actions befriended me, and not as a victim, but rather as a willing participant, I swayed.

FOURTEEN
Tide Rushes In

"WHERE IN THE HELL YOU BEEN GIRL!" demanded Betsy, yanking Solo by her arm from the chair. Betsy's force almost made Solo lose her balance. Betsy swung Solo around to face her. Solo, frantic from rushing into the club while trying to avoid Mr. Big was distraught. Also, she was equally consumed by the events of the day, Solo had no time to deal with Betsy fussing, not today.

"Sorry," Solo mumbled softly with her head downcast.

"What's wrong with you girl?" Betsy said as she eyed Solo up and down.

"Nothing, just tired," mumbled Solo.

"Speak up girl! Why are you acting like a little Milly Mouse?" Betsy inquired expressing a little concern. She was sincere, given Solo was her star and her favorite of the girls.

"You know MB has warned you repeatedly of being late. It's disrespectful to him and the customers. You know he's gonna fire you. Then what you going to do? Clean rich White folks' homes, walk the streets selling your precious jewels?" Betsy snickered. "See how long that lasts before you wish you abided by MB's rules. Do you understand I have a mind to kick you out right now?"

This was only to get Solo's attention. Betsy would never let her go. She was hers. "And all you got to say is *sorry*. Bullshit, if you were sorry then you'd get your black ass here on time."

Solo did not respond and stood in the same spot with her head held down. Her body began to tremble.

"Are you crying?" Using two fingers, Betsy lifted Solo's head and saw her face was streaked with tears.

The door opened and one of the girls walked in. "GET OUT OF HERE!" yelled Betsy, as she held Solo close to her chest. The poor girl jumped in fright and rushed out of the room, closing the door behind her. She did not want any part of Betsy's wrath. She knew all too well Betsy could give a good ass-whipping.

"Come on now," Betsy said sweetly as she held Solo in her arms. Betsy's comforting only made Solo cry harder. She was unaccustomed to such a show of affection from another woman, but it felt good to be held and comforted. Solo allowed her emotions to take over and released all her pent-up feelings. Her legs almost gave way, so Betsy had to hold her tightly, if not, Solo would have sunk to the floor.

Lord, please don't let this child be ill. Trying to sound calm, Betsy asked, "Does something hurt you? Just show me where."

Betsy slowly walked Solo over to a nearby chair, peeled Solo's hands and arms from her body, and lowered her gently to the chair. Solo put her face in her hands and sobbed. Betsy kneeled in front of her. She was frustrated with Solo, trying to ignore the lingering thought every second she was losing money. Normally Betsy would not have tolerated such shenanigans from one of the girls. She would have demanded the girl stop the fuss and get her Black ass back to work or get packing. On more than one occasion, Betsy had escorted a girl to the door with just the clothes on her back. But this was Solo, and she knew it was best to take it slow with her. Surely it was just something stupid, like a fight with that trifling man of hers. Whatever it was, Betsy thought, *we need to get it resolved right now.*

Betsy reached down in her enormous bosom and took out a clean, lace hankie embroidered with tiny flowers (*it was her only possession from her Maw and she kept it close*). She took the pretty hankie and carefully dabbed Solo's wet face, stained from the onslaught of unyielding tears. The nearness of Solo made Betsy grow all warm all over. She felt beads of sweat form on her forehead, and her armpits grew sweaty. Her breast ached, heaving up and down. Her nipples grew erect and hard. Not to mention, the other parts going wild. With her two right fingers, Betsy slowly and delicately lifted Solo's chin and stared into her eyes. Solo's beautiful bluish gray eyes glistened with tears. They looked right back at Betsy as if they were staring into her very soul. This made Betsy's heart quicken so, she had to look away for a minute.

"Ok, now tell Aunt Betsy, what's ailing you?" Betsy said sweetly without showing any sign of emerging frustration.

Solo hesitated momentarily. She struggled with forming the words that were causing her so much distress. She shuddered. "I...I think...I think..." she repeated, pausing for a moment while Betsy looked on with a puzzled expression on her face. Solo continued, "I think," she lowered her head and the tears silently streamed down her face. "I'm with child."

The words came spilling from her mouth out so fast, it took Betsy a few seconds to comprehend what she said. "Pregnant?" Betsy stood up as she spoke. "Didn't we talk about being careful? How far along are you child?" Betsy shook her head from side to side in frustration. Damn stupid, silly girls, always getting themselves knock upped by those good for nothing, no-count men. *No matter how many times you tell them, use protection, be careful. But noooo. What do they do but get themselves burnt anyway and ruin their lives*? Betsy let out a long sigh.

"Alright, now, hush that fuss!" Betsy held Solo in her arms as she stroked Solo's long, beautiful golden hair. How she loved this girl. "Now how far long are you?" Betsy asked.

Solo stopped her sniffing long enough to think. She didn't know a thing about how to know when or if she was with a child. Through her sniffles, she mumbled, "I don't know."

"WHAT THE HELL YOU MEAN, YOU DON'T KNOW?" demanded Betsy as she pushed Solo away from her. This made Solo jump in fright. While she had heard Betsy yell and use bad words with some of the girls, Betsy's anger had never been directed toward her. "LOOK HERE GIRLIE," Betsy was still shouting as she circled Solo. "WELL, YOU BETTER THINK REAL HARD. IF NOT, YOU ARE GOING TO FIND SOMETHING HANGING OFF THOSE TITTIES OF YOURS." This made Solo afraid. She was speechless.

Betsy was still walking around and talking to herself aloud. "Let me think." She suddenly stopped and looked around the room. She walked over to a table and picked up a yellow lead pencil. She took a piece of paper from a discarded bag. She bent over and began writing fast. She folded the paper in half and handed it to Solo. "Tomorrow before you report to work, I want to go to this address written on this paper. Go alone, and please don't take that no-count man of yours. By the way, have you told him about your situation?"

With her eyes half-closed and looking down to the floor, Solo shook her head indicating that she hadn't. She didn't feel like telling Betsy that she and Jessie had argued over this very matter.

"If you are with child, is it by that no-good man of yours?" Betsy inquired. Solo looked at the floor for an answer. How could she know who had her knocked up? She didn't know how you even get knocked up, except the man had to pull it out quickly. Also, making a baby comes from love. So, it had to be by the one you love. Solo smiled, if she was with child, it could only be by Jessie she thought to herself. "I believe it's Jessie."

Betsy almost hit the ceiling with fury, "*DUMBASS!*" She wanted to scream. So clearly you don't know, which is best because that can work in your favor," said Betsy with a smile on her face. Maybe this whole situation could make her a few dollars if she played her cards right.

Betsy handed Solo the paper where she had written down an address. Through misty eyes, Solo looked at the address, which was in Harlem, 214 West 134th Street. She had heard a lot about Harlem, and it wasn't anything good, but what choice did she have?

"When you get to the address, ask for Miss Odessa. Nobody, but Miss Odessa, you understand me, this is important." Betsy said rather forcibly. "Tell, Miss Odessa, I sent you. She will let you know if you are with child and what can be done if anything, and what it will cost. Take $5.00 with you, no more, no less. She will want more. But tell her that's all you got," said Betsy. Solo continued to stare at the address on the paper, she finally looked up at Betsy with tear-filled eyes. Betsy felt so much compassion for this girl, so she gathered her in her arms tightly, and there they stood.

Solo arrived home before daybreak. It had been a long hard night. She was glad the place was slow, so she didn't have to entertain too many patrons, plus she wasn't in the mood. It was cold out when she left the spot. Of course, no Jessie waiting for her at the end of the long dark alley. How he pissed her off. He knew she hated walking down the alley by herself. Girls had been beaten, raped, and robbed. Sometimes Vick would walk with her through the alley, but tonight Vick had run an errand for Mr. Big. All the other girls had left. So here she was alone, no sight of that sorry ass Jessie.

With Jessie being a no-show, Solo had to pull a quick trick to get a ride home, but it was worth the ride. Her feet hurt, and she felt sick from too much liquor and smokes, not to mention the quick blow job. Had she eaten? She couldn't even remember. Everything was a blur after her conversation with Betsy. She didn't want to think about their talk. She needed to throw up. With shoes in hand and stockinged feet, Solo began the steady climb on the long stairwells. She hated walking on these dirty floors with her bare feet, but her feet hurt too bad for the shoes. In the distance, she heard babies crying. A burst of laughter rang out. *Somebody was having fun*, she thought. Solo hated walking up the stairs and the hallway was always dark, with things scurrying about. She tried to move at a rapid pace, scared somebody or something would reach out and grab her. Her imagination always got the best of her. With her sore feet, she moved quickly. A few neighbors had their doors ajar. *Did anybody ever sleep?* Finally, she reached her door. Her hand was shaking so it was hard to put the key in the lock. She heard the lock click and pushed open the apartment door with her shoulder. The apartment was pitch dark. "Damnit." How many times had she told Jessie to leave a light on if was not going to be home? "OUCH! SHIT," Solo screamed, striking her big toe on something hard. She limped towards the lamp by the bed and turned on the light. Solo sat down on the crumpled, unmade bed and massaged her foot. She wanted to cry but held back the tears. She closed her eyes and rubbed her foot until she felt the burning, sour vomit rising to her throat. She moved as quickly as she could to the nearby water basin, but not quick enough before her guts spilled out on her and to the floor. Between, the vomits, she made a mental note, tomorrow she would visit Miss Odessa. This needs to be over with and quickly.

    For what seemed like an eternity, Solo kneeled over the foul-smelling basin and emptied her stomach of the substance. With no food on her stomach, much of the substance was just watery-smelling liquid. When she was satisfied no more was coming, she poured the foul substance into the grimy toilet. Her head was spinning, and she felt dizzy. Solo stood staring at the foul substance in the toilet. Finally, she stripped out of her soiled clothes down to undergarments. She unhooked her garter belt to remove the torn stocking. "Another pair of stockings ruined," Solo said out loud, shaking her head. She threw the ruined stocking on the floor. Down to her drawers and bra, she ran fresh water into the basin and washed the heavy makeup from her face. The water was cold and made her shiver. She was so tired, she felt faint.

Her mouth tasted nasty, so she lit a cigarette and took a long drag until the flame glowed on the end. She walked over to her pocketbook and pulled out a small bottle of brown liquor and took a long swig. The liquor burned going down and caused goose bumps on her skin. Solo took another long slow drag from the cigarette. She looked at the nasty stuff on the floor from her guts and decided it would just have to wait until the morning. Better still, *I will leave that for Jessie*. The thought made her laugh. Solo crawled onto the crumpled bed. She took another swig of liquor, which emptied the bottle. The empty bottle was tossed aside. Damn she thought, I still need more. She felt relaxed and her eyes grew heavy. She took another drag from the cigarette and clicked the ashes to the floor. She closed her eyes, her head dropped down to her chin. The lit cigarette slowly cascaded to the floor like a swaying butterfly.

"Baby? Baby where are you?" Solo called out as she made her way through the smoke-filled room. Her throat was burning from smoke and fire loomed around her. With her hands outstretched to feel her way through the smoke-filled room, suddenly she felt her hands being touched, "Baby hold on to my hand, so I can take you out of here." Something crashed down, and fire jumped out at her. Suddenly her hand was being pulled hard. "Baby, stop pulling, this is my bad arm, and you are hurting it!' Solo yelled and the pain was running up her arm. Solo strained to see through the thick, black smoke. A burnt black hand had engulfed her hand, pulling her further and further into the burning room. Solo screamed in terror, "WHO ARE YOU? WHERE IS MY SISTER? WHERE IS BABY?" The deformed hand pulled her hand harder. Solo was frantic, her heart was pounding. She struggled and fought hard to release her hand. She felt the fire burning her hand and creeping up her arm. "No stop, please, you are breaking my arm" Solo cried out, "Who are you? Where is Baby?" She tried hard to free her hand away from the faceless terror. but the monstrous hand pulling her was too strong. The fire was getting close to Solo and danced around her like playful taunting children.

"Help! Help me!" she screamed out. "SOMEBODY, PLEASE HELP ME!" Solo screamed as loud as she could. A small, muffled voice called out to her, *"Solo, I'm burning, please help me."*

"Baby, is that you?" Solo yelled. Somebody was calling her name. The hand finally released her and as the fire danced around her, Solo saw through the smoke-filled room a figure.

"MAMA!" she screamed.

Sirens sounded, yelling, screaming, pounding, knocking, banging. "FIRE! FIRE!" somebody was yelling. Children crying, running feet. "GET OUT! GET OUT! GET OUT NOW! EVERYBODY GET OUT! The firemen yelled as they made their way through the long staircases. People were running and trying to grab some of their merger processions. Smoke quickly filled the stairwells. The firemen met people barely clothed running towards them. The firemen continued to yell, "OUT! OUT! EVERYBODY MOVE IT."

The firemen ran from floor to floor, banging on doors and even kicking in doors as they searched for people. People were in panic and had made their way down the long, wrought-iron fire escape. Children and old people were being carried. Smoke and fire quickly consumed the old unkept building. The firemen outside sprayed water onto the building, while others continue to search each floor.

Maybelline tried to bang on Solo and Jessie's door, but the door was hot and burned her hands. She had a wet towel on her face so she could breathe. *Why was the door so hot,* she thought? She noticed the smoke coming from under the door and could hear crackling sounds. The building was on fire. She panicked. *Did Solo and Jessie make their way out by the fire escape?* She wanted to make sure before she left.

"Solo! Jessie! Are you in there? Do you hear me? The building is on fire! You need to get out! Solo! Jessie!" She continued to scream until she was met by a white fireman.

"Move your ass now and get out of this building!" the fireman yelled. He thought to himself, *Always the same thing. People freeze up in a fire and are too dumb to see they are in danger.* Maybelline coughed from smoke. She heard the fireman but didn't care. With the smoke burning her eyes and lungs she struggled with her words… "My friend, I haven't seen her, she may be still in the apartment."

"I got it! You go!" the fireman yelled.

Satisfied the fireman would find Solo, she went running through the smoke-filled hallway and down the stairs to safety moving as fast as she could.

The fireman noticed the thick smoke was pouring from under the door. He touched the door, and it was hot. He knew if he opened the door, the air would erupt the fire into bigger flames, so he took his ax and began to chop down the door. He saw through the opening in the door. The place was consumed by fire and smoke. He chops away a little more to get a better look. Through the thick smoke, he could make out what he thought was a lifeless figure. The fire was fully engaged around him.

His training had taught him this was a critical situation and time was not his friend. Without any hesitation, he chipped away the remainder of the door, batting away the flames, as he tried to make his way to the figure quickly. He was acutely aware the fire was beginning to consume him, and he could barely see through the thick smoke. He patted around where he had seen the figure laying. He reached out and quickly grabbed the figure by the leg and lifted the figure over his back. It was a female. She was light. He made note she was covered with burns and was unconscious, which was a blessing, given the severity of the burns. He had no time to administer care, but he did check for a pulse, by the mercy of God she was alive. The room was dark from the smoke, but he could make what appeared to be curtains. The fire escape! With the woman on his back, he took one hand and ripped off the curtains. The window was closed, so he kicked several times as hard as he could until it the glass gave away and climbed out of the window. Smoke and fire followed them. His uniform radiated smoke, and the woman only wore undergarments. He moved quickly down the fire escape. Below he could see the people, fire trucks, firemen, and police. People were pointing and yelling. He slowly proceeded down the fire escape. The woman had been burned. He wondered what in the hell this White woman was doing in this place. He felt conflicted. His pulse was racing. She probably was one of those White women who preferred Negroes. He should have left her. He saw other firemen rush towards him. Well, he thought, with these burns, no man is going want her now. White or Black. Serves her right.

One of the other firemen gently pulled Solo off the fireman's back and continued down the remaining stairs. People started clapping and the fireman smiled. He was a hero, even though if he had known, he would have done things differently. However, many gasped as they saw Solo. They were shocked and lowered their heads in sorrow. Some prayed. However, Maybelline, seeing Solo pushed her way through the crowd of onlookers.

She ran quickly towards the fireman who was carrying Solo. Seeing Solo's badly burned body made Maybelline scream out to the fireman. "OH MY GOD, IS SHE DEAD?"

The fireman did not respond. He continued to carry Solo's limp body toward the hospital wagon. Maybelline continued following the fireman, repeating the same questions in a muffled voice, as tears streamed streaking her face leaving ashen lines.

"Is she dead? Will she be, okay? Her pretty face, her beautiful hair. She's burned."

By now the fireman was losing patience. He shouted at Maybelline, "Move out the way! I got to get her to the wagon! MOVE!"

Suddenly, Maybelline realized she hadn't seen Jessie. Surely, he would be at Solo's side. She turned to look about at the crowd.

"Where's Jessie? Did you get Jessie?" screamed Maybelline at the fireman. As the fireman continued to walk fast with Solo, he responded to Maybelline.

"Look here, I don't know Jessie. Didn't see no one else. Only this here White girl."

Maybelline, taken back by the fireman's statement ran after him shouting, "She's not a white girl! She's a Negro."

The fireman's pace slowed, but he continued towards the wagon. As he handed Solo to the waiting attendant, he whispered, "Rush her to Harlem City."

The attendant was puzzled because typically White folks were not taken to Harlem City, even if they could not pay. "Why City? That's a white woman."

The fireman shouted, "Harlem! Now! Move it!

The attendant shook his head and closed the doors. He turned on the sirens and sped down the street. The wagon's flashing lights made adults and children alike stop and give pause.

Maybelline looked as the wagon passed her with her friend inside and realized she may not ever see her again. The thought brought tears to her eyes. She said a silent prayer for the strange girl with the strange name. She liked Solo. She wondered, *where in hell is that Jessie?*

*You say I am crazy; you say I am a fool, you say I am not the
person for you and that is fine;
My behavior is unacceptable, my actions are unfathomable,
my life and ways are lost in unexplained forces that bind;
Easy to say sorry, not meaning, just happen, wanted to be
kind, not in my nature to feel internal motions or wine;
Hard not to forgive you, even when it's not deserving, just a
matter of again because it happens time after time;
Is this now it, something has changed I am not questioning
your actions, maybe I am losing my mind;
But you will never find another love because truth be told,
my love for you is one of a kind.*

FIFTEEN
Changing of the Tides

Jessie watched as the hospital wagon went rushing by him with sirens blazing. The sirens were deafening. He placed his hands over his ears to close out the loud sound as he looked around at the crowd. He thought to himself, *some poor soul was on their way to City.* He shook his head slowly because it was pounding from a night of hard drinking, sex, and gambling. Yet, it was a profitable night, the dice were in his favor. Jessie smiled and stuffed his hands in his pockets. He felt the roll of bills and stroked his fingers over them. He smiled again. But slowly the smile left, and he thought of the fight he had with Solo. He hoped she read the letter that he left for her. It was time for a change. Never mind that she may be with child. He stayed too long. Now she wants a family. He certainly didn't want any more crumb snatchers. He was already sending money back home to take care of the three youngins he had. Something he hadn't even shared with Solo, not that it was any of her business. This was his business. Plus, with all her comings and goings, how could he be certain she was knocked up by him? And no way was he taking care of another cat's baby. He had seen that happen too many times. Sleep with a woman one time and she is going to claim you as the Papa. But, for sure it was not going to happen to him. Jessie rubbed his head. All this thinking was making his head hurt even more.

As Jessie got closer to his dwellings, he could smell the burnt smoke as it lingered in the air. No, please he thought, *not another fire.* He looked straight ahead towards the building and could see large crowds of people gathered out front, some barely clothed. Fire wagons with their water hoses were lying about the street. Water poured fast and freely from the fire hydrants. Children were running about around the water as if this was playtime. There were patty wagons and plenty of patrolmen talking and laughing. Jessie cursed out loud, "What is this bullshit? Now, what in the hell is going on? Probably some fool man has caught his woman with another man or one of those bad unkept kids done set the building on fire. Damn kids always in the hallways lighting fires. Knowing good and well they shouldn't be playing with matches."

Jessie picked up his pace and began a fast trot toward the building. As he got closer, he slowed his pace so he could make his way through the crowd. He recognized some of the people from his dwelling. Some turned to look at him and they whispered to each other. Others looked at him and shook their heads. *What the f—k is going on?* Jessie thought to himself, feeling all eyes were on him. *Are these people looking at me or what?*

"JESSIE, JESSIE!" Someone was yelling his name. Jessie looked straight ahead and could see a hand waving at him and motioning for him to come. It was Maybelline, and she looked a mess. Her hair was nappy and uncombed. She was dressed in a loose-fit house coat which was not too clean and looked old and worn. She was not wearing shoes and her feet were dirty and ashy. Her face was streaked with gray stains from crying. Her lips were cracked and hard. Her eyes were red and darted about nervously. She looked a mess, which was understandable given the situation.

Jessie pushed his way through the crowd towards Maybelline. When he reached her, she went limp and fell into Jessie's body. Her body's ashy arms went around his waist and hugged him tightly. Jessie was startled. He felt very uncomfortable with Maybelline's body pressed against his. Some people turned to look at them.

Maybelline, still hugging Jessie with her head buried into his chest, spoke rapidly, as if she was being chased.

"I thought you had burned up! I asked the fireman did they get you out, but they wouldn't answer me. The smoke was coming from under your door. I banged on the door, but no one answered. I couldn't breathe. The smoke burned my eyes, but I kept banging. I yelled for Solo, then I told the fireman to help."

Jessie frantically scanned the crowd. No sight of Solo. Surely, she would be here with Maybelline. So, Jessie reached back and peeled Maybelline's arms from around his waist and forcibly pushed her back so they were face to face. He shook her and yelled, "Maybelline, where's Solo?"

"Solo, Solo!" Maybelline's mind registered what Jessie was asking her. Jessie looked at her, waiting for a response. He was somewhat puzzled and unsettled by Maybelline's lack of response. Maybelline's eyes could not meet Jessie's. Looking sad, she cast her eyes down to the concrete ground. She was momentarily distracted by her shoeless feet. Jessie followed her gaze. Maybelline began to mumble and shook her head from side to side. She spoke in a whisper, forcing Jessie to lean in closer to her so he could hear her. Maybelline whispered as if saying the words too loud would make it worse. With closed, tear-filled eyes, she spoke.

"Burned bad, Solo bad, so pretty, her hair. I knocked on the door, I called out to her, but she didn't answer. The smoke was coming from under the door, I was coughing." Maybelline slowly opened her eyes and raised her head. She looked directly at Jessie with red glassy eyes, "I tried to help, they made me leave, I had to go, she was burned, her face. My God, her face." Maybelline covered her face with both of her hands and sobbed. Jessie tried to make sense of what Maybelline was saying but got frustrated with all the crying. She wasn't making any sense. He looked around to see if there was anyone else he could get some answers from. Seeing no one, he placed both his hands on

Maybelline's shoulders and shook her again.

"Maybelline," what happened to Solo? Was she in the apartment? Did she get burned? Is she okay?"

Maybelline gazed up at Jessie and said, "Solo, not dead." She is a Negro girl, not White." Jessie threw his hands in the air. He was not getting anywhere with this fool-ass Maybelline.

Jessie looked around and spotted a few patrolmen. Maybe they could provide some information. He told Maybelline to stay put. He wasn't sure if she understood him, but she nodded. He made his way over to the patrol wagon where a few patrolmen were talking. Jessie had quickly learned a Negro man in New York City was a piece of shit to the law and best you stay clear of them. While he hated the men in blue with a passion, especially the cracker ones, he had to find out what happened to Solo.

Jessie made his way through the crowd which was now moving towards the apartment building after getting the all-clear signal. He wondered if Solo ever came home from the spot. But what was all the fuss Maybelline was mouthing about Solo being burned? Jessie was so confused. He would check the apartment, but right now he needed to find Solo. All Maybelline's gibberish about burns had made him jittery. Most likely, Solo didn't even make it home. She was probably with one of her sugar daddies. But still, best he checked.

Jessie approached the two patrolmen, who were smoking cigarettes and laughing. As he got closer, he removed his hat and interjected.

"Excuse me." The two patrolmen continued to talk, ignoring him, or maybe they just didn't hear him. But Jessie was sure they'd heard him, so he coughed and cleared his throat. He took a deep breath and spoke louder.

"Excuse me, sirs!" The patrolmen stopped talking and turned in Jessie's direction. They looked Jessie up and down. Jessie froze and looked down at the ground. The patrolmen stared at him. Finally, one spoke in an irritated and harsh tone.

"Yeah, what you want boy!" Jessie continued looking down, and not making eye contact (*which was drilled in him by his Papa*). He stuck both of his hands into his pockets and again toyed with the roll of bills. He began to speak nervously.

"Excuse me, sir, sorry to interrupt you, but I was wondering if there was any talk of a girl being burned in the fire. I was looking for my girl. Her name is Solo. I was told she was burned in the fire. Not sure if it's true, so I'm just asking." The patrolmen looked at each other.

"Well," one said, "There was a girl taken out, thought she was white at first, but turn out she was a n—r."

There was a roar of laughter between the two patrolmen. Jessie looked up and stared at them both. The laughter subsided. The patrolmen shifted uncomfortably. One spoke up, "The n--r was taken over to City Hospital over in Harlem. Don't have no name. No more information. Best you move along and go over there." Even though he wasn't satisfied with the answer, Jessie didn't want no trouble. He thanked them and turned and walked away. The patrolmen watched as he walked away before bursting out into laughter.

Jessie made his way back toward the apartment building. He looked around for Maybelline, but she was nowhere in sight. Maybe she went back to her apartment. Jessie needed to go over to City to see if the girl the patrolmen spoke of was Solo. He didn't want to jump to conclusions, but the reality was, it was possible it was her. However, first, he needed to retrieve some things from his apartment. He hadn't thought of what condition his apartment was in. As he made his way up the drenched stairs, a few people he recognized looked at him with sadness in their eyes. Jessie continued to make his way up the stairs. The sickening smell of the burnt smoke lingered in the air. Everyone's apartment door was open but there appeared to be no damage. Jessie finally reached his floor, which was saturated with water. His shoes made squishing sounds as he walked through the water. Some of the water eased into the soles of his shoes, wetting his socks. Jessie realized the hems of his pant legs were wet.

"S—t," he said out loud. "What a f—king mess!"

Hearing Jessie swear, one of his neighbors, an elderly Black man with gray hair named Nash, came out of his apartment. "Young man!" he called out. Jessie turned to see Mr. Nash motioning to him. "Shit, what now!" Jessie muttered to himself. He wanted to keep going to his apartment, but out of respect, he turned and walked back to old man Nash.

"Come on now," old man Nash motioned to Jessie. Jessie forced a small smile.

"How can I help you, Mr. Nash?" Jessie asked out of concern.

Mr. Nash, with his head lowered, spoke slowly and carefully.

"Your girl...that pretty girl of yours. Well, she was hurt bad...really bad. Just thought you ought to know. The fire started in your place. They took her out. Sorry to say, but from what I can tell, she seemed bad off. My Misses wanted to help."

Old man Nash's wife joined him in the doorway. His wife was shorter than him and plump all around. She was fair-skinned with kind eyes and silky gray and black long hair.

"Yes, my son," she began, "your lady was hurt in a bad way. We'll pray for her."

Old man Nash looked at Jessie, reached out, and touched his shoulder.

"Now son, you let us know if there is anything we can do for you."

Jessie was touched. He nodded and smiled.

"Thank you, much appreciated."

Jessie continued to walk toward his apartment. As Jessie got closer, he could see the remains of what his apartment door had been, thrown about in the hallway. Some of his other neighbors peeked out their doors as he walked by. Best to leave him be at this time, they all thought. Jessie's pace slowed. His eyes were trying to register what he was seeing. As he got to the doorway, he looked and gasped. All the furniture was broken and thrown about. The fire had burned the bed and the window curtains. The lamps were broken, and all their clothes were either burned or soaked in water. The window was broken out, and glass was everywhere. The cabinet doors had been chopped off, all the dishes and glasses were broken and scattered on the floor. Everything was either burned or chopped to pieces. He had no idea there would be such destruction. *Solo! Shit. So, she had been here. It's true, she was burned.*

Jessie's eyes looked down at what was the ruined remains of the bed he once shared with Solo. The bed sheets and blankets were destroyed. One side of the mattress was burned worse than the other. It was the side where Solo slept. The mattress was soaked with water. Jessie's heart was beating fast. He was growing hot. He couldn't think clearly. Here he was out feeling sorry for himself after his argument with Solo, drinking, gambling, and having his way with a loose woman, while his beautiful Solo was here being burned and suffering. He was not here to help her. She must have called out to him. He shook his head to get the thought out of his mind. His eyes burned with tears he forced back. Jessie was not a praying man, but he said a silent prayer for Solo. Now he understood, this was what crazy Maybelline was trying to tell him. Jessie screamed out in agony. Even though they couldn't tolerate the stench of lingering smoke, some of the neighbors closed their doors to shut out Jessie's suffering. It was hard to hear a grown man crying. Many of them had seen Solo when she was brought out of the burning apartment. It was not a pretty sight.

Jessie, overcome with grief and loss, continued to curse and cry out. "What am I going to do now? So much destruction. All is lost." His small collection of clothing was all lost, mostly burned, and damaged by water. Solo would be heartbroken. Her beautiful clothes were either burned, torn to shreds, or thrown in the foul water. *Why so much destruction?* He certainly understood the need to quickly put out the fire, which by all accounts must have started in their apartment. But this was overkill. He had heard how the White firemen would destroy Negro possessions. Everything was damaged as if an angry mob or a pack of wild dogs viciously went through their home. Hate is always alive. There was nothing worth saving, Jessie thought to himself.

Jessie continued to maneuver through the disarray. Tears form in his eyes. His heart was heavy, and his feet labored through the destruction. Even the contents of their small icebox had been emptied and tossed to the floor. The floor was saturated with water. While it wasn't much, it was what he and Solo called home. Now it was ruined. There was nothing left. There was no longer a home. It was the end. Jessie hung his head and closed his eyes and took a long hard deep breath. Best he tries to see what he could salvage before he left to check on Solo. Once he left, the greedy would take advantage of his misfortunate. Jessie began to pick up discarded clothing and other personal items. Their only table lamp was broken.

Finally, Jessie bent down and lifted the dresser, which was now overturned. The contents of the dresser had spilled onto the wet floor. Mostly, old paper and a few undergarments. But before his eyes, Jessie recognized the damp envelope. He reached down to pick up the envelope. It was the letter to Solo from her Mama, Tulip. The letter had been given to Jessie by a friend that he knew from back home. The letter had not been opened. Jessie carefully tucked the wet, soiled letter into his jacket pocket. Careful not to tear it. He picked up a few toiletries and stuffed them in his pocket. Nothing else was worth taking, all was lost. Jessie stood and looked around the apartment one last time. He took a deep breath. Lowered his head and stuck his hands in his pockets. He felt the roll of money. He walked out and didn't look back.

Old bag bones, wind-scarred face immersed with lines of age due to destruction and waste;
Once love lived there, happiness ran rampant, could not have predicted what would is simply fate;
Like an unyielding force, the storm came rushing in with high tides only to recede with a heart sprinkled down like broken crystal pieces;
The strong winds blew out the flame of passion and left a depth of emptiness;
Moving with a slow ease, trying hard to breathe, empty eyes, cloudy with lack of emotion, the mind trying to what was believed to be the past, is reality.

SIXTEEN

City Hospital #4

It was a dreary, rainy day. The low-hanging, dark clouds draped over the tall Victorian buildings, giving off a ghostly dim appearance, which made the hospital wagon screaming and flashing lights seem even more sinister. The blasting sirens screamed loudly as the hospital wagon moved quickly through the muddy, crowded streets. The sound was both deafening and frightening, which caused hearts to quicken with fear and minds to ponder unanswered questions... *Who's in there? Someone I know? What happened? Is the person hurt badly, sick, or dead? Will I be next?* Some people stopped mid-stride and paused as the hospital wagon with its hypnotic lights and loud noise, made its way down the muddy, rough streets, moving too quickly. It appears the attendants took pleasure in causing such a ruckus. Even though, some people were curious about the occupants...they selfishly prayed it was not anyone that they knew. Some men took off their hats, giving respect to the poor soul being rushed. Women made the sign of the cross and even kissed the rosary dangling from their necks. However, others were annoyed, and some looked irritated as if the fast-moving, loud vehicle was messing up their day. Fearful mothers called out to their children to move out of the path of the fast-moving hospital wagon, out of fear they would be either killed or seriously maimed. It was common knowledge small animals, children, and even adults had been run over by the fast-moving hospital wagons. However, the young sensed no harm and took pleasure in chasing the roaring hospital wagon; some children, bursting with excitement, even chased after the hospital wagon, trying with all their might to catch up with the hospital wagon. Of course, they were never successful, but the children enjoyed the chase. Time was of the essence, so the hospital wagon, with sirens blasting, twisted and turned, causing muddy dirt to fly in every direction as it sped down the roads, with its flashing lights to reach its final destination.

Inside the wagon, while two of the attendants navigated the streets, the other two attendants worked on Solo, who appeared to be greeting death's doorsteps. The attendants spoke no words, while they worked in unison. They carefully put an IV in Solo's arm and placed an oxygen mask over her face. Solo had not regained consciousness, which in some respects was good, because the pain from the burns would have been unbearable and the attendants needed her to be still as they assessed her condition. Solo's clothing had burned into her flesh. The attendant carefully peeled pieces of the burnt material stuck to her burnt skin. The work at hand made the hospital wagon uncomfortably hot and musky. It was critical that Solo's burnt skin not be exposed to infection. The attendants would leave the critical job of removing most of Solo's burnt clothing from her body to the professionals at the hospital. It was clear her skin and fabric were now merged and there was exposed fleshy fatty red meat and white bones. Beads of sweat popped on the attendants' foreheads and ran down the side of their faces. While they had seen their share of cuts, blood, and broken bodies, and in some cases even death, they still struggled to hold down nausea rising from the pits of the stomach to engulf their throats. No words were exchanged. They looked at each other as if acknowledging the gravity of the situation, but continued with the task at hand, determined to save this pitiful young girl's life. Solo's breathing was labored. Her heart rate and blood pressure were highly elevated. The attendants silently prayed they would get to City soon. Time was critical.

"HOW MUCH LONGER BEFORE WE GET THERE?" one of

the attendants yelled out to the driver of the wagon.

The driver yelled back, without taking his eyes off the dirt road, "Moving as fast as my Black ass can without taking any lives!" He yelled out of the window. "Get the hell out of the way! Move it n—r."

"S—t! Hell, the crazy asses can't see this emergency vehicle. Damn, have a little respect!"

"What's going on up there? The situation back here is getting critical. I don't know if she's going to make it!" the attendant yelled out while trying not to wake their patient.

"Doing my best, I'm not a magician, man! Only if these no-account sons of bitches would get out of my way!" The hospital wagon tilted to the side, causing the attendants to fall to the floor, but they managed to keep Solo from falling.

"Ok," said the attendant, "Do your best, but don't kill us trying."

The driver smiled and kept speeding down the road, blowing his horn along with the sirens and flipping off finger signs to no one in particular. The attendants turned their attention back to Solo. They marveled how one side of Solo's body seemed untouched, while the other side was a monstrous mess. It called to mind *The Phantom of the Opera*. Not that they could afford to see a big-time play, not off their pay, but they had seen the posters. Yes, she was beauty and the beast all in one. If she lived, how would she survive? Solo's breathing grew very shallow.

The hospital wagon pulled up to City Hospital #4. Several Negro female nurses in their crisp white uniforms, with matching white shoes, stockings, and hats, moved quickly to the wagon. Two tall, male attendants pushed a metal bed cart with long black leather straps. The cart made a rattling noise as if it needed to be oiled. Suddenly, the back of the hospital wagon flew open and one of the attendants described, in rapid succession the conditions of the patient as he walked with the nurses. "We have a Negro woman *(the nurses looked at each other and then at Solo, but didn't say a word, they had seen it all and they were no strangers to mixed-race)* age approximately between 19-25, height 5ft. 8in., weight 125. Found in the fire. No name. Suffering from severe smoke insulation, and several areas of fifth to sixth-degree burns, mostly contained to the right-side extremities. The patient is in a self-induced coma with burns on the face, head, arms, side. Blood pressure is 185 over 90, breathing is labored. Gave the patient 100cc of insulin. Open wounds are exposed and subject to infection from materials or other complications."

The nurses nodded their heads and wrote rapidly on their clipboards as they tried to capture everything the wagon attendants were saying. The attendants quickly and carefully lifted Solo and placed her onto the metal bed cart. The nurses attached the IV drip to the cart, one held the drip, as the others walked behind the cart, while the wagon attendants rolled the cart through the hospital doors, which were wide open to accommodate the incoming emergency bed carts. Throughout the whole ordeal, Solo remained unconscious. The nurse knew she was in a coma, which was the best thing for a severe burn victim.

When compared to the other New York City hospitals that only served white patients, City Hospital #4 (City #4 as it was called) served the Colored, poor, and less fortunate. The buildings were old, dilapidated, and poorly kept. The wards were extremely overcrowded. Medication and supplies were scant, and the equipment was deficient, old, and outdated. The wagon attendants found that compared to the outside, the hospital lighting was extremely bright and well-lit. The brightness made their eyes blink and strain. The smell was a combination of foul urine, food, disinfectant, medicine, and rotting decay.

City Hospital #4 had long deep corridors, which were always overcrowded with patients with varying medical and/or mental conditions.

City Hospital #4 also served the mentally ill of all ages and races as well. Patients and families filled seats in barn-like waiting rooms, and many were forced to stand for hours. All along the corridors, patients on stretchers endured the same interminable wait, terrified and alone. Some patients were in makeshift wheelchairs, while others lay lifeless on bed carts or were perched against the undecorated concrete gray walls which boasted a dangling cross, perhaps donated by some random group of missionaries or a nunnery. Many just sat on the cold linoleum floors as they waited for care, which could be days.

You could find patients lingering in open doorways or moving about the ward with parts of their naked bodies exposed through flimsy hospital gowns. Patients who caused a ruckus, mentally ill or not, could be found in straitjackets or bed restraints. There was so much movement. Nurses and doctors moved at a rapid pace and avoided patients who reached out to them or required their attention. Nurses' shoes clicked against the floor as if they were musical instruments. Cigarettes dangled from some of the hospital staff's mouths and the smoke formed halos around their heads as if they were angels in disguise. But mostly, patients suffered, and the pain was paramount. There were pleas for help, mourning, praying, and crying intertwined with children singing off-beat nursery rhymes or playing patty cake.

City Hospital #4 offered no separation between sick children and sick adults, females, and males, or physical and mental illness. When it came to Negroes, patients were all mixed in together. No screens or partitions for privacy. Some patients stared blankly, while others yelled and reached out to the nurses as they walked by, trying to get their attention, especially mothers with sick kids. However, most were ignored. Some were given a pat on the head or an adjustment of bed linens. It was clear City Hospital #4 was understaffed as well as a training ground for new and aspiring Colored doctors and nurses.

There were never enough doctors or nurses. In some cases, patients endured exams performed by hurried and overworked interns with little experience. If the patients were fortunate to have a little money, they could slip it into the hand of an attendant or nurse for faster and better service or just a few meds to make them or their family member more comfortable. In most cases, however, these patients had no money to spare for healthcare, so they were at the mercy of home-based remedies handed down from generations, such as roots or the local neighborhood "doctors." When all else failed, or in an unforeseen dire emergency, they turned to what "free" City Hospital #4 care could afford.

Daily shifts required one nurse to care for more than thirty patients at a time. One doctor could be on call for up to three days without a break. The hospital staff did their best for the sickest patients, such as ones with intravenous solutions running into their arms, catheters running out of their bladders, or severely burned patients. Doctors, nurses, and attendants were so overworked, patients' survival could be attributed less to good nursing and the use of new remedies, than to the recuperative powers of the human body, the strength of the human spirit, and prayers to their God. Nurses usually found one or two vomiting or others moaning in pain or children crying for their mothers. This was not hell, this was "City Hospital #4!"

Separate but equal they say, no part does race play; but here I endure from the interrelation of my race, inadequate treatment on all levels; no right or wrong, simply because they can and to my detriment, I think of them as friends;

My skin cannot change, my blood runs red, my kinky hair will remain, my heart bears no indolence for the continuous onslaught of generational bigotry of blame because it is my visible skin that is thought to be the source of shame;

For I am not naive to the injustices or blind to the actions of those who have bitten from the poison fruit, their hearts seek to instill fear or worst make me dead;

I am fully aware my skin color is the force of their fear; it begs the question…

how can I fully embrace my will to live, when the roadblocks of hate are blocking my path to my life dreams to be sealed?

The past has a record of the misjustice of my ancestors or others simply based on their color, the present continues the suppression in a different style of dress, but the future provides the opportunity for us all to come together regardless of race, and just try our God-given to be our best.

SEVENTEEN
This S—t is Getting Real

Patients looked on as the fast-moving gurney made its way down the long hallway. Some tried in vain to get a look at the dear soul laying lifeless on the stretcher. Some patients jumped in fear of the stretcher running them over. Not speaking any words, the nurses and attendants knew time was critical for burn victims, so they continued to quickly push the stretcher carrying Solo down the long, crowded corridor without engaging any patients, or hospital staff. Time was of the essence. As they passed the reception desk, one nurse called for Doctor Frank to be sent to Operating Room Blue Section A *(operating rooms were identified by color and sections)*. The nurses and attendants continue to their destination.

The nurses and attendants made their way into the operating room. Once again, Solo was moved carefully from the metal cart to the cold, hard operating table. Solo remained unconscious, oblivious to everything happening around her. Her beautiful, mangled, burned hair cascaded down the side of the operating table. One Negro nurse began to cut away at Solo's remaining locs. Even the nurse even marveled at how beautiful her hair was, but it wasn't hers and so she took pleasure in cutting it off. The other nurses cut away the remains of Solo's clothing, while another dabbed antiseptic on the exposed wounds. Even though Solo was unconscious, it was important she didn't wake up during whatever surgery would be needed, especially the skin graft, so a gas mask was placed over her face to ensure she was sedated. This would be a long, painful process.

Freshly scrubbed, Doctor Frank entered the operating room. He stood tall, about 6 ft. 3 in., slim build, very pronounced with large facial features but small, delicate hands, which was helpful for his line of work as a surgeon. His smooth skin was caramel color with light brown eyes which were almost translucent. He was serious about his work, as a result, he had no time for foolishness. Doctor Frank rarely smiled. *What was there to smile about working in this hell hole?* But when he did flash a smile, magic… his big white teeth sparkled like stars in a dark sky and his eyes twinkled. Doctor Frank wore his black hair slicked back, like one of the New York musicians, but his was not processed. he just had *good hair* because of his Indian heritage. He was a good-looking man, and he knew it. Needless to say, the female nurses, along with a few of the male nurses had wet dreams about him.

Doctor Frank was an older established surgeon who had worked in various hospitals throughout the city that served New York City's destitute. He longed to work in one of New York's affluent hospitals where his skills would be appreciated, and he could gain the respect he so well deserved. However, being a Negro Doctor, he was relegated to hospitals serving the destitute of all races—Jews, Irish, Asians, White, and Negro—where it was felt he was best suited. While he had no delusions as to why he was at City Hospital #4, he could still dream. He had been there for ten years and had seen a lot. He really didn't care about the patients he served, but his moral code required he give them the best care possible. But sometimes that was not possible. Many patients who came to City Hospital #4 had serious mental illnesses and they were confined to the subhuman mental wards. Patients needing his skills were far and in between. In most cases when they arrived at the hospital they were already knocking on death's door. But every now and then, Doctor Frank would have a patient requiring his expertise, and severely burned victims just happened to fail right into that category.

"So, what do we have here?" Doctor Frank asked as he strolled causally into the operating room. The head nurse spoke rapidly as she draped Doctor Frank with a plastic operating gown and gloves. Doctor Frank's focus was on his patient. He looked down at the Solo who remained unconscious and was heavily sedated as well. The head nurse briefed Doctor Frank on Solo's condition, which was getting graver by the minute. Her blood pressure was elevated, and her heartrate was erratic. She was a Jane Doe. No information yet on her or her family. Doctor Frank continued his slow visual assessment of his unconscious patient. "WOW," he thought to himself, she's a beauty, clearly a mulatto, seemly, yet could easy be mistaken for a white woman. He should know because he was married to one. Even the burns didn't take away the fullness of her beauty. *So young, she couldn't be no more than 20 years of age or so, such a pity and waste.* As Doctor Frank took a long survey of Solo's body, he had to stay focused because his manhood was certainly reacting. Interestingly, the serious burns were concentrated on her right side, while the left side only sustained minor damage. Doctor Frank slowly let his hand stroke Solo's unharmed side. Poor kid, her family must be devastated.

"Young lady, can you hear me? Can you tell me your name?" but no response. "I am Doctor Frank, and I am going to take good care of you." He pushed her gently. Still no response. This part of the process was very important to ensure the patient was fully under sedation. Didn't want the patient waking up in the middle of the skin grafting, which was beyond the tolerable threshold of pain.

"OK, folks let's get started," announced Doctor Frank, as if he was starting a show or race. "First, we will try to save her right arm, with the skin grafting from her back. There are exposed bones, so a lot of repair work. It appears this arm most likely sustained a serious injury in the past, maybe broken as a kid, and did not properly heal. Keep the gas pumping, don't won't our dear young lady waking up during the process. As you know this is going to be painful."

Doctor Frank always found burnt patients to be the worst. It was never a true recovery. Most burn victims succumbed to their injuries, and others died from infections and improper care. City Hospital #4's burn unit was very limited in the care it provided, including proper care for burned patients. Mostly the care was to keep them comfortable. Depending on the severity of the burns, some recovered and the remaining just went nuts due to the constant pain, lack of care, and disfiguration.

Doctor Frank knew this patient would be seriously disfigured and would require long-term rehabilitation. Recovery was possible but would be hard, long, and costly. Of course, with a lot of pain. He knew a major key to the recovery process for burn victims would be family and a strong mental attitude to survive. He didn't know this girl, so it was no way for him to judge.

"Okay everyone, this will be a very delicate process so please check to see if there is any family or someone for this poor soul."

A student intern quickly left the room. It was her job to keep the family updated and get needed supplies or medication.

Take away my burden, take away my pain, for as truly as a child of God, I am the cause of my suffering and shame, for the life I so willing chose to live is not the blame;
Look upon my weary soul and judge not what you see, for we are the same, yes, you and me;
My suffering is hard, my tears stream like a fast-rushing river, shackled by demons or evil spirits of another name, for they have claimed my fame;
Long gone are the days I so causally tossed to sea, not caring if another one come because I was in charge of my spirit, I was free;
Now here I lay, scarred, broken, and damaged, my faith has been tested, eyes wide open staring at a new life ahead of me, only time will tell what it will be or maybe my lost days will return from sea, I can only wait and see and ask God to be with me for he holds the key.

EIGHTEEN
Got to Find Her

As Jessie stepped over the broken apartment door, he heard fast-running feet behind him.

"Jessie! Jessie!" someone called out. It was a woman's voice. Jessie's ears burned, his heart quickened, his mind raced. *Could it be?*

He stopped walking and turned slowly hoping Solo's face would appear through the smoke-filled hallway. As the footsteps got louder and closer, some of the other tenants peeked out of their doors to see what was going on.

Jessie rolled his eyes as he realized the source of the ruckus was none other than that crazy ass Maybelline. She was half-dressed, hair undone, and barefoot with her arms frantically flailing about. Jessie didn't have time for her foolishness, so he turned and started walking in the opposite direction.

"No Jessie, wait up! I got news about Solo!" Maybelline yelled as she tried to catch her breath. The mention of Solo's name made Jessie stop in his tracks. His mind was racing, his hands were sweaty, and his heart was pounding. Did he really want to hear any news about Solo? All this was probably her fault. He was done with her and knew it was time to move on. *I should have left a long time ago,* he thought. On the other hand, he needed to know if she was okay. Maybelline slowly approached Jessie with one outstretched hand, while the other held tightly onto her flimsy clothing. She placed her hand on Jessie's shoulder for support as she bent over heaving for air. She held out one finger indicating she needed a minute to catch her breath. Jessie rolled his eyes impatiently but waited, nonetheless. He was curious about what information she had about Solo.

Finally, Maybelline took her hand from Jessie's shoulder and stood tall. Jessie's eyes grazed her body and landed on her tits as the sheer fabric she wore exposed her big black nipples. Maybelline quickly gathered her clothing and held it close to her body. *No freebies here. Men always got their minds in the gutter.* She knew there was no time to dwell on any of that. She had more important things on her mind.

"Well?" Jessie prompted rather roughly, "What news you got about Solo?"

Maybelline began, "This is what I learned. It seems the fire started in your apartment. They think Solo may have fell asleep with a lit cigarette. She was always so tired from working so hard. It wasn't her fault. Oh my God! She was so pretty. Now, her hair, her face…Jessie…it's bad. Real bad."

Jessie took both arms and forcibly shook Maybelline's shoulders. "Look girl," he yelled. "I got no time for your foolishness! Where in the f—k is Solo? YOU BETTER SAY SOMETHING REAL QUICK BEFORE I SLAP THE S—T OUT OF YOU!"

"Hey, stop treating her like that! She's just trying to tell you your lady was burned really bad, and they rushed her to City Hospital #4 up in Harlem," yelled out a neighbor in Maybelline's defense.

Jessie stopped shaking Maybelline.

"Sorry," he mumbled. "And thank you."

Maybelline cried even harder. Jessie gently patted her shoulder. Along, with his few belongings in tow, he turned from Maybelline and ran quickly through the water and smoke-filled hallways. *CITY HOSPITAL #4,* his mind repeated over and over.

* * *

The sun had set as the clouds parted. Looming before him, Jessie saw a massive brown structure looming before him. He tilted his head as far back as he could to take in the fullness of the gothic-themed building. It was truly a scary sight. To Jessie, the hospital didn't look like a place of healing. Instead it seemed like a place for bad people, very bad people. The black cast iron gate completely enclosed the structure, as if its main purpose was to keep people out rather than invite them in. City Hospital #4 covered more than two long city blocks that spanned more than twenty acres of land. It had multiple adjoining red brick structures with high peaks, looking like old castles. Iron bars covered the windows like a prison. Bright lights escaped through each window giving a ghostly appearance. Jessie had heard City Hospital #4 was used to treat the insane and mentally afflicted. It was also the only hospital to serve New York City's less fortunate population and the services were free. Even though the poor, homeless, and immigrants went to City Hospital #4, it was commissioned to serve as a training hospital for future Negro doctors and nurses and to only serve people of color. If you were Colored and got sick, had a baby, or went crazy, you were taken directly to City Hospital #4, hands down. You were not given a choice. If uppity Coloreds couldn't afford a private room, they found themselves in beds alongside less fortunate Coloreds or poor degenerates.

Jessie had his meager belongings close to him as he looked up at the old brick building. He walked down to the open iron gates where an ambulance wagon was pulling in. He walked through the gates and took the long path to the hospital entrance. People dressed in various uniforms rushed about near the entryway. Jessie stopped in his tracks. When the ambulance wagon's back doors swung open, two men dressed in white hopped out and began to lower a person onto a stretcher. The body appeared lifeless and unresponsive. Several nurses ran out to assist other patients as the two attendants from the ambulance moved quickly with the stretcher through the wide-open hospital doors.

Jessie lowered his head and walked in behind the nurses who were rapidly directing questions to the attendants, which must have been about the person on the stretcher. No one paid Jessie any attention.

As he turned to walk toward the entrance, he stuffed his hands in his jacket pockets and felt the letter. He looked around one last time. There, moving swiftly, he saw a young Colored girl, dressed in brown and white with white shoes and stockings. A little white hat was perched on her head. Jessie thought she looked too young to be a nurse, but she carried a clipboard and seemed to work at the hospital. Jessie watched her as she moved about talking and smiling. He thought to himself, *maybe she can help. Nobody else has and this is getting a little frustrating. What the hell, I got nothing to lose.*

Jessie ran to catch up with the young girl. She was a fast walker. Finally, he caught up with her and moved quickly to face her, which forced her to stop and look at him. For a few seconds, Jessie and the young girl stared at one another. He looked down at saw a name tag that read: Hi, My Name is Julie. Suddenly, she smiled, showing off her pearly white teeth. Jessie let out a sigh of relief.

"Hello," she said. "My name is Julie, and I am a hospital volunteer. Given you are blocking my path, I can only assume you are in immediate need of assistance." She looked down at the paper on her clipboard. With pen in hand, she asked, "Are you sick or hurt? Is someone else sick or needs help? Are you looking for a patient?" Jessie was amazed at how the questions seemed so rehearsed. For a moment, all he could do was stare at her.

"Sir, how can I assist you?" she repeated. Jessie gathered his thoughts and took off his hat (*out of respect for the young lady*).

"I'm looking for someone who may have been brought here. There was a fire, and she may have been hurt. I was told she was brought here," Jessie replied as he fumbled with his hat.

Julie smiled at Jessie and responded, "I'm here to help you with that. First, what is the patient's full name? Please speak slowly and clearly, so I can get it right." She put her pen on the paper and looked at Jessie with a smile.

"Her name is Solo," Jessie said rather quickly.

"And how is that spelled?" Julie asked still smiling.

"S-O-L-O."

"And what is Solo's last name?"

"Her last name is Thornton," he stated slowly.

"And how is that spelled?"

"T-H-O-R-N-T-O-N."

"Okay," Julie said, "Now you said it was a fire and she was brought here today, correct?"

"Yes," Jessie said, a little huffy. This little girl was really getting on his nerves.

"And what is your name?" Julie asked. Jessie gave out a long sigh and mumbled his name.

"Please spell that slowly," Julie stated. "First name first."

Jessie was about to lose his temper but instead complied with her request.

"Thank you," Julie said, sensing Jessie's frustration, which she was no stranger to. "What is your relationship to the patient? Are you kin?" Julie inquired as she looked at Jessie because only kin can receive information on patients.

Jessie hesitated and realized the predicament. He lowered his eyes and stared at the floor.

"She's my wife."

Julie read his body language and knew he was lying, but still wrote down his response. Having the required information, she smiled at Jessie and instructed him to follow her. They walked down a long corridor lined with people lying on beds as nurses and doctors passed by quickly. Jessie struggled to keep up as they made several turns. Finally, they stopped at a massive desk surrounded by nurses speaking and going about their routines. The girl approached the desk and showed one of the nurses what she had written on the clipboard. They both looked up at Jessie and lowered their heads to talk some more. The nurse smiled at Julie and thanked her. Julie feeling proud, walked over to Jessie and said, "Please have a seat in the chair and Head Nurse Mary Pierce will be right with you. It shouldn't be too long."

Before Jessie could thank her, she was off with her clipboard seeking out someone new to help. Jessie turned and sat in one of the empty chairs against the wall. As he twirled his thumbs, he hoped the wait wouldn't be too long.

Several of the nurses stood around laughing and talking. Head Nurse Mary Pierce had walked off without even acknowledging Jessie's presence. The voice in Jessie's head screamed at him. *Man, get out of here. This is not your godd—n problem. What if they say you have to pay? You shouldn't have said she was your wife.*

Regardless of the thoughts in his head, Jessie felt obligated to ensure Solo was okay. Just as he decided he would leave the letter and go, he noticed two elderly Colored people walk up to the desk. They spoke quietly to one of the nurses.

"We have been waiting for hours to hear about our son. Is there any news?" they asked in unison. The nurse, looking sympathetic at the couple replied with a smile.

"The doctor will be out soon to talk with you, please have a seat. Can I get you some water?" The couple declined as they walked back slowly to their seats. "It shouldn't be much longer," the nurse called out to them.

Jessie knew he was in for a long wait. He put his cap over his face and leaned his head back against the wall. *Might as well catch a nap while I wait.*

*Our conversations in the dark will now be exposed
in the light;
For I am seeking answers to the questions we only shared in
the night;
I searched my soul for you, as you are, I see us together. To
share in your world seemed to be my blight;
I want to run, I long to escape, I feel you drawing me near,
but my wings want to soar, this is only your plight;
You got me feeling like belonging, I remember the way we
make love, but not loved. I never had that in our sight;
We have run our course like a bird in the sky, it is time for
me to take flight.*

NINETEEN
Long Road Ahead

After twelve long hours, Doctor Frank, with sweat dripping from his face, eyes red, cramped legs, and a growling stomach, let out a slow sigh. The procedure had been long, delicate, and difficult. The burns were deep, and the burnt skin had seared into the bones. Unfortunately, the patient, a beautiful young woman, would be physically and emotionally scarred for life.

He was able to save her arm even though the burns caused additional damage to the nerves and muscles, and it hadn't healed properly from the past injury. Doctor Frank was sure the unfortunate girl would not have full use of the arm though. It would dangle lifelessly by her side. He was not sure if her fingers would be functional, but with the proper physical therapy, they might regain some use. But worst of all was the severe burns to the left side of the patient's face. There had not been much skin to graft, due to the severity of her burns. Her left earlobe had to be removed but when her hair grew back, it could hide the deformity. Doctor Frank figured, due to the high concentration of the burns to one side, she had most likely been on her side in a drunken sleep when the fire started. She still reeked of cheap booze whereas he preferred a good bottle of cabernet sauvignon. Time would tell if cosmetic surgery was possible and if she could afford it.

Doctor Frank believed the patient had a thirty to seventy percent chance of survival. Hopefully, no respiratory failure, sepsis, or other organ failure would occur, which usually causes the death of most severely burned victims. The major problem faced was leakage of fluid and salts, loss of circulation, and insufficient blood returning to the heart for it to maintain blood pressure. The pain would require the patient to remain sedated. If she survived, once she saw herself, she could possibly go into cardiac arrest or go insane. There could be depression, anxiety, and mental problems. No happy ending here.

Doctor Frank stripped off his mask and gloves and took one final look at his patient, who, even with the bandages covering her face, was still beautiful. He announced his directives.

"Okay, let's clear her out of here and get her to the burn ward. Keep the pain drip and IV in for the next forty-eight hours until we reassess her recovery. Let me know if anyone shows up asking questions. Family, friends, whoever." He walked slowly from the room. He would check on her tomorrow. *What a waste. She was once a beauty. Beauty and the Beast.*

Several of the nurses quickly moved Solo from the operating room. The was no concern about her comfort because they knew she was unconscious from the amount of drugs administered during the procedure. The double doors opened, and they wheeled away the bed. The quiet of the operating room was a contrast to the crowded hallways littered with moaning patients, crying children, and laughing nurses. With Solo strapped securely to the cot, the nurses entered a large elevator to take their unfortunate patient to her new home, City's Hospital # 4 Burn Unit. One nurse stayed behind to see if anyone had inquired about the patient.

City's burn unit for severely burned patients was located on the twelfth floor of the hospital, which happened to be the top floor. The patients were isolated from the other units because of their continuous screaming and crying from their conditions. Their situations required constant care such as bandage changes, bathing, administration of pain medication by the hospital staff. The death rate was disproportionately high for severely burned patients, mostly due to infections and a lack of will to live. Therefore, it was best to keep them isolated from the other patients. Also, City's mental ward was located on the same floor as the burn unit, but in a different wing. Many of the burn victims ended up being transferred to the mental ward. It was like the hospital treated their burns as mental health problems, rather than physical health problems. Visitors were only allowed on Sundays, and they were limited to immediate family and only two a day, a policy implemented to reduce the risk of infections.

City's burn unit was nothing fancy or to write home about, rather it was a big non-descript open cold room *(the temperature was kept cold to reduce the chance of infections from sweating)* with pull curtains between each patient's bed. There were about forty patients, no windows, and very limited privacy. The adjacent small operating room was used to continue skin grafting and treat open wounds. In some cases, the patients were awake for the procedures, which was extremely painful even with medication. Some patients passed out from the intolerable pain.

The operating nurse passed by Jessie, who was now in a deep sleep. The events of the previous night and the hell of the day had completely exhausted him. His head leaned against the wall, his mouth hung open, and a trickle of spit eased from his mouth and down his bumpy, unshaven chin.

The nurse had not paid any particular attention to Jessie. She was used to seeing people waiting for news about their loved ones and most of the time, they were asleep because the wait was long. The nurse approached the desk. After exchanging greetings and a few moments of small talk, she gave the other nurses a detailed breakdown of her most recent patient's condition. The nurses behind the desk usually spent their days processing the paperwork of incoming patients or collecting information from family members when the patient was incapable of providing it directly. Their job could be very mundane at times, so they lived for the juicy news from nurses who were either in operating rooms or had inside information on new patients. As a result, the gossip about Solo quickly gained the attention of all the nurses. The telephone rang but went unanswered as the nurse told the others about her severely burned patient from the slums who came in with skin as white as day, greenish-blue eyes, and blonde hair, but was Colored and reeked of liquor. The girl didn't have any identification on her and couldn't be more than twenty years old.

"She's burned so bad, she'll be damaged for life if the poor chile live."

The other nurses were fully engrossed as the operating nurse updated them on Solo's condition. They covered their mouths as they could not believe what they were hearing. Surely, this unfortunate patient would not survive. They shook their heads in pity. Finally, after they finished their gossip *(which they couldn't wait to share with other nurses)*, they pointed to Jessie. He was the only person who had come in inquiring about a young woman in a fire. Solo fit the description.

"Sir! Sir," the operating nurse called out to Jessie as she gently shook his shoulder. She thought to herself, *this is a good-looking man, even asleep. He must be having a hell of a dream.* Her eyes traveled down Jessie's body and blushed at his reaction. It was obvious he was into her and she was definitely into him.

Jessie slowly opened his eyes at the urging of the nurse. The nurse stood fully upright and smiled. *Is she flirting?* Jessie took a minute to collect himself. He rubbed his eyes and took a long breath. How long had he been there? No way to tell without any windows. There were different nurses behind the desk than when he first came in. His neck was stiff. He patted his pocket. His money was still intact and his belongings were still there. The nurse spoke softly as she slightly bent back over toward Jessie.

"I understand you were inquiring about a young lady who was in a fire and based on your description of her, she may be the patient in our care. I need to get some information from you and then you'll be able to follow me so we can confirm. I understand the woman you're looking for is your wife."

"Yes," Jessie answered.

"Okay, because only immediate family are allowed to see patients after surgery."

At this point, Jessie stood up. He towered over the nurse.

"What kind of surgery?" he asked panicked.

The nurse looked at him and spoke calmly.

"Sir, after we confirm that this is your wife, Doctor Frank will talk with you."

The nurse took a deep breath. She was used to family members wanting a full account of their loved one's conditions, but that was not her job. She didn't want to lose her job over this man no matter how cute he was.

"Sir, please follow me." The nurses behind the desk watched the whole scene between Jessie and the nurse *(while the phone continued to ring)* and began to chatter as they walked away.

The smell hit him first. *What is that smell?* Jessie thought before coughing into his hands. As he walked behind the nurse, she moved quickly through a large open ward, ignoring the pleas from the outreached hands. There were patients on both sides of the room. Some were bandaged from head to toe like a mummy, while others, both men and women, lay naked—fully exposed. Jessie's paced slowed as he looked from side to side. Some patients were covered with open wounds and meaty flush oozing with green substances. Jessie's stomach turned. Surely, Solo was not here among the living dead. Several nurses moved about caring for the patients, offering water and words of comfort. It seemed there was nothing more to do. Finally, the nurse stopped and asked another nurse the whereabouts of Doctor Frank's recent female burn patient. The nurse pointed to the very last bed on the left. Jessie looked and all he saw was a body wrapped in white bandages from head to toe. The nurse walked to the bed and inspected the clipboard dangling from the end of the bed.

Jessie stood silently looking at the person laying immobilized. *This cannot be Solo,* he thought. The nurse walked over to the opposite side of the bed. She told him to come closer.

"Is this your wife?" she asked compassionately.

Jessie looked down at the lifeless body, covered in bandages and with an IV needle stuck in her hand. The only visual body part was one eye, which was tightly shut. Jessie looked at the body and back at the nurse. He doubted it was Solo. He just stood silently. The nurse tried to maintain her composure but was losing patience with Jessie because she had other work to do before her shift ended and she didn't want the head nurse on her case. So, she repeated her question.

"Take your time sir. I'm sorry, but you never told me your name."

"It's Jessie Freeman." *(He realized he had given Solo's real last name)*

Suddenly, someone screamed in a blood-curdling voice, "NURSE, SOMEONE HELP ME! PLEASE GOD, LORD JESUS HELP ME!" The nurse looked in the direction of the screaming as all the other nurses continued to tend to other patients.

"Please excuse me, Mr. Freeman, I will be back in one moment." The nurse left to assist the screaming patient.

Jessie shook his head while he continued to look at the motionless body. *What is that smell?* It was making him sick. He continued to look at the body but couldn't recognize who it was. Even the hands were wrapped.

"How in the hell do they expect me to tell who this is?" he mumbled in frustration. His thoughts raced. *I need to get the hell out of here. This is ridiculous. Maybe it was Solo, maybe it wasn't. What difference does it make because this body here is at the point of no return.* He needed a drink and a smoke. He patted his jacket pocket for his smokes and felt the crumbled letter. He turned and looked around to see if anyone was watching him. The nurse who brought him was busy changing a patient's hanging bag, just like one for this body. He reached into his pocket and pulled out the crumpled letter. He figured he should leave the letter in case this *was* Solo. At least they would know who she was and find her family. But what if it wasn't Solo, then what? Well, it wasn't his problem. What if she was somewhere else here in the hospital? But they said there was only one burn victim brought in that day. "I need a drink and smoke," he repeated to himself. Plus, his head was pounding, and the smell was making him sick to his stomach. He looked around again, no one was looking at him. Jessie took the letter, being careful not to disturb the body, and stuck it between the mattresses. He looked down once more and spoke softly.

"Solo, if this is you, I'm sorry but I got to go. I want you to know I did care for you. You never did tell me if there was a baby, but if it was, it's gone now. I'm sorry for that, but it's for the best. I hope you get better. As you know, I am not a praying man, but I hope the man upstairs makes you better."

Tears gathered in Jessie's eyes. He lowered his head. "Where are you, Solo? What did you do? You crazy girl! What did you do?" He wiped his eyes, put his hat on his head, stuck his hands in his pockets, lowered his head, and quickly walked out.

* * *

Deep in Solo's subconscious, she drifted, searching for something, someone, a place. What she was searching or seeking, she could not fully comprehend. She felt a sense of peace consume her soul. Her nostrils caught a strong scent of sweet flowers, even though she saw no flowers. How sweet they smelled as she hummed and slowly drifted, neither walking nor floating, just peacefully drifting towards that sweet smell. Suddenly, far in the distance, she thought she saw a shadowy familiar figure. As she drifted closer to the figure, it moved farther away. Maybe the figure was frightened. She tried to call out to the figure, but while she mouthed the words, no sound bellowed from her mouth. Her arms and hands reached out, but the figure slowly drifted away like a cloud in the sky. Solo yelled out. *Who are you? Please don't be scared, I just want to talk to you.* Even then, no sound came from her mouth, Solo sensed the shadowy figure understood her. Suddenly, the sweet scent of the flowers was replaced with something that now smelled like burning flesh. Solo wrinkled her nose in disgust as the untouchable shadowy figure disappeared into a sea of smoke. The cloudy smoke encased the shadowy figure.

Solo tried desperately, but to her dismay, she could no longer see the figure. Once again, she was all alone in a strange place. She was overcome with fear. Her eyes teared and burned from the smoke. *Come back, please come back! Please don't leave me! I am lost and all alone.* She pleaded to the shadowy figure, but once again, no sound reached her ears. Without any warning, an onslaught of the black, thickening, foul smoke swirled around Solo, engulfing her, making loud hissing sounds like an angry mob of invisible people. All around Solo, red and orange flashes of flames teased her as if they were playing a mean game of touch-me-not. Solo could not see through the thick black smoke. No longer could she see the shadowy figure. Fear paralyzed her body. The fire was getting closer. She tried with all her might to run from the fast-approaching angry flames, but they attacked her skin as if settling an overdue debt. Starting at her feet, Solo watched as the red flames scorched them until they were no longer there. The pain was so intense and cruel. Her skin cracked and melted into a slow puddle. The foul smell of her burning flesh invaded her nostrils. Solo, screamed and screamed, begging for mercy, as the fire slowly crept up her body. They tried to comfort her. They shook their heads because they knew there was no way to completely stop this poor girl from suffering. They increased her pain medicine, to make her as comfortable as possible. For Solo, this scene would play out for many years to come.

The attending nurse understood the thrashing about was due to the patient being in a deep sleep, not pain. The nurse checked Solo's vitals and proceeded to tuck in the bed sheets. That's when she noticed a piece of paper stuck under the bedding. The nurse, being curious, reached down and pulled the paper from the bedding. It was a soiled envelope. *How strange*, she thought. Just as she was about to inspect the contents, a patient yelled out. With duty calling, the nurse stuffed the dirty envelope in her front uniform pocket and went off to provide much needed care. She made a mental note to deal with the envelope later.

Surely the day will come when you have to pay
for the wrong that was done;
No one gets a pass; good fortunes may come and life is rich
and even immense with unbelieve pleasure and fun;
Be assured that when a debt is owed, no human can
determine the due date or payment for the unpaid sum;
Death does not complete a life, for parts of it remain either
in others or in unfinished acts of that what's to come;
If you lived as the person your God put you on this earth to
be, then you have no need to fret or worry because as surely
as night comes so will the sun;
Therefore, take grace in your actions, walk carefully in your
words, let not your work or deeds be the source of someone's
misfortune that cannot be undone.

TWENTY
Tulip

Life had been a struggle for Tulip, but the years had been kind and graced her physical appearance. She had become what one would call a good-looking woman. While she was thick around the hips and thighs, her waist was small, her stomach was flat, and her rump dipped low in the back and protruded out in a nice round form with plenty of jiggle when she walked. Tulip was now thirty-six years old. One would never guess she had birthed seven children. After marrying Carson and moving to Maryland, she found God and became a devoted Catholic. She didn't drink *(except for communion wine or a little spiked homemade eggnog at Christmas)*, smoke, or curse. Overall, life had been fair. Gone were the silly girl's delusions of love and romance. A life of a woman without a man and no education was a hard life. After the heartbreak of losing her beloved Malcolm, she forgot about her children and herself while becoming reckless with drinking, smoking, and running around with men. She was lucky to have met Carson. Even though he drank and smoked a little too much for her liking, he was a good man and provided for his family. Tulip told Carson all about Malcolm and their children. He accepted it all and promised he would never leave her, and her children would be welcomed in their home. Therefore, as Tulip moved through life with Carlson and her new children, she was neither happy nor sad. Deep in her heart, she longed for her other children. After learning about the death of Baby, Tulip knew she would never be content until she had Solo and Little Henry home with her, where they belonged.

The small sharecropping town located in Saint Mary's County is where Tulip, her husband, her husband's mama *(who was eighty years old, blind as a bat, toothless, had a great sense of smell, and mean as the day is long), ten-year-old* Paul, nine-year-old Veronica, and seven-year-old twins, Joseph and Magdalene.

The farmhouse had a kitchen and a large room where there was a table, two chairs, and two long benches on either side. On one side of the room, there was a bed for Tulip, Carson, and the twins. The other side was for Mama Barnes and the other two children. Together they worked the twenty-acre corn and hog farm for their keep and food. The farmhouse had no electricity, only a small wood-burning stove, and Kerosene lamps throughout for lighting, which was subject to blowing out due to the strong wind creeping through the many cracks and openings. There was an outhouse, a well for water, a chicken coup for chickens and fresh eggs, a horse and buggy, and a few piglets. There was a small garden where they grew their own vegetables. Life was hard but good, and they were happy even though Tulip planned for the day when all her family would be together. But the best of plans can go astray.

Southern Maryland's weather was fickle. Summers were long and scorching hot, with temperatures reaching the 100s, while winters brought freezing rain, heavy storms, and brutally cold temperatures.

So, it was no surprise in the winter of 1946, when southern Maryland experienced one of its worst snowstorms since the 1922 Knickerbocker Storm. It was recorded that the blizzard took lives and caused major destruction throughout the region. While this snowstorm was in no comparison, it was still just as deadly. Lives were lost along with valuable livestock, pets, and other animals. It was as devastating to the small island. For more than twenty days, the snow fell along with ice-cold strong winds. The snow forced trains off tracks with constant snowfalls and drift. Telephone poles were blown down with black wires cascading on white snow like snakes, and electric power lines sagged dangerously near the snow-covered ground, some unseen to the naked eye, which presented deadly consequences. The visibility for traveling was poor to none. All waterways (rives, ponds lakes, beaches) were frozen to sheets of ice. Even wells were frozen. Dirt roads were nonexistent and blocked by snow drifts. Folks hankered down, too afraid to venture out in fear of being lost, frozen to death, or buried alive in the snow. The wind made hollowing sounds like a female cat in heat.

The mounds of snow covered Carson and Tulip's small farmhouse like a freshly-washed sheet. Everyone was told to hunker down until the storm blew over. There was no work to be done and no place to go. Carson and Paul had struggled to make it home from town where they'd gathered up some last-minute supplies and a letter the shopkeeper was holding addressed to Tulip. As Carson tucked the envelope into his coat pocket, he hoped it was the news Tulip was waiting for.

Carson and Paul could barely see through the heavy snow as it fell to the ground. Large snowflakes and the icy wind blew around them. Their poor horse, Charley, led the way home. Veronica watched out the window, looking for Papa and her brother. She strained her eyes looking through the snow, using her elbow to wipe the condensation from the glass window.

She stood on her tip toes and finally yelled, "I see Charley! That's my Charley!" She jumped, clapped, and squealed with joy.

Mean old Mama Barnes stomped her right foot down hard and yelled out to Veronica. "STOP THAT DAMN RUCKUS! DAMN CHILDREN NEVER QUIET!"

Tulip, sensing the start of a crying session from Veronica, who was very sensitive to being yelled at, went over and gently stroked her hair.

"You are a good helper." Tulip peered out the window. "That is

Papa and ya brother Paul!"

Mama Barnes let out a grunt. "Still no sense in making all that ruckus."

Tulip grabbed her shawl and pulled the door open. The wind was so strong, she had to tug hard. She was met with wet, hard snow attacking her face. Carson and Paul, whose arms were full of goods, literally tumbled across the threshold as though they had been pushed by the wind. They were covered in snow. Tulip and Veronica rushed to help with the goods. Carson told Paul to get the horse settled in the barn and to bring in some more wood just in case it was needed for the stove. Tulip was relieved, Carson and her son Paul were home safe. She didn't let anyone know, but she had been worried sick. She went about putting up the goods which included a sack of flour, sugar, rice, beans, and peppermint candy sticks for children.

"Where's my stuff?" Mama Barnes yelled in the direction of her son Carson.

"I got it right here Mama. Just let me take off these boots. I don't want a mess on Tulip's clean floor."

Mama Barnes let out a favored grunt. "Hmph!"

After Carson removed his boots, he walked over and warmed his hands by the fire. He looked over at his family with a sense of comfort, he was glad to be home. Carson reached in his pocket and pulled out his mama's stuff and the envelope for Tulip.

"Okay, Papa's home and he got something for everybody," he announced playfully. Tulip stopped what she was doing and smiled at her husband. She liked to see him happy and in a good mood.

"Okay, here my dear, lovely mama, is your stuff," Carson said loudly as he bent down and placed the items in her hand.

"Go away from here," Mama Barnes said playfully to her favorite son.

"Now who is next?" Carson turned to the twins, while Veronica watched and waited her turn.

"Me, Papa!" the twins squealed in unison as they jumped up and down clapping their hands in anticipation of the unexpected gift. How they adored their papa.

Of course, their behavior was rewarded with a grunt from Mama Barnes. "You both are just too loud," she mumbled to herself.

Carson leaned over to each of the twins.

"Here's your favorite candy treat." The twins could hardly contain their joy as they took the candy from his hands.

Tulip said, "Now where are your manners? Did you forget something?"

Remembering their manners, the twins responded quickly, "Thank you, Papa."

Tulip chimed in again, "Now, you know the rules, no sweets until after supper."

They didn't respond but stared at their favorite candy bar. "You hear?" asked Tulip firmly.

As if they were shaken back to reality, the twins jumped and replied together, "Yes, Mama." They walked off holding their candy tight.

Veronica looked and was happy for the twins. She hoped her papa had remembered something for her. Papa was so full of surprises. He looked at Veronica, whom he affectionately called Ronnie, and said, "This is for you." He handed her a brown paper-wrapped package.

Veronica smiled and quickly held her gift to her heart. Next, she carefully removed the wrapping, and found a leather-bound diary to write down her dreams and thoughts.

"Papa," she said, "you remembered. Thank you, Papa!" And she walked off with tears forming in her eyes.

"Now for you," Carson said as he walked towards his loving wife whose back was turned to him. Tulip didn't respond. Carson called out, "To you, my beloved, I bring good tidings."

As Tulip slowly turned to face him, she saw Carson bent over, head down, one hand behind his back and the other outstretched towards her holding an envelope. Tulip looked at her husband. He could be a silly jester at times. Tulip offered a smile as her eyes traveled to the contents of the outstretched hand. She wiped her hands on her apron, not wanting to soil the paper. Her eyes filled with tears. Carson stood up straight and faced her. A gust of wind suddenly blew Paul through the door with an armload of wood.

Later, everyone, except Mama Barnes, huddled closely under homemade quilts near the wood-burning stove. Mama Barnes rocked in her rocking chair, a gift from Ernest, the eldest of her seven sons, with a knitted shawl across legs she no longer had use for. Even though she could no longer see, she could knit and smell food cooking a mile away.

Now with supper finished, everyone gathered around to hear Tulip read the letter she received from her friends up North. Her family knew she had another family before them. But Mama Barnes didn't like it one bit. She didn't understand why a mother would run behind a good-for-nothing man and leave her youngins. It didn't sit well with her one bit.

The envelope was the last piece of mail Carson retrieved from the town's grocery/postal store before the storm hit. He was so excited for his wife and prayed for God's divine grace that it was good news. The devil had camped out at their doorstep too many days.

When Carson handed his wife the letter, she could only stare at the envelope, like her eyes were seeing, but her brain was not comprehending.

"Go on now," Carson urged his wife. She waited, holding the faded envelope that possibly held hope. Tulip didn't recognize the writing, so her heart gave a flutter and her knees buckled. It wasn't from the Chiles. She looked up at her husband. Carson smiled but said no words. Tulip closed her eyes. They felt heavy. She said a little prayer for this to be good news from Little Henry or maybe even Solo.

After the Chiles got word to her about Baby's death, Tulip was in shock. She grieved hard. She blamed herself. Maybe Baby would be alive if she had not left or had come back to get her, as she had promised. She was overcome with grief. To make matters worse, Little Henry had joined the Army and Solo had run off. But at least Little Henry was in communication with the Chiles and even sent money home to them. He considered them his Maw and Paw, which deeply hurt Tulip, and rightfully so. Nevertheless, she harbored no ill feelings toward her friends. Kin was kin. She was confident they would be back together one day. However, she had not reached out.

Here lately, Tulip dreamed of outstretched hands extending to her. Someone calling out to her, pleading with her, needing her help. But, as soon as Tulip would get close to the figure, it would disappear in a cloud of smoke. She could not reach it in time. But God as her witness, Tulip knew deep down in her heart it was Solo calling out to her. She needed her. So, Tulip would wake from the dream and pray to God and her Mama to watch over Solo until she could bring her home safely. Let no harm come to her.

Now here was the letter. This precious letter Tulip held in her hands had to be the answer to her prayers. Her family all gathered around her, even mean old Mama Barnes, quietly waiting to hear the words. With Maggie at her feet, Tulip tore open the fragile envelope, took out the letter, inhaled deeply, and wiped away tears. She began to read…

Misses Tulip,

I hope you and your family are well. I won't be long in this letter for what I have to say. With years gone by, I don't know if you remember me, but my name is Jessie

Freeman and I was a good friend of your late husband, Malcolm. You may recall me visiting your home on several occasions. In fact, in our younger years, we even kicked up some dust together. I recall you were a hell of a dancer.

What I have to say, must be said and I take no pride in saying it. I know the whereabouts of your daughter Solo. You see, me and her ran off together to New York City. At the time, I didn't know of the fire that claimed your youngin's life. Solo told me I was in danger for my carrying-on with her being that she was underage and me being much older. I couldn't afford no trouble with the law. Please know that I did not mean anyone any concern or harm. I am ashamed, so I will spare you the details of my relationship with your daughter.

I ran into a fellow from back home and he told me about the death of Malcolm. I was so sorry to hear that news. He was a decent man and good friend, and you were fine folks. However, the fellow went on to tell me about the fire and the death of one of Malcolm's children and how Solo had run off and how Mr. and Mrs. Chiles and town folks had been looking for her. Thought maybe she too was dead or had something to do with the fire. It was very disturbing to hear this news of the worry that I had caused everyone. I didn't know what to do. But as time went on, it worried me so and not knowing your whereabouts, I sent this here letter to Mr. and Mrs. Chiles and asked if they could somehow help this letter find its way to you.

Please know that she is with God in heaven, and you have my condolences. I must say, after hearing this painful news, it was only fitting that I pay my respect to the Chiles, who also were pained by this tragedy. If I had known about the fire, I would have done things different. However, no use now and that is now water under the bridge.

Out of respect to my friend Malcolm and you, who always treated me kindly, I wanted you to know that Solo was safe and that she didn't know about the fire, let alone that her sister had died so tragically. I still don't have the heart to tell her, I figure I would leave that up to the family. But, to make a long story short, Solo was with me the night of the unfortunate fire. At the time, I didn't know about the fire. Solo told me Mr. Chiles and some other men folks were after me. I was scared they were out to cause me harm because I was messing around with her, being underage and all. I was going to leave by myself, but she begged to come with me. I know I should be ashamed of myself because I was old enough to be her Paw and she was just a child. Against my better judgement, we ran off together to New York City.

Please know I did not mistreat her or cause her any harm. No harm has come to Solo, and she is as beautiful as the day is long. But I see now I was wrong, and I want to make things right. So here is the address where you can write to Solo or come and get her. It is time for her to go home and be with her family. Not saying this in a bad way, it's just time.

Write to:
c/o Jessie Freeman
The Sylvania Apartment
59 W124 Street
Unit 401
New York City

I hope you can find it in your heart to forgive me.

Your friend, Jessie

The room was still. The winds of the winter snowstorm blew its musical sounds as it swirled around the little house. Somewhere in the distance, there was a cry of a hungry wolf. The only sound in the house was the creaking of Mama Barnes's rocking chair. Carson, with eyes closed, quietly blew smoke from his pipe. The children, too young to comprehend the significance of the letter, stared at their mama who seemed to be frozen in time. There was no movement from Tulip as she quietly re-read the letter again to herself. She turned it over in anticipation of more on the other side. Because she was holding her breath, she felt lightheaded. Finally, her chest rose to the heavens and ascended downwards as she slowly let out a long breath.

Forgetting Maggie was at her feet, Tulip leapt up and clapped her hands, almost kicking her daughter. The poor child jumped in fright while her mama was dancing around and loudly giving praises.

"Thank you, Lord. Thank you, God. You are so merciful. I give you all my honor and praise!"

Carson rushed to comfort the baby and check for any injuries. The children huddled together, with their mouths agape and eyes open wide as they watched their mama shouting and praising the Lord.

Mama Barnes was disgusted with Tulip's display of emotion. "Girl done gone plum crazy," she huffed. "Knew she wasn't right in the head," she continued mumbling to herself as she shook her apron. "All this fuss over some wench of a daughter. Best she leaves well enough alone."

"Babies, your mama done found your sister!" Tulip said as she tried to catch her breath, placing one hand over her heart and the other raised to the heavens to give thanks and praise.

"Mama, our sister coming home?" asked Paul.

"Soon baby, real soon. Y'all will get to meet your sister real soon. God has answered my prayers," Tulip said with a big smile on her face and both hands on her heart.

"Soon baby, real soon," Tulip repeated with closed teary eyes.

Carson stared off into the distance. He felt conflicted. Sure, he was happy for his wife, why wouldn't he be? But the reality was these were hard times, and they were barely getting by. Now there would be another mouth to feed. He was hoping to move his family to Washington, D.C. where talk had it that there was work to be had on the railroads for Colored men. He was not an educated man, but coming from a very large country family, hard work was in his nature. He just hoped his beloved would not spend their little bit of savings to go looking for this youngin who was fitting to be a grown woman by now.

Run off like she did. Sounds like trouble, yes trouble she is as sure as the wind blew. Mama is plum right as always, Carson thought to himself. *Best we leave well enough alone.* But he knew in his heart she wouldn't, and he had to stand by her no matter the consequences, and given that letter, there would probably be many.

Everyone had fallen asleep in their designated places. A homemade curtain was pulled in on one side of the large room to give she and Carson some privacy, while the children *(except for the twins who slept with her and Carson)* and Mama Barnes sleep in one large bed on the other side of the room. Like most nights, after everyone was sleep, Tulip lay in bed with her eyes wide open. She listened to the musical sound of the wind that thankfully drowned out the loud disturbing noises both Mama Barnes and Carson made as they slept. Some nights she didn't know who was worse between Mama Barnes snoring and letting out foul-smelling farts or Carson breathing loudly with his mouth wide open and rumbling stomach. Most nights, she tried her best to block it all out, tossed and turned, and prayed for better days until sleep came, but tonight was different.

Slowly, Tulip moved from the bed. She took the blanket and made a barrier around the twins so their Papa wouldn't roll over on them. He slept hard. She gave the babies a gentle kiss on their cheeks and stroked their thick manes of coarse, black hair. She lovingly smiled down at her babies as she eased from the bed. Cautiously, she pulled back the homemade curtain just enough for her to pass through. The room was dark except for the fire glowing from the wood-burning stove, which kept them from freezing to death.

Tulip looked over at Mama Barnes and the children who were all tangled together because even though Mama Barnes was child-sized herself, she took up most of the bed. Mama Barnes let go of a fart that quickly permeated the room. Tulip shook her head in disgust, and silently prayed, *Lord, give me strength*. She carefully walked over to check the logs in the wood stove and decided to add one more. She poked the fire to make sure the new log caught. Her eyes caught something scurrying across the floor, probably a field mouse, more scared of her than she of it. She moved Mama Barnes's old rocking chair closer to the warmly lit stove. Not only did she stay warm, but she also needed the light from the stove to reread the letter. Tulip needed to be focused.

She blocked out the sounds of her sleeping family and concentrated on the tune of the wind playing a sweet melody as it swirled around her home. She took a deep breath, inhaled, and released the air slowly. Tulip read her precious letter again.

After reading the last word, Tulip's eyes burned and watered from straining in the dimly-lit room. She eased her head back, patted her itching nape, closed her eyes, smiled, and let her mind drift to another time and place. Misses Chiles' letter already told her Solo may indeed be with Jessie. She thought often why Jessie would take up with such a young girl, let alone Malcolm's daughter.

Tulip recalled her first introduction to Jessie the night she and Malcolm were on their way to the dance in the barn. She had leaned forward in the wagon to get a better glimpse of the loud, smiling man. Right at that moment, Jessie also leaned forward to pass a bottle of moonshine from his wagon to Malcolm, which he accepted happily. She and Malcolm had been on their way to a dance. Her very first. The excitement of the memory made Tulip's heart flutter. Jessie's wagon had been full of other partygoers, mostly Colored girls around her age. She had felt uncomfortable and out of place when the girls eyed her up and down and whispered about her. Nevertheless, good ole Jessie was smiling, loud, full of life, and not bad on the eyes. He was a good-looking young Colored man and at the party, all the girls had eyes for him.

In fact, that night at the barn dance, Jessie was only the second boy she ever danced with after Malcolm. Even though Malcolm could cut a rug, Jessie could also shake a leg. Tulip covered her mouth so she wouldn't giggle out loud and wake the family. Mama Barnes already thought she was plum out of her mind—*bonfire crazy*, she would often say out loud to no one in particular. Tulip let her thoughts drift back to that night after the dance. She and Malcolm made passionate love in the loft of the Chiles' barn. It was the first time he hit her spot. The thought made her blush and tightened her thighs. She cried out internally, *Malcolm, my dear Malcolm.* Over the years, Jessie and Malcolm's friendship grew and they became like family. Even with the uncomfortable knowledge that Jessie was a little more than sweet on her. So, this was troubling and gave her heart a pause, to think Jessie was with her baby girl, in a man and woman way. Her mind couldn't comprehend Jessie with Solo. He was there when she came into this world. *Why, he was kin, her uncle in sort of a way.* Tulip's heart began to beat faster. She shook her head from side to side. *Best Malcolm has gone to be with his maker because hearing this would have surely killed him, or he would have killed somebody.* While it was troubling news, in her heart she still appreciated Jessie coming to his senses and writing to her. She recalled her mama saying, "You never know what plans God has, but you better take heed of the devil's."

Tulip got up from her chair and drew her shawl tightly around her. She made a mental note to drop a log on the stove and quietly walked over to her knitting bag and pulled out a sheet of paper and a pencil. She picked up a log and tossed it into the stove, the flames jumped angrily as if they did not want to be disturbed. She could hear her babies, her husband, and Mama Barnes breathing peacefully. She was glad everyone was sleeping hard because it gave her time to herself, and that is what she needed most right now.

She sat down in her chair, took a deep breath, and wrote the letter that had found its way to Jessie's procession.

Who said God will make a way and
your life will be right;
Said just let God do his work and you will see the light;
No need to worry, or try to seek things out with your might;
You got to surrender and have faith and get down on your
knees at night;
Because only God knows what path he wants you to take, so
no need to fight;
All that worrying, sadness, and crying, when all you need
was to have faith in the almighty.
For he is your savior, he is your provided, he will not lead
you blindly, he is your sight;
Who said God will make a way and you be right, now that
God got your attention, as he who always said, follow him
in life and you are goanna be alright.

TWENTY-ONE
Nightmare Alley

Hearing a loud commotion outside of his office, Doctor Frank opened his office door and asked rather loudly to several nurses, including a young Colored volunteer named Cincy, "What in the hell is going on here? Why are you outside of my office cackling like a brunch of hens? Don't you have patients needing your attention or bed pans to empty?"

The nurses, who were huddled together, kept their eyes on the floor, not making eye contact with Doctor Frank or answering his questions. Growing frustrated with their silence, Doctor Frank slowly began to speak.

"Okay, in one second somebody better start talking or get back to work or lose a day's pay." His deep voice echoed throughout hallway. The nurses all jumped, but no one answered.

Finally, the young volunteer spoke up and blurted out rather rapidly, "There is a problem with the burned Jane Doe patient."

Doctor Frank looked puzzled.

"So, fix it. Why all that fuss? Did she finally wake up from her coma on her own?" He inquired.

"No…" Cincy replied softly.

"Well, is she dead?" Doctor Frank asked impatiently with clear worry lines saturating his forehead. He didn't want another death on his hands.

"No Doctor, she is far from dead." Cincy lowered her head and peeked up at Doctor Frank, afraid to hold his pensive stare.

Doctor Frank took a deep breath before he spoke. He always thought the nurses were too sensitive, and he had no time for tears.

"Then please tell me what in the hell is needing my immediate attention? I don't have time for this damn silly back and forth. My time is valuable. Come quick with it or get back to work."

The older nurse, sensing Cincy's discomfort, stepped forward and spoke sternly.

"Doctor Frank, we need you to come with us to examine Jane Doe. It is a grave situation needing your expertise."

"Who is the Doctor on duty? In the last six months, I have not been involved in that case. I only asked a few times for an update. Let the doctor on duty handle whatever this situation is." Doctor Frank proceeded to wave the nurses away from his office, signaling he was done with the unnecessary intrusion.

The older nurse stepped in front of Doctor Frank and looked him straight in the eyes and said, "This is a matter needing your expertise." She turned and walked away with the other nurses, including Cincy scurrying behind her. Doctor Frank paused at his door, holding the handle as he debated with himself. After a few seconds, he said, "What the hell?!"

He caught up with the nurses, looked at each one, and said as he pointed his index finger toward them, "This better not be a brunch of nonsense. If so, each of you can pack your bags and get the hell out of my hospital TODAY!" He stormed off to the burn unit taking rapid quick long strides. The nurses had to do a little trot to keep up with him.

Doctor Frank hated going to the burn unit. All the moaning and crying, and the smell of burned flesh along with the bloody and soiled bandages made him feel dirty. It was not that he lacked compassion, he was the one credited for saving their miserable lives. While he was briefed on patient progress, he didn't deal with their daily or immediate care. He left that to his subordinates. However, he did make an exception with the Jane Doe case. Since he performed surgery on her, he often thought of her and on occasion would inquire about her condition. He wanted to see her eyes and the level of scarring she'd ultimately endure. It's a possibility, depending on how she heals, cosmetic surgery could be an option, but the state doesn't pay to make someone look better, only to keep them alive. However, some patients, because of the pain and deformities from the burns, preferred death. Some would take their own lives or died from various complications.

As he hurriedly walked through the ward, some of the patients called out to him and he gave them a wave and smile. His only thought was to hurry and get out of there. Some of the nurses looked up from caring for patients and smiled at him. Fortunately, it was not visiting hours and he didn't have to deal with any family members who always had tons of questions. He finally made it to Jane Doe's bed. He looked down at her. She still had bandages on most of her body. Blood and pus oozed through the bandages, giving off a foul smell.

"When was the last time these bandages were changed?"

One of the nurses pulled the chart hanging on Solo's bed and began to read the notations.

"There is no record of that doctor," a nurse replied.

Doctor Frank turned and looked and shook his head from side to side.

"Well, I want them changed today," he said firmly, with his discontent on full display. *Such incompetency,* he thought. "Alright I'm here, what is the issue that so desperately needed my attention?"

The nurse pulled the curtain around for privacy and pulled back the covers fully exposing Solo. Doctor Frank looked down and immediately saw the issue.

"What the hell? It can't be." He adjusted the stethoscope dangling around his neck and then placed the lower end of the telescope on

Solo's abdomen, locating her uterus. He could not believe his ears. He pressed down on her abdomen and could hear the heartbeat of a fetus. Did he hear a heartbeat? He checked the patient's pulse, it was rapid, indicating that she was in serious distress. Doctor Frank looked at the nurse and told her to arrange for a pelvic exam immediately.

Doctor Frank turned to the nurses, "How come this is just being discovered? If this confirms my suspicion, she either has a large tumor or is with child." The nurses looked at each other but did not speak.

"By tomorrow, I want a full report of her visiting doctors and nurses, anyone who has been in contact with her. Has she had any outside visitors? Please understand this is a very delicate situation and must be kept quiet. Heads could roll if this is leaked. Do not write anything on her record. This is strictly confidential. Let me know when she is ready for the pelvic exam." Doctor Frank turned, with his head down, and slowly walked out of the ward.

A few hours passed before Cincy knocked on Doctor Frank's office door.

"Please come in," he instructed.

"They are ready for you, Doctor," said Cincy shyly. She didn't have much contact with the doctor, so she was a little intimidated.

Without looking up from his work, he acknowledged her. "I'll be there shortly."

The hospital's basement was used to house the morgue. It also served as a place for doctors to perform sensitive and critical medical procedures, such as abortions, amputations, sterilizations, and even cruel, inhuman experiments such as brain shock therapy. The basement was dark and cold with cement floors and low-hanging fluorescent lights encased with spider webs. The harsh lights constantly flickered on and off. It was a scary place. The basement location was restricted to only authorized staff. The corridors were long and formed a maze. Each corridor had designated rooms used to perform these sensitive procedures on patients. Consent was either forced or simply not obtained. The room doors were windowless and made of heavy metal to block out sounds such as screaming and pleas from unwilling patients.

As Doctor Frank entered the room, Head Nurse Mary Pierce (Nurse Mary) was assisting the doctor and one other nurse monitoring the IV. They were waiting for him to perform the exam. Nurse Mary placed an unconscious Solo's hands in leather restraints and her legs open wide with each ankle restrained as well. Doctor Frank took a good long look at the naked patient with her privates fully exposed to him. He shook his head and thought, *what a waste*. Even in this state, she was still a beauty. He placed one hand on her pelvis and pressed down gently as he inserted two fingers inside her vagina and began to explore. As he poked and pressed, his face became intense, and his brow formed lines on his forehead. Sweat formed on his face, perhaps from the task at hand, perhaps from the lights emitting heat.

No one spoke as Doctor Frank conducted his exam. Nurse Mary watched as he appeared to look concerned. Suddenly Doctor Frank motioned for her to push down on Solo's abdomen as well.

"Push hard!" he shouted. "Do you feel what I feel?"

Nurse Mary nodded in agreement.

"Well, I be damned! There are two of them!"

The nurse monitoring Solo's vitals let out a gasp. Doctor Frank gave her a stern look, displeased with her show of emotion.

Nurse Mary continued to press down on Solo's abdomen and announced, "Is she in early labor?"

Doctor Frank was flabbergasted. His mind was racing. *How could this be possible? She must have been with child when she suffered the burns. How has this gone undetected? Was blood work done? How could I have missed this? Why didn't she miscarry during the surgery? Well, abortion is not an option.*

Nurse Mary and the other nurse stole a sly glance between them as they quietly waited for Doctor Frank to speak. Finally, he turned to both nurses and said, "This is a very unfortunate situation, and I must ask for your complete discretion. I want no mention of this to anyone, am I clear? Do you understand?"

The nurses nodded in agreement.

"Okay, please take the patient back to her room. One other thing, let me know if there have been any inquiries about a burned Jane Doe. Let me know what you find out. This is a delicate situation. I trust I can count on your cooperation."

The nurses looked at Doctor Frank and nodded their heads in unison, acknowledging agreement. Taking a long look at his patient, Doctor Frank said, "Okay, let's get her back to her room."

Doctor Frank spoke directly to Nurse Mary and sternly said, "We need to prepare for emergency delivery, so until then, I want you to be solely responsible for this patient's care. No one else. This probably means working a double shift. I hope that doesn't pose a problem."

"Whatever you need Doctor, I'm available. I will get her all cleaned up and report to you as soon as I can on whether there have been any inquiries."

Doctor Frank thanked her as well as the other nurse, took one more look at Solo, turned, and left the room.

As she pushed Solo onto the bed cart, no attendant was needed. Nurse Mary thought to herself, *this is the break I have been waiting for. This could prove to be quite profitable for me.* She smiled.

Doctor Frank headed to his office and immediately picked up the telephone and dialed. After a few seconds, he spoke into the receiver.

"Hey, it's me. I got an urgent situation at the hospital that needs your special skills. When can you get here? Yes, nine is fine. See you soon. Come directly to my office. I'll be waiting. This is strictly confidential."

Doctor Frank walked from his desk, opened a wooden cabinet, and pulled out a bottle of aged whiskey and two glasses. He placed both glasses on his desk and carefully poured a double and drank it down quickly. He did not want to waste a drop. He had expensive taste. The drink was just what he needed. The burn was good. He put the glass down and returned to his chair and waited.

A little after 9:00 PM Nurse Gloria Mae White's heels clicked on the linoleum floors. She moved quickly in her patent leather, black shiny four-inch heels, tight straight black skirt with a long open back split, and a red silk blouse with the top two buttons undone to reveal a lacy bra that exposed her small, but plump breast. Her coat was neatly draped over her shoulders. Her makeup was nicely done and of course, she wore red lipstick that she touched up a bit as she walked.

Not knowing what the love of her life wanted, she dressed in anticipation for what she wanted because it had been too long. For about ten years, Nurse White trained under Doctor Montgomery Frank. She was taken by him from the moment their hands accidentally touched during an examination of a patient. She knew he was married, but that did not deter her. She pursued him as hard as she did her nursing profession *(secretly longing to be a doctor one day)*. She was pleasing to the eyes—light-skinned with reddish curly hair, big light brown eyes, and narrow lips. She was tall for a woman, around 5'9 which means she met most men at eye level. She had slim long legs with a flat behind, a girl can't have everything. She was smart and one of the few Colored nurses who fully understood the female anatomy and even served as a mid-wife *(even though women still preferred to have a male doctor to deliver their babies and treat their female problems)*. Mostly she assisted other doctors in treating women's problems. Now married with two boys, her life was reasonably content, but she always answered her dear friend's call, who she affectionately referred to as Montgomery. She saw no reason to be formal, they were colleagues.

In anticipation of his visitor, Doctor Frank's office door was slightly ajar with a soft glow throughout. Nurse White observed that his office was open, mostly for her, but for a little tease as well as out of respect, she gave the door a light flirty tap. Not expecting any other visitors, Doctor Frank caught a whiff of her sweet-smelling perfume, which she wore just for him, or so she said.

"Come in Mae," he said as he poured more whiskey into the empty glass. He had been waiting for her. She entered the room and stood before the love of her life without speaking, she wanted him to take her all in. Doctor Frank slowly let his eyes cascade up from her long slim legs to her small breasts, stopping there. His eyes met hers. For a moment they stared, no words were needed.

"You look stunning, as always. Old man time has been good to you." Doctor Frank smiled as he motioned for her to take a seat. Mae, being the dramatic woman she was, let her coat fall from her shoulders to the floor as she moved toward her friend. She took a seat and opened her legs wide for his full view before she crossed them. Doctor Frank leaned in for a quick peak, he noted she wore no panties. *This woman is so tempting.* He pushed the glass of liquor toward her.

"For me?" Mae asked pretending not to already know the answer.

"Just like you like it, strong and hard."

She winked and raised her glass, "Cheers."

Doctor Frank raised his glass and smiled back at her before his demeanor grew more serious.

"Mae," Doctor Frank folded his hands in front of his face and spoke in a low tone. "I have a very delicate situation. I need your full discretion and trust. I must have your word you will never discuss this situation with anyone, not even Mr. Wonderful."

While Mae was disappointed the call was not for what she anticipated, the reference to her husband got her attention. Doctor Frank rose from his chair and motioned for Mae to follow him. He stopped suddenly and pulled his friend to him and said, "First, a kiss."

She moved in closer and smelled the hot whiskey on his breath. Her hard nipples pressed against his chest. He let his hands move from her back to her nice round bottom. He stroked gently as his nature rose. The kiss was long and passionate. Doctor White caressed her friend's privates. For several minutes they were lost in ecstasy. The task at hand could wait.

Together they walked down the hospital corridor as two professionals, not like two people who were caught up in pure sexual rapture only minutes prior. Doctor Frank talked rapidly about patient Jane Doe, who had been unconscious since he treated her more than six months ago.

When he mentioned full-term pregnancy, Mae stopped in her tracks. "Did you say full-term pregnancy?"

Doctor Frank, suddenly aware she had stopped walking, turned to face her.

"Yes."

"But how is that possible? She was severely burned, you treated her, and she's been unconscious. My God, is it possible someone impregnated her here? That would be a scandal."

"No, no, that is not the case," said Doctor Frank. "As I said, she is full-term, so she was pregnant when she arrived at the hospital. She is ready to deliver. That is why I need you to perform an immediate cesarean section."

"What the hell!" exclaimed Mae, raising her voice. "That would be unethical. I could lose my license. What about her family?"

Doctor Frank sensed Mae's hesitation. He walked towards her and wrapped his arms around her and felt her trembling. With as much sincerity as he could muster, he spoke lovingly.

"Mae, I will take full responsibility if this ever gets out. Nevertheless, I need you to do this for me. You are the only one I trust to deliver these babies."

Mae pushed him back angrily.

"DID YOU SAY BABIES?"

Doctor Frank was growing weary.

"Look one baby, two babies, what's the difference? I need this procedure done tonight. Now can I count on you or not? I must know you are here for me."

Mae was speechless. Her mind was racing. It seemed like hours had gone by, but it had only been minutes. Finally, she spoke.

"What's going to happen to the babies?"

"You don't have to worry. Arrangements have been made for their care until their mother recovers or we can locate family members. However, I must tell you that given the mother's state, their heartbeats were not strong, so action is crucial to their survival. Mae, can I count on you?" Doctor Frank looked somber and stretched his hand towards her.

Mae looked at his hand. "I'm not dressed for surgery."

With that, he smiled. "I am sure we can arrange for something more suitable. But until then," he let his hand gently stroke her rear end. "I want you."

*If only I had stopped and walked away,
would my life path have been different;
Acting on impulse set a course of action that
could not be undone;
Like a raging bull, I dove in fully committed with no regard
for the lasting outcome;
It was not a decision but rather an emotional impulse to
satisfy an immediate desire;
Foolish some would say, at the time,
it seemed to be the only way for that day;
Now I ponder my choice, I question my own logic,
I am my judge and jury;
My sentence for self-gratification is life,
it is the price I paid for monetarily play;
Now I regret, oh now I have logic, now I spend the time to
reflect and try to sustain my inner fury;
So the question remains forever unanswered, would my life
path have been different if on that day I just walked away;
Who's to say?*

TWENTY-TWO
A New Reality

"Solo, it's time to wake up baby! Come on baby, you can do it. WAKE UP"! Hearing the voice calling out to her, Solo struggled to open her eyes. She twisted and turned, thrashed about, but something or some strong force was heavy on her body. Her eyelids felt as though they were glued shut. But the voice kept calling out to her, encouraging her to open her eyes. The voice was shouting in her mind and the sound vibrated throughout her whole body. It was frightening. The voice was relentless.

Solo tried in vain to open her eyes and obey the commands. She thrashed about in her bed, but her hands and feet were restrained. Her body shook as if she was having a seizure. "HELP ME, SOMEBODY, PLEASE HELP ME!" Solo screamed out in her head. No sound came from her mouth, she had no voice. Her lips were dry and seemed to be stuck together. Beads of sweet covered her forehead, snot ran from her nostrils, and tears stained her cheeks. With all her might, Solo continued to thrash about her bed, while making strange sounds from her voiceless mouth. She sounded like a tortured, trapped animal. Some patients were frightened by her sound. The nurses only gazed in her direction but did not try to comfort her. They were told to keep their distance. They just wished they could help her.

Fearing for Solo's condition, one nurse immediately ran to get Nurse Mary who was assigned to Jane Doe. Nurse Mary had strictly instructed that in her absence, if Jane Doe either gained consciousness or there was a drastic change in her condition, immediately get word to Doctor Frank.

After three years, most of Solo's burns and grafts had healed. Some were better than others, but most were not so pretty. Due to inadequate care, many of her burns became infected and required more skin grafts. Sadly, as with most burn victims, she suffered daily from debilitating pain due to the tightening of the skin grafts. But, even with the deformities, Solo's physical beauty still shone through. However, her mental state was questionable. The doctors and nurses had many burn patients who suffered mental breakdowns. For their patients, the doctors and nurses worked quickly to treat their physical conditions so they could return to their normal lives. Those patients who suffered mentally because of their conditions were immediately transferred to the mental ward. That is why the nurses and a few doctors found it very peculiar that Jane Doe was still hospitalized in City #4 burn ward and had not been transferred to a long-term mental health ward. It was clear no more treatment was needed for her physically. Her care was minimum. She was being fed intravenously, vitals monitored, bed sores treated, and she received monthly baths. Her hair was kept short to avoid lice. She was mute but was known to have sudden outbursts with unintelligible sounds. She never had any visitors, and no one ever inquired about her. She was labeled as a charity case. She was still referred to as Jane Doe or the patient in bed #6.

Fearing Solo was having a convulsion, a nurse rushed over to her bed and picked up the IV pole from the floor. Fortunately, the bag did not burst. Solo was moaning and thrashing about with her hands and legs pulling against the restraints. (Nurse Mary felt it was best to restrain Solo to prevent her from harming herself because she was subject to seizures, which was a side effect of both the drugs and her condition.) The nurse took a moment's pause to really get a good look at Solo. She thought Solo's eyes were both strange and beautiful all at once. All the nurses had wondered what Jane Doe looked like before she was disfigured. Her eyes told it all. She must have been unbelievably gorgeous. With her hand on her heart, the nurse spoke in a compassionate voice.

"Sorry dear, but you gave me a fright. I wasn't expecting to see you staring at me." Solo didn't attempt to respond or even move, she just continued to stare at the nurse with her eyes open as wide as they could. Finally, after a few long moments, Solo struggled to form some words, but nothing came out. The restraints hurt her wrist. Solo looked at the nurse, then down at the restraints. The nurse, finally comprehending what Solo was trying to communicate, placed her hand on Solo's shoulder and lifted her restrained hand to check her pulse. As she expected, her pulse was too rapid. This could cause a seizure.

The nurse spoke clearly. "Okay dear, I know you are frightened and have tons of questions, but I need you to try and lay back and relax. Can you do that for me?"

Solo nodded, with her eyes pleading for answers.

"Good girl," said the nurse. Now we must call the doctor and he will be so happy to see you awake and he will answer all your questions. We were all so worried about you. Now let's get this IV back working, got to keep you hydrated and get you all set for Doctor Frank."

Solo was confused, and slowly let her eyes look around the room. What she saw frightened her even more. Most of the patients were wrapped in bandages, some from head to toe. Some patients lay fully exposed, but their skin looked strange like it was deformed. *What the f—k is this place?* She tried to sit up in the bed, but the nurse held her down, but not before the covers slipped and exposed her ugly, scarred body. She screamed. Surely, she must be having a nightmare. After so much screaming and her mind unable to handle the magnitude of the situation, she fainted.

"She is coming to Doctor," said the nurse.

Doctor Frank had managed to come down shortly after Solo had fainted. Since that faithful night three years ago, and not wanting to raise any unwarranted suspicion, he kept his visits to Solo at a minimum. Nurse Mary would update him on her condition. But over the years there had not been much change. It was surprising she had not succumbed. Given her years in an unconscious state, her memory will not be able to recall many events, but maybe it would this time, which would be a problem.

Solo's eyes slowly opened. Her head felt heavy, and she tried to raise her right hand, but it was still in restraints. She groaned but was aware of a face moving close. Her breathing became rapid, but she tried to focus on the face leaning in close to her. Her mind raced. Her eyes darted in quick motions from side to side. She thought to herself, *I know this face. Who is he? How does he know me? What is this place? Looks like a hospital. Yes, a hospital. He must be a doctor. What about her, who got that silly grin on her face? His nurse most likely. But why am I in the hospital? When I try to speak, no words come out, my throat hurts. I need water. Why don't I have no voice? Why was I tied up like a wild animal? My hands move. I can wiggle my toes and lift my legs.* Solo's inner thoughts were suddenly interrupted.

"Don't be frightened," the man said as he leaned over her, shining an annoying light into her eyes. He spoke emphatically, "My name is Doctor Frank and I'm here to help you. You are in the hospital. You were hurt in a fire and have been here for over three years."

Solo could not speak, but her mind was screaming. *No, it wasn't me in the fire. It was, was...why can't I remember? How did I get into a fire? Did I get burned? Yes, now I remember. Those ugly scars on my arms... It was me.*

Doctor Frank continued, "I know you have many questions, but you cannot talk at this moment. You will be able to soon enough. Please relax, I am here to help and when you are ready, I will answer all your questions. If you understand me, just move your head up and down for 'yes' and from side to side for 'no.' Okay, let's give it a try," Doctor Frank continued. "Are you in any pain?"

Not taking her eyes off the Doctor, Solo moved her head from side to side, indicating no to his question.

"Okay, that's good. Very good," said Doctor Frank. "Now can you tell me your name?"

Solo thought hard, *What is my name? I know I must have a name. Everybody has a name. Why can't I remember?*

Solo squeezed her eyes together as hard as she possibly could, causing hot tears to fall. She gripped the bed sheets. Her fingers were stiff and ached. *I NEED MY NAME*, she yelled within. *Think, think, name, name*. But no matter how hard she tried to recall her name…nothing. It was not happening. Finally, Solo lowered her head, embarrassed, and shook her head quickly from side to side. She looked frantically around at the nurse and then back to the Doctor. She was scared.

"Okay, no problem. It will come to you but for the time being, we will call you Jane Doe," said Doctor Frank. "Is that okay with you?"

Solo nodded her head.

Doctor Frank looked at her and analyzed her stare. It was unnerving like she had a deep secret. It was something very sexy about her stare. *Her eyes are beautiful.*

He continued, "I am going to listen to your heart. Please try to remain very still." Solo closed her eyes as the Doctor moved the sheet covering. Then he gently pulled down her hospital gown to expose her chest. Solo's heart was racing. Her mind was bouncing with so many thoughts. She didn't like it and shivered as the cold metal pressed against her chest.

"Nice and strong heartbeat," said the doctor. "Now I need to check your reflexes. If I untie your restraints, you must promise not to move about or try to get out of bed. You have been sleeping for a very long time, so it will take time for your muscles to get strong. So, can I depend on you to remain calm?"

Solo nodded. Doctor Frank instructed the nurse to remove the restraints. After the restraints were removed, Solo could feel the blood coming to life in her hands, making its way through her arms. It felt good. She looked around as the nurse was undoing the last restraints. She watched as the doctor was busy looking at the papers on the clip board. This would be her chance. No more than a second as the nurse pulled free the last restraint, Solo lounged forward, taking both the doctor and the nurse by surprise. But Solo was unstable and dizzy, and together they all fell to the floor. Doctor Frank's clipboard flew up in the air, making a crashing sound as it landed.

Everything seemed to be in slow motion. Nurses, doctors, and orderlies came running to assist Doctor Frank and the nurse. For Solo, this was her opportunity to get free and escape. She ripped the needle out of her arm, blood shot upwards like a fountain. Her eyes darted. Her legs felt lifeless. She crawled on her hands and knees, making animal sounds. Seeing the orderlies running towards her, she crawled under the bed. As they tried to grab and pull at her, Solo fought them fiercely. She caught hold of one hand and sunk her teeth into it. The orderly cried out in pain. Finally, the bed was moved, exposing her. She kicked and growled at anyone who came near her. Doctor Frank managed to reach a syringe and with precision befitting his order, injected Solo. Within a few seconds, her body became limp and her eyelids drooped. Doctor Frank instructed the orderly to lift her back onto the bed.

He turned to the nearest nurse and said, "Move this patient immediately to Ward B isolation."

The nurse, knowing Ward B isolation was for the severely mentally ill patients, lowered her eyes in sorrow and left to make the necessary arrangements. With nothing left to do for Solo, Doctor Frank collected his clipboard and walked slowly from the burn ward ignoring the other patients who called out to him. His heart was heavy. He had hoped she would recover and maybe, she could have been good as new. As he had feared, the patient's mind was gone and there was no fixing that.

> *It's not the time in life that we waste, but rather the space*
> *that we fill in the moments of living;*
> *We try desperately to carry out our selfish expectations while*
> *pushing down into those non-reachable places any thoughts*
> *or desires that may lead to feelings;*
> *It is that very small thing called nature*
> *that may direct your actions or lack thereof that drives*
> *beyond internal glass ceilings;*
> *Control, thinking things through, not being compulsive may*
> *lead to the road of recovery and much needed healing;*
> *For you are your own destiny, regret is only a term and as*
> *defined, does not determine one's forgiveness.*

TWENTY-THREE
New Experiences

Three long years had passed since Tulip sat down and wrote a heartfelt letter to Solo. Tulip had hoped to have the letter on its way within a matter of days, but because of the snowstorm, it was months before it was finally headed to Solo by way of Jessie. Tulip waited and waited for the roads to clear so weekly mail service could resume. She was on pins and needles, constantly asking Carson about the conditions of the roads. Therefore, when Carson finally announced the roads were clear enough to make his way to town for much needed parcels, Tulip seized the opportunity and gave the letter to Carson to take with him. She explained to her husband it would be months before Mr. Jakes, the old White man who worked for the local postal service, would make his mail rounds to Colored folks. The fact being, the White families would get their mail first, which was understandable because they were White and that was just how it was.

Tulip needed answers, she didn't want to wait any longer, she just couldn't. The waiting was making her more fearful, plus it had been way too long. Carson, sensing his wife's suffering, agreed to take her precious letter. He understood her fear, and how she longed for her first-born daughter (which he didn't understand given they had more than enough children), but that's a woman's way for you.

Tulip was overjoyed because the letter was finally on its way. Now all she had to do was wait. Soon her beautiful Solo would be back with her.

After such a long delay due to the storm, word got around that mail service had resumed. Once a week, mainly on Thursday, between 2:00 PM and 3:00 PM, Tulip would rush out to greet Mr. Jake with a silent hope and prayer that this would be the day she would get a letter from Jessie, even possibly Solo, or anybody. Tulip waited and waited for months and then years but she never got the anticipated response. She scolded herself repeatedly when her mind would run rampant and a sudden chill would come over her body...maybe Solo was hurt or even dead, like Baby. Maybe she didn't want to be with her Mama. Maybe Jessie was dead or didn't care to write back. Maybe it was too late. But Tulip would fight the streams of doubt. She couldn't lose both daughters that she and Malcolm (in her mind Malcolm was Solo's father, she had blocked out any memory of the rape, which resulted in Solo) created out of love. So, it was decided she would make her way to New York City and find Solo.

In the early 1940s, times were hard and jobs were scarce in rural areas for folks to make a decent living and keep a roof over their heads and food in their bellies. While crabbing, fishing, and hog raising provided a good source of income, it still was not sufficient to provide for a large growing family. There weren't many skilled jobs, so most men found work for the State clearing roads and building, while the women did day work–cleaning, child-rearing, and cooking for well-to-do White families. This was true for both Whites and Coloreds. There was no separation between poor Whites and Coloreds when it came to making a living. They worked and lived side-by-side. Hell, they even married and had children. However, even though it was never spoken out loud, the Coloreds still felt inferior to the Whites. So, when Carson's oldest brother Melvin decided to move to Washington D.C. to find work and provide a better life for his family, Carson wished him well and promised to join him if things worked out. Carson knew he would miss his big brother, who was the oldest of his six brothers and one sister. Being the last boy to be born, Melvin was more than fifteen years Carson's senior. After Papa died, Melvin became more like a surrogate father than a big brother.

Being tall, with caramel-colored skin and exotic features, Melvin was a good-looking man. Carson looked up to his brother and usually followed his lead. After years and no communication, Melvin showed up one day unexpectantly, driving an old black "deuce in a quarter" *(another name for an Oldsmobile Electric 225 where the first two represented the deuce and the twenty-five stood for the quarter)*. The car had white wall tires and a red interior. It shined like a new baby's behind. Melvin stepped out of his car, keys in hand, grinning, looking dapper, and busting with excitement. He leaned back on the car allowing all eyes to take in the scene. S—t, his nappy hair was even slicked back and lay flat from the magic of lye. Carson eyed his big brother from head to toe and let out a slow whistle.

"Man," Carson said with a big grin, "That is a beauty."

Melvin smiled. "Who me?"

"Hell no! That ride," Carson replied laughing. Carson was overjoyed to see his older brother, but at the same time, felt a little inferior with his dirty overalls and uncombed, bushy hair. He yelled loudly to his mama, "Mama! Your prodigal son has returned!" The two brothers laughed, embraced, and slapped each other on the backs lovingly. While Melvin was happy to see his little brother, he also needed to see Mama, who upon hearing her first-born's voice, clapped her hands in glee. He tossed his car keys to Carson and headed inside the house.

Hearing all the fuss, Tulip went to the door to see what was going on. Seeing Melvin walking towards the door, she smiled. Tulip opened the door for her handsome brother-in-law, who preceded to pick her up in the air and spin her around *(he secretly always had a crush on Tulip, thought she was a real good looker, shapely and sweet)*.

Tulip squealed with joy and yelled to Melvin, "Now, put me down before you drop me!" They both laughed as he slowly let her down. Holding her close to his groin, his nature rose. Tulip didn't notice.

Hearing Melvin's voice, Mean Old Mama stretched out her arms and called out to him. "Put that fussy girl down and come over to yo Mama."

Melvin did a little jig and walked sideways to his Mama, playfully calling out to her. "Here I come to get you!"

With a big wide toothless smile, Mama said, "Boy stop that nonsense and get over here. I might not can see you, but you're still not too big for a butt whipping."

Melvin quickly ran to his mama and kneeled at her feet. He lay his sleek back greasy head on her lap. Mama smiled and patted his head gently. By this time, all the kids had gathered to watch all the goings on.

After supper, Melvin and Carson decided to drive up to the local night spot, Happy Land, for a quick drink and much needed catching up. Happy Land was the only joint in Southern Maryland for Coloreds only. It was just a little hole in the wall, dark and smoky, located on the edge of town. They served good liquor, cooked food, and sometimes would have a live band or singer. There was a jukebox and folks made room to dance. But mostly, Happy Land was for drinking, cheating, and letting your hair down after a hard day at work.

Melvin and Carson were relieved it wasn't too crowded, so they were able to find a couple of seats in a secluded area to talk. Melvin told his little brother that up in Washington, D.C., he had landed a good-paying job with the Southern Pacific Railroad. While the work was long and hard, if you did your job and reported on time, they were fair, and it was good honest money. Coloreds and Whites worked side by side and as far as he knew, were paid the same wages. There was also a Union to ensure you got paid and worked in safe conditions. Melvin went on to tell Carson he had a house with plenty of room for his family. He and his wife, Lorraine, even had their own bedroom with a door to close out the youngins. They both laughed and raised their drinks.

As they drove back home, Melvin told his brother to come to D.C. The railroad was still hiring, and he already talked to his boss about him. Further, Melvin told Carson he didn't have to worry about where they would live because he had more than enough room for his family, even Mama. Carson was thinking and nodded in response. When they got home, it was late, so Melvin had to get back to D.C. He wrote down his address and gave it to his brother. Carson looked at the piece of paper and promised he would talk it over with Tulip. The brothers embraced and Melvin got in his car and Carson watched the taillights until they were out of sight. He was deep in thought. When he turned towards the house, he was surprised to see Tulip huddled in the doorway. He walked and announced they needed to talk.

Carson jumped at the opportunity to move to Washington, D.C. Within a month, the entire family and their meager belongings were on their way. Not too long afterward, Carson landed a laborer job alongside Melvin at Southern Railroad. The work was minimal, long, dirty, and hard. Carson's job was to keep the cars and tracks clear of trash, keep bums from trying to hitch a ride on empty cars, run away the hookers, and repair and install rail tracks.

Both Tulip and Carson found it very stressful living with Melvin and his family. They shared one bedroom, while Mama slept in her rocking chair, and the children slept on the floor. So, after a few months, Carson moved his family, including Mama, to a larger home in D.C. It was within several blocks of his brother. The old house had no electricity and an old coal stove for heat. There was a well for water, an outhouse, and a yard big enough for a few chickens and a vegetable garden patch. The rent was affordable, but money was tight with their growing family. Tulip worried she would never be able to save the money to go to New York City to find Solo. Lorraine had told Tulip about available work cleaning for White families. The pay wasn't much, but it helped. Lorraine's daughter was old enough to help

Veronica out if she couldn't be home to make dinner for the family. Tulip picked up some day work from some of the White families uptown. Mainly just washing clothes, stripping down and making beds, ironing, sweeping, mopping, and dusting. The homes she cleaned were never really that dirty. White folks just didn't seem to be dirty. The hardest part of her work was waiting for the streetcars, which were always too full or late. Even after she got off the streetcar, there was still a long walk to her house. Her feet and legs constantly ached. She was somewhat thankful for the alone time walking home which gave her a chance to think about her how her life had evolved. It seemed her life after losing her mama was a distant memory—almost forgettable, yet lingering. Long gone was the *field of flowers*. The memory of her life with Malcolm seemed like a sweet dream. However, the love for their children was still very real. Solo, Little Henry, and Baby would always hold a special place in her heart. Now she made room in her heart for Carson and their children. They were family, but the family was incomplete without Solo.

Living in the Big City was a real adjustment for Carson, Tulip, and Mama. In comparison to the country, where birds sang beautiful songs, green grass grew, butterflies flew, and gentle winds blew, the Big City was loud, noisy, and trashy. There were always people moving about at all times of day and night. There were open-air markets where a variety of purchases ranging from fresh fruits and vegetables to clothing were sold. Additionally, daily fresh meat and produce wagons crept along the streets selling their goods. Coming from small towns, Tulip and Carson found their new life very strange and sometimes a little frightening. They made sure the children stayed close to home and did not venture out. Mean Old Mama complained constantly. She did not like the big city one bit and wanted to move back to the country. She complained about the living conditions, even though the farmhouse had only one room. There was no pleasing her. Nag, nag, nag–day in and out. The children liked seeing their parents hugging and kissing. Mean Old Mama found it disgusting and said so. Her constant complaining made life difficult for Carson and Tulip, but they made the best of it.

The city offered plenty of night life for those seeking a little relaxation after a hard work week and most took advantage of it, except for the God-fearing souls. Uptown, it was called, was where you could find a bunch of beer gardens, bums lying about, dance halls, restaurants with live entertainment, gambling, shoe-shiners, hair parlors, barber shops, men-only clubs, and street women. You name it, Uptown would have it. Uptown was an adult playground. Most nights there were fights and sometimes even murders. Paddy wagon sirens would ring with flashing lights racing fast through the streets. After dark, children were forbidden from going Uptown and surely would be escorted home by the local policeman when caught and spanked when they got home. Given that the city was predominately made up of Coloreds, it was the destination of most popular Colored entertainers. Posters would be hung, children handed out flyers, or word of mouth would pass along when well-known Colored entertainment would be performing. Mostly Coloreds folks went to Uptown, but White folks would also seek out Uptown because of its nightlife.

From his brother Melvin, Carson and Tulip heard talk of the goings on in Uptown. Tulip, now a devoted Catholic, did not want nothing to do with that part of town. She had heard of nothing but bad things about that part of town. Drinking, fighting, and loose women. Plus, there was no money for Carson and Tulip to waste on Uptown. Carson's money was used for paying their high rent and buying needed food. The little money Tulip made from her work was spent on the children's needs, and the little she managed to put away was for a special occasion and not for such foolishness. But, even so, Tulip was only human, and she missed the fun in her life. Therefore, when Carson learned that Nat King Cole, one of his favorite singers was coming to Uptown, he was full of excitement. Leaving work, a little Colored boy hurriedly jammed the wrinkled flyer in his hand, and there it was. Nat King Cole was appearing at the Howard Theatre. During that period, it was the largest Colored theater in the world and dubbed, "The Theater for the People." Seldom did Carson display emotions, but he couldn't wait to tell Tulip about Nat King Cole coming to town. Plus, it had been years since he and his wife had spent alone time together.

Tulip was so full of excitement, the straightening comb burned her ears and she let out a little scream.

"Did you burn yo ear Mama?" asked Veronica, her oldest daughter who was now a teenager.

"Yeah baby," answered Tulip. "Hand me that jar of salve."

After fetching the jar of salve for her mama to put on her burned ear, she continued to watch Tulip straighten her hair. Tulip wanted to be finished with her hair and dressed before Carson got home so she wouldn't be in his way. For weeks, all she could think about was them going out to see Nat King Cole. When Carson first showed her the flyer, she just stared at it. They didn't have any money to waste on going out, plus she only heard bad things about the Howard Theatre, but Carson had reassured her it was not located in Uptown, and it was near the University, with the same name, where rich Colored people sent their children to be educated. In fact, Tulip had done day work for well-to-do Colored families whose children went to Howard University. She often fanaticized about her children going to college one day. Preferably, to the highly acclaimed Howard University. But it was only a fantasy because she and Carson didn't have the money for no fancy uppity Negro college.

Tulip called out to her daughter Veronica. "Put the iron on the stove and let me know when it's hot."

"Yes, Mama," Veronica replied, getting a little tired of doing her mama's errands, but she knew better than to refuse.

"And don't forget to take your papa's shirt and pants off the line, they should be dried by now," yelled Tulip. Hearing no response, Tulip raised her voice. "Girl, did you hear me?"

"Yeah, I mean yes, Mama," Veronica responded nervously.

"Well answer me when I'm talking to you, do you hear? And don't forget to check on the twins." Tulip was getting frustrated, she had too much to do before Carson got home.

"Yes, Mama," Veronica replied reluctantly. She always had to do everything, it just wasn't fair. Her brother Paul was never home. Instead, he was always hanging out in the streets up to no good. However, her brother Little Henry was different. Since he had come to live with them, Veronica found him to be kind and always willing to help Mama and her around the house.

Hearing the back and forth between Tulip and her daughter, Mean Old Mama rocked hard in her chair and let out a big "HUMPH!" Talking out loud to no one in particular, she went on.

"Y'all are running around making all this fuss to waste good money. Frying hair, bathing, stinking up the place. Just ain't right. Call yourself a Christian! Now you go play in the devil's playground. Don't think I don't hear you forcing my boy to waste good money on foolishness. You need to be home with your youngins. Here I am stuck in this God-forsaken hell hole place while you are getting all dolled. Ain't right I tell you. I told my boy you were no good. He got to work hard all day and now you want to go fretting up and down the streets. For what? Just ain't right I tell you. Always leaving me alone to take care of these no-good, hardheaded youngins. Where's my supper? I'm hungry."

Tulip completely ignored her. She was always running at the mouth saying nothing new. Same old same old.

Suddenly, the door flew open. Both Melvin and Carson rushed in. Tulip, still in her slip and bra, rushed to cover herself. She wasn't expecting Carson home for hours. It was too early for him to be home.

"How's my sweet girl?" Carson asked, kneeling in front of his beloved Mama. He gently stroked her hair. Mean Old Mama loved when her favorite son sweet-talked her, he was the only one who did, so she responded, "Boy, go away from here with your foolishness."

"Got something for you, Mama," Carson said playfully as he shook the bag he held in one hand, while other bags lay resting at his feet.

Mama asked in her sweetest voice, "Now what you done did?"

"Oh, just a little something, something," Carson said playfully.

Tulip had quickly put on a housecoat and worried about all the things that needed to be done before they went to the theatre. Upon hearing all the fuss, Veronica and the twins ran into the house.

Carson reached into the bag and pulled out the cutest white kitten and placed it in his Mama's lap. He took one of her hands and put it on the kitten. For once, Mama was speechless. Tears moistened her dull, lifeless gray eyes. The kitten purred in response to Mama's touch. The twins cooed in unison. They wanted to run to their granny to see the kitten, but Veronica held their hands tight. She knew her granny needed that moment.

At that moment, Little Henry and Paul walked into the house and saw the pretty little white kitty sitting in granny's lap. Paul, being the smart aleck that he was, blurted out, "Maybe the cat can catch that pesky mouse if the mouse don't catch him first."

Everybody laughed, even Mean Old Mama as she lovingly stroked her prized precession.

Carson turned to Veronica and the twins and said here is a bag for you. Veronica, still holding the twins' hands tightly, walked over and took the bag from her papa. Handing the bag to her, Carson said sternly, "Now don't eat of this until after supper and give your granny some, you know she is fond of sweets. Your mama and I are going out together for a while with your Auntie Lorraine and Uncle Melvin. Little Henry will be in charge." This was the first time the children heard of their papa and mama going out at the same time, so it was a little confusing.

While Veronica didn't mind Little Henry helping out, she didn't need anyone to be in charge of her. Thinking she was grown, she protested, "But why, I don't need him to look after me."

Carson said, "No sassing. He's the oldest and he is in charge, and that's final."

Paul let out a giggle and thought to himself, *he will never be in charge of me.* Secretly, Paul thought Little Henry was soft. Veronica lowered her eyes to the floor and squeezed the twins' hands so hard they yelled out.

With that settled, Carson turned his attention to his wife. Grinning like a chipmunk, he said, "Now for you, my sweet." He playfully reached into another bag and pulled out the most beautiful satin red dress with ruffles on the sleeves and a big black bow at the bosom. Tulip's eyes grew wide, and she covered her mouth so she wouldn't scream out in joy. "Carson, what have you done? Have you done gone plum crazy and lost your mind?"

Carson walked over to his wife whom he loved with all he had and handed her the dress. "Tonight, I want you to be the prettiest lady at the show."

Tears formed in Tulip's eyes, "But can we afford this? Carson please, you must take it back."

"No, it's okay," Carson said pulling Tulip into his arms. "I ran into a little luck, so there is no need to worry. In this bag are also a few personal items. Now run along and get pretty for your man."

He kissed his wife on her head. The children all laughed and covered their eyes.

Mean Old Mama spoke up, still stroking her new gift, "What she got there?"

Carson responded, "A beautiful new red dress."

"Red!" yelled Mean Old Mama, "Serves her well, a whore color."

"Now Mama, behave yourself!" Carson said very firmly. Mean Old Mama, giggled and made the sign of the cross.

Standing in the alley of the Howard Theatre, Tulip held onto Carson tightly. She was taken aback by so many Colored people, all dressed in their Sunday's best. But, even more surprising, there were White folks in line as well, standing along a sign reading "Colored Folks," laughing and talking, like it was the most natural thing to do.

Lord, Tulip thought to herself, *now I have seen everything.* Everyone was there for the same reason, to have a good time. In anticipation of what was to come, Tulip was full of excitement.

Colored folks were mingling around, without any order, waiting to be let into the theatre and see their own, Nat King Cole. Even though some were making a fuss, others were dancing about and cutting up with foul jokes. On the other hand, White folks were lined-up orderly and talking quietly among themselves, being careful to keep their distance and not stare too hard at the Colored folks acting up.

Carson and Melvin shared a flask filled with brown liquor and smoked cigarettes. Melvin passed his flask to his wife. She took a quick swig and let out a loud, "Whoop!" So much of this to Tulip was déjà vu except back then they had been riding in a wagon and the liquor was in a jug. Tulip felt a little lightheaded, memories flooded her mind like rushing water. She closed her eyes and held on tightly to Carson, who didn't seem to notice her discomfort. Tulip began to focus on her feet, which were killing her. Carson along with her beautiful red satin dress and had even brought her stockings and matching high heels. She wasn't used to wearing heels so high, so she hoped she didn't fall and make a spectacle of herself. The dress was tight, so Tulip constantly tugged at it. The dress accentuated all her assets. While she felt very self-conscious, Carson gave out a sensual whistle when he saw his wife. Yet, it was just too tight.

How much longer did they have to wait in this alley? she wondered. It was getting chilly, and the crowd seemed to be getting drunk and a little restless. A loud chant started, "OPEN THE DOORS! LET'S GET THIS FUNKY GROOVE GOING! COME ON MAN, OPEN THE DOORS!" People started to clap, and some began to sing.

Melvin asked, "Hey brother what's your favorite groove by the King?" Tulip smiled because she knew the answer immediately. As soon as the song came on the transistor radio, Carson would start singing "You better straighten up and fly right." The two brothers gave each other a high five like they were part of a secret club.

After the White folks had entered the theatre, *finally*, the Colored folk's line started moving. Given the condition of the alley, Tulip was pleasantly surprised the theatre was grand inside. Beautiful drapes, massive chandeliers, red velvet seats. Tulip felt like a princess. There were a lot of steps to climb for their seats, and Tulip's feet were now on fire. She didn't mind because this was something she had never experienced. After they were seated, the lights went low. Carson was like a kid in the candy store and when the loud music started from the stage and the curtains slowly opened, everyone, including Carson, stood to their feet, clapped, yelled, and stomped. Tulip was frozen in her seat. Her eyes were glued to the stage. It was nothing like she had ever experienced. She even felt pretty, even though the dress was too tight, and her feet were screaming to be set free. Tulip was scared to take off her shoes in fear she would never be able to get her feet back into them, and Lord knows she was not going to walk in stockings back into that nasty alley. Suddenly, Tulip looked up and saw her husband on his feet grinning like an alley cat that just caught a nice fat rat. It warmed her heart to see him so happy.

"Man, what a show!" exclaimed Carson as they walked to their car. He twirled Tulip around and around.

"Stop silly man, before I fall on my face," Tulip said as she tried to catch her breath. Melvin and his wife laughed out loud, both a little tipsy from way too many drinks.

"Okay folks, my chariot awaits," Melvin said as he stumbled and almost hit the ground laughing.

"Where to? Where would you two beautiful ladies like to go? The night is still young." Melvin wanted to keep the party going.

Carson spoke up as he took a swig out of his nearly empty flask.

"Yes, the night is young, and I know just the place where it's jumping. Bro, head on up to Jimmies on 14th & U."

Tulip tugged at Carson's jacket and whispered, "Don't you think we need to get back home to the children? It's pretty late, and you have to go to the Balls' in the morning."

Overhearing Tulip, Melvin quickly chimed in.

"Oh come on now Sis, don't be a sour pus. I heard you like to shake that thing."

Tulip almost turned red, and playfully slapped Carson upside his head. Everyone laughed, and chucked down a drink, except Tulip.

Jimmies was right in the heart of the city "Red Zone," where the nightlife offered a little of everything; drinking, prostitutes, dancing, eating, hustlers, drugs, pimps, gambling, and more (if there could be more). Tulip had heard gossip about the red zone and had forbidden her boys from going there. News on the radio always announced the goings on there—fights, shootings, raids, even murders, God forbid. Tulip grabbed Carson's flask and took a quick sip.

"Now that's what I'm talking about!" Carson shouted.

Carson was right, Jimmies was not only jumping but it was smoky, sweating, loud, and crowded. People were everywhere, laughing, drinking, smoking, dancing, you name it. Jimmies was just a little hole-in-the-wall joint, no frills. It was small and dark. There was a little stage and a small dance floor. Still, no one needed a dance floor because people were dancing everywhere. Tulip let her eyes take everything in. She recalled joints like this when she was at her low point after leaving her children and learning of Malcolm's death. Jimmies brought back not-too-nice memories that she preferred to keep buried. Yet even though she hated the place, and her feet were beginning to ache again, she longed to dance.

It was magical and then she smelled the sweet fragrance of the "field of flowers."

In the wake of time,
one will discover that life is truly undefined;
As the saying goes, nor will you know the hour of the day
when your life passes away;
So, truth be told,
the precious moments are like a fine glass of wine;
Therefore, I say, walk gently in your steps,
let your footprints be your guide, listen with your heart, and
let not your ears betray;
Life's path has been predetermined,
there are no shortcuts or unknown signs;
Our eyes are free to unlock the truth, we only have to open
them to see the reality of what is to be...

TWENTY-FOUR
Monster

After spending two years confined to City #4 hospital's mental ward, Solo's burns had healed very poorly, leaving her severely scarred and in constant pain. Her mental state was even worse and quickly deteriorating. She didn't know who she was and she cursed at staff and fought other patients. She constantly scratched her skin until it bled profusely, and constantly tried to escape and fought anyone trying to stop her. She spat her food out at staff, defecated on herself, and speared the foul-smelling contents on herself and anyone who dared to get near her. She laughed loudly, made grunting animal sounds, stripped off her makeshift gown, and danced naked around the mental ward. Doctor Frank and Head Nurse Mary, for her safety, as well as the staff, kept her heavily sedated and/or bound to her bed or in a straitjacket. No one ever inquired about her family or friends. There appeared to be no foreseeable improvement in Solo's mental condition. She was in dire need of long-term care that the mental ward could not provide. With a heavy heart and no foreseeable recourse or improvement in Solo's mental state, Doctor Frank committed her to one of New York City's notorious state hospitals for the mentally retarded and criminally insane.

Constant screaming, laughing, crying, running, praying, and the smell of sorrow. The state mental hospitals were a dumping ground for insane or feeble-minded Negroes and epileptics throughout the 30s and 40s and operated under shameful and unimaginably humiliating conditions. The most horrible, unbelievable cruelties were inflicted upon anyone unfortunate enough to land in one of the facilities. Therapies would include, but were not limited to, sedatives, hydrotherapy, insulin shock, or malaria treatment. These treatments were both subjective, pure torture, and nightmarish. Patients would scream out in terror. In some cases, patients were used as guinea pigs to test out new treatments, which in many cases left them in worst condition than they were before.

Not only was the treatment barbaric, but the wards and living conditions were also equally just as cruel as well as unspeakable. Dirty, unsanitary, foul-smelling, and crowded. There were few attendants assigned to ensure the patients did not harm themselves or to prevent abuse by other patients. Many of the physically able patients would care for the helpless ones. Some patients would be completely naked or wear old or oversized clothes stained with days-old food. During the day, there were no formal activities. Most patients were left to their own in a big, open, crowded day room. Many would just walk about, while others would lay all day on the bare floor. At night, all patients were given sedatives.

Solo was conscious. While her eyes remained tightly shut, her ears pinged into unbearable, animalistic cries. For what seemed like an eternity, she laid there stiff as a board while her mind tried to comprehend the situation. She had died and this was hell. She had voices yelling in her ear. Solo violently shook her head to stop the nagging voices. After the voices seem to calm down, she willed herself to open her eyes, which proved to be a daunting task. Her eyes seemed to be glued shut. Solo struggled to open her eyes. Finally, bright lights screamed at her, which made her quickly shut her eyes. The lights pained her eyes, but she had to see, she needed to make some sense of her reality. Her eyes finally adjusted to the bright light, but she kept having to squint as her eyes darted around the large room. She tried to lift her head, but it was heavy, and she felt dizzy. Hence, for now, she would let her eyes do the work. Solo looked around taking in her surroundings. There appeared to be more than 100 women of all shapes and sizes moving about. Most were fully dressed in the same, ugly, gray makeshift tent of a dress. Some were naked, except for what appeared to be a baby diaper. No bars. Most were either bald or had short, cropped hair, which made Solo think of her hair. She thought to herself, *I have beautiful golden long hair.* All were shoeless. There was so much noise from the laughing, crying, talking, shouting nonsense, calling for God or Mama, which made Solo think to herself, *Mama, I have a Mama.*

Why is that lady staring and pointing at me?

The lady saw Solo look directly at her and she screamed out, "Look, look! The monster is alive!" Others looked in Solo's direction and began to scream and point at her. Solo was afraid and tried to get up, but she was dizzy. She realized both her arms and legs were in leather restraints. The women continued to scream "Monster! Monster!" and some began to move close to her. Solo was in a panic. *Why are they calling me a monster? Where am I?*

Finally, the sea of women parted as a tall, heavyset, dark-skinned man dressed in all white made his way through and with a voice of authority said, "Calm down, let's calm down, let me through. Bertha, stop pulling out your hair. China, put your dress down. Okay, let me see what's going on. Everybody just go to your assigned places." And just like that, the women all scattered—some immediately sat on the floor, others moved to various parts of the room. Some got on their carts. It was like watching a performance.

The man looked at Solo and smiled. He slowly walked over to her, taking caution with each step. Some of the patients yelled at him to stop while some closed their eyes or pulled their clothing over their heads exposing themselves. Solo struggled to sit up. She began to sweat. Her heart raced. She tried to scream, but no sound came out. The voices were whispering in her ear, *don't trust him, kick him, kill him.* Solo was trapped. She closed her eyes and turned her head away from the approaching man.

"Are you trying to play possum?" the dark-skinned man asked. Solo liked his nice voice. The man continued, "Now, I know you are not sleep because I just saw those big, beautiful blues of yours." He let out a slight snicker. Solo wanted him to leave her alone. The man continued.

"All the ladies here call me Fred."

Saying his name aloud caused a chanting of his name from some of the women. "Fred, Fred, Fred, Fred, Fred, Fred."

The man laughed and said, "Okay, ladies, that's enough." Some of the chanting stopped, but a few continued. Fred turned his attention back to Solo. In the years since her arrival, she had been out of control, attacking anyone who came near her. After so many instances, it was decided to keep her sedated during the shock treatment sessions. That was fine with Fred because when he was alone at night with the women, he had his pick. Sex was sex, even if you were crazy. With what he had to put up with, this was just an added benefit of the job. Most of the women were nothing to look at and some stank so bad, even Fred didn't want to go near them. The comatose ones, like Solo, were kept pretty much clean to keep down the bed sores and other infections. Sometimes he even made a little money by sneaking his buddies in for a little fun. He charged less than the regular hookers, plus they didn't talk back. All in all, Fred had his fun from the moment he saw Solo, even though she was crazy as shit. But even with the ugly scarring from the burns, she was still a looker and had a nice fat ass. But more importantly, she was a Jane Doe. No family to worry about, which was perfect.

"Are you thirsty?" Fred asked Solo. He knew she just had a recent shock treatment and, in most cases, it made the patients extremely thirsty. Solo, still trying to make sense of her situation, didn't trust Fred. She kept her head turned away and refused to look at him or ask for water, even as thirsty as she was. Voices yelled in Solo's directions from everywhere, "DRINK THE WATER, WATER, WATER DRINK IT!" Some were screaming, while others were laughing hysterically. Solo wanted to cover her ears, to shut out the noise. The voices continued to yell at her to drink the water.

Fred asked again, "Do you want some water? I'll be right back. I'm going to get you a cup of water. Now, don't you go nowhere." Fred said very kindly. Solo turned her head slightly to see Fred walking away. She looked at the people singing, talking, dancing, and laughing. Solo only peeked through her eyes, she didn't want them to see her and start another commotion. Her throat was so very dry. She really was thirsty and wanted water. Where was that man named Fred? She wished he would hurry back with the water.

Solo was still confused as to why she was hospitalized. The restraints, the lights, the noise, they all added to her confusion. There was not a familiar face in sight. She wondered where was Jessie.

"Are your eyes blue or are they green?" Fred asked, looking straight into Solo's eyes and holding a cup. "I have a nice cup of water for you. Now, I can hold your head up and let you sip the water, or I can undo the restraints and let you try to hold the cup. But, if you make a scene or try to hit me, I will sedate you and put you back in restraints. Your choice."

Solo looked directly at Fred. He was a big Black man, dressed in all white with big, humongous hands with short fat fingers. He was not a good-looking man at all. Everything on his face was large—his nose, mouth, and eyes. His teeth were yellow and showed signs of poor dental care. Solo had the urge to laugh, maybe the women were calling him the monster and not her. She turned her attention back to Fred and merely nodded at him.

"Good girl," Fred said as he proceeded to undo her restraints.

Hours had gone by since Solo had encountered Fred. After drinking the water and having her hands and feet free from the restraints, she was overwhelmed with a sense of dread and confusion. She didn't ask Fred any questions. He had explained to her that a doctor would come and see her shortly, so she should just lay back and relax. Solo was itchy all over. She scratched the back of her hands to no relief. Solo raised her hands to take a better look. Her eyes took in the ugly, twisted, disfigured skin. She could not believe what she is seeing. She turned each hand from front to back slowly taking in the awful appearance of each hand. Solo sat up straight in the bed to get a better look, maybe her eyes were deceiving her. She slowly pulled on the sleeves of her gray gown. Her arms were worse than her hands. Eyes traveled down each arm and took in the twisted red, purplish skin that was now in place of once beautiful, smooth skin. She forcibly kicked back the covers to expose her legs or what was now left of her once beautiful legs. She pulled up the ugly gown to see more even damage. Her heart was racing. *NO! NO! NO! This can't be possible,* she thought to herself but was actually screaming out loud, which frightened the other patients, and the screaming began with a chant, "THE MONSTER! NO, NO, NO!"

Solo, now standing upright, ripped off her gown to fully expose her ugly, scarred body. She shook so hard that urine slowly released from her to the floor. Shaking her head "no," she began to slowly walk like a newborn baby with her arms outstretched. Some patients screamed, others huddled in the corner afraid of the monster. Solo looked around as if searching for something. Struggling to walk and keeping her sanity, she spotted a silver tray. As she moved slowly towards the object in her sight, two men and two women dressed in white entered the room and began to gather the patients. Some were yelling and stripping off their same ugly gowns. Solo finally reached the silver metal tray.

Blocking from her mind all the chaos surrounding her, she momentarily stared at the tray. She reached out and grabbed it with both hands. A scared patient thinking Solo was going to attack her with the tray, screamed in horror and ran.

A soft, calm voice was talking in her direction.

"Jane, I know you are scared, but please put down the tray. We will not hurt you. I am Doctor Hertz. I've been treating you."

Still holding the metal tray, she continued to back up while the doctor crept slowly closer to her.

"Now hand me the tray and we can sit down and talk. I know you are confused and even afraid and have a lot of questions. First, I want you to know that I understand, and I will not harm you. This is a hospital. You were in a fire and hurt bad," Doctor Hertz spoke slowly looking, directly at Solo, with his hands stretched out toward her. "I want to help you. I know your name is not Jane Doe. Can you tell me your name?"

Solo held the tray closer to her body as a barrier of protection. Her mind was racing. *Did he say fire? Was I in a FIRE?* Solo shook her head from side to side, trying to remember. Thoughts invaded her mind. *NO, NO, it was Baby in the fire. It wasn't me.* Solo looked at her arms, then at her legs. *MY GOD, I WAS BURNED!*

Tears rolled down her face and she slowly raised the metal tray to her face and looked at the monster before her. She fainted, and her distorted, grotesque body crumpled to the floor.

Beauty is in the eyes of the beholder, so it is said not what's on the outside, but rather what's on the inside;
Our eyes take in the visual and the pleasure of its pleasing effect that in some cases is one of a kind;
What we see is what want it to be and not a real interpretation of the reality of what it will turn out to be in a matter of time;
So the question remains, can beauty be truly defined, or rather is it a mistaken manifestation of the unexplainable in-depth function of our mind?

TWENTY-FIVE
Jane Doe

Finally, after years of begging and empty promises, City Hospital #4 received money to expand its overflowing burn ward. A whole new wing was constructed just to treat the increasing number of burn victims. This new wing came with increased staff, more beds, more space, and the latest technology to treat severely burned patients.

With all the changes, moving day was here for City Hospital #4 burn ward. There was much to be done, patients to be moved, offices to be packed, equipment to be moved, supplies to be ordered, and more. Doctors, nurses, attendants, and volunteers were moving quickly about trying to provide patient care, while at the same time helping to assist with the massive move. It was beyond chaotic for both patients and hospital staff, but it was getting done.

Head Nurse Mary maintained all the patient records as well as staff files. Over the years, her office had become overloaded with paper, and she didn't have time to get it organized. In preparation for the move, she recruited one of the young nurses to pack up her office. The young nurse was impressed the Head Nurse had selected her, and she was more than eager to perform the task. As she entered Head Nurse Mary's office, she took a long sigh thinking of the task ahead of her. Her instructions were to trash all outdated papers. Some documents were more than thirty years old including past and current patient files, mail, books, pamphlets, documents, and letters to patients. The young nurse stood with both hands on her hips and scanned the room. She knew it was a daunting task so she had better get busy. At least she would get a break from the patients. Caring for burn victims was a heartbreaking task, days filled with seeing the flesh melted away from bones and open wounds oozing foul-smelling pus. The tortured screams and moans of unbearable pain haunted her dreams. These thoughts made the young nurse shiver. For her, while this task seemed overwhelming, she smiled knowing it was a blessing in disguise.

She closed the office door behind her, rolled up her selves, and said aloud, "Let's get busy." Hours passed while sorting through dusty papers and files, but finally, she was seeing a little daylight at the end of the tunnel. She was getting hungry and thirsty so she decided to take a break. As she stood, an envelope slid to the floor. The young nurse stared at the envelope trying to decide if it should be trashed. It looked old. It was dirty and even a little burnt. Curiously, she bent down and retrieved the envelope from the floor. She stared at the address and name, Mr. Jessie Freeman. *It must be a letter for a patient that was never delivered or forgotten.* While she didn't know every patient in the burn ward, the name Jessie Freeman did ring a bell. One of her responsibilities was to deliver mail to all staff and patients. For some reason, the name on the letter seemed familiar. She recalled when she was a volunteer she had found a letter on the floor near Jane Doe's bed. She remembered looking at the name. Strange that she would recall such.

Well, it was none of her business and probably was nothing, but she had to decide whether to trash it or give it to Head Nurse Mary. Deciding it may be of importance, she put the unopened letter in her apron pocket to give it to the head nurse. After finishing her work, she took a long look around and was pleased. Boxes were neatly packed and stacked, ready for the movers. Her task was complete, time to call it a night. As she was about to leave, she reached down in her pocket and touched the letter. It was a split decision. She placed the letter on Nurse Mary's desk, cut off the lights, and shut the door.

It had been a long day. Head Nurse Mary stared out the window into the darkness and let out a long sigh. She had stared out that same window for more than twenty years. She would miss the view, seeing the lights of the city at night. *My, how time has flown by.* She had to admit the young nurse she assigned to pack her office had done a fantastic job. Head Nurse Mary let her eyes roam her office. *Years of work all packed away.* Her eyes traveled slowly to the top of her desk where a lonely envelope lay in the center. *What could this possibly be?* She reached down and picked up the envelope. On the outside was scribbled "Burn victim." This was puzzling. The letter was addressed to a Mr. Jessie Freeman. Head Nurse Mary knew every patient's name, except for Jane Doe, who was now committed to the infamous State Hospital for the Mentally Retarded and Criminally Insane. She did not recall a patient named Jessie Freeman in the men's ward. She continued to look at the envelope, her fingers trembled as she nervously opened it. She began to read, "My Dearest Solo…"

After Head Nurse Mary finished reading the letter, she slumped down in her chair. *NO! NO!* she screamed internally, *This can't be possible. Well, I be damned, after all these years, really the answer to Jane Doe's identity was right here in my office. She had family, people who were trying to find her. All this time, Jane Doe had a name, isn't this a bitch. She has a unique beautiful name, "Solo," she also has a family, people who loved her and would have taken care of her.*

Tears trickled down Mary's face. Her heart was heavy. How was it possible this letter was lost? She was always strict when it came to patients' family members. She was compassionate and understood how critical it was to the patient's progress for them to have the support of their families. She understood that medicine could cure, but absent of love, sometimes it has been proven to be ineffective. Knowing the power of family, Mary took pride in assuring patients were in contact with caring family members. In many cases, these were the people who would have to provide the long-time care. She also had the same level of compassion and concern for Jane Doe, especially given the events that happened. As a result, over the years, Head Nurse Mary as requested, made sure Doctor Frank was kept updated on Jane Doe's progress. But, while her physical health improved, her mental state deteriorated to the point that she was moved for long-term care and confinement. Mary had conferred with Doctor Frank, and he agreed Jane Doe's mental condition could not be treated at City #4's mental ward. She needed more intervention than they were equipped to offer. It was agreed she would be moved and no longer be their responsibility.

While both Head Nurse Mary and Doctor Frank knew this was surely a death sentence for Jane Doe, unless by the grace of God there was some miraculous intervention, most likely Jane Doe would be the ward of the hospital for the remainder of her unfortunate life. It was all so very sad. By finding this letter, Head Nurse Mary contemplated whether she and Doctor Frank had acted too hastily and failed to take the necessary measures to locate Jane Doe's kinfolks. She had to admit this was a long shot. The letter may have nothing to do with Jane Doe, let alone her family. It may be possible this may not even be Jane Doe's family. Yet still, there was no patient by the name of "Solo" under her care and she made it her business to know each patient by name, out of compassion.

It seemed like time had stood still as Head Nurse Mary pondered what to do and finally, she opened her desk drawer looking for writing paper. None was there because as she had instructed the young nurse, she had dutifully packed everything away accordingly. She searched her office reading the labels affixed to the boxes. Finally, on top of her desk, there was a box labeled "writing materials." She took off the top and pulled out a wad of writing paper, an envelope, and a few ink pens. She took a seat at her desk and moved some of the boxes aside to make room to write. She held the pen in her hand but stopped before she made one stroke. She thought to herself that maybe she should consult Doctor Frank first. This probably was not even Jane Doe's family and then Doctor Frank would be upset because she bothered him with such nonsense. Even still, who was this person looking for? The letter sounded so loving, but desperate. Head Nurse Mary had to know. She took a deep breath and began to write...

"Dear Mrs. Barnes,"...but then she suddenly stopped. But, what about the babies? There would be an investigation, she could possibly lose her job. There must be another way. She felt sorry for Jane Doe or this person named Solo locked in that deplorable state mental hospital. She doubted if the patient even had any knowledge she was even pregnant, let alone delivered babies. How could she? Beads of sweat popped up on Head Nurse Mary's forehead. She got up from her chair and began to pace around the office, twisting her hands together. Sweat from her underarms began to soil her uniform. *Think, Think.* How could she help Jane Doe, possibly Solo, without implicating herself? Head Nurse Mary thought to herself, *it would be so easy to just tear this letter up and throw it in the trash and be done with it. No one would ever know, but she would. Had her past caught up with her?* She was an excellent nurse and always wanted the best for her patients. However, in the case of Jane Doe, she used poor judgment because of her feelings for Doctor Frank. While she wanted the best for her patient, her feelings for Doctor Frank directed her actions, which she now regretted. It was clear Doctor Frank didn't care about her, she talked out loud to herself. "Him and his happy family." Where was her family?

As a young nurse, she had been so impressed with Doctor Frank. His talents, overwhelming compassion, and care for his patients. She was so flattered when he requested her assistance. They worked side by side in the operating rooms and spent long hours together discussing cases. The love affair started gradually. First, with just warm embraces and slight quick kisses. His eyes would follow her when she passed him in the hospital corridors. Gradually, the kisses and touching became more probing and intense, until one magical night their passion and desire overtook their better judgment and moral compasses. They would steal kisses and have quick love-making sessions in his office. She didn't mean to fall in love with him. Doctor Frank made it very clear from the start that if their affair was discovered, it would be a scandal and most certainly the death of the careers they sacrificed and worked so hard for. While Negro nurses had it easier, it was very hard for a Negro doctor to get an assignment in a top-notch hospital. Because no hospital would take them, they were usually assigned to hospitals serving Colored, poor, and newly-arrived immigrants, and these posts were far and few in between. So, Doctor Frank, even though he was top of his class, felt fortunate to be the Head Burn Surgeon at City #4. Besides his most prestigious career, he would never leave his wife because of her family wealth and connections that played an instrumental role in his placement at City #4. Needless to say, Doctor Frank had a lot to lose. Head Nurse Mary fully understood. She was not stupid, but she wanted him regardless of the limitations and consequences. So, she willingly welcomed their clandestine love affair. Now so many years had passed and she was older and so much wiser. No longer a naïve, wide-eyed young nurse, her job was now her lifeline. No longer did she need hot passion to validate her self-worth. She was excellent at her job. Her hard work and dedication alone earned her the title and respect as Head Nurse. It was a worthy accomplishment and she was proud. As a result, her respect for her position, coupled with her compassion for her patients drove her sense of responsibility and care. Her staff, patients, and their families trusted her. Head Nurse Mary thought to herself *if Jane Doe had family who was searching for her and could give her a chance at a better life, then, who am I to stand in her way?*

"My God, she has a right to know her family." Mary moved

frantically around the room and talked aloud, "What about my love? I gave him my trust; I cannot betray him, this would ruin him. But I took a professional oath to give my patients and their families 100 percent care, honesty, and trust. This letter probably is not even related to Jane Doe. I should just tear this letter up and that would be the end of it. Probably nothing anyway. Why start an unnecessary fuss that may prove to be nothing or lead to professional ruin and heartbreak?"

Nurse Mary felt light-headed. She closed her eyes and laid back in her chair for a little clarity. Other than the sound of the rain pounding softly on the window like white cloud noise, for a moment, her world was quiet.

Life is funny, you never know when it may take a turn for the worst or best;
Every second is a new experience and sometimes an unwanted adventure or the most wonderful of all;
Living is like going on a trip or acting on a stage; you never know what to expect, which way it will turn, and you take an unexpected fall;
The unknown is present every day, it takes on different forms, and we all are on call;
Enjoy the ride, take it all in stride; it is nice to be alive, so take my advice and live each day as the last and have a ball.

TWENTY-SIX

Such is Life

It was a beautiful evening; Tulip exited the streetcar for a short walk home. It had been a long day. While she was tired, her job was not done. Tulip shifted the bags in her arms. Mrs. Bond, the White lady she worked for, always gave her something to take home. Usually, it was discarded clothing and leftover food. While Tulip was very prideful, she wasn't stupid. Many times, she didn't want to take this White lady's leftovers. For some reason, it seemed demeaning and made her feel inferior. She knew very well what White folks thought of Colored people. While in the country, White folks and Coloreds work side-by-side, shared meals together, watched over each other's children, and even helped each other out when times got rough. Overall, country folks were almost like family. It seems they were all in the same boat trying not to sink.

However, these big city Whites and even uppity Coloreds were cut from a different cloth. While their lips would smile, their eyes showed contempt. You would feel the air sucked out of you in their presence. In the city, you didn't share a meal with White folks, you only worked for them. That would let you know quickly you were not their equal or friend. As a result, when they had hand-outs, Tulip would swallow her pride, nod in appreciation, and take them. Times were hard and the money Carson made from his work was barely keeping a roof over their head. She never let Carson know she took the handouts from the White families. The fact is, the children needed clothing, especially the little ones. Even still, Tulip had to admit, while some of the White folks' clothes were very worn and needed mending, some clothes were as good as new. Now when it came to the food, that was a totally different animal. While she didn't mind taking home leftovers she cooked, leftovers from White folk's parties, holidays, or food that wasn't cooked by her was a different story. With her large family, extra food was always good to have. If she didn't cook it, she carefully inspected it before being eaten by her family. Tulip didn't want to take a chance of her children getting sick or hexed. Some of the White folk food items had strange names and smelled awful. The cookies with fruit fillings and fruit cakes were always stale and the only one who would eat them was Mean Old Mama.

As Tulip walked along, she smiled to herself as she thought of her life. Sometimes her thoughts would go back to Mama and Malcolm. The memories would start pleasant but eventually, make her sad. The walk to her home was about four long city blocks and took about an hour. The city streetcar didn't go in the direction of her address so, she had to walk. As she walked along, Tulip took it to the bustling city sites and tried to block out vulgar catcalls from the seedy-looking men directing her away. She cherished this slice of alone time. No man or no children constantly wanting something from her. Now with Mean Old Mama's health failing, it was even more work having to change her soiled clothing and keep her clean. Every day was endless hours of cleaning, cooking, washing, mending clothes, and running after the kids. It was extra hard on the days Tulip traveled across town to do her day work, but the little extra money was greatly needed.

As Tulip walked, she always reflected on her life. Is this what she expected her life would be? Did she ever have any expectations for her life beyond a man and children? Was she happy? Would life have been different if Malcolm had not left? So many what-ifs and unanswered questions. One thing for sure, there was always work to be done. Now to make matters worse, it seemed Carson was always gone, especially on weekends. She was left home to deal with the children and Mean Old Mama. For some reason, it didn't sit well with her.

After buying a car, Carson traveled down to southern Maryland on the weekends to work his side job for a White family named Ball who had a very large corn and hog business. When Carson's papa was living, he worked for the Balls. When he and his brothers were old enough, say around five or six, they also went with him to work the Ball's land and livestock. After Carson's papa passed on and his brothers drifted away, he continued to work for the Balls.

Carson liked the Balls, they were good to him and treated him like family. They always remembered the children's birthdays and even gave them Christmas presents. As a result, he had no problem traveling back to the country and continuing his work for them. Seemly, just as important, going back to what he considered home gave him a chance to visit his kin and hang out a little in his old stomping grounds with his no-account friends. So, here lately on weekends, Tulip wouldn't see Carson until he returned home on Sunday nights. Stinking of liquor, funky underarms, stale cigarettes, and Lord knows what else. Talk had it that Carson was keeping women in his hometown. Talk even had it that there was another child. However, Tulip paid no mind to such foolish talk. She learned a long time ago that people liked to gossip about others, especially when they were jealous. Tulip knew her husband was a good man and did right by her. He treated Little Henry just like he was his natural-born son. Helped him to get a job and proudly introduced Little Henry as his son. This made Tulip happy. Little Henry even called him Paw. She knew Little Henry had it hard after both she and Malcolm left him and his sisters in the care of the Chiles. Then having to deal with the loss of Baby, coupled with Solo disappearing, poor thing. He had been all alone but he never blamed her. So, when he wrote her asking if he could come and live with her, she cried. Little Henry wanted to be with his family. While she was more than grateful for the Chiles looking after Little Henry, it was time for him to be with his kin. Tulip of course had to seek her husband's permission for Little Henry to live with them. It was a serious matter of another mouth feed. Yet, Little Henry wasn't a child. He was nearly twenty years of age, a grown man who had fought in the war, risking his life for his country. He would be expected to earn his keep.

For weeks, Tulip struggled with how to approach Carson with the subject of having Little Henry live with them. She had already written to the Chiles telling them her son was more than welcome. Little Henry was expected to arrive within a week, so time was of the essence. Then finally one night after the family had all retired for the evening and Tulip laid in the bed snuggled next to her husband, gently rubbing his private, she approached the subject of Little Henry. Carson, without hesitation, put Tulip's fears to rest. Of course, Little Henry was welcome. Tulip was overwhelmed and lifted her nightdress and straddled her husband. But, even with this rush of happiness of having Little Henry with them, she still knew her life would not be complete until Solo was home with the family. Not a day would go by that her heart still didn't pain for her daughter. She felt the call of her lost daughter, like the call for her own mama many years ago. Mother and child. Tulip felt the pain in her bones, like a dull ache, no matter bad or good, a mother knows when her child was hurting, even if she is causing the hurt.

Carson left instructions for Mr. Jake, the town's mail carrier, to give his mail to his brother Sam. In return, he would get it from Sam when he visited. But still, Tulip was concerned Jessie's letter might not find its way to her, and Solo would be forever lost. When Carson would return home from his weekend side job, he would bear gifts—fresh meat from a killed hog, baby chicks for the kids, fish or crab, canned goods, and a Sears and Roebuck catalog. But never the much longed-after letter from Jessie. In one year, Tulip had managed to save enough money to cover her expenses to New York City. She still had Jessie's letter with the address, so she began her plan.

"New York City, here I come! Solo, your mama's coming." Tulip smiled to herself. She recalled that terrible blizzard in 1946 and the joy in her heart when she received Jessie's letter about Solo. How she sat down and wrote a heartfelt letter back. But she never received a response. She pondered for a minute but quickly dismissed it. She didn't want negative thoughts to venture into her mind. Four years had passed. Tulip thought to herself, *my Solo is a young woman now, twenty-two years of age.* Tulip shook her head from side to side. "It's been at least sixteen years since I saw my firstborn. My, how time has flown," Tulip whispered out loud.

With so many thoughts, Tulip didn't realize she had reached the front rickety broken gate to her home. A few chickens scurried about, and their fleabag dog ran up to greet her, wagging his tail in hopes of getting some food scraps.

"Hey Lady, slow down there," Tulip heard the voice from a neighbor, Maureen Phelps who lived next door with her husband and seven unkept, bad ass kids. Tulip stopped walking and replied.

"Yeah, another day the Lord made."

"Yes, praise God," Maureen said smiling as she walked toward the wrought iron fence separating their homes. Tulip set her bags down and walked toward her neighbor.

"Hey girl, how was your day with your tribe?" Tulip asked laughing out loud. Hearing their mama's voice, Tulip's children came bursting out the door and ran to greet their mama, hoping she brought home some treats.

"Here come your tribe, like raging bulls," chuckled Maureen.

Tulip looked at her youngins. Her girl's hair looking nappy and uncombed. Tulip shook her head and put hands on her hips and looked over at her children. She left specific instructions for Veronica to do her baby sister's hair. Look at it, an embarrassing mess. Before she could fuss, Maureen interrupted her and said, "Now don't be too cross, you know these kids today have a one-track mind."

Tulip just shook her head as she yelled to her children to take the bags into the house. She took a deep breath and turned to Maureen.

"These crumb snatchers just don't mind what you tell them to do. Here I am slaving all day to make sure they don't starve or go naked. Now I got to come home and slave some more. Every day it's the same thing. Never mind what I tell them. Well, I tell you what Maureen, if I walk through those doors and the floor has not been swept, clothes washed, and beds made, there is going to be some butt whipping." The two ladies looked at each other and let out a big loud laugh.

"Well you might as well get your switch off the tree and get your arms ready for some butt whipping. The other day I was whipping that oldest of mine and pulled a muscle in my arm. The pain nearly killed me. Made me so damn mad, I commenced to whipping everybody in sight." This brought a real hard laugh between the two ladies.

Tulip began to walk away saying, "Girl let me get into this house before that man of my mines come home. You know that's another story for another day." They laughed and promised to talk later.

As Tulip walked inside, her eyes surveyed the room. She acknowledged what had not been done and began to call out the kids by their God-given names.

"First, what did I tell you to do today? I said to sweep the floors and get your brothers to help you hang the rugs outside to be beaten. And didn't I tell you to comb and plait your sister's hair? Look at her."

Veronica turned in her sister's direction. She held her head down in fear of what was coming next. Tulip went to sit down and remove her shoes when the twin, Mag, came over to her to be picked up. Tulip reached down, picked her up, and kissed her on the cheek while affectionally stroking her head. She allowed herself to be caught up by

Mag's sweetness. Coming back to reality, Tulip yelled to Veronica, "Where are your brothers?"

Veronica replied with a sarcastic tone, "They haven't come home yet from work...if they even went to work."

Tulip suddenly felt something was out of place. She looked over and saw that Mean Old Mama's rocking chair was not in the living room space. Her stomach formed knots. The boys knew she had to be pushed from the bedroom to the living space. Tulip turned to her daughter who was still frozen in the same spot.

"Did you feed your grand maw today and give her the medicine?"

Veronica looked sheepish and quickly replied, "I tried, but she been sleeping all day and wouldn't wake up. Mama, you know that she hits you with the cane when you try to wake her up, so I left her alone."

Tulip was beside herself and took a deep breath as she kicked off her old worn shoes and rubbed her tired feet. The rubbing felt so good. She closed her eyes for a minute to enjoy the pleasure before she had to deal with the wrath of her mother-in-law, who once she was awake would be on a war path and sure to tell her beloved son, Carson, how she was neglected by his no-good wife and worthless children.

Tulip slowly opened the door to the small bedroom where the girls and Mean Old Mama slept. As soon as she opened the door, the foul smell of urine and loose bowels attacked her nostrils. She stared at Mean Old Mama who was slumped over in her rocking chair. Tulip's eyes tried to register the scene before her. Mean Old Mama's head was slumped to one side. Her mouth was frozen open as if she was trying to call out. Her lifeless eyes were wide open. Tulip, hearing the children calling out to her, turned and quickly shut the door to the bedroom. She didn't want them to see her in that condition. Tulip noticed one of Mean Old Mama's hands dangling to the floor as if she was reaching for something, while the other hand tightly grasped her favorite old worn button-down double pocket apron. The smelly urine leaking under Mean Old Mama's rocking chair had formed a small pool of yellow cloudy water. Tulip stared at Mean Old Mama, she was frozen in her space. It was no doubt she had passed on, but this was different from seeing her own mama's dead body. Even though Tulip was a mere child, she saw her mama seemingly at peace. Even in death, Mean Old Mama looked pissed and angry, just like she lived. It was clear she wasn't ready to meet her maker.

> *In the dark or light, it comes,*
> *stealing both the old and young;*
> *No one can escape its path, you can run, you can hide, but*
> *to death, this was just a game of fun;*
> *Leaving this world for what is unknown is a prize that we*
> *all compete for and won;*
> *Yes, I say to you, live the life you have been given, enjoy it to*
> *the fullness, be young, be old, be good, be bad, be sad, be*
> *happy, be giving, be selfish, but for each of us, the end will*
> *come. So, say GOD, let it be done.*

TWENTY-SEVEN
Home Going

"And ye shall seek me, and find me when ye shall search for me with all your heart. Jeremiah 29:23…so let not your heart not be heavy today. In the year of the Lord nineteen hundred and fifty-five, we sent our beloved Sister Barnes home. She was ready to meet her maker, for she fought a good fight and won the battle. So, let's not be weary, but give praise for this day because this is her homegoing and praise be to God."

Pastor Teals spoke passionately as he stood over Mean Old Mama's casket, clutching a worn-out Bible close to his chest. The family and mourners all nodded in acknowledgment. There was an overcast of clouds when they laid Mean Old Mama to rest on the family burial grounds, which dated back as far as the late 1700s. Big, blackbirds sat perched on the decaying headstones as they too were part of the festivities. Many of the headstones were crumbling from age. Even some of the graves had caved into the earth. The trees that hung over the burial grounds gave a ghostly appearance. Weeds sprung over many of the graves. Vines curled around the headstones as if they were lovers. It was not well maintained. In fact, it was poor in condition. After the slaves were freed, Mean Old Mama's folks and other family members became sharecroppers and worked the fields for the same White family who previously owned them as slaves. After Emancipation, which freed the slaves, some of the White owners allowed their former slaves to have a small patch of land to work and grow crops to eat and sell, as long as the profits were shared with them. When most of the White family died or moved on or just lost interest, sharecroppers, like Mean Old Mama's folks and kin continued to work the land. So, it was only fitting they were provided the opportunity to buy the land from the Whites. And that is how the Barnes family burial site came to be.

Carson and his seven brothers and only sister Lilly took their Mama's passing hard, even though they all knew it was way beyond her time on this earth. She had outlived their Papa Robert Barnes by more than thirty years and pretty much raised her children on her own, notwithstanding the help of family members and kind neighbors.

When she was as young as five or so, along with her Mama, Papa, and eighteen siblings, she worked the White family's tobacco farms. It was said she was not only a quick study, but she was strong as an ox and worked hard.

At the time of her passing, she was a ripe ninety-four years of age. She lived through the Great Depression, wars, famine, deadly outbreaks, deaths, and much more. It was told that in her youth, she was not a looker, but pleasant enough to grab the interest of a few local men, especially, her late husband, Robert Barnes. She stood a natural 4 ft. 11 in. but was mean and feisty as hell. Maybe that accounted for her mean-tempered spirit. At one time, she was the "root doctor" known for her potions to cast off a spell or put on a spell. She could fight like a man. After her husband Robert passed on, she never had time for men. She said could be both father and mother to her offspring and never remarried. She worked the farm and sold goods to support her large, fatherless family.

After the boys came to age, most went to fight in the wars or look for other work besides sharecropping or farming. On occasion, some would send money home, but they never returned home. Talk had it that two of the brothers, Ernest and Levi, moved to New York City to live a freer lifestyle. They were said to be "funny" or homosexual. Only Carson, his brothers, Melvin, Robert Jr. (called Bobby), Samuel, and his sister Lilly stayed on the farm with their mama. After Lilly and Robert Jr. married, it left just Carson and Melvin. Finally, Melvin got married, and moved on to start a family, and that is how Mama was left with Carson. However, for Carson, the death of his mama was a great loss and he was deeply grieving.

People mingled around the burial site getting reacquainted and sharing old memories. Children, sensing the funeral had ended, began to run and play games of tag. The men gave out loud shouts to long-time friends. They gathered to catch up, share a taste, and smoke cigarettes, while the women returned to the church to prepare the food for the repast.

Tulip gathered her thin sweater to block out the chill from the weather as she walked quickly to the church. She hoped it wouldn't rain, but it was a cloudy and gloomy day. It made the funeral even sadder. With her little ones in tow, she looked around for her oldest three children. She noticed her daughter…smiling and laughing with a few girls, and her two sons were talking to a group of boys.

Tulip stopped in her tracks, put hands on her hips, and yelled out loudly, "Miss Veronica Barnes! Stop all that lollygagging and get to moving. You know your help is needed."

The twins, hearing their mama's voice, looked toward their sister. Instead of acknowledging her mama, Veronica rolled her eyes at the twins and stuck out her tongue. Tulip, growing impatient, yelled again at her daughter, with much more sternness.

"Don't make me walk over there and get you!" Veronica quickly said goodbye to her friends and made her way to her mama before she died of embarrassment while thinking to herself it was not fair that her brothers, Paul and Henry, got to talk to their friends and never had to do any work.

The small church was bustling with people moving about. Tables and chairs were being moved. Prepared food was set about everywhere.

It was a long-standing tradition to prepare food for the grieving family. It was thought this would relieve their burden of the worry of feeding family and guests who came to pay their respect as well as for the family to have food to eat during their grieving. Many in the small town attended funerals in anticipation of the good food that would be served. It was also well known that many of the women competed for the title of best cook and flourished under the compliments of their cooking.

Tulip handed the children off to her daughter and instructed her to get them something to eat and then join her and the other ladies. Tulip also handed her daughter a sweater because the small church was getting overheated from the people moving about. The aroma of fried chicken, pig's feet, greens, hog maws, corn pudding, yams, chicken livers, butter beans, biscuit, gravy, poor crackling, green beans, cakes, pies, and more filled her nostrils. Tulip's stomach began to grumble. She suddenly realized she hadn't eaten all day, but eating had to wait.

Tulip made her way over to a few of the ladies she recognized and greeted them with a warm smile and a very shy "hello." At the sound of Tulip's voice, the women looked up from their tasks. Beatrice, the oldest of the ladies, walked around and gave Tulip a bear hug. The sweat and smell from Beatrice's wet underarms made Tulip feel dizzy, but she managed to return the hug. The other ladies offered their condolences and gave Tulip forced smiles. Tulip, feeling uncomfortable, thanked the ladies with a nod and quickly asked how she could help. Beatrice told Tulip she should get a cool drink and take a seat, but Tulip wasn't having none of it, she insisted.

After the food was all set out and the church was filled with kinfolks, visitors, and guests, the pastor offered his blessing.

"Oh our merciful God, we come to you on this day to break bread together to honor the homegoing of our dear friend. We ask that you welcome her home with love and grace. Bless this food and drink. Bless the preparers of this food for they gave unselfishly. Oh God, since you redeemed us so dearly and delivered us from evil, as you gave us a share in this food so may you give us a share in eternal life. This food is just mere nourishment for our body, but you God are the food that feeds our soul. Amen."

"Amen," everyone said in unison. The pastor and the Barnes family took their seats to be served. The ladies insisted Tulip sit with Carson and her children and be served. Tulip wanted to help, these were her husband's kin and friends. For some reason, she was never close to any of the other family members, except for Melvin and her sister-in-law Lorraine, who is now her best friend. So, she felt like a guest. Tired and hungry, she took a seat beside Carson and the youngins. She kicked off her shoes under the table and swiped the sweat from her forehead. One of the twins reached for her, so Tulip placed the baby on her lap and waited to be served some of that good food.

Flies swarmed around the food and laid around on the discarded plates. They attacked the food like an angry mob. Some folks swiped at the flies, but most just ignored them as they made homes on their hands and other exposed body parts. The tight room was hot, so many of the guests moved outside. The men needed a drink of liquor. Fast women wanted to flirt with the available or unavailable men. Some women wanted to gossip. The young children were eager to run freely about and took advantage of their family being immersed in conversations and not paying them much attention. The teenage boys also began to sneak out seeking any young girl for a little alone time and maybe even a possible feel. Married secret lovers stole silent looks and made plans for quickies. Faithful servants of the church (*mainly old women or widows*) collected and removed discarded plates and trash. Most of the leftover food was shared and packaged to be sent with the grieving family. However, some of the women did take some food to feed their families the next day. The young women who didn't manage to sneak out helped with washing the dishes, pots, and pans as well as ensuring they were returned to their rightful owners. The elders of the church (all men) put the table and chairs in the proper place for the Sunday church service. In no time, the church was restored to its proper state.

Tulip had to stay with the ladies of the church to help with the cleaning. The boys had run off, of course, but she made Veronica stay to help and keep an eye on her siblings. It had been a very long day; she was physically and emotionally drained. They had to leave home sometime around dawn to arrive on time for the service. Tulip was beyond tired and ready to hit the road and get home to her bed. She was tired of fake smiling, loud talking, cooking, cleaning, and meeting people. Her children were restless and pretty much worn out. Needless to say, she was fit to be tired when Carson told her to have Veronica take the little ones to her Aunt Martha's house because they were all going to Happy Lanes for a little grown-up fun. Out of respect for Mama, the owner had invited them there for free drinks.

Tulip smelled the liquor on Carson's hot breath as he breathed heavily on her neck. She tried with all her might to hold her temper, keeping her back to her husband because she did not want him to see the expression on her face. With her hands balled tightly into fists and through clenched teeth, she spoke calmly.

"We need to gather up the childrins, say our thanks, and get on the road. It's getting dark and we have a long ride back to the city. I don't want us traveling on these roads when it's late and dark. Just not safe for the childrins. I'm just about done in here, so we can leave soon. It's been a long day and I am tired, and I know you must be as well. If we go out drinking, it will be too late to be traveling on those dark roads," she could only imagine what could happen. "Plus, you will be all liquored up and tired."

Carson placed his hands on his wife's shoulders and turned her to face him. He took a good look at her and said, "I understand, but this may be the last time I see my family for a while, and these people took their time to pay respect to Mama, and Mr. Whitney (the White owner of Happy Lanes) done invited us. Just wouldn't be right for us to up and leave. We don't have to leave until tomorrow, which is Sunday." Carson smiled at his wife.

"But Carson," Tulip protested, "I didn't bring extra clothes for the little ones."

Carson quickly quieted her and said, "They will survive."

After getting the kids settled, Carson, Melvin, Lorraine, and Tulip rode up to Happy Lanes. The joint was jumping, in full swing with most of the family and friends from Mean Old Mama's funeral. Big yells came from the crowd when the group walked in, along with kisses, pats, handshakes, and big bear hugs. Drinks were quickly shoved into Carson's and Melvin's hands and a loud cheer exploded from the crowd, both men and women alike. They were quickly ushered away by a group of men, leaving Tulip alone. The music was deafening, but that didn't stop loud laughing and conversations. Everyone was talking at once. A group of people tried to dance around near the Jukebox, which was bellowing out a blues song.

Tulip looked around the darkened room for a place to sit or even hide. Her eyes burned from the thick smoke that had formed about her head. Lorraine yelled in Tulip's direction and motioned for her to come over. Tulip squeezed through the crowd, offering apologies for pushing or stepping on feet. Greedy hands squeezed her butt as she pushed through the sweaty crowd. Maybe it was intentional or maybe it wasn't, but she couldn't even attempt to protest, so she pushed forward. As Tulip scanned the crowd for her husband, she found Carson was nowhere in eyesight. Finally, she caught up to Lorraine, who was now standing on an available chair in front of a small table frantically waving at her with a big smile, a drink in both hands, and a cigarette dangling from her mouth, shaking her big butt. Tulip shook her head and said to herself, *It's going to be a long night.*

"NIGGA, YOU AIN'T S–T!" someone yelled. Another male voice balked back, "Nigga, you ain't worth two cents or my time of day. Looking like yesterday's leftovers."

There was loud laughter and high-fives. Tulip looked around to see where the ruckus was coming from. A couple of men were shoving and pushing each other and cussing up a storm. She had never heard so many MFs or SOBs in her life. Tulip shook her head and thought to herself, *With all the drinking, it's just a matter of time before these no-account heathens go at each other. Colored folks and liquor…so predictable.*

Carson sashayed over to where Tulip was sitting, grinning from ear to ear. "There's my sweet honey pie," he giggled. Tulip looked up at her husband approaching her with that silly, clearly drunken look on his face, grinning like a Cheshire cat. She was so damn annoyed at him. She fully understood Carson should spend time with his family and friends, so this was expected. He just buried his beloved mama and who knows the next time he will see his kinfolks again. What Tulip didn't appreciate was Carson's lack of attention to her since arriving at Happy Lanes. He never checked on her or saw about her well-being, even though she was with family and friends and there was no need, still Tulip was angry. Secretly, she had been watching her husband like a hawk as he paraded around the room, hugging, kissing, and laughing with other folks—especially women, which was not normal for him, as far as she knew. What was really making Tulip angry and very uncomfortable, was there was one woman who seemed to linger on her husband just a little too close and too long for Tulip's comfort. This woman wasn't familiar to Tulip, possibly a distant cousin. Watching her all up on her man was making Tulip heat up. She wanted to ask Lorraine who the woman was but didn't. Knowing her sister-in-law, she would make a scene. When the woman walked across the room to dance and shake her big ass to the music, Tulip got a good long look at her. She was fairly attractive for a redbone, *(almost white)*, with creamy skin and curly hair *(almost like Solo)*, nice toned legs, and big breasts about to jump out of that too-tight dress she was wearing. She wore red lipstick and long dangling earrings. She wasn't bad if you liked that type. Apparently, her husband did.

"Hey there baby girl," Carson yelled a little too loud to Tulip. He did a quick step and spin and held out his hand towards her. "Come here and dance with your husband." He wanted to laugh and dance, but she was mad and didn't want any of his foolishness. So, she didn't look at him and completely ignored him. Carson, feeling good from the liquor and just being plain happy to be with family, didn't realize his wife was feeling a little put-out, it never crossed his mind. Therefore, he reached down and scooped up her, even though she protested fiercely. Carson dragged his wife to the corner where people had gathered to dance and held onto her tightly. Far away from Tulip and Carson, someone was watching them closely, as she slowly sipped her drink. The red-bone woman eyed them with envy. Her fully exposed large breasts rose up and down quickly as she clutched her glass tightly. She thought to herself, *He was mine first. That Black heifer stole my man with all those babies.* She snapped her head around so hard that her hair smacked her face. *Just she wait and see, wait and see.*

Rolling her eyes, she yelled loudly, "Hey, what a lady got to do to get a drink around here?"

Someone in the distance hollered out, "First, be a lady," which brought on a loud roar of laughter.

Hearing the comment, she replied, "Ha ha, very funny."

Tulip, hearing the laughter as well, stared at the red-boned woman, who was staring directly at her. Suddenly, Tulip felt Carson quickly pulling her through the open door, as he got high-fives from several drunk men, heckling, "Don't hurt 'em now," followed by more high-fives and laughter.

"Carson, I can't breathe. You are heavy and your breath is so funky," Tulip protested as she and Carson attempted to get a little piece in the backseat of their car. They had to make a bed in the car because his brother Bobby's house was already crowded with his children and who knew who else. After they had dropped off Melvin and Lorraine to their car, they went inside the house to check on the children. Martha, her sister-in-law, had made pallets on the floor for the children to sleep. Tulip pulled the covers up on the twins who were huddled under their big sister. Little Henry was over in the corner, curled up on the floor, and knocked out. He was such a heavy sleeper. She looked around in the small dark room for her other son, Paul, but he was nowhere in sight, of course. No telling what that boy is up to.

While Carson pounded away on her in the backseat, Tulip let her mind recall the day's events. She couldn't shake the feeling that something was up with him and that redbone. *What did they call her? Tootsie, yeah Tootsie my ass.* She saw her and Carson whispering in the corner before they left Happy Lanes.

"Carson slow down, what's your hurry?" He was always in a hurry when he had sex like his nut wasn't coming fast enough. Tulip really couldn't understand what the fuss or big deal over sex was besides making babies. She found more pleasure with herself than a big hard thing poking up in her privates usually leading to some unwanted pain or Lord forbid, an unwanted infection or baby. Maybe because he was the first, but sex was different with Malcolm for some reason. Tulip let herself drift to the past for a minute, she closed her eyes and began to move in motion with Carson, as she thought about loving Malcolm. Her thoughts were all over the place.

Finally, Carson flopped down on her and let out a slow moan, this brought Tulip back to a sudden reality. She squirmed free from his dead weight and tried her best to sit up. Carson never opened his eyes and proceeded to snore. Tulip shook her head. He hadn't even bothered to pull on his undergarments and pants. Everything just exposed. It was hard to maneuver, but Tulip managed to get his pants up and zipped. She needed to get a little rest before the sun came up. They had a long trip back home.

Tulip gently laid her husband's head in her lap and made herself as comfortable as possible, considering the circumstances. She closed her eyes and listened to the country night sounds…crickets and frogs croaking, and an owl letting out a night call. How different country sounds were from the Big City. So still, so quiet, so gentle. While the city's night sounds were almost the same as day…honking cars, sirens, people yelling and cursing, streetcars, loud music, babies crying…never quiet or still. How she missed the country. It was home. As Tulip drifted off to sleep, the vision of the field of flowers invaded her dreams. The sweet scent of the flowers was almost too real and there was that sweet voice of Mama calling out to her.

The loud bang on the car window made Tulip jump in fright.

"Hey, you two love birds," yelled Melvin as he knocked on the car window. Tulip looked to see him and Lorraine grinning big smiles.

Tulip rolled down the car, "Morning."

Still grinning, Melvin replied, "Good morning to you. I hope you guys didn't sleep in the car all night. He looked at his brother who was still sleeping, holding his "johnson."

"Looks like somebody had a good time."

Tulip shook her husband to wake up. Carson sat up looking confused, trying to get his bearing. "Wipe that silly grin off your face," he said in the direction of his brother.

"Well, good morning to you too dear brother," Melvin said with a hearty laugh. Carson rolled his eyes. He had a terrible, pounding headache, probably from the moonshine.

Melvin continued to laugh. "I'll see you two in the house," he said as he walked off.

Tulip leaned forward to look at herself in the rearview mirror. She patted her hair and wiped at her eyebrows. She needed to wash her face. Maybe a little lipstick would help. So, she reached into the front seat and retrieved her purse, and pulled out her lipstick. Carson, watching her carefully, asked if she had any powdered aspirin packs. He was trying to get himself together. Tulip was prepared, without speaking, she handed her husband a BC.

"Thanks," Carson mumbled and proceeded to open the package and pour the contents on his tongue. As he swallowed, he shook his head as the medication took a quick effect. Tulip stepped out of the car and stretched her arms out wide. The sun immediately attacked her. It was early but already hot. She attempted to smooth the wrinkles out of her dress, but to no avail. Her back and neck ached. Carson stooped behind her and let out a loud yawn. Tulip turned to face him and said, "You need a bath," and walked off. Carson lifted his arms to get a smell. He didn't think he had a smell. "Women," he said to himself as he walked towards the house.

The twins screamed, "Mama," as they ran to greet their mother.

"Hello babies," said Tulip as she patted the top of the twins' little heads. The house was crowded with people moving about and smelled of fried bacon, biscuits, grits, fried potatoes, and more. Tulip's stomach rumbled in anticipation of devouring some of this good food, but she knew if they sat down to eat, they would not be getting on the road until late. Tulip looked around for her oldest daughter who was in the kitchen preparing plates. Tulip looked around to see most of Carson's brothers and their families were there, along with friends and neighbors. Even the pastor was there. It couldn't be any later than 9 AM. *How did everyone get here so early?* If only she had woken up early, maybe she could have convinced Carson to get on the road since they both had to work but it was too late now. She would never be able to convince him to leave his family. Tulip had been to enough country funerals to know it was a several days long affair. The food, drinking, talking about old times, tears, fighting, even standing feuds. Tulip had a change of clothes for herself in the trunk of the car. She needed to freshen up and change her clothes. Seeing Veronica helping with the meal serving, she called out to Little Henry. She told him to get his Papa's car keys and get her brown bag out of the trunk.

After Tulip was cleaned up as best she could *(she had to wash her face, underarms, and private areas with her hands with cold well water)*. She walked into the kitchen where her sister-in-law Martha was still serving up heapings of butter grits, fried fatback, and red-eye gravy. Martha was a redbone with blonde nappy hair. Some said she was White, but because she had been around Colored folks so long, she was Colored. She and Bobby never had kids of their own, but Martha had a couple of good-looking *(half-white)* brothers with good hair who they raised as her children. One thing for sure, she could burn in the kitchen. No one turned down her cooking, especially a free meal. Most of the women helped with preparing the food and serving the men and children. The women would only fix their plates after everyone had eaten and the men and children were out of the way. Together, they would kick off their shoes, sit and chat. Tulip desperately wanted to bring up the question about who this Tootsie was who always lingered on Carson, but she thought better of it.

It was now sunset. Tulip had rounded up all the kids except for Paul. He would find his own way home. Martha had packed up food for them to take to eat on the road. She told them to say thank you and share goodbyes, then get right in the car while she fetched their Papa. Tulip knew she had to tear Carson away from his brothers. Finally, after many hugs, tears, last drink, high-fives, and empty promises, they were ready to hit the road. They blew their horns, and the car wheels kicked up dust from the dirt as they sped away. A few dogs barked and chased after the car. Tulip sat back to enjoy the ride. No more than a few miles down the road, they heard the honking of a horn and saw a pickup truck's lights flashing. Thinking something was wrong with the car, everyone turned to look to see who was making such a commotion. Carson pulled the car off the road. The pick-up truck stopped as well. Carson told Tulip and the children to stay in the car so he could see what was going on. Of course, curiosity as well as frustration was killing Tulip. Hopefully, this was not another relative or friend who wanted to talk. Tulip watched in the mirror as Carson approached the man standing outside the old dusty pick-up. She recognized him. It was their old postal delivery man, Mr. Jake. She had heard his wife was sickly so he wasn't able to attend Mean Old Mama's funeral. He probably just wanted to pay his respect to Carson.

Tulip watched as Carson and Mr. Jake greeted each other with a formal handshake. Mr. Jake was holding a paper in one hand. While Tulip appreciated the respect, she hoped this would not be a long conversation.

The twins asked, "Mama, who Papa talking to?"

Tulip responded, "Hush now and stay out of grown folks' business. But, if you must know, that is Mr. Jake. You might be too young to remember, but when we lived here, he delivered our mail."

"Mama, can we live her again?" asked one of the twins.

Before she could answer, Veronica said, "Don't be so stupid. You know we can't live here."

"Why not?" one of the twins countered.

"Because we just can't, that's why. Now just hush as Mama told you before you get hit!"

Tulip was still watching Carson and Mr. Jake talking. She was tempted to call out to Carson and tell him they needed to get moving, but that would have been rude. She watched as Mr. Jake handed Carson the paper he had been holding. Carson patted him on the arm, shook his hand again, and turned towards the car.

Tulip smiled and said, "Well that wasn't too long and now we can be on our way."

Carson got in the car grinning like a Cheshire cat. Tulip looked at him and wondered why he was so happy after talking with Mr. Jake.

"What did he say to make you so happy?" Tulip continued to stare directly at her husband waiting for a response.

Carson still smiling replied, "Oh, I don't know, just happy, I guess. Always, good to see old friends." In unison, the twins yelled loudly, "Yay, Papa be happy!"

Tulip said, "Okay, enough with the happiness. Let's get moving."

Carson said jokingly, "Are you rushing me lady, my beautiful ebony queen, the mother of my brown princess and princes, the keeper of my place of love?"

Now Tulip was getting irritated, she didn't feel like playing his silly games. She wondered, *Why he so happy today after just burying his mama? Probably because of that no-account wrench who kept hanging around him.* Tulip folded both her arms in front of her and stared straight ahead.

Really enjoying this game, Carson looked at his wife and said, "Oh, are we mad now? Well then, I guess I will keep this here letter to myself. What do you think, my children? Should I keep it or give it to your mama?"

Veronica was getting irritated herself. She was tired and just wanted to enjoy the long ride home, sleeping with no yelling children. But that was not about to happen. The twins began to yell in unison laughing, "Keep it, Papa, keep it!" They loved playing the game to make Mama mad at Papa. Veronica yelled at the twins to cut the noise and rolled her eyes. All this just made Carson crack up. He could barely focus on the road because he was laughing so hard, maybe just a little too hard given the situation.

Tulip abruptly turned to face her husband; her heart began fast palpitations. With wide eyes, Tulip turned to look at her husband, blocking her children's chatter, and asked in a low tone, "Did Mr. Jake give you a letter for me? Was it from New York City?"

Carson looked at his lovely wife. While he wanted to tease her more, seeing the tears moist in her eyes, he could no longer hold back. He slowly handed her the letter. Tulip's hands trembled, as one tear slowly passed from her eye, down her burning cheek like a slowing-moving stream.

What's in a "homegoing," a passage from one life to another,
so you think;
Looking above to the heavens and
praying it is really there;
Looking down to hell knowing it is truly from the life you
lived that you fear;
Every minute of life is a new beginning;
but not knowing what's waiting
on the other side is a reality
that is not real because you are dead;
We live in this flesh until our spirit is really for another
journey or is called home, so they say;
Taking every breath for granted, living for the minute, not
knowing if this is the final destiny of your state of being;
So spread your wings, soar high above the sky, you are home,
there is no going.

TWENTY-EIGHT
Vulnerability

Rushing of quick feet, the low voice talking rapidly. "HOW COULD THIS BE POSSIBLE?" the heavy-set, Colored nurse yelled in the direction of several other nurses and a couple of attendants. With their eyes downcast, no one said a word. The heavy-set Colored nurse's was named Nurse Viola. She was the overseer of the nurses and attendants for New York's State Hospital for the Mentally Retarded and Criminally Insane, specifically, Ward C, which housed the mentally insane female patients who were mostly non-verbal, violent, and suffered from various medical conditions.

Nurse Viola had been assigned to Ward C for over twenty years. While she was a heavy-set woman, she was tall and stood over six feet. She was strict, no-nonsense, and ran a tight ship. Nurse Viola was held in high regard by both doctors and nurses alike. But the patients feared her. She was known to dish out harsh punishment for those who failed to obey the rules and refused to eat or take their meds.

The patients in Ward C were housed in an open room, with no windows, and neatly lined up with wooden cots or old metal gurneys that had been discarded from other hospitals. It was brightly lit during the day but pitch black at night except for the light radiating from the nurse's station, which was a wired cage at the entrance of the room before the locked prison iron bars that lead into the patient's room. There was only one way in and one way out. All staff carried heavy keys to unlock the main gate that led into the patient's room. The floor was white linoleum that was always cold—summer, winter, fall, and spring.

But always very clean and shiny. There was no privacy. Ward C had over 100 female patients, varying in age from sixteen to ninety-four years of age. They had been placed in Ward C because of their severe mental conditions and psychosis, which made them good candidates for experimental drugs and procedures. Most of these patients were destitute and did not have any family to speak of. The ones who had no contact with their families had their rights freely signed away, which relieved the family of any financial obligations. Meals were served in another large room which was also the makeshift playroom. Patients were hosed down with water for bathing. Most patients used their bathing time to relieve themselves of body contents, which would quickly go down the drain into the public sewer system. All patients wore the same hard, makeshift gray shift dress, with no undergarments. Menstrual bleeding was controlled with buckled-on rags, which many of the alert patients would constantly strip off and discard on the white, shiny, clean linoleum floor. Patients were drugged, fed, and experimented on. Most patients never found their way back to their families or even society.

So, now here Nurse Viola was having to deal with this unfortunate situation. This wasn't the first time a patient was discovered to be with child, but rarely was it discovered during delivery. To prevent these situations, she had implored the Hospital Board to allow them to sterilize these patients, but the Hospital Board refused. She took no pleasure in killing babies, she was a devout Catholic. Hence, in most cases, sterilization could only be performed on the most critical patients.

Nurse Viola was no fool. She knew orderlies and even some doctors took advantage of these patients. It was not the patients' fault—it was rape. Nurse Viola knew if these men could seek comfort in streetwalkers and whores, they would settle for an unfortunate, vulnerable mental patient. They were as good as any prostitute. Plus they were free and always willing to do anything being asked of them, probably for a mere piece of candy or just something sweet. Nurse Viola was sure most of these low-life men preferred the comatose patients or if they were young and not bad looking, like this one…Jane Doe, even with her burns. To these men, pussy was pussy.

Nurse Viola walked quickly down to the examination room where Jane Doe was being held for her examination. Her head ached with tension. These types of situations always frustrated her because it was her patients who always suffered in the end. Notwithstanding the unfortunate children brought into this world who never knew their true family, let alone how they came to be. Nurse Viola recalled Jane Doe arriving from City #4 mental ward about two years ago because of her mental decline after being severely burned in a fire. From what she recalled, she was committed because she had gone completely insane as a result of the trauma bought on by her medical condition. She mostly stayed sedated because of extreme outbursts and constant violent behavior toward staff and other patients. Most times she was non-verbal, except when she had her loud outbursts and screams. She couldn't hold a conversation and would only grunt when responding to questions. Her burns had left her so disfigured to the point she looked like a monster, which was very sad because it was very clear that at one time, she was a beautiful young lady. She never had any visitors, occasionally an inquiry would be received from one of the doctors at City #4 basically about her progress, which was very compassionate. However, the reply was always the same…no change. As far as Nurse Viola was concerned, Jane Doe would live out her days at City, like many of her other unfortunate patients.

As Nurse Viola approached the patient examination where Jane Doe had been taken, she heard loud screaming, which was not unusual. Nurse Viola finally reached the examination room and pushed open the heavy metal double doors. There were two male orderlies and two female nurses on each side of Jane Doe, who were forcibly trying to restrain her while she thrust about and directed profound obscenities at them. Nurse Viola could see Jane Doe was in full labor. Not what she expected. She asked out loud for an update. One of the nurses, a very young one, quickly responded, "The patient is about eight centimeters, and the baby's heartbeat was rapid."

Nurse Viola asked, "As best you can tell, is this a premature or full-term pregnancy?"

The nurse spoke up nervously," She is full-term, and it appears to be a multi-birth. It is not her first."

Nurse Viola paused for a moment. "Did you say, twins?"

The young nurse who was not making eye contact nodded her head up and down. Nurse Viola took this as a yes and said, "S—t!" as she watched Jane Doe.

Nurse Viola asked the young nurse, "Did I also hear you say it appears this patient has possibly delivered before?"

The young nurse pulled back the blanket from Jane Doe and pointed to a long raggedy scar across her lower abdomen. A Cesarean scar. Nurse Viola walked over to were Jane Doe lay outstretched on the gurney to get a better look at where the young nurse was pointing. It was possible the scarring was from the burns, but it was clear this was not her first child. Nurse Viola asked for her file. She needed to review this patient's history to see if there was any mention of prior surgeries. All the notes made were related to the painful procedures Jane Doe had undergone as a result of her severe burns and mental condition. She stared hard at Jane Doe, whose agony was escalating rapidly. It was clear she was at the peak of delivery. Nurse Viola gently placed her hand on the lower part of Jane Doe's uterus and pushed down and could feel the contractions. She placed a cold stethoscope on her stomach to listen to the baby or babies' heartbeat. This caused Jane Doe to raise her head, yell, and spit out obscenities at Nurse Viola. The veins in her head and neck protruded as if they were going to pop at any minute. Nurse Viola recognized this patient was in crisis, and she didn't like being touched. Solo began kicking her legs, waving her arms wildly. Nurse Viola was sure she would pull out the IV. She ordered Solo to be retrained.

Nurse Viola asked, "When was the last time Jane Doe had any medication?"

The young nurse spoke up softly and tried to explain to Nurse Viola that after becoming aware of Jane Doe's condition, the medical staff was advised to cease all medications until her condition could be confirmed. Best she could estimate, it had been more than the last three weeks since Jane Doe had been medicated because once her condition was confirmed, she went into labor. Now Nurse Viola understood what she was dealing with, a severely mentally ill patient, absent of much needed psychic meds, going into withdrawals and labor...what a mess. She shook her head and took a deep breath.

Once Nurse Viola placed the cold stethoscope on Jane Doe's stomach, she heard one strong heartbeat. She moved the stethoscope slowly, and there it was, a faint sign of another heartbeat. She smiled and said out loud, "Twins it is." She bent over Jane Doe closer to check her heartbeat. While cold and wild, she looked into the most beautiful eyes, which were staring back at her with pure fear and hate. Despite the burns, which had consumed and disfigured eighty percent of the patient's body from head to toe, her beauty still stood out. No wonder some low life saw fit to help himself to the merchandise. *Who could it be?* Most likely one of the night attendants. Nurse Viola had her suspicions, but how could she prove it? In all honesty, no one would really care. It was not the first time this situation had happened and unfortunately, it would not be the last.

"We need to get moving quickly. Give Jane Doe 50ccs of Bertine and move her to the procedure room and call St. Ann's Children's

Home to see if they can accept two babies. Please explain they must come ASAP and discuss this matter with no one. Let's move it, folks, we got work to do. This is very serious and if this gets out to the public, we could all be sued and fired. So let each of you be warned, KEEP YOUR DAMN MOUTHS SHUT!"

> *Freely exploring the parts of my body*
> *that are most private only to me;*
> *How dare you touch there and say that it's ok;*
> *Should I protest or just let it be; what can I do, when I am*
> *powerless; you say that is what I wanted you to do;*
> *I cannot breathe, the fear and pain is overwhelming;*
> *Not fully understanding what is happening, but knowing*
> *that something about this just is not right;*
> *Upon release, you toss me aside this a used dirty rag; I feel*
> *humiliated and damaged;*
> *So onward I go, hiding the violation like it was a secret that*
> *I must never expose;*
> *It is a burden, I must now carry, how do I form the words to*
> *say something so outside of God's plan;*
> *While my inside is yelling out, please somebody help,*
> *my lips smile, so I hide;*
> *You come again and again; when will this end;*
> *So day by day, I go on my merry way, pushing the violation*
> *way down inside, and living my life in disguise.*

TWENTY-NINE
Once Again

Solo felt foggy as if she was floating outside of her body. She couldn't move. Again, she had no concept of where she was. Her mouth was dry and her limbs were restrained.

An obese woman was staring at her. She had large, black moles covering her entire face; the whites of her eyes were yellow, like some type of beast. Her big, purple cracked lips drooped with a trickle of saliva hanging loosely. Not a speck of hair covered her head. Instead, in the place of hair was only a multitude of knots and abrasions. Unbeknownst to Solo, this unsightly creature always watched her, night and day. She feared Solo. In her mind, Solo was a demon sent there to attack her. She feared this grotesque monster that constantly fought her caretakers. She had witnessed firsthand Solo's sudden outbursts and rages that would send the other patients running in fear. Because her cot was positioned directly in front of Solo, she had a birds-eye view of this creature. They called the monster Jane Doe. Even though the woman knew better, she was "Lucifer." She knew the day would come when Lucifer would come for her, and that day had arrived. The woman sat on her cot and watched Solo as she looked around and raised her head up. They made eye contact. The woman pulled her blanket up to her face and yelled out as loud as she could, "THE MONSTER IS ALIVE! IT'S ALIVE, LUCIFER IS HERE!"

The room busted into sheer madness. Solo was startled as well as fearful of this woman's sudden outburst. The woman, who was obviously crazy, continued to scream about some monster and somebody named Lucifer. Now others joined in yelling and screaming. Solo closed her eyes and lay back on her cot.

"WHY ARE YOU POINTING AT ME?" Solo screamed out loud. "STOP POINTING AT ME, YOU UGLY B—H!"

The woman got louder with her screams, as she continued to point at Solo.

"STOP IT! I SEE YOU, UGLY HEIFER! STOP POINTING AT ME! WHEN I GET LOOSE, I AM GOING TO WHIP YOUR BLACK ASS!"

Because of the cruel onslaught, Solo was exhausted. So, she laid back on the cot and closed her eyes. She shook her head from side to side and thrashed about kicking her legs and flinging her arms in an attempt to block out the nasty names being directed her way. Solo questioned, *Am I the monster? Why are they being mean to me? I am not a monster, I am beautiful. Somebody, make them stop, please stop!*

Hearing all the ruckus and the obscenities being directed at Solo, several nurses made their way to the patients and attempted to calm them down and distract them from Solo. At the same time, the heavy-set Colored nurse, Viola, saw Solo in distress. She quickly grabbed her push cart which contained a water pitcher, cups, cloths, bandages, as well as medication.

Reaching Solo's bed, she saw her glistening with sweat, so she quickly lifted the pitcher from her cart and poured a cup. She spoke to Solo in a very soothing voice.

"Hey there, you must be thirsty. Now I will give you a cup of nice cool water, but you first got to calm down." Nurse Viola placed her hand on Solo's forehead and stroked it very softly. Solo began to relax. Nurse Viola lifted Solo's head and said, "Okay, now drink this slowly. Take slow sips."

Solo opened her eyes and gulped the water down quickly. The room had gone quiet, no screaming or yelling. Solo tried to raise to see that ugly bitch who kept pointing at her.

"No! No!" the young nurse said. "You must lay back and take your time. If not, you will choke. Now let's try it again, slowly you go."

As if she was talking to a child, Nurse Viola said, "My name is Nurse Viola and I am here to take care of you. Now let's drink a little more. Good job, Jane. You drank all of your water!" Solo thought to herself, *Who in God's name is Jane?* Yet, she didn't mumble a word, she wanted the water.

"Okay, that's enough for now," said Nurse Viola as she placed the cup on the metal tray. She reached for Solo's hand and began to speak. "You gave us quite a scare. How are you feeling? Are you hungry?"

Solo did not respond, she just looked at the young nurse.

"Okay, you don't have to answer right now. But when you are ready, I'll be here to help you," said Nurse Viola. "Do you understand?"

Solo nodded.

Nurse Viola continued, "Good, we are making progress. Would you like to sit up or move around a bit? You have been in bed for a while."

Once again Solo nodded her head, obviously not ready to let words come from her mouth. Never taking her eyes off Solo and smiling, Nurse Viola raised her hands and made some type of jester or signal. She sat still for a few moments as if she was waiting for something or someone. Solo did not know what to do, so she just laid very still. Suddenly at the foot of her cot stood two burley, unassuming Colored men. Solo felt afraid and cowed at their presence. Nurse Viola, sensing her distress, quickly spoke up.

"No, it is no reason to be afraid. We are all here to help you. You must trust me, no one is going to hurt you. Now, if you want these restraints off so you get up and walk around, then I will need your full cooperation and these two nice gentlemen are here to help make that happen. Ain't that right gentlemen?"

The two men nodded in agreement as they stared down at Solo

with cold unblinking eyes. Solo stared back at them. "Okay, so we all aboard," cheerfully said the nurse. "Is that right Jane?"

Solo wanted to scream at her, *my name is not Jane, stop calling me got damn Jane.* Yet she knew that wouldn't help so she just nodded in agreement. Nurse Viola took off the hand restraints, while the two men took off the ones attached to her feet. She reached behind Solo's back to raise her into a sitting position. Solo felt lightheaded and woozy. She wanted to throw up, but she forced it down. She looked to see if she saw that ugly woman that was pointing at her and calling her a monster. But the cot was empty. It must have been a dream. Nurse Viola, breaking Solo's thoughts said, "Now you are going to feel a little lightheaded because you have been out for a while, so we are going to take it slow." Solo nodded.

Nurse Viola reached down and lowered the bars on Solo's cot. The two men walked up closer to Solo as Nurse Viola raised Solo from the bed. She felt like dead weight. While holding onto Solo's back, Nurse Viola motioned for the two orderlies to help support Solo's legs and feet off the cot. Solo frowned when the men pulled back the covers and flinched at the sight of her disfigured body. While they had seen worse, it took them by surprise. The orderlies proceeded to undo the restraints and carefully lift her legs from the cot to the cold, white linoleum floor. Both the orderlies' hands on her body and the cold floor made chills run through her body, and she shuddered. Sensing her fear, Nurse Viola assured her she was safe and no one was going to harm her.

With the assistance of the orderlies, together they lifted Solo off the cot and attempted to stand her up straight. One of the orderlies was holding firm onto Solo's ass. She wanted to protest, but the words couldn't reach her tongue. Her legs buckled and she was lightheaded. Her skin itched and was burning. Solo wanted to lay back down. Her mouth was dry. She couldn't do this. Her heart was pounding, she was on the verge of screaming. She slumped, but the two orderlies pushed her up straight, while the young nurse continued to coach her.

"Okay, just take your time Jane, no rush. You have not walked in a while, so you will feel a little out of practice, but we got all day."

Solo thought to herself, *what in the hell is this Jane s—t?!*

As Solo struggled to walk from her cot, she noticed eyes on her. Once again, there was screaming and yelling. Shouts rang out from Nurse Viola, the orderlies, and other nurses for them to quiet down. Some cooperated and huddled in place, using their arms to cover their faces. Others sat down on the floor while some ran and jumped on their cots covering themselves. Others continued to make muffling sounds. Solo tried to ignore the irritating chaos as she made attempts to walk. She thought to herself, *If these are sick people, why are they acting like animals?* As she began to move, she felt a sense of heavy pressure, as if something was weighing her down. Her bladder released spontaneously. A warm strong odor of yellow pee ran down her thighs. She didn't have on any undergarments. Nurse Viola, taking in the situation which happens often, waved for someone to clean up the mess. She didn't want the patients playing in it or even trying to drink it. Trying to still focus on her movements, Solo didn't have time to be embarrassed about wetting herself. She just needed to move her limbs which seemed so damn hard to do. Slowly Nurse Viola and the two orderlies walked Solo up to the entrance of a very wide and tall gate that had a massive iron lock. Solo noticed Nurse Viola pull out a ring of heavy keys and unlock the gate. It made a loud clicking noise that cause some of the patients to rush forward, but the young nurse closed it quickly using her massive key to lock it back.

Solo was confused. While she had never been in a hospital, it still seemed strange there would be gates, bars, locks, and keys. Once outside the gate, Solo looked to her right where there was another large room with several women who appeared to be nurses. They all had on outfits like Nurse Viola. As Solo looked, one rather tall, big-busted

Colored nurse with a smirk on her face and her hands on her hips said very sarcastically, "Well look who is up and about."

Another rather thin, petite nurse, smiled and said, "Good to see you up and about, Ms. Jane." While shaking her head, another nurse chimed in and said, "Oh my goodness, here comes trouble."

Solo quickly turned her head to look in the direction of this nurse and stared directly at her in the most hateful way she could summon. The nurse quickly lowered her eyes. Solo thought to herself, *Was she referring to me?*

Slowly, Nurse Viola, Solo, and the two burley orderlies proceeded into the long corridor where the lights were even brighter and more people were moving about. No one even looked at Solo and she was relieved. Solo felt her legs getting stronger and didn't seem to need much support. She felt heavy as if her body was carrying weights. She took slow baby steps. She raised her head and began to look around, trying to take in her surroundings and make sense of things. Looking at the people or patients moving about, she didn't think they appeared sick or injured. Instead, these people looked lost and even simple-minded—talking to themselves, pulling their hair, walking in circles, and laughing out loud. She recalled seeing people like them wandering around all hours of the day and night in her neighborhood. They were pitiful souls and sometimes very scary. What type of hospital is this? While it was foggy, she knew she had suffered great harm. Bits and bits flooded her mind. She had been burned, but how…when? Like a light bulb went off in her head or reality became clear. Solo stopped in her tracks. She was frozen in place. She saw Nurse Viola's mouth moving, but no words reached her ears. Her ears were ringing. She snatched her body away from the two orderlies. She looked at her arms, and to her disgust, they were scarred and ugly. She ran her hands across her face. One side felt soft and smooth, but the other side felt raggedy, rough. Tears formed in her eyes. She reached up and let her hand stroke her head; there was no hair. *Where is my hair? My beautiful hair. I am one of these people. I am in a crazy house.*

The full realization was clear as day, but she needed to maintain some control. The pounding of her heart was deafening. She tried to scream, but no sound came out of her mouth. She wanted to run, but her body would not move. Her body went limp. Nurse Viola, realizing Solo was becoming panicked, said gently, "Okay Jane, you had a long day. Let's get you back to your bed for some rest. I know this is very confusing. So, let's get you settled, and I will send for the doctor to try to explain things. Is that fine with you?"

Solo nodded in agreement. She just wanted to lie down. Was this a nightmare? She needed to think. How long has she been here? Why did they put her here? She continued to scream out loud, "WHERE THE F—K IS JESSIE? I DON'T BELONG HERE! I AM NOT CRAZY, PLEASE GET JESSIE, SOMEBODY GET JESSIE."

No one answered her. Solo was getting dizzy. Her final thought before she fainted was, *Where is Jessie?* Nurse Viola instructed the orderlies to take the patient back to her room while she fetched the doctor. Nurse Viola watched as the orderlies slowly guided Solo back to her room. Her heart ached for this poor unfortunate girl. The things she heard had happened to her were just cruel and unimaginable. The rape, shock treatments, various medical procedures, and months of being sedated with heavy drugs. Not that she could validate it, but there were whispers among staff that Jane Doe had delivered two babies, twins, as a result of being sexually attacked. Her being in the mother way was not discovered until she was ready to deliver. Poor Jane Doe wasn't even aware she was an expectant mother. To make matters worse, this unfortunate creature had to bear this all alone without the support of family and any knowledge of how this came to be. If true, this is very sad. The thought of one of her patients being so horribly violated was just terrible. Nurse Viola shook her head as she walked, tears forming in her eyes. This girl couldn't be no older than herself.

Even with her disfiguration, the nurse found Jane Doe to be very attractive. She thought to herself, maybe it was Jane Doe's whiteness of her skin or delicate features that made her stand out from the other Colored women patients. Sometimes when she was heavily sedated, she looked like an angel. But when awake, her behavior was wild like an animal. Rightfully so, she was labeled a freak. Where did she come from? How did she get so severely burned? Nurse Viola feared that if she didn't get better and leave this place, she would perish here.

"Where is her family? Poor girl, she is now a ward of the state. Fully believing God is merciful, and maybe just by faith, someone is looking for her but doesn't know where or how to find her. Maybe there is hope for her. There is always hope, and I can help her. I will help her!" Nurse Viola's steps picked up some pep and a smile came on her face.

There once was a little girl who everyone said was cute;
The little girl thought she was cute too, but to her dismay,
love didn't come her way;
So the little girl thought, "I have to find a way." But to her
dismay, for love, you must pay;
So she smiled, flirted, and freely gave herself away;
Love came the little girl's way, but it was a game she
continually played. If not, the love would stray;
When the baby came, the little girl thought she finally had
the love she prayed for but soon discovered, a baby's love was
only child's play;
So the little girl went back to her game of giving her body
away to promises of love that would stay;
The little girl is no longer cute.

THIRTY
Coming to Terms

Doctor Hertz nodded and gently touched the patients who reached out to him. Some followed behind him, talking rapidly to themselves. He greeted several of the nurses he passed. He hadn't had a chance to look at the file of the patient he was going to visit. To avoid distractions from other patients, he preferred to meet with patients in his office, but he was informed this was a very sensitive case, and the patient was incapacitated.

Since arriving in Ward C, the patient, Jane Doe, had been assigned to several doctors and was assigned to him a few months back. The only background information on Jane Doe was regarding the various treatments and surgeries for her severe burns and transfer to the State Hospital for the Mentally Retarded and Criminally Insane. No family, no name, no address, no inquiries, nothing. Since arriving in Ward C, her file contained complete notes from various doctors, which detailed their assessment of her condition including performed medical procedures, prescribed medicine, diagnosis, etc. The conclusion seemed to be that Jane Doe's case was hopeless, and she should be committed for life. Doctor Hertz strongly believed proper care, support, professional therapy, and medication could lead to a normal life outside of the confinement of a mental institution. He was known for his compassion for patients, and since arriving at the hospital a little less than three years ago, has successfully rehabilitated and released about twenty patients. He took on the most hopeless cases. He had not had an opportunity to fully assess Jane Doe because when she wasn't in a comatose state. She would become so hysterical or agitated and had to be kept heavily sedated for the safety of staff, patients, and herself. She had fought with staff and other patients—cussed, screamed, and displayed what could be labeled as animistic behavior. Doctor Hertz wanted to determine if she was mentally ill before she was burned or was the mental illness a result of the trauma. As he pondered that question, he stopped to fill his pipe with tobacco, took a few puffs, and waved at the nurse to unlock the gate.

Doctor Hertz was glad it was activity time, so most of the patients were not in the room. As expected, the few remaining patients ran to him for his attention. Not giving the patients any attention and with the assistance of the nurses, they quickly lost interest in him and moved away. Doctor Hertz asked one of the nurses if she could direct him to Jane Doe. The nurse shooed the patients away and began to walk swiftly. As she walked, she began to inform Doctor Hertz that the patient may not be lucid because of the effect of the drugs. The nurse went on to say in the last few weeks, the patient has been much calmer, making eye contact and even responding to verbal commands. However, because of her past behavior, it was deemed necessary to keep her sedated and confined to her bed. Doctor Hertz listened very carefully and did not respond. The nurse stopped, leaned over Solo's cot, and touched her shoulder. Solo jumped at the sudden touch. She did not like being touched, especially in the dark when the touching hurt her, and she couldn't breathe.

"Jane, you have a visitor today, this here is Doctor..." but before she could finish, Doctor Hertz touched her arm very gently and said, "Thank you, but I have it from here." The nurse looked at Doctor Hertz for a moment, and said "I will be in the booth. Just press the button if you need any assistance." She walked away and took a quick look back at Doctor Hertz who was just standing there staring down at Jane Doe. The nurse thought to herself... *How odd!*

Doctor Hertz took a long draw on his pipe, but the fire had died out. Still, he chewed on the end of the pipe as he took a visual study on his patient. He thought to himself, *She looks so innocent, a mere child.* No age could be confirmed. If he had to guess, maybe late teens or early twenties. One of those mixed bloods. Why do they insist on shaving off these women's hair? He shook his head in detest. *So degrading. No wonder they act like animals.* As he looked at Solo, he flipped through the papers of her file. *Very interesting*, he thought. The burns were about 80% on the left side of her body. The right side of her body only received superficial burns. Well, that explained why the side of Solo's face and arm that was exposed to him showed no signs she had been burned in the tragedy.

Solo lay very still. She could smell the scent of tobacco smoke. She knew someone was standing there. *Why don't they say something? Who could it be?* Her hands drew into tight balls. She willed herself not to move. Maybe it was one of those nurses who was always bothering her. *Why don't they just leave me alone? They don't even know my name, and I am not telling them nothing. I will not talk to no one. I just want to sleep.* Her legs began to cramp, and she needed to move but she was scared that whoever or whatever was hovering over her would notice. She began to sweat, it was getting hot. She needed water. Slowly, she opened her eyes, but she didn't turn to see who was watching her. Maybe she could peek and see who it was without moving, but no such luck. She knew what would come next. A hard shot in her leg leaving her motionless and speechless. She was so vulnerable. *No, I need to get some control if I am going to find out where I am and how to get the f—k out of this nightmare.* So, with all her might, she flipped over to her other side and coldly stared at the person in front of her.

Doctor Hertz had been watching Solo the entire time. He knew eventually her curiosity would get the best of her. It always happened, no surprise there. Doctor Hertz had learned a long time ago in his practice it was best to let patients who had demonstrated aggressive and uncontrolled behavior make the first move. It was about territory, and most of these types of patients don't like anyone intruding into their space. It becomes necessary to keep these types of patients sedated to render the most basic care without the fear of being hurt. As a result, these patients could not receive the rehabilitation needed to improve their mental health.

For a moment, Solo and Doctor Hertz stared at each other. Solo's one good eye locked onto this person. Doctor Hertz noted the thick scarring ricocheting down the patient's face. Her left eye drooped and was partially closed with no eyebrow. Her ear lobe was completely gone. In place was a hole. With no hair to hide her head, the blisters oozed cloudy pus. There were plenty of old sores along the side of her bald head. She did look like a monster. But his work had proven that monsters were not born, they are created. The challenge was to help the patient get free from the demons and live the best life possible. He didn't believe in the word "normal."

Doctor Hertz let a few more minutes pass. *Okay, this is a stubborn one.* He moved closer to Solo and said, "Hello." No response. "My name is Doctor Jermaine Hertz, but I prefer the short version either Doctor Hertz or just plain old Doctor. Do you mind if I light my pipe? I have been chewing on it for a while and I really need a smoke. I know what you are thinking, bad habit. I know, but it's my only vice. Trust me, everybody needs at least one vice. Do you smoke a pipe?"

Solo couldn't believe what he just asked her. She wanted to laugh. *Do I smoke a pipe? I don't know, maybe I do. Why did he ask me that? I don't know, I tell you, I don't know. Go away,* she wanted to scream at him. *No, stay, he sounds nice.*

Doctor Hertz interrupted her thoughts and said rather cheerfully, "Okay, I will take that as a yes." He lit and puffed on the pipe. The smoke swarmed the high ceiling in little circles. The smell of smoke evoked something deep down in Solo. Memories came rushing like an ocean raising high waves crashing into the sand. She thought to herself, *I know that smell.* She sniffed at the smell. She rose and sniffed like a dog trying to catch a scent. Doctor Hertz chuckled to himself. It always worked. Before Solo knew it, she was sitting still with her eyes open taking in the sweet smell of the pipe smoke. It relaxed her. It smells like a friend. Doctor Hertz was watching her every move. Now fully exposed, she looked like beauty and the beast.

The nurse watched Doctor Hertz and Solo very carefully. She wasn't taking any chances and had the two orderlies standing nearby just in case their services were needed. When Solo raised up, the nurse made a move closer. Doctor Hertz did not want to have this moment with his patient interrupted, so he put his hand behind her and waved for her and the two goons to stand down. He continued to blow the pipe smoke in the air. With her unscarred hand, she reached for the smoke like a little child reaching for the sky.

"Do you like the smoke?"

She responded with her good eye growing wide.

Doctor Hertz took that as a "yes." They were communicating. *Progress.*

"Jane?" No response. "Jane." Doctor Hertz repeated. He made a quick note in the file, "Her name?"

For a moment Solo didn't feel scared anymore. No eyes were on her. This man, this doctor, *What was his name? He said his name.* She thought hard, but her mind was confused and her thoughts were disjointed. She couldn't remember. He seemed kind. Solo wanted to talk to him, but she couldn't find her voice. Her mouth was dry, the words would not reach her tongue. Yet, her eyes said everything. They darted rapidly around the room, then back to the Doctor, then around the room again. Solo clasped her hands tightly around the thin cover on her bed. Doctor Hertz, who was closely observing her, recognized she was struggling and might go into a panic attack. He didn't want her heavily mediated, so decided it was enough for today and would schedule a follow-up session tomorrow in his office. He will instruct the nurses not to give this patient any heavy sedatives no matter what, only a mild sedative to be administered. He needed her mind at least half clear. As so many questions ran through his head, Doctor Hertz continued to stare at Solo and said very calmly, "It was nice meeting you, lovely lady, and if it is okay with you, I would like to talk again. Maybe tomorrow? Maybe I will smoke again and you can smell my smoke?" Doctor Hertz chuckled.

Did he just say lovely lady? No, no, I am a monster. But he said lovely lady, I heard him. She drew her legs up to her chest and did not respond. Doctor Hertz looked at her, smiled, turned, and walked away. Solo didn't know why but she wanted to beg him to take her with him, but she closed her eyes.

Doctor Hertz instructed the nurse to give Jane Doe or whatever her name was a good bath, because she smelled something terrible, and for God's sake, give her a new gown without any holes. It looked like she was wearing rags. "Also," he stated emphatically, with his index finger pointing and shaking directly at the nurse, "Tonight, and in the morning only give her a mild sedative that I have written in her file. I reviewed her file and the level of drugs that have been pumping into her would drive anybody out of their mind or make them a complete vegetable. No wonder she acts like a wild animal." He said very sharply. "Under no circumstances do I want her drugged. Have her brought to my office tomorrow by 10:00 AM sharp."

He then turned and started to walk off, but stopped and said, "One more thing. Please treat those open sores on the patient's head and I am sure she has bed sores all over her body as well." He puffed his pipe and asked that the gate be opened.

The nurse took down Doctor Hertz's instructions and nodded. She looked down at Jane Doe who was now balled up in a knot. Even now, unmedicated, she had never seen Jane Doe this calm except for when she was sedated. But with the other patients now returning, she wasn't taking any chances. Jane Doe was overdue for her meds, and they had to be administered before her dinner. If not, her food would become a weapon and she would have to be force-fed. However, she would try to follow Doctor Hertz's instructions. She hoped his method worked.

Solo was still huddled in a fetal position when the noisy patients stumbled into the room with their loud laughing, singing, crying, and non-stop chatter. But for some reason, Solo didn't focus on them. Quite frankly, she didn't care, her mind was elsewhere. The scent of the Doctor's sweet smoke still lingered above her head. It made her think of another time. She felt calm. Her mind was getting quick snapshots. Her lingering thought was *He called me lovely. I am Solo. My name is Solo. My name is Solo,* she repeated over and over until she drifted off into a nightmarish sleep of smoke and fire.

> *Dreams don't lie; they are the reflection of your very inner thoughts and living life in your soul;*
> *The past intertwined with the present, which leaves you sweating or shaking from the cold;*
> *Disjointed figures and flashes of people distant and far, different times, no longer young or old;*
> *Time passes as flashes of light, colors shine like a burst of daylight taking on sudden scenes of a life not yet told;*
> *Calling out names, touching hands, traveling through time, being something new and different, not shy or bold;*
> *The simple truth is a dream in a reality that will never truly take hold.*

THIRTY-ONE

A Breakthrough, My name is "Solo"

Solo sat very still. She picked at the scars on her arm. They itched something terrible. Sometimes she would scratch and scratch until her arm oozed with dark red blood. The nurses bandaged her arm to prevent her from scratching, but she would just tear off the bandages. Just for spite, she would scratch even harder. Since the nurses stopped shaving her hair off, her head even itched and she had bugs in her hair. She didn't care. She liked having hair; the bugs were her friends since they lived on her. Head and eyes cast downward, Solo curled her feet up in the hard chair and pulled her gown down over her legs. She wrapped her arms tightly around her body. Her hair had grown, so now strands dangled down her face, which was good; she hid her ugly side. While looking down and picking at her scarred hand, she was curious as to what the doctor was doing. So, she raised her head slightly and peaked at the doctor. The doctor was looking down and seemed to be busy writing. He was always writing. However, she didn't mind because she liked coming to the doctor, listening to him talk and watching him smoke his pipe. She loved the smell of the smoke coming from the pipe. How she secretly wished he would let her smoke his pipe. When he smoked his pipe, he was quiet and not talking so much. Sometimes he made Solo's head hurt, always asking the same questions over and over until she was ready to throw things at him. His questions were always the same. "How do you feel today? What is your name? How old are you? How did you get those burns? Do you have family?" Sometimes she wanted to scream out, *How in the hell do you think I feel looking like a f—king ugly monster, confined in this hellhole with these damn crazy lunatics. Why am I in this s—t of a place here? I am not crazy, I don't belong here. Please, please, let me out of this f—king nightmare. This s—t can't be for real.* Even still, Solo had to admit to herself, even with the doctor's never-ending questions and relentless probing, she looked forward to their weekly visits.

Anything to get away from the watchful eyes of those nosey nurses. Always looking at her and whispering about her as if they cared. Yet, her dear Doctor Hertz was very nice to her and always gave her special treats like chocolates and cookies. Even though his office was always cold and had a lot of stuff like books and paper, it was still nice to be there. She could stay there all day. She hated that big room with all those crazy assholes and the nurses always watching her. *F—k all of them*, she thought to herself. Solo refused to talk to any of them. Even though she didn't remember what exactly happened to her, how the hell did she end up in a f—king looney bin? She knew the doctor would help her. He had told her so many times and she trusted him. She so desperately wanted to talk to the doctor, but the words just wouldn't come out. She tried on many occasions, but she just hadn't found her voice yet. To her amazement, the doctor didn't seem to mind. He was so kind. He told her to take her time, which apparently, she had plenty of.

Doctor Hertz stopped writing, laid down his pen, folded his hands together, and looked at his patient. It had been more than six months since he and Jane Doe started their weekly visits. Little by little, he had reduced her medications and relied on shock treatments, which he hoped would jar her mental faculties. She had made some progress. No more uncontrollable outbursts or fights with staff and other patients. She appeared to be coming to terms with her conditions, but with the exception of nodding her head, she was non-verbal. So, today he thought he would try a different approach. He brought in a small record player and had a few vinyl 45s of various artists. Research had shown that after shock treatments, the introduction of something familiar to the patient had proven effective in getting the patient to open up. Therefore, he looked through the stack of records and decided on Billie Holiday, which was fitting for this situation. The music started playing, but he kept his back turned to the patient. Solo was busy chewing on the sleeve of her sweater, a gift from a nurse to conceal her scars. With the sweater hanging out of her mouth, she suddenly stopped to listen. The music seemed to attack her senses, familiarity came to her. Solo's mouth gaped wide-opened. The sweater sleeve dropped from her mouth. Her eyes sparkled. Her legs were untwined and her feet went to the floor. She slowly stood up and walked over to where the doctor was standing. Doctor Hertz didn't move, but he felt her presence behind him. He began to talk, "This is one of my favorite songs, by a famous artist named…" but before he could get the words out, Solo hoarsely whispered, "Billie Holiday."

Doctor Hertz closed his eyes tight, and a wide smile spread across his face. *Finally, a breakthrough.* The record stopped, so he quickly moved the needle and restarted the record as Solo continued to inch closer and closer. Doctor Hertz was completely aware of how close she was, but he didn't turn around. He felt no fear. This was good and he didn't want to lose momentum, so he quietly asked, "Do you like music?" Complete silence. Seemed like a lifetime passed, but Doctor Hertz waited. Finally, in a very low, child-like voice came a "Yes."

Doctor Hertz smiled to himself and said, "That's good because I like music as well. Billie Holiday is one of my favorite artists. She has her share of demons, but she is a talented and strong woman. I've seen her several times in concert."

The record stopped so Doctor Hertz removed it from the player and gently put it back in its sleeve. He turned to Solo, facing her, and thought, *Her beautiful eyes always amaze me, even with her scars she is still beautiful.* Looking into Solo's eyes he said, "Please, let's take a seat."

He took her hand (Solo didn't resist) and guided her to the chair as if she was a sickly invalid. Together, they walked with his hand gently supporting her back. After Solo was seated, Doctor Hertz returned to his seat behind his desk. He had a plan and wanted to try something new with his patient since it seemed that at this very moment, he had gained her trust. Experience had taught him the importance of seizing the moment because once it's gone, it would be maybe months or even years before the opportunity would present itself again. He smiled to himself because this was the very first time this patient had verbally communicated with him.

Doctor Hertz leaned back in his chair and slowly turned away from Solo and began to talk, "So I see you do have a voice and if I must say, a rather nice voice at that. But what troubles me is that after all this time we have been together, I am curious about what to call you. I know your name isn't Jane Doe and here at the hospital we have to give that name to patients when we don't know their name and have no way of finding out unless they tell us."

He turned around and faced Solo, who was holding her head down and staring at her hands. Doctor Hertz continued, "So, I know your name is not Jane Doe and I refuse to call you that, but since we are friends…we are friends, aren't we?"

Solo, who was continuing to look down, didn't respond. Moments went by. Doctor Hertz figured this would be a waiting game, but she would answer. A few more minutes went by. Slowly, Solo looked up from her hands, made eye contact with Doctor Hertz, and nodded her head up and down. Doctor Hertz let out a quick breath, chuckled, and said, "Good girl, for a moment I thought you didn't like me." He noticed the change in the patient's facial expression, almost a smile. Doctor Hertz went on, "So since we have established that we are friends and you know my name, it is only fair I know your name. Can you tell me your name?"

Solo began to shift in her chair, she started to scratch at an imaginary itch on her scarred arm until it was beginning to turn red. Her heart raced fast. Her tongue felt heavy and thick. She was thirsty. The room grew hot, and she began to sweat. She wanted to run, get away. *Why am I afraid? I like him, he is my friend. Jane Doe is not my name. I don't like when they call me that ugly, disgusting name. Even worse they call me a monster. I am not a monster; I am not Jane Doe. I have a name. A beautiful name. He thinks I made it up. He doesn't believe me. No, he is my friend. I am his friend. I want to tell him my name.* Solo was so nervous, and this internal debate continued within, making her fretful. She was on the verge of having a meltdown. Doctor Hertz was aware of her struggle. He had anticipated such a reaction, it happened when patients began to regain control of their senses...a breakthrough. Doctor Hertz got up from his chair and walked over to a stand that was holding a large silver tin pitcher of water and several tin cups. He poured water into two of the tin cups and walked over to Solo. He handed her one of the tins. She greedily grabbed the tin and drank the water down so fast that most spilled down her chin to the front of her gown. Doctor Hertz still standing, took a sip of his water and returned to his seat. Solo finished her water and gripped the empty cup tightly. Doctor Hertz looked at her and said, "Here let me take that from you." Solo lean forwarded toward Doctor Hertz and handed him the cup. She then took the back of her hand and wiped her wet lips dry. Doctor Hertz smiled and said, "Now back to my question. I really would like to know your name."

Looking shyly like a lost little girl while tugging at her dress, she coughed and said almost inaudibly, so quietly, Doctor Hertz had to lean in closer to hear her, "Solo."

Doctor Hertz was confused and didn't quite get what she said, so he asked, "Did you say Sophie, Sondra?"

Solo looked at him and repeated with a little more force and so loudly, it even frightened her, "SOLO! SOLO! SOLO! SOLO!" As she repeated her name, her voice grew louder and louder. She felt giddy and free. She stood up from her chair, dropped to her knees, and raised her hands in the air, and with tears streaming down her face, she calmly said, "My name is Solo!"

Being lost and trapped inside one's own created delusion with no visual way out, I pondered the path I should take; Should I keep straight, go right, or go left, my mind is going in circles trying to make sense of this approaching tragic reality that I cannot shake; Escaping is not an option, hiding is exposing me in plain sight, I cry out to closed ears, trying to make sense of my plight, must I try to navigate alone; My patience is running thin, loud voices holler within, heating my flesh as if some force has cast me into my own personal hell to which I yelled, "For Christ's sake!" As the hook reels me in, I flap about regretting all my sins, realizing this surely must be my end, the last birthday cake.

THIRTY-TWO
Grieving

As one traveled down the open roads passing others along the way, does one ever wonder what's going on in those people's lives as their cars scurry by? Minding their business and certainly not minding yours. Still, you can't help but wonder, Are they happy or sad? Lonely? Sick or lost a loved one? Lovers? A family? Rich or poor? Dying? Changing towns? Just traveling along the road. You are passing them and they are passing you.

One evening in 1955, a car slowly traveled along the dusty roads carrying Tulip and her family. One filled with so many mixed emotions, some good and some bad.

The gentle, warm breeze traveled gingerly through car windows, and the car vibrated from the rocky road, sometimes causing them to rise out of their seats. Tulip, still overcome with emotions, raised the letter Carson had received from their former mailman in Southern Maryland and held it close to her heart. She didn't look at the sender, not yet. She wanted to savor the moment as she said a silent prayer to her Lord and Savior. She prayed the letter would lead her to her lost daughter. She didn't want to rush the moment, so she closed her eyes and was still. The twins, Magdalene and Joseph, were watching their Mama closely and asked, "Papa, is Mama hurt? Why is she sad?"

Keeping his eyes on the road, Carson took a quick look at his wife. Her eyes were closed as she held the precious letter to her chest. He hoped it was good news, just for her sake. After losing his mama, they needed some good news. He answered the children and said, "No,

Mama is not sad. Those are happy tears. You know how you get a gift, and you are happy? Well, that letter is a gift for her. So, she is happy."

Magdalene sweetly responded, "But it's not Christmas." Everyone in the car burst out in laughter, even Veronica.

Tulip wanted so desperately to open and read the letter. She didn't recognize the writing on the envelope and her curiosity was killing her. One thing she knew for sure, the letter was not from her friends, the Chiles. Since Little Henry had come to live with them, she had ceased writing letters to her friends. Rather than writing, Tulip would use Mr. Carver's market telephone to call her friend. Letters between them had become infrequent. She loved hearing her dear friend's voice, it felt more personal.

Tulip didn't want to rush the moment just in case it was not good news. She waited this long, so a few more hours wouldn't make a difference. Tulip tucked the precious letter in her dress pocket for safekeeping and drifted off to the sweet smell of flowers. She was happy.

It was dark when Tulip's family pulled up in front of the house. Recognizing the sound of their car, their dog barked loudly and incessantly. Secretly Tulip had wished the dog had run off, but Mr. Fleabag was still there. Carson got out of the car to retrieve their belongings and yell at Mr. Fleabag to stop the damn barking. The dog went quiet. All the children were fast asleep.

Tulip reached back and shook Veronica's leg very gently saying softly (she didn't want to wake the little ones), "Baby girl, baby girl, come wake up now. We are home."

Veronica stretched out her arms and rubbed her eyes to get some focus. Tulip continued, "Come on now, it's late. And get Maggie to carry her. I will take care of Joseph, please don't wake them." Without acknowledging her mama, Veronica opened the car door and slowly lifted Maggie from the seat and walked to the house. Tulip was right behind them carrying her sweet little Joseph. As she walked to the house, she kissed him on top of his head and realized he was getting heavy, so she had to take her time. As Tulip reached the house, Carson passed her going back to the car. He didn't say anything to her, just walked by with his head down. Tulip noticed he had not muttered another word the entire trip home except for his joking when he first gave her the letter. Just sipped out his flask and kept his eyes on the road. Tulip figured he was just tired. It had been a very long weekend.

As Tulip entered the house, she took a deep breath and thought it was nice to be home. She went to the children's bedroom. Even though it was dark, she saw Veronica and Maggie were still fully clothed and knocked out sleep. She put Joseph at the foot of the bed and took off all the children's shoes, including Veronica's. The house was very cold, so she covered her sweet babies with a big heavy blanket. As she was leaving the room, Tulip looked over at Mean Old Mama's rocking chair. She could have sworn she saw the chair moving, but she was too tired to dwell on it, so she cast it off as her imagination. She would take care of going through Mean Old Mama's things tomorrow. She would give her things to the church. Even though it was not much, it was no sense in letting things go to waste when others had less. As Tulip walked from the children's bedroom, she rubbed her back and smiled to herself, thinking either her little one is getting too heavy for her to carry, or she was just getting old.

She began to unbutton her dress as she entered her bedroom to get comfortable so she could read her letter, but the letter would have to wait. Tulip stopped in her tracks because Carson was sitting on the edge of their bed with tears streaming down his face and his whole body was quivering. Tulip panicked and could not ever recall seeing her husband crying. Men don't cry. She dropped to her knees in front of her husband and grabbed both of his hands. She looked up at his face and spoke.

"Honey, what is the matter? How can I help you?"

Carson did not reply. He just continued to sob. Tulip took the hem of her dress and lovingly wiped her husband's face. He was pulling at her heartstrings, so she hugged him tightly, cradled and rocked him like one of her precious babies.

Tulip continued, "Carson, honey please tell me what is going on, are you hurting? Are you in pain?" Carson said nothing.

She held him tighter and said no more. After what seemed like an eternity, she heard a low moan, then a mumble.

"Mama is gone," Carson said in a low husky voice. "She's gone," he continued. Now Tulip understood her husband's tears. She had failed to recognize that maybe her husband was grieving the loss of his mama. Coming home with all the reminders and sensing the loss brought back the memory to Carson that his Mama had gone home to be with her maker. She will never be physically present to him again until he joined her and his papa. For Carson, the sense of loss was unbearable.

While personally, Tulip did not really grieve for Mean Old Mama since she was not the nicest person to her, Tulip had empathy for her husband. She knew of such loss since she had suffered and grieved when her Mama passed. She had grieved when Baby died in that awful fire. She knew loss and her heart ached for her husband. However, unlike Carson, he would not suffer his Mama's death alone because he had her. So, Tulip got up from the cold hard floor and gently laid her husband down on their small bed. She only removed her shoes and then his. She cut off the oil-burning lamp and climbed into the bed joining her husband. His eyes were shut tight, and his breathing was hard, but his tears were no longer flowing. And together, husband and wife lay fully clothed. They fell into a deep slumber. As the night passed and the different sounds of night shackled in the wind, love was in the house. For there is no greater love than the love one can share with another in a time of need or loss.

Deep in sleep, Tulip could smell the sweet scent of the flowers. The sky was blue and bluebirds flew above her head, chirping along and bringing her greetings. She felt a deep sense of happiness. Suddenly, there was her field of flowers. She ran full steam ahead dragging her hands along the sweet colorful flowers. She closed her eyes and let the scent of the flowers engulf her very soul, but she felt a presence. She was not alone. Tulip slowly opened her eyes and off in the far distance she could see a shadowy figure. She squinted her eyes to try and make out the figure. The figure seemed to be floating in the air. She could hear a voice in her head. The figure was calling out to her, motioning her to come closer. *Come to me baby girl, come.*

"Tulip, Tulip come on. Wake up, girl. I am off to work, and you need to get up before the childrins start to stir," said Carson, standing above Tulip.

Tulip opened her eyes and rubbed them to get some focus. Her husband was hovering over her still wearing yesterday's clothes, looking like he was carrying the whole world on his shoulder. Tulip, realizing she overslept, quickly jumped out of bed She was still wearing yesterday's clothes, and her braids had come undone.

Tulip looked at her husband, reached out, and touched his face lovingly. She said, "Why don't you stay home today? It's been a long weekend and you could use the rest."

Carson looked at his wife, turned, and began to walk away without responding. Quickly he put his hand on the bedroom doorknob, "No sense in laying around feeling sorry. What's done is done, plus we need the money. The last of our savings was used to bury…," he hesitated, unable to complete the sentence. He walked out the door and closed it slowly.

Tulip sat up on the side of the bed. She couldn't bring herself to respond to Carson. She needed to get her thoughts together. She wanted desperately to tell her husband she had saved money for her trip to find Solo. This made her feel bad for hiding money from him, knowing how desperately the family needed clothes and food. There were also bills to be paid. But she had worked hard for the money and only skimped off a little a time. She never spent any money foolishly or even on herself, and Lord knows she was long overdue for some decent undergarments But she made do. However, she still struggled with guilt about her secret stash.

"It ain't fair," Tulip mumbled slowly as she stood to lift her now wrinkled dress over her head. Time stood still as the small, stained, crumpled envelope slowly cascaded, sailing through the air like a baby bird's first flight. She watched with wide eyes as the envelope softly made a home on the cold linoleum floor. With so much going on, she had completely forgotten about the letter in her dress pocket. She hesitated before reaching down to retrieve it. She knew this could be good or bad news. It was too late for her to read the letter because she needed to get ready for the day. She had to get the kids up, get them fed, and then be off to her day job working for the White folks. Once again, the letter had to wait.

*Say, I am melancholy, but as they say,
when it rains it pours.
Never knowing what tomorrow may bring is certainly an old cliché, but I freely walked through open doors;
Living life in the moment, taking for granted limitless time, not adhering to the golden rule, forsaking all for the immediate, self-gratification for pleasing, never giving, "Why…what for?"
Time lived, seems like it was just yesterday, but of course, the reality is that I remain unequivocally attached to my mother's core;
When death brings that separation, it is like the value of my own existence is now fully exposed, and takes on a form of pain that radiates through my mind and body like a never healing infected sore;
I grieve for what was, here I no longer want to be, as I look up to heaven, pleading for my mother that cannot be, I see my very spirit raise from the floor and I am no more.*

THIRTY-THREE
The Cost of Freedom

Solo was so excited she could hardly contain her emotions. The big day had finally arrived. She could not believe she would be leaving this awful place. *Farewell crazies.* It had been more than two years since she had started visiting Doctor Hertz. He was truly her lifesaver. His efforts combined with shock treatments, medications, and their many hours of talking helped her to become better. While she had not fully regained her memory (due to the heavy meds, shock treatments, along with mental blocks because of the trauma…some memories were lost forever).

However, Solo almost had a major setback when she realized a total of eight years of her life were gone, lost forever. She knew who she was, and that was the most important thing. She was able to recall her real name, her birthday, Jessie, and a few other details about her life in New York City before the fire. But she didn't remember the fire. Unfortunately, her memories of family or relatives, specifically her Mama, Papa, and any siblings, appeared to be lost within the deep black hole of her mind or she chose subconsciously to keep them hidden. Try as she might, she could not recall having a family, except for Jessie. Eventually, she gave up trying to remember. However, good old positive-thinking Doctor Hertz assured Solo that in time, her memories would come back, and she could look for her family. Even though Solo adopted the attitude that if her family were so concerned about her, including that no-count Jessie, then why hadn't they visited her or a least sent a letter? She surmised that they didn't care. "*So, f—*

k 'em! *Who needs them anyway?*" However, there was some news proving to be even more devastating, shocking, and unimaginable. Solo had no recollection of being pregnant and giving birth. Who would want to impregnate a crazy, scarred, lifeless woman? Doctor Hertz understood fully her concerns.

But he felt it was important to her full recovery that she knew about the birth, even though in the long run, it would serve no purpose. The twins had been immediately taken from her at birth and put up for adoption. How could she care about something she had no knowledge of? She wasn't ready to be anybody's mother, especially to a baby who she didn't where they came from. Anyway, what would she do with a baby? Who was the father? Some other messed up person like her. She was ready to start her life, maybe find Jessie, and just live. No time for babies. When the time was right, she and Jessie would start a family.

Doctor Hertz kept his promise to Solo. He had found a boarding home that would take her in, even with her disfiguration and mental issues. However, she would be required to work and live by their rules…no drinking, no men, no staying out late, helping with chores, paying rent, etc. Solo didn't care. She would have agreed to anything, just to have her freedom from this hell hole. While she feared facing the world in her condition, she was ready.

There was nothing for Solo to pack. The nurse had given her a used paper bag for her belongings…toothbrush and toothpaste, comb and brush, and a few other toiletries. Some of the patients made her farewell gifts which she planned to trash as soon as left this place. *Who wanted reminders of crazies?* Solo wanted to forget everything about this nightmare.

Solo's least favorite nurse came up and asked sarcastically, "So, Miss Solo, you got your little bit of belongings packed? You must be so excited to be leaving this place. And if I must say, we are happy to see you go. We take pride in the work we do to help our patients transition back into society. So please behave yourself."

Solo looked at the nurse and nodded her head up and down.

The nurse replied, "Now remember Solo, we agreed that you must use your voice. We don't want no one to think that along with being ugly, you are also deaf and dumb."

Her words stunned Solo whose eyes misted. She wanted to reach out and strike the nurse, which she had done in the past. But, not today. Solo was determined she would not let the nurse cause her to spend one more day in this place. So, she took a deep breath, as Doctor Hertz had taught her when she needed to take control of her emotions, and replied "Yes, ma'am."

The nurse smiled and said, "Okay, that's a good girl, follow me." A few of the patients yelled in unison, "Bye, bye!"

Solo walked behind the nurse, moving quickly to keep pace, keeping her head down. Some of the other nurses and attendants wished her well. Solo didn't acknowledge them or provide any response. One attendant walked quickly by her with his head lowered and did not make eye contact. For some reason, that attendant always made her feel uncomfortable, but she could never figure out why. Solo held tightly onto the brown paper bag containing her meager belongings. The shoes they gave her were a little tight and began to hurt her feet. They made a heavy sound on the clean, waxed floor. Her dress was a little big, but she liked the blue and yellow flowers matching her blue sweater. She was happy with the sweater covering her scarred arms. Her hair had been washed and brushed. It had grown long and swayed onto her face which pleased her because it concealed the one-sided ugly scarring.

Together Solo and the nurse walked. Solo didn't want to get her hopes up, but she was pleased when the nurse stopped and they stood in front of Doctor Hertz's office. She didn't want to leave this place without saying goodbye to him. She secretly had a crush on him and would often fantasize about them being boyfriend and girlfriend, just a harmless fantasy because she knew deep inside no one would ever love her again. The nurse knocked on the door and announced their presence.

Doctor Hertz, in his nice gentle voice, told them to enter as if he was expecting them. Solo could hardly contain her emotions, she wanted to push the nurse out of the way, throw her arms around Doctor Hertz, and smother his face with kisses.

Doctor Hertz continued to write. The nurse turned and looked back at Solo and rolled her eyes. Solo felt flushed with embarrassment and wondered if the nurse could read her thoughts. Finally, Doctor Hertz put his pen down, looked up, and smiled. He waved for Solo to come forward. The nurse, feeling a little put-off, moved aside for her. Doctor Hertz stood up behind his desk and said, "Well look at this young woman in this pretty dress. So, this is your last day here before you go into your new life." Feeling the mean nurse's eyes on her, Solo smiled and nodded.

Doctor Hertz said, "Now Solo. Do you have a voice?"

The nurse interjected, "I told her Doctor Hertz that she must use her voice. I am really concerned she is not ready to be released…"

The nurse wanted to voice some of her concerns about Solo. But before she could continue, Doctor Hertz held up his hand, silencing her. He did not want to put doubt and fear into his patient. He politely said, "Nurse, thank you. If Miss Solo's discharge papers are in order, I will take charge from here. You are excused."

The nurse started to protest because this was highly irregular, but she knew better than to cross Doctor Hertz.

She handed over Solo's paperwork, then turned and looked at Solo saying, "Please take care and I am sure we will cross paths again." With that, she turned and walked towards the office door, thinking to herself, *That b—h."*

Doctor Hertz said, "Nurse, please have someone buzz my office when Miss Solo's ride is here. Thank you." Without turning around and hand on the door now, the nurse replied, "Yes, Doctor Hertz." She then walked out the door with her head held high.

"Finally," Doctor Hertz said, "we got rid of her."

They both laughed. "Come, dear, have a seat. Let's chat for a minute before you leave."

Still clenching her trashy brown bag, Solo took her seat. She didn't squinch her legs up in the chair. Instead, she crossed her legs like a real lady, touched her hair, and smoothed out her dress. Doctor Hertz watched her carefully and marveled at this young woman now sitting before him. What a long road they had traveled.

Speaking in a serious tone, Doctor Hertz spoke. "First, I want you to know that I am going to miss our talks. You are one of my favorite patients." Solo smiled.

He continued, "You did the hard work and now you have a chance to take control of your life. So, as we have discussed, your mental breakdown was directly related to the trauma you suffered from the fire. You are not crazy, but you must continue to take your medications as directed. These medications are to help you. Maybe one day you will no longer need them. But for now, they will help you get better. You must mind the rules at the boarding house. The woman who runs it is named Misses Hathaway. She is my friend. But she is strict and no-nonsense. Respect her, obey her rules, and everything should be fine. Now, there will be other young ladies like you living in the boarding house. Please try to get along. You will have a job and you will earn a little money to spend on yourself. Know that you will be expected to help around the house. That is your home for as long as you want it, and that's what's important. I think you will do great if you follow the rules and take your medication. I am confident you are going to do well. Okay, let's part with a handshake. You have my phone number.

You know how to reach me. If anytime you need to talk, just have Misses Hathaway give me a call and we can chat. Do you have any questions?"

Solo started to shake her head, but she looked at Doctor Hertz and quietly responded with a verbal "No."

Doctor Hertz smiled and said, "Good girl, you are going to be just fine."

Doctor Hertz reached down under his desk and pulled out a small, wrapped gift. Solo put her hands to her mouth and her eyes open asking, "Is that for me?"

"Yes, Miss Solo, it's for you to take with you. It's my way of saying job well done."

Hesitantly, Solo reached over and took the gift from Doctor Hertz. She was excited and started to talk rapidly, "I don't think I've ever had a gift before."

She carefully pulled off the red ribbons, wanting to save them later for her hair. She pulled the tape from the little pretty wrapped box and stuffed the silver wrapping in her dress pocket. She wanted to keep everything. She gently opened the paper box, trying with all her might not to tear the box to pieces. Inside the box, she noticed a small black velvet box. She gently lifted the black velvet box and opened it. To her amazement, there was a pair of white pearl earrings. Solo could not believe her eyes. She couldn't ever recall receiving such a beautiful gift. She was at a loss for words and tears formed in her eyes and slowly streamed down her eyes onto her blushing cheeks. Solo tried to find the right words. Doctor Hertz handed her a handkerchief. She carefully tapped on her face not wanting to stain his clean handkerchief. Finally, she coughed and found her voice.

"Thank you, Doctor Hertz, for everything. Thank you for the gift and for helping me. These are the most beautiful earrings, and I will treasure them all of my life. I owe you my life."

Doctor Hertz was overcome with emotion.

"No need to thank me. I wanted you to have something that was yours and to remind you that you are special."

The phone rang loudly, which startled them both. Solo let out a loud sigh. She knew the time had come. Doctor Hertz picked up the phone, nodded his head, and gave Solo a wink saying, "Okay, she will be ready when you get here." Solo felt her heart beating wildly. She doubted herself and a thousand questions were running through her head. *Was she ready? People are going to laugh at me and stare. What if they don't like me? What if they throw me in the streets? Or even worse, return me to the hospital.* So many ifs. She needed a plan. She had to find Jessie.

While Doctor Hertz and Solo waited for the nurse to pick her up, together like two old friends, they sat and chatted until they heard a soft, rapid knock on the door. Solo's heart quickened. Doctor Hertz summoned the nurse.

"Solo's ride is here. Is she ready?"

Doctor Hertz replied, "Yes, she is more than ready. Isn't that right Solo?"

Solo looked directly at Doctor Hertz. He felt her pain, so he stood from his seat and motioned for Solo to do the same. No sense in delaying the inevitable. As they stood in silence, many unspoken words traveled through them. The nurse was also consumed with the tension in the room. She had experienced this before. The doctor and patient saying their farewells. Solo reached down and picked up the brown paper bag that carried her few possessions. She closed the bag tightly, and turned towards the nurse, but hesitated. She held her head down and her small delicate body began to quiver. The river gate opened, and she started to cry. Doctor Hertz, seeing Solo in distress, moved from his desk, walked over to her, and placed his hands on her shoulders saying, "Now, now, we're not going to have none of that.

Come on look at me."

Solo turned to face the doctor.

He continued, "I know you're scared and it's okay to be scared. Sometimes I get scared. The world can be a scary place. Now you remember what we talked about?"

Solo nodded.

"Yes, but just remember Solo, this is your life and only you are in control."

Solo wiped her face with the back of her good hand, turned from the doctor, and walked toward the nurse. She turned back one time and looked at Doctor Hertz and smiled. She took a deep breath, grasped her bag, and walked out of that awful place to what she hoped was a new beginning.

As I walked toward my destiny, I saw my shadow; it swayed and bent like a growing tree;

My path is unknown; it is not clearly defined, but the vision before is a free life;

No longer regretting what was, what could have been, is it now filled with what will be;

So, I laugh at those memories locked in my own prison, because now I have the key;

As a famous poet once said, "To Be or Not To Be" I know now that is me.

I AM OUT!

THIRTY-FOUR
Red Stone House

It was a cloudy, rainy, cold day. No sun was shining, only dark forming clouds moving along the sky like sailing doves. The sprinkling rain caused little puddles on the dirt streets. People moved about clenching their coats tightly. Some held umbrellas to shield them from the rain while others seemed oblivious.

For more than two decades, Misses Hathaway had run a boarding home for the mentally unstable Coloreds. The house had five spacious rooms that had been divided and subdivided into small sleeping rooms. All residents shared one bathroom and ate in the common room. Misses Hathaway's boarding house had the feel of an institution, not much different than the one Solo had just left.

Misses Hathaway's boarding house was the only one in New York City exclusively for Colored mental patients. Over the years, she had been successful at placing these women in jobs as maids, servants, seamstresses, cooks, and warehouse workers. However, some patients had not been successful in their employment and were eventually returned to the asylum. Some patients ran away to God knows where, while others left to live on the streets or become drug addicts and prostitutes. Truth be told, Misses Hathaway supplied some of the women to pimps and received a nice payment. She, herself, was once a woman of the streets. When she first arrived in New York City from the Jim Crow South, she had no money, family, or job. As a result, selling her body as well as running other hustles were the best options for an uneducated Colored woman. To her luck, one of her clients who will remain nameless, let her rent his home. This client also had contact with big-time officials throughout the city. There was an outcry throughout the city regarding the inhumane treatment of the mentally insane. So, Misses Hathaway told her client his house was big enough to accept the Colored, mentally insane women and help them find employment for a small fee. They both could make money. Over the years, with her client's connections, many women, and in rare cases even children and newborn babies would pass through Misses Hathaway's doors. So, when she got a new patient from New York City Hospital for the Mentally Retarded and Criminally Insane, she made the trip once again.

Misses Hathaway, with an unfiltered cigarette dangling from her big, red lipstick-covered lips trudged her way up to the front entrance of the hospital. She saw a nurse who she recognized standing with what looked to be a young White girl. She thought to herself, this couldn't be possible because they knew she only took in Colored crazy women. Maybe she was waiting for someone else. As she got closer, the nurse, recognizing Misses Hathaway, gave her a big smile. Now Misses Hathaway was getting concerned because she was not going to take in no crazy White girl. That would be just asking for trouble. Plus, the city had laws against mixing races. She flicked the cigarette to the ground. As she got closer, she noticed the girl kept her head down with her long stringy, blonde unkempt hair hiding her face. Misses Hathaway looked down at her legs, they were decent enough, she thought.

"Hello, Misses Hathaway," said the nurse smiling.

"Hello," Misses Hathaway said with reservation.

The nurse stepped forward to Misses Hathaway and said, "This is Solo Thornton."

Misses Hathaway stepped back from the nurse, shaking her head from side to side.

After handing the woman some papers, the nurse turned to Solo and said, "This is Misses Hathaway, and you will be going with her." Then the nurse bid her farewell and good luck.

Solo did not respond to the nurse. As instructed, she walked quickly behind the large Colored woman, who did not greet her or say a word. Clutching her sweater tightly around her thin dress, Solo kept her head down and did not utter a word. She wanted desperately to shout to the world, "I'M FREE!" but such an outburst would bring attention to her, and she didn't want that. She could just imagine they would take her right back to the hospital with the rest of the crazies. Solo continued to follow the large Colored woman who was moving rather fast given her weight and size. Solo wanted to laugh as she watched the woman's enormous ass bouncing up and down like a rubber ball with each step she took. She found this to be pretty funny, but of course, she kept her thoughts to herself and didn't even crack a smile, as much as she wanted to.

Solo noticed the waiting beat-up dirty old automobile. As they got closer, Solo looked up quickly and saw an old thin, Colored man in a cloud of cigarette smoke sitting behind the wheel. She pulled her hair toward her face in a futile attempt to cover her scarred face. She didn't want anyone staring at her.

"Come on now you, move quickly. We don't have all day and I ain't fitting to stay out in the s—t cold with my old aching bones. Get a move on now!"

The woman was annoyed. Solo picked up her pace, but it was hard to walk with the shoes she was wearing that were flopping on and off her feet. She almost lost one. Finally, they reached the car and the large Colored woman reached and opened the back door. She turned to Solo and said, "Get in," while pointing at the back seat.

Solo quickly bent down and got into the car. Her heart was about to explode, She was literally shaking. Not from the rain, not from the cold weather, but rather from the unknown.

With Solo in the back seat, the woman struggled to get into the front seat. Once she was finally settled, she immediately lit a cigarette. After taking a long draw until the flame burned bright red, the woman blew circles of smoke and let out a loud sigh. The strong smoke quickly filled the automobile. Solo wanted to cough, but she held it in, fearing a cough would bring on unwanted attention.

With the cigarette dangling from her mouth, the large Colored woman said, with much irritation to the Colored man behind the wheel, "What your dumb ass waiting for? Get moving. Lord Christ, with exception of the crazies, you must be the dumbest person I've met. For Lord sake's I don't know why in the damn hell I keep you around. I must tell you everything. Drive, dumb ass, drive!" She rolled her eyes and lit another cigarette.

The old Colored man didn't respond. He took one more drag off his cigarette and stubbed the butt out in the filled ashtray. Before pulling out, the man nervously looked around as he slowly pulled the automobile into the oncoming traffic. There was always a lot of traffic near the hospital, which included a combination of automobiles, incoming and outgoing hospital ambulances, wagons being pulled by horses, and men pushing carts selling their wares. The old man was used to driving in the mess of traffic. For over fifteen years, he had been employed as Misses Hathaway's driver. While Misses Hathaway was always rattling his chains, the pay was decent. Plus, there were a few additional incentives. He never feared getting fired because he knew some of Misses Hathaway's secrets, especially related to the crazies picked up from the insane asylum.

The old man took a quick look in the rear-view mirror at the passenger in the back. She was a sight to see. *Got dammit, she is damn near white as the day would have it.* He couldn't see her face, because she kept her head down. He thought to himself, *Another lost pitiful,* soul...well she better be ready because nothing good was waiting for her. He had seen it too many times after picking up hundreds of these young crazy Negro women, both young and old. Many of them couldn't cope and would end up right back in asylum. Some would run off to work the streets, but most just worked those long-hour jobs supplied by Misses Hathaway and took their drugs. Like he said, "poor souls."

Solo felt the man's eyes on her and wished he would stop staring. She wanted so desperately to look out the window and take in the sights. Maybe she could recall something that looked familiar. But that was not going to happen as long as this creepy old man kept watching her. Nevertheless, she wanted to look so bad. The need to look gave her a painful thundering headache. Plus, to add to everything, she was hungry and thirsty. She hadn't eaten since early that morning and that was just some thick, cold nasty oatmeal and toilet water tea. She hoped the place where she was going would have some decent food at least. She could hope.

To Solo's relief, the old Colored man finally turned his attention to driving, as he should have been doing along. Now she felt comfortable enough to look out the cloudy window. Solo was amazed there were so many people moving about, but the noise was most unsettling. Even with the closed windows, she found the outside sounds were almost too much to bear. She willed her mind to stay calm and took deep breaths as Doctor Hertz had told her to do when she felt frightened or nervous.

Misses Hathaway did not talk to either Solo or the old man driving the car. She just kept her head turned towards her window, seemingly in her own little world. As they zipped past the different streets, the driver would occasionally honk the car's horn and shout obscenities out his window. Solo stayed focused on the sites. Now and then, she would look up to see if she recognized the names of any of the passing streets. She thought hard to recall the name of the street where she lived with Jessie, but to her frustration, she couldn't. However, Doctor Hertz assured her that over time, her memory would return. What was more concerning to Solo is she couldn't even remember the fire or the last time she was even with Jessie. Her heart raced when she thought, *Maybe Jessie died in the fire.* She shook her head, not wanting to accept the thought. *Maybe Jessie was looking for me.* But there was evidence he ever came to the hospital looking for her. She never had any visitors or letters. Surely Jessie must have known she was in the hospital. Didn't he? Solo contemplated the thought. The palms of her hands grew sweaty. She knew she was working herself into a frenzy. *Think, think…what did Doctor Hertz tell me to do? Take deep breaths. How could Jessie find me when they didn't even know my name? Jane Doe. What a f–king joke, a Negro girl being called Jane.* Solo suppressed her laughter and directed her attention to the passing streets. She had to remember…she *will* remember, her life depended on it.

The old Colored man started to drive slowly, passing rows of similar looking red stone houses. Solo could not recall ever seeing houses that were straight up and high enough to reach the clouds in the sky. She counted at least five different levels, all with windows. To Solo, the houses were most daunting. As the car moved slowly down the dirt road, she noticed the houses varied in color from pink, red, orange, even purplish. But they all had either a red brick-front or white limestone-front. It was very quiet, with only a few Colored, nicely dressed people walking slowly by. Solo's thoughts were suddenly interrupted by the sound of the large woman's voice.

"Alrighty Joe, pull over here. That's good, right here," the woman said. The driver slowly pulled the car from the street and came to a complete stop. Solo grew nervous as she watched Misses Hathaway open her door, step out, and take a long stretch. Misses Hathaway reached back, opened Solo's car door, and said rather roughly while motioning her hand, "Come on you! Make haste. I don't have all day. Grab your belongings and get out of the car and follow me."

Solo hesitated for a moment, nervously looking at the woman, and turned to look at the old man who was once again watching her. The woman commenced to yell rather loudly, "Get your crazy ass moving, ain't got all day!"

Solo jumped at the loud command and quickly gathered her meager belongings and stepped out of the car. Her legs, heavy and stiff from the long ride, made it somewhat difficult to walk.

As Misses Hathaway walked up the long concrete steps towards one of the red-brick houses, she slowly took one step at a time because of her aching, crusted, dry, fat feet and swollen blackened ankles, the result of a lifetime of squeezing her fat feet in too small shoes. There were a lot of steps, so not only was Misses Hathaway moving slowly, but she also rested in between making a loud breathing noise. Walking close behind Misses Hathaway, Solo watched her dress flap up and down which was clearly due to her rather sizeable rump. Her dress was even hiked up in the back exposing fat layers of chunky thighs. However, Solo's eyes were still fixed on the motion of Misses Hathaway's big ass flapping up and down like a bouncing ball. She wanted to laugh because it was a funny sight to see, but instinctively knew this was not the right time for laughter. Further, when she turned her head slightly to look behind her, and spotted the old man still watching her. *Creep!* she said to herself.

Once they reached the top of the steps, Solo was overcome with a sweet smell. She looked to her left and saw the most beautiful flower garden that reminded her of the flowers back home. *Wow.* The flowers really stirred up some deep familiarities. Solo stepped onto a large red, brick front porch. She took notice of five wooden rocking chairs, all lined up neatly and seemingly moving slowly along with the brisk wind. Baskets of flowers adorned the red stone house's white window sills. Solo thought it was a pretty place. She hadn't seen such beautiful flowers since she left her home in Connecticut. Interesting enough, Solo found to her amazement that she recalled how her Mama loved flowers. The thought of her old home and her Mama sent a cold shiver throughout Solo's body causing her to pull her sweater closer.

"God have mercy, one day these steps are gonna be the death of me," Misses Hathaway announced as she exhaled loudly and rested on the porch railing trying to muster up the strength to continue. The sudden outburst made Solo stop in her tracks. As she waited for Misses Hathaway to make her next move, the front door to the house suddenly flew open and there stood a stocky, wide-hipped, short, and very dark complexioned woman with deeply dimpled cheeks and large round brown eyes. She was wearing a flowered apron, very worn black shoes, and a headscarf while sporting a big wide grin from ear to ear, showing off her near-perfect brown stain teeth. Her name was Harriett, and she was the maid.

Harriett had been there since the inception of the boarding house. She was loyal to Misses Hathaway and Misses Hathaway trusted her immensely. Harriett ran the house like a prison, and she was the warden. She was not strict, but compassionate. And truth be told, no one could pull the wool over her eyes, or so she thought.

"Hello, Misses Hathaway," said Harriett as she shuffled her fat feet aside and backed up her big behind to let Misses Hathaway pass through the front door. As Misses Hathaway walked past, she didn't make eye contact with Harriett. Rather, she gave the nervous woman a slight nod of her head and said with a tone of exhaustion, "Thank you, Harriett. Hell of traffic, just a mess. Really works my pressure."

Misses Hathaway paused as if to catch her breath. After a brief moment she continued.

"Is everything ready for our new guest?"

Smiling at Misses Hathaway, the woman quickly responded, "Yes ma'am. I put her with Sally."

The woman took a quick peek at the mess of a girl hiding behind Misses Hathaway, shaking like a newborn puppy. Were her eyes deceiving her? The woman's mouth hung open, not believing her eyes...*a White gal, no way*, she thought. *We don't do know white gals.*

"HARRIETT!" yelled Misses Hathaway, snapping her out of her trance.

"Yes ma'am," Harriett replied quickly.

"Stop your gawking and take this gal to her room," said Misses Hathaway and shoved Solo rather hard towards Harriett.

"By the way, her name is Solo. I know, I know, it's strange, but we are used to strange. And she is not a White gal. Just one of those, what you call them, mulatto or something like that. Now because she looks White, there will be no special treatment. So remember, no extra food, soap, covers, nothing. Give her the same as others. You got that Harriett? I mean it and if I hear otherwise, there will be hell to pay. I said my piece. Go on now!"

Harriett nodded in agreement and started to walk. Misses Hathaway once again shoved Solo.

"Go on now, follow Harriett. She will take good care of you."

With that, she gave Harriett a slight smile.

*Birds fly high up in the blue sky, no one can explain, we
really don't know the reason why,
as they move from one to a pack of ten;
Flapping their wings, soaring with the wind, letting their
senses guide them because for them, it's always a win;
Their life is free and they live without fear, they only seek
what they need to spend time with their kin;
No today, not tomorrow, no regrets, and no sorrow,
their life is just around flight around the bend;
But, the beauty of it all,
is that unlike humans, they do not SIN.*

THIRTY-FIVE
Home

It had been a couple of weeks since Solo had arrived at Misses Hathaway's. While she was still trying to adjust to the transition from the hospital to the rooming house, it had not been without problems. To start, Sally, Solo's assigned roommate, was scared of her and was a basket case herself. Sally constantly screamed in horror when she saw Solo's burn scars. The girl was frightened to be alone with Solo, let alone share a bedroom with her. She was driving Harriett crazy with her constant complaints and tears. "Solo this, Solo that," on and on, "She is so ugly, I am scared of her," on and on. Sally would cry real tears.

Even the other residents would not go near Solo, and like Sally, complained about her scars. None of the residents interacted with Solo. So, Solo tried her best to hide her scars, but that was hard to do when she bathed or undressed. Misses Hathaway was aware Solo had suffered bad burns and was severely disfigured. However, when she got a real good look at Solo, even she was taken aback by the severity of Solo's condition. The doctor and hospital staff had not fully disclosed her condition. She looked like a monster.

Misses Hathaway felt she had been duped into taking Solo. No matter what the state paid her, she had a good mind to cart this, *whatever you want to call her*, right back to the asylum where she belonged. Locked away where no one could lay eyes on her. Misses Hathaway felt not only was this poor girl crazy, but she was also a freak. *How could she work and make her money?* Her home was no side-show *(even though she knew some men would get off on such things)*. However, Misses Hathaway was no fool and she didn't want to lose the little money the government paid her for taking in these crazies. Until she could figure it out, this freak needed to be out-of-sight. She couldn't have this mess of human upsetting the other residents and cause her to lose money. Best that this thing was kept away from the others as much as possible.

There was a creaky, narrow winding staircase leading up to the attic. If one was standing outside looking up at the red stone house, they would see a little window, the eyes of the attic. From its inception, it was never meant to be occupied by humans, but the room held a lot of secrets. Rather, it was there where old casted-off items such as furniture, clothing, books, trunks, rugs, etc. were kept. Even the previous owners would scare their children with ghost stories of the attic as punishment. In the winter, it was extremely cold. In the summer, it was stifling hot to the point where one could hardly breathe. The dust was thick and spider webs draped the room, casting an eerie ghostly shadow. The residents were warned to never venture into the attic. In fact, the attic was used as a source of control over the residents. Harriett often would lock a resident in the attic when they talked back or disobeyed the house rules. The attic was where the monsters lived, so it was only appropriate that this would be Solo's new home. There, she would be away from the other residents as well as any visitors.

Solo was moved to the cramped, dark, musty, rat-infested room. No explanation was given to her as to why she was being moved, but she was glad to get away from the annoying half-wit girl always looking at her and talking behind her back just like in the hospital. She was glad to go. As she followed closely behind Harriett up the tight, winding steps, Solo felt excited. But also, fear of the unknown crept into her soul. She heard Doctor Hertz's kind, soft voice in her head, *Now Solo, my dear, take slow, long, deep breaths…in and out. Good girl.*

Harriett turned the knob and opened the attic door. She gave it a hard push and it made an awful crying sound as it opened slowly. Harriett stepped into the room, moving quickly. Solo followed her taking short, slow steps. Solo gagged and coughed from the smell. She carefully looked around at her new home. She noticed the little window was so covered with thick dirt and dust that it offered very little light. The room was dark, so Harriett lit the oil lamp she had brought with her. Spiders and other unknown bugs crawled about freely; some moved quickly to avoid the human crush. The attic floor was covered with trash, dust, and dirt. It was a poor sight.

As Harriett looked around the room, she avoided making eye contact with Solo. She knew the room was not fit for a human. No matter if she did look like a monster and had very little sense, she was still a child of God.

With her back turned to Solo, Harriett quickly said, "This is where you will sleep and spend your time after you finish your work."

However, Solo did not see either a bed or a cot. Harriett went on, "I'll give you some cleaning supplies, so you can clean it up best you can." Harriett moved towards a big old, black metal trunk that seemed to have seen better days. She opened it and pulled out some smelly old quilts. While handing them to Solo, she motioned to a mattress on the floor in a corner and said, "You can sleep there."

Solo took the bedding and looked to where Harriett was pointing. Next Harriett handed Solo an oil lamp and instructed her on how to tell when the oil was running low. Also, she pointed to a crusty, black bucket in another corner and told Solo it was for her personal business. She must bring it down every morning to be emptied and cleaned, along with any used dishes from meals. They didn't want to encourage the rodents, which also lived in the attic. Harriett informed Solo that on Saturday mornings, she could take a bath before the others awakened. On other days, she would just wash up in the kitchen.

Harriett told Solo she was forbidden to roam the house freely among the residents. No trips outside, except to empty her pot or throw out garbage. Until Misses Hathaway could find suitable work for her, she would help with the housework such as washing dishes and clothes, scrubbing floors, ironing, cooking, and whatever Misses Hathaway or Harriett saw fit. This was no free ride. At the rooming house, everyone, no matter their illness or condition, was expected to pull their own weight, and Solo would be no exception.

For the first couple of months living in the attic, Solo was overcome with grief due to her living conditions. She cried constantly and lived in a state of terror. She longed to call Doctor Hertz or return to the asylum. Every crack, ping, or scurrying of something across the floor, made her jump in fright. Her thick scarred skin itched and ached. Something was always crawling or biting her; it was a never-ending battle. She scratched until her skin bled and in time, got infected. Her hair hung loosely around her face, matted and tangled. She smelled from the lack of bathing. Over time, her condition was deteriorating. She was becoming unhinged. But she found that even with the disgusting living conditions, she didn't mind living alone in the attic. She preferred to be alone, away from the looks of others. Plus, it gave her the freedom to fantasize about her past life where she was a beautiful princess. Yet, more importantly, the solitude gave her time to plan her escape from this nightmare as well as search for Jessie. Surely, he must be looking for her. Let them think she was a monster, soon she would escape and be free. She had a plan. However, with no mirror in her room, Solo did not see what she had become.

Every morning, except Sunday, which was the Lord's day, Solo had to wake by 5:30 AM to wash her face and private areas in the basin of cold cloudy water with the harsh lye soap. Harriett would bring her medicines and a glass of lukewarm water. Just like in the hospital, in fear of overdose or abuse, no residents were allowed to self-medicate.

Harriett always watched Solo to make sure the pills were swallowed. She had experienced the wrath of those who did not take their meds. It was not an experience she wanted to repeat. After Solo took her meds, she dressed, made up her makeshift bed, poured the cloudy basin water into the pail that held her bodily fluids and more, then began her day.

Solo had to be down in the kitchen promptly by 6:30 AM, no excuse was accepted for tardiness. One of her jobs was to assist Harriett in preparing breakfast for Misses Hathaway and the residents. Also, lunches had to be made for the residents who went off to their day jobs cleaning homes, sewing in factories, and working in the mill. Some of the residents worked at night. Solo wasn't sure what they did at night. Perhaps they danced at a joint as she had done in a time that seemed like a lifetime ago. After the residents had eaten and went about their respective business, including Misses Hathaway, Solo ate whatever food was left. Sometimes it wasn't much, but Solo was getting better at hiding a little more food. Solo would clean up the kitchen and help Harriett with other house duties. Harriett was meticulous and would reprimand Solo when tasks were done incorrectly. Sometimes Solo was made to do a task over and over again until it met Harriett's approval which was often. But on a few occasions, after she completed her work and Harriett gave her approval, Solo could roam about the empty house without the watchful eye of Harriett. Solo really enjoyed the freedom to herself. She made mental notes of each level of the red stone house.

On the first level, there was a long narrow hallway with several large fully furnished adjoining rooms. There was a kitchen and a sitting room. The dining room, where all the residents took their meals, had a long wooden table with about twenty matching chairs. The table was always adorned with a beautiful lace tablecloth and matching dollies which Solo had the duty of washing and ironing each week. In the hallways as well as the sitting and dining rooms, there were old, but beautifully framed, pictures of Misses Hathaway, children, *and* grayed old men and women. There were various pictures of Misses Hathaway surrounded by several different women. Even Harriett was posed proudly in the group pictures. Some of the framed pictures were neatly arranged on tabletops, while the others adorned every inch of wall space on the first floor, even going up the stairs to the second and third levels. There were no pictures leading to the attic. What really caught Solo's attention were the pictures of the children. Solo stared deeply at the pictures. Her mind conjured up memories of her own siblings. She smiled and gently touched the pictures. Her eyes grew moist and deep sadness entered her soul. She quickly moved away from the photos.

Misses Hathaway's sleeping quarters were also located on the first level, away from the residents. Solo looked at the closed door. She only entered the room with Harriett to clean, make the bed, and wash the linen. Her hand slowly reached for the doorknob. She hesitated, quickly drew back her hand, and proceeded on with her adventure. The house had indoor plumbing, so there was one small bathroom with running water and a flushing toilet. Also, below the first floor in the center of the kitchen, was a trap door leading to the dark, creepy, disgusting house cellar. Solo had only gone into the cellar a few times, and only with Harriett. She liked it even less than the attic. Like the attic, the cellar was creepy and dark with rats as well as spiders calling it home. But for Solo, it always felt as though something evil was lurking in the corners. God only knows, but it was something there watching. (Later, Solo would learn it was used to punish residents who refused to follow the rules.) The third and fourth levels were sleeping quarters for the residents, including Harriett. But, once again there was a locked door. Solo put her ear to the door and she swore she heard deep breathing. Goosebumps rose on her arms. Solo backed away, staring at the door. There was someone in there. Solo found it interesting that on each level of the house, there was a least one room that was kept closed and locked. Solo had noticed the keys attached to a dangling brown, leather belt tied around Harriett's waist. Harriett used those keys to lock the kitchen pantry (a necessary precaution to prevent the residents from stealing food and their medication) and other rooms in the house. *What was behind those locked doors?* She wanted desperately to find out, but Harriett was never without those keys. Finally, on the very top level, was an attic used for storage, unwanted junk, and unused old furniture. But for Solo, for the time being, it was home.

> *The eyes of the beholder or your formed version of reality are only part of the whole picture;*
> *Believing what we perceive to be the real instead of facing the cruel fact that life has dealt you a raw deal;*
> *For some, it seemed the simple act of being born was designed to be unfair; the pendulum swayed in their unfortunate directions, creating a living hell;*
> *Eyes open wide, seeing clearly the actions and attitudes, one cannot mistake the beat of drums from the entitled, "WE SIMPLY JUST DON'T CARE;"*
> *Shout and cry out to empty ears, in your everlasting agony and desperation, the realization hits you that life, as you know, will never be fair...*

THIRTY-SIX
Slave

Two years had passed since Solo had arrived at the red brick house. It was Misses Hathaway's tradition to use the resident's arrival date to honor their "birthday." Harriet would bake a cake and adorn it with a single tall candle. It was time to celebrate Solo's birthday, well, more of an anniversary.

The residents huddled together and sadly sang "Happy Birthday" to Solo as she hung her head low, scared of the attention and too frightened to make eye contact with anyone. Some of the residents shouted to her, "How old are you?" but Misses Hathaway would tell them to hush and mind their business, and then she would give Solo a roughly wrapped gift of harsh coarse paper. The residents stared with drooping lips and eyes of greed. They begged Solo to open her present, and she hesitantly complied. As she slowly ripped the coarse paper, she felt the envious, cold eyes watching her every move as they grew more and more agitated. Solo didn't care; this was her day and her gift, and she would not be rushed. Finally, she opened the gift revealing a bar of sweet-smelling soap. It was a welcome gift. She wanted to smile because this was one special day and a happy day compared to her miserable daily routine.

Because of her monstrous looks, Solo was not allowed to work outside the house. Misses Hathaway did not want to scare off her paying customers. As a result, Solo would rise early, work the entire day, and go to bed late to earn her keep. Her free time was very minimum, mostly just taking time to wash herself and eat a cold meal. On the bright side, her mental condition was improving, and unbeknownst to Harriett, she even managed days without medication. Harriett was very strict about administering the medications, but she had come to trust Solo. As time passed, Solo had come to terms with her physical condition, the scars, the ugliness, constant pain, and night terrors. But the loneliness and longing for companionship were hard to accept. She needed to be touched and told she was beautiful. Touching herself was pleasurable, but she longed for more.

Given the tight quarters, Solo could not avoid running into one or two of the residents each day. Of course, they didn't speak to her, and most would move quickly out of her way to avoid getting within her reach or making any physical contact. However, some were very mean, and stuck out their tongues or made disgusting faces at Solo as if she smelled of something unpleasant (which most times she did). As a result, Solo's extended interactions with the other residents, except for Harriett, were limited, much to her dismay. Mostly, Solo did what she was told and kept to herself.

Most times Solo took her meals alone in the kitchen. However, on occasion, Harriett would sit with her to take her meal and to rest her aching bones, as she would call it. Solo found having Harriett near her rattled her nerves to the point she felt faint and nauseous. So, when Solo sensed Harriett was going to join her, she quickly scarfed her food down to avoid talking to Harriett, who was always prying. *Is that your real name? How did you get those ugly scars? Were you in a fire? Was your mother or father White? How old are you? Where are your folks from?* On and on Harriett would go with her endless questions. Solo simply didn't want to share any information about herself. However, even though Harriett put on a hard front, she was not uncaring. From the first day she laid eyes on this half White, half Black halfwit with a strange name, she knew some tragedy had come her way. Poor thing feared her own shadow. Harriett pitied her and tried to draw Solo out, but of course, Solo wasn't having it and did her best to avoid Harriett's probing questions.

Solo's loneliness was never-ending, especially at night in the dark cold, creepy attic she called home. She would listen through the door to the residents below laughing, talking, and having fun, oblivious to her daunting conditions. Faint sounds of familiar music would find their way through the dark halls and up the long creepy steps to Solo as if the beats of the music were purposely seeking her out. This made her happy and fond memories of her past life invaded her consciousness. She had flashbacks of life where she danced and brought the crowds to their feet when she hit the dance floor. Over time, she began to remember the "joint." It wasn't her imagination, it was her real past life. She would smile to herself when she thought of how everybody at the joint loved her. And boy, could she dance. Solo tried hard to recall the name as well as her friends but to no avail. She longed to dance and laugh. Her mind and body connected with the sounds floating up to her room. She had to contain herself from breaking out into a spontaneous dance. She smiled recalling those times. But those times were few and far between. Most nights Solo prayed to return to the hospital. At least there she could talk to Doctor Hertz. She missed him terribly. Where was her family? Where was her beloved Jessie? Why wasn't anybody looking for her? These thoughts would keep her up at night. In her mind, she was still a child. She was still a young girl of seventeen *(not realizing five years had passed, and she was now a woman of twenty-two)*. But thank God for the sweet music from below. It was like heaven to her ears and helped to silence the never-ending questions in her mind.

Solo twirled around and around in her creepy, dark, rodent-invested room. Her mind imagined she was back at the joint dancing with Jessie. She would hike her dress up real high and kick her feet out in rapid succession, being careful not to make too much noise fearing someone would hear her and stop the beautiful music. This would bring an end to her brief moments of joy. Dancing and dancing, she would go endlessly until exhausted and sweaty. She would then fall onto her makeshift floor bed. Those were her fun times until the bad times returned, especially at night.

When Solo slept, the memories of her previous life ran like an old black and white silent movie show. She dreamt of a life with the Chiles. She battled with the memories of her Papa, Mama, Little Henry, and most of all, Baby. The dreams were always of fire, constant screams, and smelly skin being burned. Fires surrounded her and engulfed her body. Most times she was alone, but other times she would be searching for her sister, Baby. She cried out to Baby to run from the fire, but instead, she watched as Baby's beautiful brown skin melted right before her very eyes. Baby did not cry out. Instead, unspoken words invaded Solo's head... *Why did you leave me? Help me, Solo. Help me, Solo. I don't want to die. Why Solo, why?* It was torment for Solo. Her flesh would burn, smoke raised high above her. Her beautiful hair was in flames. The pain made Solo scream out in agony. These memories were unbearable and painful, but they seemed to be becoming more and more real. Solo didn't understand why she had mixed emotions about her Papa and Mama. *Where is my family? Why did they leave me? Did they blame me for Baby's death?*

"Mama!" Solo would cry out in her dreams. "Help me, I need you!" But, in her dreams, her Mama's back was always turned away from Solo as flames engulfed her.

Solo loved her family, but the dreams about them scared her. Her longing or sadness was not for the absence of her kinfolks, but rather for her lover Jessie, whom she had passionate dreams about. Recalling their time together after fleeing Connecticut, but not fully understanding why they left their beloved home for New York City. Yes, she remembered. She needed her man to fill her arms and take away her pain. Surely, he must have gone mad not knowing her whereabouts and searching endlessly for her. She must find Jessie, and get word to him. But, being confined to this place, it was not possible. She needed to find her man. How? This was a question Solo pondered every day. With no money, no job, and no friends, what could she do? She had to try before she went mad.

Solo knew she needed a plan. She felt stronger physically, but sometimes her mental state was off. It didn't take her long to figure out it was because of the prescribed medication. She knew the daily dosages of medication kept her dazed and made her move like a zombie as if she was in a trance. The thought of not taking the meds was frightening. She didn't want to be carted off back to the looney bin as she had seen happen to some of the residents Harriett said had refused to take their medications. She had promised Doctor Hertz she would take her medication. But, why? She was never crazy, just burned.

Most days when they were so busy, Harriett would just simply hand Solo her meds to take and walk away without ensuring she took them. So, Solo would simply place the pills in her mouth, take a small slip of water and when she was sure Harriett wasn't watching, she would spit them out in her hand and throw them out with the rest of the garbage. She was a little nervous because sometimes the wild dogs and cats would eat the garbage and she didn't want to hurt them. But she couldn't worry about that. Her mind needed to be clear to devise her plan of escape and if it meant hurting a few animals, so be it. She could just put her meds in the food. That would teach them for laughing at her and treating her like some common "Negro slave." Devising her plan made Solo feel giddy and alive. Feelings she had not felt in a long time. Solo was back!

Freedom, freedom they cried. We are free now! But what is it to be free when your life or mind is in bondage? I am free to be me they say, but who am I?
"I want to fly like an eagle, let my spirit carry me...till I'm free," so the song goes;
But this is not a song; this is my real life, playing out on center stage.
Curtains fall or fly high like a sky.
My captured mind, hidden from all to see, locked away in pain, constant agony.
No peace, no matter how hard I tried, with my mind asking why.
Not a day goes by that I don't try to be free to wander with no questions, why.
How I would love to sail high in the sky like a plane, free from fears, no worry, and pain, just me, as God meant for me to be in his name.

THIRTY-SEVEN
She's Alive

"Whew!" Tulip let out a long sigh as she headed to the back of the streetcar, praying there was an available seat. She was too tired to stand for the trip home. It had been a long, hard day. She had been so distracted by her thoughts of the letter, money, and guilt that for the first time, she broke a glass. The glass made a thunderous sound when it the floor. She heard approaching shoes and knew she was in for a good tongue-lashing or even termination. Mrs. Bonds called out to Tulip as she entered her spotless kitchen with the latest Sears appliances.

"Tulip, dear, what in Christ's name is going on in here? You just about gave me the fright of my life!"

Tulip was on her hands and knees trying desperately to pick up the glass pieces without cutting herself. Keeping her head down and avoiding eye contact with Mrs. Bonds, Tulip fumbled to find her words.

"I'm sorry, Misses," Tulip said, a little too loudly, "but this here glass just slipped right out of my hand. I am truly sorry, and you can take it out of my wages."

Mrs. Bonds helped a reluctant Tulip to her feet.

"Get up and stop before you get a glass splinter. Get the broom and sweep up the pieces. It's just a silly old jam glass. Nobody is going to be losing wages for some silly glass."

Tulip stood up and was almost in tears. She couldn't lose this job, she needed the money.

"Thank you, Misses, I am truly sorry," Tulip mumbled so softly Mrs. Ball had to struggle to hear.

"Now hush with the apologizing and sweep up the mess," said Mrs. Ball. Mrs. Ball walked out of the room, chuckling to herself. Thankful for Mrs. Ball's understanding, Tulip quickly cleaned up the mess and left to make her way home.

Tulip finally saw a free seat on the streetcar. She slumped down, exhausted. As she dozed in and out of sleep, she heard the driver announce her stop. Tulip gathered her belongings and made her way off the streetcar. She still had a long walk home, which was fine with her because she needed time to think. *What if the letter was bad news and her precious daughter was hurt or even worse, dead?* No, Tulip thought to herself, get those thoughts out of your head, that is not God's plan. Solo is now twenty-two years of age and she hasn't seen her in more than sixteen years. *What does she look like? Is she married with a family? Maybe I am a grandmother.* Tulip smiled to herself. *Yes, my beautiful Solo, with golden hair and strange eyes, is alive.*

The God-sent letter waiting for her at home was good news, *yes, good news!* Her beautiful daughter was alive, and she was going to find her if it took the rest of her life. That is a mother's love for her child. With these thoughts, Tulip's steps had a little more pep as she made her way home.

The house was clean and quiet, and the little ones were fast asleep. Carson had passed out right after dinner and Little Henry was on his bed reading, which made Tulip's heart flutter. The older he got, the more he looked like his Papa, her dear Malcolm. She closed her eyes and allowed herself a very brief remembrance of her long-gone beloved, but quickly moved on. Paul was not at home and God only knew what mischief he was getting into. Tulip worried the streets were getting her son and Carson needed to take a firm hand to him before it was too late. She made a mental note to speak to Carson. But for now, there was something very important to tend to.

Hearing his Mama moving around, Little Henry looked up from his reading and watched as his Mama took a seat at the table in her favorite spot. She placed her spectacles on her eyes. Tulip didn't like wearing the ugly glasses. They made her look old, but lately, it was hard to read in the dim light. The sight of his Mama wearing those funny-looking glasses made Little Henry laugh. Tulip was startled by his laughter, but tickled none the same.

"Boy you better go on now with your studying and stop minding my business," she said lovingly to her favorite son.

"Yes, Mama," Little Henry replied with laughter in his voice and went back to his reading. Tulip looked up from her specs at her son and gave him a smile. How she loved him.

Tulip slowly retrieved the envelope from her dress pocket. She stared at the postage…New York City. It was addressed to her, but to her previous address in Maryland. It had to be from Jessie. He was the only one she had written to in New York City, but the return address was from New York City Hospital. *Why?* She prayed Jessie was in good health. Tulip opened the envelope.

The first thing she noticed was the beautiful penmanship. Clearly the letter was not from Jessie.

> *March 10, 1950*
>
> **Dear Mrs. Barnes:**
>
> **My name is Mary Pierce, and I am the Head Nurse for the New York City Hospital burn ward. Please accept my dearest apology for the timing of this letter. But only recently your letter to Mr. Jessie Thornton, inquiring about your daughter, Solo, came into my possession. I know you are wondering why a hospital, let alone a burn**

hospital, has knowledge of your daughter. However, some years back there was a very bad fire in the lower Manhattan slums. A severely burned, unconscious victim was brought in with no identification. The burns were so bad, she was not expected to make it. However, she did, but she remained unresponsive and comatose for more than a year. There were never any visitors, and no one ever inquired about the patient. Over time, her burns healed, but unfortunately not without severe scarring, pain, and deformity. Further, the patient had no memory of the fire, who she was, or even family or friends. In fact, her mental condition bordered on insanity, and rightfully so, given the state of her physical condition. As a result, she was moved from the hospital burn ward to the mental ward, which was more equipped to treat her mental illness. Please know in my years of treating severely burned victims, it is not uncommon for them to suffer a mental lapse.

I know this must sound very troubling, and I am not confirming that the patient known as "Jane Doe" is your daughter. But, given some of the important details in the letter, it may be possible that Solo and Jane Doe are one in the same.

I want you to know if this information had come to my attention earlier, we would have made every attempt to contact you. But I must say, the story of Jane Doe does not end here. Trust me, it is very complicated, but I will try to explain. After a couple of years of trying to treat the patient's mental condition, there was no progress.

The patient became extremely violent and was deemed a threat to herself as well as the other patients. As a result, the patient was confined to the New York State Hospital for the Mentally Retarded and Criminally Insane and is under the care of Doctor Montgomery Frank.

Again, it is no way to confirm this is your daughter. However, I would recommend that you reach out to the hospital directly and speak with Doctor Hertz about a patient transferred from City Hospital #4, formally called Jane Doe. I can't make no promises, but it may be worth it.

The address is:

462 First Avenue
Manhattan, New York, New York

On behalf of New York City Hospital #4, please know every care was extended to the patient. I hope this letter provides you with comfort. We wish you well and God's speed.

Sincerely,

Head Nurse Mary Pierce
New York City Hospital #4

Tulip's eyes glistened and warm happy tears rained down her soft Black face. She smiled and held the dear letter to heart, closed her misty eyes, and said a silent prayer to thank her God. She read the letter over and over.

"What's wrong Mama?" Little Henry asked startled by seeing his mama's face wet from streaming tears. He raised up higher to get a better look at her in the dimly lit room. She didn't answer him. He roughly threw back his covers and stood tall. At that moment, Paul who was clearly inebriated, stumbled loudly through the door, swaying as he walked. Befuddled, he looked at Little Henry who was standing in his underwear, who was staring at Mama sitting at the table holding some papers to her heart with her eyes closed, head thrown back, and crying like a baby. Paul swore. He did not expect to come home to an audience in his condition. Now here he was, facing the wrath of Mama.

"Sorry, Mama," Paul blurted out quickly, with stumbling words. "I didn't mean to use the Lord's name in vain. I...I...was just overcome, seeing you so upset, and Henry standing there looking like a ghost. Meant no disrespect."

Tulip stared at Paul. She had too much love in her heart at that moment to be angry. So instead, she said lovingly, "Boys, I found your lost sister. I found her. I found Solo. She is alive, she is alive! Praise God, she is alive!"

Little Henry and Paul exchanged looks and confirmed in harmony, "She's alive?"

Tulip jumped up from her seat and raised both her hands above her head, stomped her feet, and yelled, "YES, MY BABY IS ALIVE!"

Hearing the ruckus, and fearing harm was coming to his family, Carson quickly put on his pants and stepped out of the bedroom he shared with Tulip, only to see his two sons watching their mama having some kind of a fit. Hearing their mama's loud yelling, Veronica pulled the twins, who were also awakened, along with her to investigate. Together, the family all watched as Tulip twirled around. She gave thanks to God, fell to her knees, and cried out, "My baby, your sister, she's alive! She's alive!"

No life is set in stone, there is a road map that eventually in living time will grow cold, and old in the earth's soil.
Some believe God's plan for each living human is pre-determined, not by happenstance or left to fester like a mole;
Others say the world is a stage, and we are stars in our role of life as incepted in our living soul;
Beauty of it all is we each graced our presence on this earth and our physical domain we left a personal legacy to be forever told.

THIRTY-EIGHT
Bye-Bye Birdie

Baked turkey, yams, collard greens, pig's feet, ham hocks, chitterlings, hog maws, macaroni and cheese, fatback, ham, corn pudding, yeast rolls, fried chicken, giblet gravy, sweet potato pies, corn bread, fried okra, stewed tomatoes, and butter beans all had to be prepared for the upcoming holiday. It was 1953, and in just two days, it would be Solo's third Thanksgiving at the red stone house. In preparation for the annual feast, she had to work extra hard helping Harriett prepare the feast for the house residents as well as their family members. Additionally, Misses Hathaway would invite her personal guests. Solo rose at 3:00 AM and worked until 10:00 PM. She and Harriett had to shop at the local market as well as pick some vegetables from the small garden they had planted the previous year. Harriett was constantly shouting orders at Solo, "Do this, do that, no not that, do this!" It had been more than six months since Solo stopped taking those awful meds. However, she kept up the pretense around others, especially Harriett, that she was mental. But she felt great. Her recollection of past events was getting better, and her childhood memories had fully returned. Solo felt strong and confident. No one was the wiser and she loved it.

The kitchen was filled with meats, vegetables, baked pies, and cakes. Solo couldn't think straight. She just followed Harriett's instructions as best she could. Harriett was a pro and pretty much had everything under control. She was an excellent cook and prided herself on her culinary skills. As Solo peeled white potatoes, which seemed to be endless work, she did not make eye contact with Harriett, but she was aware that Harriett was frustrated.

"Solo," called out Harriett hastily.

"Yes, Auntie?" Solo rushed to answer not wanting to upset Harriett.

"Take this note and run down to Mr. Mott's market. Just hand the butcher the note and he will do the rest. Don't dolly and make haste. I know you never been by yourself, but I got the stove going and I can't trust anyone with my cooking. Now, do you understand? Do have any questions?" asked Harriett, handing Solo a piece of folded paper.

Taking off her apron, Solo's heart was beating fast. Did she hear correctly? Harriett wanted her to go to the market alone, by herself. *FREEDOM*, Solo screamed to herself.

"Now you know the way, child. Don't talk to anybody, walk fast and hightail your Black ass back here as fast as you can. Do you hear me, girl?"

Beads of sweat formed on Solo's head as she nodded and nervously took the wrinkled note from Harriett. With that, she was out the door.

It was cold out. Winter was coming. The clouds hung low as if they wanted to fall to the ground. A cold, brisk wind blew gently. Solo pulled her worn secondhand coat tightly. Even though it was too big for her small frame and smelled of mothballs, it was warm. She checked to make sure her headscarf was covering her scarred face. When traveling to the market with Harriett, Solo always wore a scarf to cover her head and face. She didn't want people staring or being frightened of her, like the red stone house residents.

With everything in place, Solo hugged herself tightly, shivered from the cold, and preceded on her way. Excitement filled her body. This was the very first time she had walked the street alone without Harriett leading the way. She needed to do good and please Harriett. Walking alone on her mission, Solo felt a sense of happiness, a feeling she had not felt in a very long time. She kept her head low, her eyes down, and walked quickly without making eye contact with the many passersby, who out of politeness, greeted her or nodded their heads. Solo did not return any greetings. She just moved along quickly, stopping for traffic. After about thirty minutes, she arrived at the market, she squeezed the wrinkled note in her hand, ensuring it was not lost. She took a deep breath and felt a sense of pride that she had made it to her destination. Harriett would be proud. As she entered the market, bells loudly chimed announcing a new arrival. The market was crowded with tons of patrons, no one looked as she entered. Before she went any further, Solo patted her face to make sure the scarf was securely in place, *no sense in causing a scene.*

Solo knew what to do so she took her place in the line for the butcher. With Thanksgiving approaching, the market was overwhelmed with last-minute shoppers. So, the wait would be extremely long. Unbeknownst to Solo, when she lifted her head to see how long the line was, someone noticed her. Not quite believing her eyes, the scantily-dressed Colored woman with heavy makeup, waiting to buy a pack of unfiltered cigarettes, screamed out.

"NO! IT CAN'T BE! SOLO! SOLO!" The outburst caused some of the customers to look in the scantily-dressed woman's direction. She frowned and rolled her eyes in disgust. Solo also looked up after hearing her name called. The woman threw money on the counter, grabbed her pack of cigarettes, and grinning from ear to ear, moved quickly towards Solo. Solo didn't know what to do, she was frozen in place. *Who was this person? How did she know her name?* Solo stood perfectly still and some of the customers watched as the woman approached Solo with outstretched arms. She struggled through the crowd and told some to, "get the f—k out of her way." Finally, she reached Solo, who by this time, was about to s—t her pants. She couldn't leave and return home without completing her task. Harriett would be so disappointed.

So, Solo wrapped her arms around her even tighter hoping this strange, crazy woman would not approach her, but that was not the case.

"Solo! Solo! It's me, your girl, Maybelline." The woman grabbed Solo and kissed her cheeks, leaving marks of the bright red lipstick on the side of Solo's face. *Who is this woman?* The woman, still grasping Solo with both hands, looked her directly in her face and said cheerfully, "Don't you remember me? It's me, Maybelline. After that terrible fire, I thought you were dead. I went to every hospital to look for you, but I could not find you. Where have you been? That no-count man of yours, Jessie, was no help. After the fire, he got his things and left with no word about you. I saved you. God knows I tried my best to find you. That fire just about destroyed everything in your apartment, but I managed to get a few of your things and kept them for you. Everybody said no way you would survive that fire, but I knew you weren't going to let no stupid fire take you from this earth. I just knew you were alive. I told my man, Johnny Boy, you were alive. You remember my man, Johnny Boy? Man, the fun you, me, and Johnny Boy had together. In fact, come with me, Johnny Boy is right outside."

Solo could only nod her head. Tears formed in Maybelline's eyes and taking both of Solo's hands in hers, pulled Solo from her spot in line towards the door.

Solo's mind was in overdrive. Somewhere deep in her subconscience was a familiarity with the woman. She knew her, but from where? Solo was so confused. Yet, she lacked the will to protest as Maybelline pulled her through the crowded market, knocking into people. Maybelline was oblivious to their complaints and vulgar language and continued holding tightly to Solo's hand in fear she would lose her again.

As they exited the market, a blast of cold air hit Solo's face. With her free hand, Solo drew her scarf tighter around her face.

Suddenly, Maybelline stopped moving and frantically looked from side to side. "That dumb-Black ass Negro, I told him to stay right here while I run in to get some smokes. But did his dumb ass listen…hell no!"

Maybelline continued to rant while looking up and down the streets. She tapped the bottom of her cigarette pack, tore it open, and retrieved one short white cigarette. Her ranting stopped as she took a long draw from a burning cigarette into her lungs. Solo was beginning to panic as she struggled to remember. She hadn't taken her meds in months and now the old feelings of doom and dread were creeping into her mind. To calm herself, she dug her nails into the palms of her hands. She felt Harriett's note still clutched in her hand. She was losing control and just as a scream was about to exit her throat, a black long, shiny automobile stopped directly in front of them. The driver of the car, an obese, Colored man with slicked-back black hair looked at them and smiled.

Maybelline put both hands on her hips as she looked into the car and yelled, "What the f—k? I told your Black ass to wait right here. I was only gone one minute to get my smokes. You know my feet hurt in these damn shoes. But no, you had to go about your merry way." Maybelline rolled her eyes and took another draw off her cigarette.

The man leaned over, and with greedy eyes undressed Solo from head to toe. "Get your sweet ass in this car. Who that you got with you?"

Maybelline, throwing the lit cigarette to the ground and stomping it out with her shoes, quickly forgot her anger and remembered Solo was with her.

"Look here sugar, you remember my friend? The White girl, Solo. You used to give her a ride to the joint. You remember Solo?"

Maybelline motioned for Solo to come closer to the automobile. "Come on Solo, you remember my man Johnny Boy."

Solo's body was frozen in place, she didn't budge.

Maybelline urged Solo towards the car.

"Well, I done died and gone to heaven, if it's not the White girl. We thought you were crispy fried. You looked like hell run over," said Johnny Boy laughing. Now Solo remembered. *Who wouldn't remember this greasy slime ball?*

Maybelline opened the automobile door and slid in motioning for Solo to do the same. "Come on Solo and party with us like old times. It's Thanksgiving," Maybelline pleaded. Solo didn't move.

Johnny Boy was getting impatient. "Look, I ain't got all day, I got things to do. Plus, that girl don't look right." Maybelline gave Johnny Boy a mean look and turned back to Solo and motioned for her to get in.

Solo was confused. She wasn't used to making decisions, so she slid in the automobile beside Maybelline and closed the door as she let the crumpled note drift to the ground.

"That's my girl, it's going to be just like old times." Maybelline smiled as she patted Solo's leg. Maybelline had seen the scars on Solo's legs. She also noticed how Solo kept one side of her face hidden, *probably more burns from the fire,* she thought to herself. No matter, men can't see in the dark, and pussy is pussy.

Solo sat silently and listened as Maybelline talked nonstop. Back at the red stone house, more than two hours had passed since Harriett had sent Solo to the market. *Dumb ass girl. Probably got herself lost and out there wandering around the streets. Well, I ain't got time to look for her now. I should have known that dumb wit would get lost. I thought she had a little common sense. I hope she's okay though. No sense in worrying now, too much to do.* Harriett knew Solo had flown the coop, she had seen it too often. She was no fool and knew Solo had been skipping her medication. The girl wasn't crazy. She had been a hard worker. Deep down, even though Harriett wouldn't admit it to anyone, she had grown fond of the halfwit. She would miss her. Harriett fought back the tears.

> *Nothing like a rainy day to make the sun go away and like clouds, my feelings are on full display;*
> *My life is like the raindrops that fall astray along the open path of heartache and pain;*
> *Consumed are my inner feelings of wanting to belong like the lyrics of my favorite love song;*
> *I feel the bondage of empty promises that to get love, you must pay;*
> *So, like my slave ancestors, on my knees, unto the divine, I pray you will come my way.*

THIRTY-NINE
Getting Closer

On a cold February day in the year of our Lord 1955, Tulip stepped onto the platform of Penn Station in New York City. She reached up to pat her hair and then ran her hands down her clothes to press out the wrinkles. It had been two days since she left home. The trip had been long, but she had gotten much-needed rest. Though she was excited about the prospect of finding her lost daughter, her heart was still heavy about leaving her family, especially the little ones, who were not accustomed to their Mama being gone. Also, her dear Carson didn't feel right about her setting off to the Big City on her own. It was his duty to protect her, his wife, the mother of his children. But Tulip, understanding and touched by her man's concern, looked deep into his eyes and explained that there was barely enough money to cover her train fare, room, and board for a few days. Further, just in case blessings were stored upon her, and she found Solo, Tulip needed to have extra money to cover her train fare home. She went on to explain to Carson that because he had to tend to Mama's homegoing, he could not afford to miss any more days from his job. It was bad enough she would miss the money she earned from her day job with the Bonds.

Tulip had lied to the Bonds saying she had to go out of town for a few days to take care of a sick relative. She hated lying, but she couldn't tell them the truth. Plus, she got Lorraine to take over her work with the Bonds. So, it worked out for the better because her sister-law could earn a few dollars while she was gone, Lord knows she could use it, and the Balls would have their work done. So, everyone would be happy.

Tulip had to put Veronica in charge of the house, which meant caring for the twins, cooking the meals, cleaning, washing, and ironing clothes. Of course, Veronica protested, folding her arms and demanding to know why she had to do all the "women's work." Why couldn't she go with her to New York City? Veronica's rant made Tulip look away so her daughter wouldn't see the smile on her face and thought to herself, *this new generation of girls is something else.* Tulip calmly explained to her daughter that she trusted her and depended on her to keep their family and house in order. The twins were older so they could pretty much take care of themselves. Tulip was more concerned about her husband and under no circumstances did she want Paul bringing any roughnecks into her house. She would talk to Carson about keeping him straight. If needed, Little Henry would help for sure, but he was now married with a family of his own. Tulip and Veronica both knew once Paul learned of his mama's absence, he would use it as an opportunity to get into trouble. All she did was nag. He didn't even care about the strap his papa would take to his hide. He was a man now. Too old for whippings. He had kids of his own but refused to marry or leave home. Tulip promised Veronica she would bring her something special back from New York City, maybe one of those new tailored, button-down blouses. Veronica, now eighteen, was engaged and would marry soon so something nice would be good for her. Tulip said a silent prayer she could keep that promise to her daughter with what little money she had. Tulip felt guilty, but she needed Veronica's help. She could not make the trip without it. Tulip made the sign of the cross.

Tulip stepped off the train toting one heavy, aged brown leather bag, and looked around. Smells invaded her nostrils. The air held a combination of human sweat and smoke from the train burning black coals. The air was thick and made it hard for her to breathe. Tulip stood momentarily looking around and holding her bag. She needed directions to the Colored Young Men's Christian Association (YMCA).

When she was on her own looking for her late husband Malcolm, she stayed at the Colored YMCA, which provided daily guest with rooms at a cheap rate. Years back, the YMCA was segregated. She didn't know if that was still the case. If not, she needed to find cheap sleeping quarters before it got too late. New York was a dangerous place at night for women.

Tulip noticed an old Colored man dressed in a porter's uniform.

"Excuse me, sir, I was wondering if I may ask you for your assistance?"

The old porter, with his grayish twinkly eyes, smiled at Tulip. He appreciated her politeness and took off his hat.

"Why certainly, Miss, that is why I am here," he said cheerfully.

Tulip explained that she was seeking Colored accommodations, perhaps at the YMCA.

"The nearest one that comes to my mind that serves good, decent lady folks like yourself is the one located on West 63rd Street. Let me see here, you will need to go through these here two doors," he pointed straight ahead, "and cross over the street and take the number 77 uptown streetcar, for, let me see," he counted as he talked, "for one, two, three, four, five, six, seven stops. If you go eight stops, you have gone too far and will have to walk a very long block back. Now, remember to get off the streetcar after seven stops and the YMCA will be there in front of you. Now don't go talking to anymore. You are a good-looking lady and there are some bad people out there in the streets, so you be quick and keep to yourself. Wouldn't want any harm to come to such a pretty lady such as yourself."

Tulip smiled at the stranger's concern for her well-being. It made her think of Carson. She reached in her handbag to find a dime for the man, a thank you for his help. He refused the token. So, she thanked him and made her way through the two doors and onto the street.

The old man put his hat back on and thought to himself, *In my day...* as he watched Tulip walk through the doors, he began to hum and returned to his work.

By the time Tulip stepped off the Number 77 streetcar, it was nightfall. The air had turned crisp, and she took in a deep breath. Before her was a stone, faded gray building that stood twenty feet tall. The large, engraved sign read "63rd Street YMCA." The building was brightly lit as a welcoming sign to those who cared to venture in. Looking at the nondescript building brought back a rush of memories Tulip cared not to conjure up. She held her bag tightly, looked side to side for any oncoming traffic, and walked up to the front of the building. As she approached, she saw a single glass door with a sign in bold black letters: ALL ARE WELCOME.

The lobby was spacious and empty. Tulip stood still and looked around for help. Finally, she saw a plump middle age Colored woman sitting behind a desk. The woman had her head down and was busy writing, so Tulip made her way over to the desk. Tulip cleared her throat to get the woman's attention.

The woman said, without looking up, "I know you are there, just hold your britches, Missy."

Tulip started to protest, but she just let her lips form an ever-so-slight smile, *talk about northern hospitality*. The woman finally looked up and gave Tulip and good once over. She thought Tulip seemed to be a decent woman, unlike some who sought rooms. "Now what can I do for you, Missy?"

Tulip wanted to turn and leave, but she couldn't roam the streets looking for a place to stay.

"I would like to inquire about a room for rent?" The woman almost chuckled at Tulip's politeness.

"The daily rate is $2.00 in advance, you must pay for the whole day regardless of the time you arrive and leave. If you plan to stay for more than one day, it must be paid upfront. Each day you stay, you must pay." The woman suddenly laughed out loud at her rhyme and repeated it. "Each day you stay, you must pay, now that's a good one," she chuckled."

Tulip was tired, she had to pee, and was trying not to lose patience. It had been a long day. "I will be paying for three days."

The woman said, "That would be $2.00 in advance." Tulip nodded and with her back to the woman, she reached into her secret hiding place for her change purse. After retrieving it, she opened it and took out some wrinkled one-dollar bills and loose change. Tulip carefully counted the money. Being satisfied, she turned and spread the money on the desk in front of the woman and firmly said, "That should be $6.00 and I will need a receipt."

The woman quickly picked up the bills as if they would disappear, she licked her thumb and counted each bill. She spread the change out across the large brown desk and counted that as well. The woman had been cheated before, so she wasn't very trusting. Confirming the amount of money was correct, she retrieved a large set of keys dangling around her neck and resting between her breasts. With one key, she opened the top drawer of the large brown desk and took out an old metal box, securing the money inside. She scribbled out a receipt and told Tulip to follow her.

They walked down a quiet corridor. Stopping in front of a closed door, the woman unlocked it, revealing a room with two single beds and a desk. It wasn't a large room, but it was clean and would do. The woman went on to explain where the bathroom and showers were located and suggested she try to bathe early in the morning before others. For right now, Tulip was the only one occupying her room, but that was subject to change. The woman handed Tulip a single key and then left.

Finally, Tulip was alone. She placed her bag near one of the neatly made beds. She was exhausted and needed sleep. Tomorrow was going to be a busy day, but first, she needed to find the bathroom. She had been holding her water for too long and her drawers felt soiled.

Startled by the loud sound of horns blowing, Tulip opened her eyes to the sun streaming into the room. She had slept hard. It took her a minute to get her bearings. She looked at the little alarm clock she had brought with her and placed it on the nightstand before she fell off to sleep. It was 7:45 AM. *Hadn't the woman told her to get up early to use the bathroom?* Tulip quickly grabbed a towel and washcloth. She sniffed them both and they smelled of soap. *Never can be too careful.* She put on her robe. Once out in the hallway, she looked both ways. She heard voices, but there was no one in her eyesight. Walking as quickly as she could, Tulip made her way to the showers.

Dressed and ready to go, Tulip locked her room door. She needed to call her sister-in-law so she could let Carson know she arrived safely and where she was staying. Hopefully, Veronica was managing okay. Tulip felt a pang of guilt for leaving her family. Her stomach was in knots, but she couldn't worry about that right now. As she made it to the open foyer, she looked towards the desk for the woman who helped her last night, but there was no one at the desk. She needed to find a phone. Finally, she saw a pretty, neatly dressed young girl, who looked to be no older than what Solo would be about now.

"Excuse me, would you happen to know where I can find a telephone?"

The girl seemed happy to help and led Tulip to a black pay phone mounted to a wall. Tulip picked up the telephone and pushed "0" for the operator. A friendly voice on the other end answered and asked how she could be of assistance. Tulip slowly called out the number she wanted to connect to. The operator told her the price for the connection. Tulip deposited the $.10 for five minutes. The telephone on the other end rang loudly about two times. Finally, a sweet voice said, "Hello, may help you?" It was her sister-in-law, Lorraine.

Since other people had now gathered in the foyer, Tulip took a seat in the wooden chair and cupped the mouthpiece of the telephone with her hand, whispering in a hushed tone.

"Hello, Lorraine. It's me, Tulip."

Lorraine yelled happily, "Tulip, that you? Lord child you just caught me before I left for the Bonds'. Did you find her? I forget her name…Sailor, or something?"

Tulip made a slight chuckle at Lorraine mispronouncing her daughter's name.

Lorraine continued, "How in the hell are you? S—t girl, we have been worried sick. Carson stopped by last night to see if you had called. Mercy child we thought you had been kidnapped or murdered, some s—t like that. You know New York City is a bad place for women, especially us Negro women."

With Lorraine's yapping, Tulip could not get in a word. Finally, she yelled loudly, "Lorraine, Lorraine, calm down girl. I just arrived last night, and my daughter's name is S-O-L-O. Look, I only have a few minutes left on the call. So, please let Carson know I arrived safely and I am staying at the 63rd Street YMCA."

Lorraine interrupted Tulip, "Hold on a minute girl, I can't remember all of this, let me get something to write with," and left the call.

Tulip tried to stop her, "No, No Lorraine! I don't have time." But Lorraine had already laid down the phone. The operator chimed in and said, "If you would like to extend this call, please deposit $0.10 immediately, if not, this call will be disconnected." Tulip needed to save what little money she had, so she hung up the phone.

Tulip walked away from the telephone, she needed to find her way to the New York City Hospital for the Mentally Retarded and Criminally Insane. She pulled the letter from her pocketbook to find the address. She saw the woman from last night sitting at the brown desk. Tulip approached her. Once again the woman's head was down, and she did not acknowledge her. Tulip took a deep breath and said,

"Good morning!"

The woman's head popped up. "Oh, it's you. Good morning, I trust you found your accommodations suitable."

Tulip replied, "Yes, everything is fine."

The woman interrupted her, "You paid for three days, are you ending your stay early?"

"No, I just wanted to ask…"

Once again, the woman interrupted her, "Well, how can I help you? No more linen can be provided. You cannot change your room…"

This time Tulip interrupted her. "I just need some directions. Like I said everything is FINE!"

The woman made a huffing sound and asked, "Well why didn't you just say so?" Tulip could have hauled off and smacked the s—t out of her. Instead, she continued.

"Need to know how to get to the New York City Hospital for the Mentally Retarded and Criminally Insane."

The woman put her hand on her heart and looked at Tulip very hard. Being familiar with the hospital's location *(she had family members who had spent time in the facility)*, she was able to give Tulip specific directions. Tulip thanked the woman, but as she was turning to leave, the woman mumbled, "Just one more thing. We do not allow crazy people here, so keep that in mind. You have a nice day."

Tulip clenched her fists tightly.

The streets were bustling with people as they walked about. Some carrying bags, some looking lost. Mothers gripped their little one's hands tightly as they rushed along. The little ones were trying desperately to keep up. Men were reading newspapers as they walked. Carts of food, meats, and other items straddled the streets. Children ran about, ducking through the carts and traffic, laughing without a care in the world. Tulip watched through the streetcar window, so many people were making their way to their destinations, just like she.

Caught up in people-watching, Tulip almost missed her stop. The conductor had to get her attention. When she exited, Tulip had a spring in her step. Her heart began to race. *Could this really be happening?* Her feet were moving so fast she almost lost her balance. She verified she was headed in the direction of the hospital and continued her journey by foot.

After walking a few blocks, Tulip stopped in her tracks and stared at the monstrosity looming before her eyes. It was a foreboding place. Tulip could only imagine the awful things that happened there. To think that her beautiful precious daughter was in this awful place brought an onrush of tears to Tulip's eyes. *Has Solo gone mad? Maybe she won't recognize me. I did abandon her. She probably blames me for her papa leaving. She hates me. What if she doesn't want to go with me?* Tulip's mind ran rampant. She couldn't control her negative thoughts. Tulip realized she had come too far and waited much too long to end her journey on the sidewalk of hell where her beloved daughter was inside. She prayed for forgiveness, and she prayed for strength. She took a moment's pause to think of her own mama and their common ground, the field of flowers. Peace flooded her soul. *Baby girl, Mama's here! Your Mama's here!* The wings of angels blew a slight breeze that crossed Tulip's face. She accepted it with grace and walked through the large open doors that swallowed her whole.

My, my, what a life I have lived with the talents I was given, but, for some reason, I can't seem to distinguish between a blessing or curse;
In my futile attempt to put the art of loving my life first...I loved, been loved, returned love, and lost love, but in between a tremendous amount of hurt;
I walked among the living, giving, receiving, and feeling now only to end up in a long black rented old hearse;
Little did I know the choices I made, and the way I lived my life, made it worse, to my dismay, living does not provide space or time to rehearse;
So heed my words, show respect for this vast universe, but importantly, take a minute of life to reflect on a bible verse..." I will bless the LORD at all times; His praise shall continually be in my mouth." Psalm 34:1

FORTY
Solo

"Girl, you better work that mouth," said the trick Solo was servicing in the alley behind Yung Ho Chinese joint. Solo stopped what she was doing and looked up at the trick with little emotion.

"You sure do want a lot for your $2.00," she said very matter-of-fact.

"That's the name of the game, baby, and I ain't got no shame," he replied. He enjoyed his pleasure from this freak of nature. The word around town was that she was half beauty and half monster, but she gave the best and cheapest blow jobs in town.

Solo needed to wrap this trick up. She had already spent more than the allotted time on his pencil. Plus, her knees were aching from the hard ground. She began to work hard on him until he finally finished. She quickly stood up, wrapped her scarf around her face, and walked off, leaving the trick with his pants down…pencil hanging.

It had been more than two years since Solo left the market with her friend Maybelline and drove off with her pimping, good-for-nothing boyfriend, Johnny Boy. In the beginning, she was confused and frightened. Some would say the daily consumption of drugs and alcohol kept her sane. Maybelline made space for her in a small, cramped dwelling located in the basement of a small market. Maybelline said the rent was cheap, and the owner got a little extra from her on the side. Solo would come to learn the same was expected of her. While Solo found her new accommodation had less space than the dirty, musty attic at the red-stone house, she didn't mind. At least she could share a bed with Maybelline and not sleep on the floor. Also, she didn't have the day-to-day hard work of cleaning, cooking, and washing clothes. This was just fine with her, despite how she was expected to earn her keep.

In the beginning, Solo took great pain to keep her body and face hidden from Maybelline and the daily string of men. Over time however, it became extremely difficult for her to keep up the pretense. Also, Maybelline was persistent in her efforts to stop Solo from hiding her body. She eventually became less self-aware of her deformities.

Solo was paranoid that Harriett and Misses Hathaway were looking for her and would whoop her silly once she was found. The thought of this kept Solo on edge, but as the days and months passed by, she soon came to realize no one cared about a disfigured crazy girl. Eventually, Solo didn't give the red stone house a second thought. Without any meds, Solo eventually turned to drugs and large sums of alcohol. On several occasions, when she was completely stoned, she would ring the hospital and ask for Doctor Hertz but would hang up when he answered. She just wanted to hear his voice. The sound of his voice, even if just for a moment, provided her with a sense of comfort. It was short-lived because life had taken on a different type of hell.

After servicing that nasty john in the alley, Solo was done for the night. Her feet were killing her, plus she was downright tired. This life was not easy, but given her condition, it was the only life for which she was suited. Solo staggered home. The flat was eerily quiet and dark. Maybelline was off doing work for her pimp, Johnny Boy, with his trifling self. Solo had come not to like him, not one bit.

Solo patted the wall for the light switch and flipped it up. The dim light barely lit up the room. She retrieved the wrinkled dollar bills and loose change from her bosom. The bills felt moist and damp from her body heat. Fifteen dollars in bills and another two dollars in change.

Not bad for one night of work. Once she gave Maybelline her cut, she would still have plenty for herself. Solo reached her hand under an old wooden brown dresser. She secured two bills into an old cigar box. This was Solo's emergency money. She had learned from living with Maybelline that you should always put a little something away for a rainy day. Plus, that greedy Johnny Boy always had his hand out, calling it protection. Solo always carried a switchblade with her. It was enough to scare the rough johns she encountered. Also, most knew she was one of Johnny Boy's girls and they didn't want to lose their lives over a two-dollar whore, and a beast of one at that. Solo kicked off her shoes, pulled off her underwear, and stripped off her clothes. She made a mental note to wash them tomorrow.

She walked over to the basin and poured in some fresh water from the pitcher. After she washed, she put on a silk red dress she had recently bought. She needed to make haste before Maybelline and Johnny Boy returned. She sprayed a little of Maybelline's cheap perfume (Maybelline sworn it was from Macy's department store, but Solo knew better). She combed her hair and put a scarf tightly around her head and face, making sure it was nicely secured. She slipped on her stockings, tucking in her switchblade, and high heels. Looking back to make sure her stocking seams were straight, she picked up a few dollars, leaving five as well as the loose two dollars in change. That was plenty to please Maybelline and Johnny Boy. She stuffed the money down her bra and patted her bosom to make sure the money was nesting safely. She grabbed her purse, put on her dark sunglasses (even though it was nighttime), and put on her jacket, closing the door behind her.

The night air was crisp, but the glow of stars in the sky shined like new-cut diamonds. Even though it was past midnight, people never slept in New York City. Solo walked down the streets slowly. Soon there were the catcalls and shouts from the Colored men lingering around with no obvious place to be.

"Hey, baby girl, you looking for me? I got just what you are looking for," they yelled while grabbing their crotches.

As Solo continued walking, an old beat-up black jalopy slowed down. The driver's sweet voice rang out, "Hey beautiful, you need a ride?" Solo looked at the nice-looking, uniformed young Colored boy. She kept walking and the black jalopy kept following her. She stopped, the black jalopy stopped.

Solo looked and smiled at the grinning boy. She smiled and asked, "Are you a soldier boy?"

The Colored boy laughed out loud. "I ain't no boy, Mama, but I am a soldier of the U.S. Army 101st Airborne Division, at your service."

Now, this tickled Solo. He sure did have a lot of spunk.

She asked, "Are you heading uptown towards East 125th Street?"

The young man, still smiling, answered, "At your service," and swung open the passenger side car door. Solo tugged at her tight dress and slid in.

With a sexy smile, Solo offered her appreciation for the ride.

The young Colored soldier, still grinning, responded, "No problem pretty lady. Out of curiosity what is a fine lady of your kind doing in these parts?"

"If you mean White woman, trust me sugar, I am far from White. You can call me Solo and let's get going."

"Yes, Mama…I mean, Miss Solo." The young soldier put the car in gear, stepped on the gas, and pulled off.

The old jalopy was cold, so Solo rolled up the window, but she kept it cracked a little so she could blow out the smoke from her lit cigarette. This was a big night for her. It had taken Solo months to plan this outing, and she was ready. Solo and the soldier rode for a while in comfortable silence, except for Solo giving a few directions. As they rode along, the young man occasionally took quick peeps at Solo's boobs, which were about to pop out of the dress. Of course, Solo was fully aware of the soldier's eyes on her breasts. She found it flattering. The dress was working. Breaking the silence, the soldier announced they had about fifteen more minutes to ride. Solo just nodded. Working up his courage, he cleared his voice, and nervously asked, "So, Solo, are you a wife or a working woman?"

Solo knew what he was getting at, so she decided to play along. "No, never been married, but one could say I am sort of a working type of girl."

"So, what type of work to do you?" He played along.

"Well, I am in the pleasure business," Solo continued seductively. She thought of Jessie and instantly regretted it.

The young man interrupted her thoughts.

"No disrespect, but I could sure use some pleasure. Being shipped out tomorrow. Don't know if or when I will get home again."

Solo barely heard him. They had arrived.

"Slow the car down. Stop here."

The confused driver complied. Solo recalled the many times she and Jessie walked this alley. *Was she ready to face her past?* The street was dark, and no one was walking about, just a few strays looking for food. Solo looked around and let out a deep sigh. She opened her purse and took out a little compact, stealing a quick glance. She closed the compact and pulled a little tightly wrapped paper, which she opened to reveal a white powdery substance. She took her pinky nail and sniffed some of the substance up both nostrils. William James, not knowing what to say or do, just watched her. After a moment of silence, Solo opened her eyes and looked at his handsome face. She turned to him and began to undo his belt buckle. William James didn't know what to do. He closed his eyes and relaxed. Solo wanted to kiss his sweet-looking lips, but she decided that wouldn't be wise to do. Instead, she would kiss something else. As she lowered her head and made contact, he let out a moan.

Both, lost in the heat of passion, did not notice the police car pull behind them. Solo's head popped up and she quickly wiped her mouth with the back of her hand. William James was struggling to get his pants on when the big White cop tapped on his side of the car window with a billy club. There was also another White, tall skinny cop standing outside of Solo's window, motioning for her to step out of the car. Solo hesitated to gain her composure. She was shaking. She knew what White patrolmen did to Colored women. Instead of stepping out of the car, she rolled down the window slightly and asked, "Yes, Officer sir, can we help you?"

The cop who was nowhere near as fat as his partner looked hard at Solo. The scarf on her head was covering her face, but he saw some flesh. "Holy s—t!" he said out loud. "I think we got a n—r lover."

His partner yelled at William James, "Get out of the f—g car before I blow off your n—r black nappy head! Now!"

William James, whose pants were still open, turned to look at Solo, who was sitting, straight up, looking forward, with a dazed expression. He stepped out tall, with his chest out proudly, lowered his eyes, and put his hands up. In the meantime, Solo was still sitting still and straight. She had completely zoned out...frozen in time. The patrolmen yelled obscenities. One thing they hated more than n—rs, was White women who loved n—rs.

Solo felt the force of the tall, skinny cop as he yanked her headfirst from the car. The silk scarf she always wore with caution and care wrapped around her damaged head and face cascaded down her face to her neck. Stringy, coarse, long blonde hair flew about her face. She was mortified and completely exposed. The tall skinny White cop, holding Solo by both her head and one arm, looked in unbelievable confusion at what was right before his very eyes. A true beauty and the beast. In the dark of the night, Solo fell hard to the ground. Broken glass and rocks penetrated her exposed skin, causing cuts and blood. The tall skinny White cop placed one of his feet on her stomach and pressed down every time she moved. *She isn't going anywhere*, he thought.

William James could not see what was happening to Solo on the other side of the car. He could only painfully listen to her screams and moans. He was ashamed. He could not help her. The anger swelled inside of him. He was helpless.

The tall skinny White cop yelled to his partner, "Man, you got to take a look at this s—t."

The big fat White cop, still pointing his gun, yelled at William James, "GET FACE DOWN ON THE GROUND BOY, NOW! BOY, THEY LET ANY MONKEY WEAR A UNIFORM. DISGRACE! I TELL YOU, DISGRACE TO AMERICA, THE LAND OF FREE. BUT BOY, UNIFORM OR NO UNIFORM, YOU DON'T GO BEING WITH NO WHITE WOMAN! NOW GET YOUR BLACK ASS ON THE GROUND BEFORE I PUT A BULLET THROUGH IT!"

William James slowly lowered his head, so they wouldn't see the humiliation on his face. He was afraid. A tear slid down his face. While he felt sorry for Solo, he was ashamed of himself as well. He called himself a soldier but was unable to stand up for himself or her.

The fat cop straddled William James to the ground and pressed his weight down on his legs, causing him to scream in agony. The cop forcefully pulled one of William James' arms behind him, which caused him to scream even louder. He pulled his other arm behind him and tightly handcuffed his hands to the car's old worn steering wheel. Being so heavy, he pressed down even harder on William James' legs, and he rose to a standing position. Satisfied his prisoner was secured, he walked around the car to see what was so pressing from his partner. He knew she was a White woman. So, what else could there possibly be? When the fat cop stepped around the car, he said, "What in the hell's name is it?"

His partner pointed at Solo who was lying face up on the cold, muddy ground, looking angrily at them as she kicked and yelled. The tall skinny cop, holding back his laughter said, "Take a good close look at her."

The obese cop, holding on to the car for support, bent over to get a closer look at Solo and then jumped back as if he saw the devil itself. He whispered, "Mary Jesus, what in world is this?" They looked at each other and burst out in uncontrollable laughter as their two prisoners silently looked on and trembled in fear as they pondered their fate.

> Traveling down the road on a path that is not specified by time or space, only a journey that I am to take;
> The trees loomed forward and the clear blue sky above me seem to be directing my way;
> My heart is driving this course of action because my mind is finally free from seeking unfilled fame that led to living a life of shame;
> No longer can I blame others for my unfilled dreams or hide inside myself with no hope because I lacked confidence and was convinced I was a fake;
> A waste of life is my sin, now my enemy is time,
> so I am in pursuit of the true me,
> I will not give that old me another day;
> The wind embraces my face with a smile, I heard the calls of the wild, and the songs of my ancestors who paved the way so I could be all that I want to be; I bow and grace;
> So my eyes followed the flying birds, they seemed to be saying, hey you, spread your wings, life is free, this beautiful earth was created by God for you and me, so soar high and fulfill your dreams.

FORTY-ONE
Tulip and Solo

Tulip let her eyes roam the around the massive building, the entrance was open. People were moving about. Doctors walked around with stethoscopes hanging around their necks, carrying large clipboards. She was overwhelmed and did not know where to begin to look for help. She noticed all the patients, men and women alike, had shaved heads. Her thoughts drifted to Solo's magnificent head of hair. Had they cut it? *Okay*, she thought to herself, *I need to focus*. She reached into her bag and took out the crumpled letter. She noticed nurses and doctors moving about. No one approached her. She was nervous and frustrated.

Finally, she spotted a nurse walking in her direction. Tulip quickly moved to her and found courage through her will. She shouted very fast, "I need to see Doctor Hertz," as she handed the soiled, crumpled letter to the nurse. Tulip continued to talk as the nurse read the letter.

"This letter says my daughter, her name is Solo, was in a fire and burned really bad. The burns made her head sick, so they sent her to this here hospital for the sick in the head and this here Doctor Hertz is helping her. I'm her mother, and I am here to take my daughter to her rightful home." Tulip was breathless as she finished. The nurse continued reading the letter.

"I know Doctor Hertz, and I will inform him you are here. But, in the meantime, I need you to be seated right over here. Please take your seat and I will take this to the nurse's station, and they will come talk with you. Now don't go wandering off. Please, just stay put until one of the other nurses talks with you."

As instructed, Tulip looked around for a vacant seat. The hospital was full, and some people stared at her. She was so tired and frustrated and to make matters worse, her feet hurt…damn shoes. She felt heat rising to her head. She had a headache. Her stomach rumbled. She was hungry. *Why didn't I just simply ask for my daughter?* She didn't need to see Doctor Hertz, she just wanted to get her daughter and go home. She missed Carson and the kids. Finally, she saw an open seat in the corner. She took the seat and waited for what turned out to be a long time.

Solo

Solo shivered in the cold cell. She looked around and saw six or seven women huddled together, whispering and looking at her. She stared back. Her scarf had been ripped away when the patrolmen pulled her out of the car, exposing her grotesque face. The patrolmen had pointed and laughed at Solo. Yet, despite her monstrous looks, they decided to have their way with her because sex was sex, and she was nothing but a low-down, White trash cunt who liked Black n—rs. They had a lesson to teach her. They threw her on the hood of the patrol car and took turns with their abuse in full site of the helpless, bound soldier. As Solo recalled the events and saw the dried blood on her legs, she felt herself retreating into the black hole that had been her prison and sanctuary, her mind. She screamed aloud for Doctor Hertz, not fearing the consequences.

An old White patrolman heard the screams and shook his head. He knew two patrolmen had brought in a deformed White girl who was caught engaging in a sexual act with a young Colored soldier. He unlocked the metal door that led to the four cells reserved for White women only (Colored women were taken to another jail). The screams grew louder as he approached the cell where the women were all grouped together. There she was, standing looking like something out of a nightmare. Blonde hair streamed wildly around her face. Clothes almost ripped to shreds. Dirty, bleeding, and yelling at the top of her lungs.

"Hold your horses, Misses, and stop the racket. I can't make out a damn thing you're saying."

He made his way toward Solo and noted the scars. When he was a kid, his baby sister suffered from burns and lived with deformity and pain until she took her own life. He knew this poor girl's misfortune.

As the patrolman got closer to Solo, she reached her arms and hands through the bars of the cells. She was frantic, she was losing it, she needed drugs, meds, something…she shouted loudly in rapid succession,

"Please, help me, I don't belong here, call Doctor Hertz, he will tell you. HELP ME! HELP ME!"

The other prisoners huddled together and watched as everything played out. The old White patrolman finally reached Solo, keeping his distance. In a low, kind gentle voice, he said, "Now looky here, young lady, you got to quit all that screaming, crying, cussing, and yelling. All that nonsense is not getting you anywhere, except downstairs in the hole and you don't want to go there."

Solo, squeezed the cell bars in a desperate attempt to calm down, and her knuckles turned white. She conjured Doctor Hertz's face in her head and tried to remember what he told her to do when she was frightened or scared. It worked. With her eyes closed, still grasping the cell bars, she took long deep breaths and exhaled the air from her lungs and through her nose. The old White patrolman coached her, "That's right breathe, breathe." Finally, Solo was calm.

Tulip

After waiting for what seemed like a lifetime, Tulip felt a hand on her shoulder, gently shaking her awake.

"Miss, Miss, Hello, Miss. Doctor Hertz is ready to see you now."

Tulip looked up and admired the crisp, white tie-up shoes with not a scuff mark. She liked things to be clean. Her eyes traveled to the white stockings, not a single run. Finally, she let her eyes travel up the clean white button-skirt and blouse, which was neatly tucked in. The nurse's lips were in a thin smile, with no lipstick. The nurse spoke softly, "Miss, I need you to follow me."

Tulip rose to her feet and swayed a little.

The nurse seemed concerned, "Are you okay? Would you like a little water?" Tulip nodded her head in agreement. She was consumed by doubt and fear.

The tall thin White nurse watched Tulip carefully. Once Tulip finished drinking the water, she took the cup and asked, "There, are you better?" Tulip nodded. "That's good," the nurse went on. "I am Nurse Tippet," pointing to her name pin. "I need you to follow me."

She spoke as she walked, "I don't know if your daughter is here or if you are who you say you are. Your letter has been given to Doctor Hertz and he is waiting to see you. But I need to get some additional information from you about your daughter. You must understand, Doctor Hertz is very busy. He is taking time away from his patients to meet with you. You didn't have an appointment. So, first things first. There are procedures we must follow. We must be certain you are a relative before we provide any information." The nurse was about business and Tulip hurried to keep up.

Solo

Solo had managed to calm down and she watched with intent as the old White patrolman approached her cell. He seemed to move in slow motion. She wanted to yell at him to move faster but she thought it was better to not. As the patrolman slowly approached the cell, he took full stock of the prisoner. She was an awful mess. He had seen some messed up folks in his lifetime, but this was by far the worst. He felt compassion for Solo.

"Please sir, help me. I don't belong here. I need my meds, please sir help me. Please call Doctor Hertz, he will tell you. I beg you please, please." She slid down to the floor. She no longer had the strength to stand.

"Okay, no need to beg. Come on now, stand up and get off the dirty floor." Solo managed to pull herself up, but she held tight to the cell bars because she was lightheaded.

The old White patrolman said, "Now that is better. What happened to your clothes?" He handed Solo a blanket he had found in an empty cell. Solo relaxed and saw kindness in his eyes.

The patrolman continued, "Now what is this about medication and doctors?"

Solo took a deep breath and explained to him she was under the care of Doctor Hertz at New York State Hospital for the Mentally Retarded and Criminally Insane. She wanted to go back to her hospital. The old White patrolman took off his hat and scratched his head.

"Now let me get this straight, you want to go to the crazy house?"

Solo nodded, "Yes!"

The patrolman said aloud, "Excuse the expression, but you must be crazy in the head if you want to go back to a crazy hospital."

Solo cleared her throat and mumbled, "Doctor Hertz can help me. He is the only one. Please call him to come and get me. Please sir, I beg you. I need him." She began to cry uncontrollably. The old White patrolman was overcome with emotion.

"Okay, let's not have none of that," he said. "Now if you promise me you will stop the tears and yelling, I will try to find this doctor of yours, but I'm not making any promises. But I will try. Are we in agreement?"

Solo's body was trembling, she ached all over. She would do anything if this patrolman would help her. She nodded in agreement.

"Great," the patrolman said. "I'll be back."

One of the other prisoners yelled to the old patrolman.

"Why are you helping that freak? What about us?"

He stopped and turned back to the cell and looked at the prisoners, and simply replied, "You didn't ask," winked at Solo, and walked away.

Solo smiled.

Tulip

As Tulip followed the tall, thin nurse through the never-ending maze of corridors, she could not help but notice the array of patients wandering aimlessly. It was a desperate situation and Tulip pitied the poor souls. She wondered what her dear Solo had endured.

Without any notice, the nurse suddenly stopped. Tulip was preoccupied with the goings-on of the patients that she almost ran into the back of the nurse. The door the nurse opened led to a small room that held a metal desk and a couple of chairs, one behind the desk and one facing the desk. The nurse clicked on a lamp for more light. There were no windows in the room, and it was stuffy and hot. There were several large file cabinets aligning the wall. The metal desk was covered with papers neatly stacked in piles. The nurse went around the metal desk and took a seat. She motioned for Tulip to take a seat, to which she complied. Tulip sat quietly as the nurse seemed preoccupied with reading over some papers. Finally, she asked, without looking at Tulip, "What is your full name and address?"

Tulip replied giving her full name and address.

The nurse's questions continued.

"Are you married, and if so, what is your husband's name and age?" Tulip didn't know what Carson had to do with this, but she reluctantly gave his information.

The nurse continued, "What is your daughter's full name and birthdate?"

Tulip responded, "Her Christian name is Solo Thornton, and she was born on July 7, 1928." The nurse wrote as Tulip talked.

"Do you know who her father was?" asked the nurse.

That question made Tulip glare at the nurse, who kept her head down on the paper. She wanted to reach over her desk and slap the s—t out of her. White folks always assumed Colored women were loose. The nurse looked up to see why Tulip had not responded to her question about the father. The nurse saw the expression on Tulip's face.

"Look, if you want to get through, you must answer these questions, your choice."

For sake of finding her daughter, Tulip swallowed her pride and said very slowly, "Yes, she had a Paw. His name was Malcolm Thornton." These endless questions were working her nerves and so much time had passed. The nurse continued.

"When was the last time you saw your daughter?" Tulip hesitated before she responded, a sense of guilt flooded over her thinking about the last time she saw Solo. As sure as if it was yesterday, she remembered the look of abandonment on Solo's face as the wagon pulled off. Tears formed in Tulip's eyes and in a less audible voice coupled with shame, guilt, and embarrassment, she whispered, "It's been twenty-one years."

The nurse stopped writing and looked up from her clipboard. "Did

I hear you correctly that you have not seen your daughter in twenty-one years?"

Tulip could only nod in response and replied, "Or more."

The nurse shook her head and said, "That should do it for right now. Please be patient while I take this information to Doctor Hertz, and I will return momentarily. Can I get you a drink of water?"

Tulip, ashamed, shook her head.

Solo

After finishing with Solo, the elderly patrolman walked slowly from the cell block, closed the hard metal door, and went to his desk. One of the other patrolmen asked, "What was all the ruckus? Did you tame the jungle?" laughing out loud. The old White patrolman pondered his conversation with Solo. He felt sorry for her. She was a mess and looked to have suffered in her life. She needed help. However, he was concerned about the hospital, surely it was segregated. *But hell,* he thought, *maybe they put all the Coloreds and White crazies together. What would I know?*

He leaned back in his chair and folded his hands behind his head and thought with great care, *Maybe this is a wild goose chase, but what harm could it do?* So, he picked up the telephone, and once the operator answered, he said, "This is Patrolman Blackwell over at the 5th District, please connect me to the New York City Hospital for the Mentally Retarded and Criminally Insane."

Tulip

Time was slowly moving, and it seemed as if the nurse had been gone for hours. Tulip closed her eyes and tried desperately to conjure up

Mama or the field of flowers. No luck. She looked at the telephone sitting on the desk. She wished she had asked the nurse if she could use the telephone to call home. Tulip needed to hear Carson's reassuring voice and she missed her babies. Maybe this had been a waste of money and time. So much doubt. The endless waiting was killing her. She closed her eyes and was drifting off to sleep when the door suddenly opened with the nurse announcing, "Doctor Hertz will see you now."

Tulip jumped so quickly from the chair that it tumbled over and landed sideways on the floor. She apologized and reached down to pick it up. The nurse said, "Please forget about the chair. Doctor Hertz is a busy man, we must not keep him waiting."

Tulip asked, "Did he say anything about my daughter, Solo?"

The nurse moved down the corridor without acknowledging Tulip's presence. She suddenly stopped in front of an old iron gated elevator, which looked to be a century old. An elderly orderly gracefully slid the gate open, which made a creaking noise as if the iron was scrapping. He nodded to Tulip and the nurse as they entered. He slid the gate closed, sat down on a little wooden stool, and said, "What floor please?"

The nurse answered, "Fourth floor, Sebastian."

The elevator creaked along the way. The man got up from his little wooden stool and, once again, slid open the old metal gate. The nurse quickly walked through the gate without a word to him. Tulip turned and smiled at him and whispered, "Thank you." His tired eyes glistened, and he nodded and closed the gate.

After a short walk, the nurse stopped once in front of the door that had a sign that read "Office of Doctor Jermaine Hertz, Head Psychiatrist." The nurse knocked firmly and a pleasant voice beckoned them to enter.

The nurse entered first, "Doctor Hertz, this is Misses Barnes."

Doctor Hertz rose to his feet saying, "Please, Misses Barnes, have a seat." Tulip accepted the invitation and took a seat as she looked around the room and thought with a smile, *Misses Barnes.* She sat in the chair close to Doctor Hertz's desk, not knowing her dear daughter had spent countless hours in that same chair. The nurse stood waiting until Doctor Hertz looked at her and said, "That will be all. I will handle this from here."

Doctor Hertz took a seat behind his desk. He looked at Tulip and could find no resemblance to Solo. "I am going to have a cup of tea. Would you like one while the water's hot?"

She nodded, afraid if she opened her mouth, the words "WHERE IS MY DAUGHTER?" would come running out.

"Great," Doctor Hertz said as he got up from his chair. "I read over your notes, and I see you have not been in touch with your daughter since she was a teenager."

Tulip spoke up, "No, that is incorrect. I have not seen my daughter since she was six years old, twenty-one long, regrettable years." Doctor Hertz nodded. Tulip's heart skipped a beat, she felt faint. After a few moments of silence, Doctor Hertz spoke.

"Your daughter suffered greatly. When she arrived here from the New York City burn ward, she was in a very bad mental state as a result of her injuries from the fire."

This made Tulip find her voice. "The letter mentioned she was in a fire."

"Yes," said Doctor Hertz. "She was burned very badly and as a result, she is severely disfigured."

Tulip's mouth dropped open. "Disfigured? My beautiful baby…disfigured?"

Doctor Hertz placed a cup of hot tea in front of Tulip and the other cup on his desk. He retrieved the bowl of sugar and placed it in front of Tulip and took his seat. He continued.

"Solo was disfigured, and it impacted her mental state. To sum it up, she completely lost her mind. By the time she came to me, she no had knowledge of who she was or how she ended up in a mental hospital. It took years of treatment before she gained some knowledge of who she was. She made great progress."

Tulip was so anxious, she blurted out before Doctor Hertz could finish, "So can I please see her? I know she may not remember me, but I'm here to take her home."

Doctor Hertz sipped his hot tea as he listened.

Tulip continued, "I don't care what she looks like, I am her mama, and she needs to be with her family."

Doctor Hertz said, "Well, Misses…excuse me. Can I call you Tulip? I hate the formality."

With her acceptance, he continued. "As I was saying, Solo made great strides in her treatment, so much so she was able to transition to a less structured environment."

Hearing this made Tulip's head hurt. She stood from her seat and began to walk about the room. In exasperation, she asked, "Are you saying my daughter is not here? For the sake of God, where in the hell is she?"

Doctor Hertz sipped his hot tea, letting the sweet fluid ease down his throat. He understood her frustration, and he wanted to proceed with care, as if she was one of his patients.

"As I mentioned, your daughter, Solo, made great progress and was moved to a home that would help her transition back into normal society. This was about two years or so ago. But recently, we were notified that Solo simply disappeared from her placement without a trace. Initially, they thought she had relapsed and been institutionalized, but we were not able to locate her in any of our facilities, which is not unusual because if she had a mental break, she may not be able to remember who she is."

Tulip looked defeated. Her mind tried to make sense of what the doctor was saying. Tulip mumbled, "She is not here, she is gone. It's been more than two years. She may be lost or in another hospital. I've come all this way. All these years. WHERE IN THE HELL IS SHE?"

Tulip began to sob uncontrollably. It was as if the years and time rushed over her like a fierce storm, and the flood gates opened. Doctor Hertz wanted to comfort her, but sometimes it is best to let the emotions run freely. Then, there was a knock of the door. Doctor Hertz thought maybe it was time for one of his patients, so he got up from the chair and opened the door. The same nurse who brought Tulip was standing there with an odd look on her face. She asked if she could speak to him privately.

Solo

The old White patrolman held onto the telephone until the operator told him the call was connected. It wasn't unusual for a patrolman to call a hospital to pick up a psychotic inmate, but it was the first time he contacted a hospital in search of a specific doctor, who may or may not exist. He expected the latter to be true. However, there was no harm in trying. The cheerful voice on the other end announced the name of the hospital.

"New York City for the Mentally Retarded and Criminally Insane, how may I direct your call?"

The cop announced himself, "This is Patrolman Blackwell over at that 5th District. How are you doing this evening?" The voice on the other end of the telephone responded, "I'm doing just fine, sir, thank you for asking. How can I be of help?"

The patrolman spoke slowly, "I got a prisoner here, a young White woman, who is in pretty bad shape, and she is looking for a doctor who helped her before."

"Well, Patrolman Blackwell, this here is a hospital for crazy people, not for sick people and most White women who have mental illness are not treated at this facility unless they are poor and homeless. May I inquire if this is the case of your prisoner?" said the voice.

"Well, I can't say for certain that is the case. But she is very insistent I find this here doctor. Hold one second, I wrote his name down somewhere. Here it is, Doctor Hertz."

"Well, you are lucky, because we do have a Doctor Hertz at this facility. Hold while I connect you and have a nice day."

Blackwell held on while the phone rang and rang. Finally, after about the tenth ring, the voice was back and said, "I am sorry, sir, I am not getting an answer from his office, but if you care to leave a message along with your telephone number, I will pass it on to Doctor Hertz." So, the old White patrolman complied and gave the voice the necessary information. He looked down at the intake chart and said the prisoner's name was Soho, Soso. Not quite sure of the pronunciation, but that was close enough. The voice said she understood, and his message would be delivered. The patrolman couldn't believe his luck and at least this doctor was for real and not a figment of this poor girl's imagination. But he didn't want to jump to any conclusion until he talked directly to the doctor. Plus, he hadn't heard a peep out of the girl. So, he just waited for the return call.

Tulip and Solo

Doctor Hertz told Tulip to excuse him why he stepped out for a second. Nurse Tippet, who'd helped Tulip earlier, handed him the written message. She watched as Doctor Hertz read. His face was emotionless.

"Finally," he said very softly. "Well, I be damned!"

The nurse stared at him, waiting for further instructions. He smiled then thanked the nurse and said he would handle it from here. As the nurse walked away, she turned back to look at the doctor, who was still standing in the hallway as if he was contemplating his next move. Doctor Hertz quietly opened the door and peeked at Tulip, who was sitting still with her shoulders hunched forward, she looked defeated. He slowly closed his office door so he wouldn't disturb Tulip and walked down the hall. He needed some privacy. After trying a few doors, he found an unlocked office. He entered and went directly to the telephone sitting on the desk. With the message in hand, he dialed the telephone number written on the paper. A very serious voice on the end of the telephone impatiently greeted him.

"This is Police Station Number 5, what is your emergency?"

Doctor Hertz quickly replied. "My name is Doctor Hertz, and I am a psychiatrist at New York City Hospital for the Mentally Retarded and Criminally Insane. I need to speak with a patrolman on an urgent matter."

The voice said, "Hold, please!" It seemed like an eternity, so Doctor Hertz made himself comfortable by sitting on top of the desk. He wished he'd brought his pipe, he sure could use a puff. Finally, the gruff voice returned and said, "Hold on while I transfer you," and preceded to yell, "Hey, pick up, it's for you, a Doctor Hertz from that looney bin."

A calm voice said, "Hello, this is Patrolman Blackwell, 5th District. Doctor Hertz, I assume? First, let me say I appreciate you calling me back. I know you're a busy man."

Doctor Hertz quickly replied, "No problem, glad to be of assistance. I must say it is truly a coincidence you called the hospital."

The patrolman continued, "Well, the situation here Doc is that a prisoner was brought in last night. White girl, maybe in her mid-twenties, but it's hard to tell with the disfigured face, but I believe I may be close in judging her age. She's pretty messed up in both body and mind. Caught her turning a trick on a Colored man." Doctor Hertz's hands were sweaty, this was more than just a coincidence.

"You said this girl is of the White race?"

The old White patrolman replied, "Well, she damn near looks White to me. I guess we didn't ask. Didn't lock her up with the Coloreds."

"Okay, I understand," Doctor Hertz said, "Please continue."

"Well, sir, she been kicking up a ruckus yelling and screaming that we call you. Only you can help her. She needs your help only."

Doctor Hertz said, "I see. I can't make out the name you gave for her. Would you mind spelling it for me?"

"Let me see here, I got it written down right here...are you ready? S-O-L-O, very strange name," the old patrolman gave a muffled chuckle.

Doctor Hertz could not believe what he was hearing, it had to be his Solo. He took a deep breath and asked, "Is it possible that I can have the prisoner brought to the hospital? I believe she may be one of my former patients and it is critical that she get here."

Doctor Hertz did not divulge to the patrolman that she was not a White woman and it may be possible her Colored mother was sitting right in his office. He feared if he told the patrolman Solo was a Colored woman her treatment would be different, and not in a good way. The patrolman responded, "Well Doc, she hadn't been formally charged and I see she needs medical attention," Blackwell paused and said, "I will bring her to you myself."

Doctor Hertz replied, "Thank you, officer, I greatly appreciate your assistance and concern."

Doctor Hertz gently placed the telephone on the receiver, clapped his hands together, and let out a big "WOOP!" Before he left the office, he called the hospital's nurse's station and asked for Nurse Tippet. He explained the situation and instructed her to personally bring the patient directly to him without delay. Now, he pondered how to handle Tulip.

The old White patrolman felt pleased with himself. It felt nice to do something good for someone. He informed the other cop he would be transferring one of the prisoners to the State Mental Hospital for observation. The other cop said, "I hope it's that ugly crazy b——h who's been screaming her head off. Maybe we can get some quiet in here." The old White patrolman shook his head and went to retrieve Solo.

Solo was sitting on the cold, hard, grimy floor with the blanket the old patrolman had given her over her head. She was tired of the other prisoners looking at her. She was tired of crying. She wanted to go home, wherever that was. *Home*, that seemed even strange to enter her mind. Everything had gone completely wrong. She was on her way to the old spot to see if anyone had seen Jessie around. But everything went wrong. Her head hurt. She was stinking. She was thirsty. Suddenly, she felt someone touch her shoulder. She jumped, ready to fight one of these White whores. But instead, she saw the old patrolman smiling at her. He was unlocking the door and motioning to her.

"Come on, get your things," he said. "You are going with me."

Solo could not believe her ears, she didn't have any things. She wrapped the blanket around her and walked towards the open cell gate. The other women prisoners just watched but gave a sigh of relief. The witch was gone.

Solo did not ask questions of the White patrolman. She was afraid of the answer. She didn't care where he was taking her as long as she was out of that cell and those hateful eyes. She just landed her head against the cold windowpane and watched the lives moving before her eyes.

Doctor Hertz walked into his office. Tulip was still in the same position. Her head hung low, with her eyes looking at her hands. She did not move until Doctor Hertz returned to the office. She was deep in thought and feared this trip was another lost cause, and her dear daughter was lost, never to lay eyes on her again—at least not in this lifetime.

Doctor Hertz needed to fill in the time while he waited. His tea was now cold for sure. So, he reached into the drawer and pulled out his pipe. He wondered if this woman smoked. He had a cigarette he kept for some of his patients. Even Solo likes to smoke he recalled.

"Would you like a cigarette?" Doctor Hertz asked, handing the pack to Tulip. She looked at him with so much pain and loss in her eyes that Doctor Hertz was almost moved to tears. He had seen that look so many times. Tulip looked at the pack of cigarettes and took one. She was not a smoker, but boy did she need it. Doctor Hertz lit her cigarette and then returned to fixing up his pipe. He looked at Tulip and said, "Why don't you tell me about Solo? How did you come to give her such a unique name?"

The thought of recalling her beautiful baby girl brought a little spark to her eyes. Carefully she spoke, "Solo was such a beautiful baby, feisty from the day she was born. Her name means, 'one who strives to do things her way, alone.' It was so appropriate for her. A head full of golden curly hair, strange blueish-gray eyes, and a smile that would just warm your heart. You couldn't help but be drawn to her. But, as she grew, she became so strong-willed and stubborn, and even more beautiful. And she used her beauty to get what she wanted. One minute, she was the sweetest and the next she could be the meanest. Yet, I loved her still the same. She was my firstborn, my first I tell you. What kind of mother loses her first child? You tell me, Doctor, what kind of mother does that?" Tulip lowered her head and held her face in shame.

Doctor Hertz handed Tulip a handkerchief to wipe her tears. She had talked endlessly, and he didn't respond. The black telephone on his desk chimed so loudly, it made him jump. Tulip jumped as well. Doctor Hertz picked up the telephone and said "Okay, that would be fine." He hung up the telephone and said to Tulip, with warmth in his voice, "Sometimes life gives you lemons, and sometimes it gives you honey. The bitter with the sweet. So, as you live, you know nothing is permanent and subject to change...meaning you get another chance. Now, it is up to the individual to take that chance and do things differently and hopefully get a different result. But you can't live in the past, you have to move forward and thank God for a second, even a third, fourth, fifth, whatever chance. That's the beauty of life."

A knock came at the door.

> *You thought it was not possible*
> *that happiness would find you;*
> *You thought happiness was for other people,*
> *never for someone like you;*
> *Could it be that sometimes a breeze of goodness flies your*
> *way, didn't linger, won't stay;*
> *Born out of no love, with one parent who struggles, setting to*
> *stage so happiness would not find your way;*
> *So, the occasional sprinkle of joy you felt was strange, surely*
> *not for you, but who;*
> *Resisting the urge to play this never-ending game knowing*
> *fully well you will surely lose;*
> *Living life searching, giving, wanting, praying abusing, in*
> *pursuit of the unattainable dream because I was a fool;*
> *The question was never, why not me because I always knew*
> *it was never meant to be;*
> *Happiness is for those who were wanted, loved, and chosen,*
> *not for a Black, fatherless, ugly girl like me;*
> *I guess what I always knew, came true.*

FORTY-TWO
Mama

Solo had dozed off during the ride. The stop gently jolted her awake. Her former home loomed before her eyes. Everything was blurry so she rubbed her eyes, closed and open them again. It was the hospital. The old patrolman opened her car door, and said, "Come on, we're here." He motioned for her to move.

Solo wanted to ask him, but for once she was quiet. The sun was setting. She took in a deep breath. The old patrolman took her by arm and together they walked through the doors.

Solo listened as the thin White nurse's shoes met the floors. She remembered the sounds; she remembered the smells. She felt mixed emotions. Maybe this was a mistake. She felt fear creeping into her. She wanted to pull away from the old patrolman, but she felt weak. If he had not been supporting her, she would have fallen to the linoleum floor. The old Colored man opened the iron elevator gate. He didn't look at the old cop, but he nodded his head and asked what floor. The elevator jerked along. Suddenly Solo knew. Yes, I know this floor. Yes, God, I know. The old patrolman took a glance at Solo, she seemed to be smiling. This made him smile. He squeezed her arm. They stopped in front of a closed door and the sign read "Doctor Hertz." The old nurse knocked and a familiar voice to Solo beckoned them to enter.

The door opened slowly. There he stood, her friend, her savior. Solo wanted to break away from the grip of the old patrolman and rush to her friend, Doctor Hertz, but she stopped because he had a person in the office, maybe a patient. Doctor Hertz encouraged her to enter.

Solo went in. She heard her name slightly whispered. Solo watched as this person slowly stood and turned to face her. Time seemed to stand still. A breeze of recognition traveled through each woman's very soul. Could this be possible? They stared at each other, each afraid to blink in fear the image would dissolve like dust. Life has a way of finding itself.

"Solo!" the voice said.

> *No matter the time, no matter the place, because with the blessings of God and the love I have, you are bound and will never be erased;*
> *Just like the sun in the sky, being blinded by clouds, but always seeking to shine, what I feel for you is deep in my heart longing to show you we will never part and true love like mist does not evaporate;*
> *Because our love was formed from equal parts like the key notes and lyrics of a lost and found love song constantly seeking to belong in each other arms;*
> *So, fret not my love trust in your heart we are forever-lasting love…I gave you life, you are my life, together we shall shut the door to the past and become as one to the love which has been cast.*

EPILOGUE

Rose

"He's home! He's home!" Rose ran excitingly to the front screen door. It had been days since her papa had been home. How she missed her Papa. Rose's little pup, Pooch, also yapped and jumped around with excitement. Rose heard the noise from the rumble of the graveling rocks as her papa's car made its way down the long driveway. She clapped her hands and bounced up and down with joy. She was only five years old, but her beauty was destined. Her glistening blonde and brown plaits moved frantically about her face as she jumped around. She leaned down and picked up Pooch and gave him a tight squeeze, which seemed to put a damper on his yapping.

Rose's mama yelled from the kitchen. You two stop that ruckus and give your papa a chance to get in the house. Rose begged, "Mama please, can I go out to the front porch and wait? Please, Mama!"

How could her mama resist her precious daughter? Her heart swelled with love."

Mama said, "Okay, only if you settle down, and promise me you won't leave the porch." With one hand behind her back and fingers crossed, Rose said, "I promise Mama!"

She bolted out the front screen door with Pooch on her heels. Now Pooch didn't make a promise to Mama, so down the stair of the front porch, he ran to meet the oncoming car of his master.

Doctor Frank could see his beautiful daughter waving and jumping around on the front porch. How he loved this little girl. She had brought so much joy to his household. After years of unsuccessfully trying to conceive a child, it was God's gift Rose was bought into their lives. He never forgot the day, he placed this little screaming, red infant into his wife's arms.

"Here is your daughter, he said to his loving wife." She looked at the beautiful baby girl. With her arms and legs thrusting about, tears of love in her eyes, and a full heart she said, "We will call her Rose because she is surely the lily of the valley.

Rose no longer could contain herself. She ran off the porch, down the steps with outstretched arms to her Papa. That's the moment he saw her…Solo!

To be continued…

ACKNOWLEDGMENTS

First and foremost, I give my honor and praise to my Heavenly Father for His continued guidance in my life. For without Him, none of this would be possible.

My family, friends, and community, thank you for the encouragement and belief in my work. Your words, texts, emails, and calls kept me motivated through this process.

To my stepson, Alexander Chambers, thank you for lending your artistic talents; you are truly a creative soul.

To Renita and her outstanding team at Mynd Matters Publishing, thank you for your professionalism. Because of your company's guidance, expertise, knowledge, and support, *The Forgotten Flowers Trilogy* is well on its way to being a bestseller.

To my readers, thank you for your support and I hope you find *Solo* enjoyable!

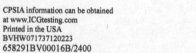